INVASION

Book Five in the Fire & Ice Series

By

Karen Payton Holt

Think 'Twilight' meets 'Game of Thrones', with a dark twist, and you are in the right mindset to enter the world of Fire & Ice.

AVAILABLE NOW:

BOOK ONE in the Series:

Fire & Ice: Awakening

Available in Paperback on Amazon
ISBN 978-1-9806710-4-6

Paperback and Hardback available in bookstores:
A5 Paperback ISBN 978-1-9996614-0-3
Hardback ISBN 978-1-9996614-1-0

FREE on Amazon Kindle Unlimited

BOOK TWO in the Series:

Fire & Ice: Survival

Available in Paperback on Amazon
ISBN 978-1-9830806-5-4

Paperback and Hardback available in bookstores:
A5 Paperback ISBN 978-1-9996614-2-7
Hardback ISBN 978-1-9996614-3-4

FREE on Amazon Kindle Unlimited

BOOK THREE in the Series:

Fire & Ice: Earth Walker

Available in Paperback on Amazon
ISBN 978-1-7181294-5-0

Paperback and Hardback available in bookstores:
A5 Paperback ISBN 978-1-9996614-4-1
Hardback ISBN 978-1-9996614-5-8

FREE on Amazon Kindle Unlimited

BOOK FOUR in the series:

Fire & Ice: Heart of Stone

Available in Paperback on Amazon
ISBN 978-1-7915462-8-1

Paperback and Hardback available in bookstores:
A5 Paperback ISBN 978-1-9996614-6-5
Hardback ISBN 978-1-9996614-7-2

FREE on Amazon Kindle Unlimited

Fire & Ice Prequel: Death of Connor Sanderson

Available in Paperback on Amazon
ISBN 978-1-9831113-4-1

Paperback and Hardback available in bookstores:

A5 Paperback ISBN 978-1-9996614-8-9
Hardback ISBN 978-1-9996614-9-6

FREE on Amazon Kindle Unlimited

This is **BOOK FIVE**, and the last in the series

Fire & Ice: Invasion

Available in Paperback on Amazon
ISBN 979-8-5593360-9-1

Paperback and Hardback available in bookstores:
A5 Paperback ISBN 978-1-8382540-0-1
Hardback ISBN 978-1-8382540-1-8

FREE on Amazon Kindle Unlimited

For the latest news on the publishing dates visit my websites:

karenpaytonholt.com

Karen Payton Holt on Facebook.

@karenpaytonholt on TWITTER.

karenpaytonholt on Instagram

Our epic journey continues, and I hope you enjoy Book Five, the final episode in the Fire & Ice Series.

Please share your thoughts and feelings in reviews.

I welcome your support

I dedicate this novel to the people who believe in me.

They drive me forward, and, at times,
give me a much-needed kick up the posterior.

This is for my mum, Sylvia,
and my friend of forty years and formatting guru, Steve.

The writing years have been hard,
and support has become more and more important.

Thank you to those family members and loved ones
who have boosted my strength.
Thank you to friends who have showed they really care.

~~~~~~~

A final thought –

this last book was finished during the Covid-19 pandemic
which raged across the globe in 2020…

As a result, my post pandemic setting no longer feels so
surreal.

Chapter 1

The vast container ship slid across the choppy water of the moonlit bay. The vessel eased from the embrace of the tidal estuary of the Scheldt and along the calm waterway, heading inland to the port. The eerie stillness on the distant riverbank gave Captain Blake pause.

When Blake grinned, air rattled through the phlegm pooled in the cavity of his mouth. He no longer had lips, so he mopped at the saliva running down his chin with a linen cloth.

The super tanker nomads were never welcome and unloading the cargo containers from the ship was a task for the crewmen alone, but usually a hive sent a party to greet their arrival as a matter of courtesy, or perhaps fear. The landscape was flat and the winds whipped along at a bone-chilling speed. The seafaring vampires, packed along the deck in a silently waiting throng, remained oblivious to the ice forming on their dead faces.

As his craft eased closer to the unloading zone designated as 'nomad territory', Blake's face bunched into a frown. The charred tight skin over his skull showed as much concern as the scar tissue allowed. The lipless mouth stretched wide.

A lantern onboard acted as the beacon which let the land-based hive members know that the food supplies they needed to keep their human herds healthy had arrived.

From where he stood at his vantage point high up on the bridge, the captain's silhouette cut a demonic shape in the glowing yellow canvas of light. Blake made another gurgling sound, and his companion and guide replied with a burst of laughter.

The lantern not only let them know the container ship was here to make a delivery, but prepared the hive vampires for the uncomfortable exchange of handing over the payment; vials of human blood.

Only Principal Julian of the London Hive still allowed a twenty strong squad of nomads to enter the City to collect the payment, most hive councils had long ago voted to honor their part of the bargain by having a truck bring the consignment down to the docks.

The Port of Antwerp, second largest in Europe, was deserted. The cobblestoned courtyard extended a hundred yards or more towards the distant port buildings; derelict and run down without a human population to 'use' them.

The Port Authority building acted as the hub of vampire operations, providing shelter from the sunshine when needed. The rows of tall rectangular windows in its walls, and those in the slate gray pagoda style roof sections, remained dark. In the moonlight, the glass sculpture mounted above the rooftop appeared to float like an angular crystal thundercloud, the segments glistening like pools of oil.

Blake transmitted his orders. *Unload the goods. If they want us to remain in the agreed zone of the port, the hive trucks will arrive soon. If not...* An eloquent shrug filled in the rest.

The mooring team scuttled over the side like cockroaches abandoning ship, and the moment they landed on the concrete causeway, chains as thick as a wrestler's thigh were tossed overboard. The movement and noise were a comedic mismatch, as if a Foley artist had used the wrong sound effects. The grinding of chain links and creaking of metal implied weight and effort, but the vampire mooring crew moved as if tossing around bundles of knitted wool.

A crucial ten minutes ticked by, and Blake and his companion, Tyrone, fixed their attention on the approach road into the port. Both focused on the point where it cut through a yard filled with cranes, the immobile jibs resembling bony fingers pointing skyward. When Blake tapped his boot on the metal floor, the entire unloading operation stuttered for a moment; the nomads telepathic link fused them together as if each crewman were a limb the captain controlled.

With the 'we've started so we will finish' attitude, even though their welcome party was nowhere to be seen in the coal-black landscape, the operation picked up speed.

As though his concerns summoned her from the bowels of the vessel, a slight Spanish girl appeared outside the salt-encrusted glass window at the top of the stairway to the bridge.

Tyrone's expression reflected the surprise his captain's features could not convey.

He pushed open the three-inch thick metal door and held it still with one hand as if the gales whipping in through the space did not exist.

Hera rushed inside in a flurry of flapping fabric and fur. Her cheeks glowed red and she blew on her fingers to warm them as the door shut, and the cocoon of calmness in the room muted the roaring wind to a whisper.

"Why are you here?" asked Tyrone.

Hera looked at Captain Blake. "The humans. You think we are in danger?"

"How did yo-?" Tyrone knew the answer to his own question and stopped speaking, but she replied anyway.

"I can hear the captain's thoughts."

Hera's steady slow heart rate made Tyrone's mouth water and the guide took a step further away. Her hybrid physiology was easier to resist than pure humans, but still, she was warm and vital and would taste of nectar.

Blake's breathing hissed, and Tyrone settled back and accepted being a broken link in the telepathic conversation. Blake was her maker and Hera had *only* drank from him, so Tyrone could not 'hear' *her* thoughts, but she took pity on him and spoke aloud. "Are our humans in danger?"

All I can know for sure, is that something is wrong here. Tyrone feels it, too.

"Should I move the others into the panic chamber?" asked Hera.

It was a polite name for a bulkhead compartment deep inside the vessel with reinforced steel walls, padded inside – which included ceiling and floor. The purpose was to mask human heartbeats and smells – the thickened walls would not withstand a vampire attack, but intruders would have to find them first.

13

Blake nodded sharply. *Yes, do it, and stay there until Tyrone gives you the all clear.*

Hera reached out and caught hold of Blake's hand, pressing her fingers into his palm. The captain stroked his thumb over her smooth skin before snatching his hand away.

Tyrone opened the door at the same moment as Hera turned to go, her shoulders slumping. He escorted her down the open metal stairway, shielding her from the worst of the wind as he guided her below deck. Returning to the bridge, he shared a new discovery with the captain.

There is a rancid smell coming from inland. Tyrone's screwed up face illustrated his feelings about the stink that Blake's seared senses could not detect.

The captain fixed his attention on the view from the bridge, and Tyrone joined him, becoming Blake's eyes as he watched the unloading process and gave his captain a telepathic running commentary on everything he saw.

Nomads, working in pairs, secured winch hooks to all four corners of each container marked for offloading. When the crane lifted the cargo from the deck and the metal box swung gracefully from side to side, the vampire riding over with it to the quayside stood on the roof, like a statue carved in ash. The garb the nomads wore had been black, once upon a time, but encrusted sea salt made it stiff and frost gray. The crewmen who had leapt ashore first climbed up into the cabins of the dockyard cranes and worked in effortless coordination. At no point were any member of the ship's crew still, they flowed back and forth like a school of fish, flitting in and out through the spaces as if using sonar to detect the location of the rest of their team. They resembled bats swooping and swirling within the fluid confines of their own work party.

In one abrupt act, as if the power driving each nomad was cut, the cranes stopped moving, the crew on deck froze in mid step, and the riders standing on the containers all turned to peer in the same direction. Blake emerged through the door at the top of the metal stairway which led to the bridge, every muscle in his body tight, like a hunting dog on point. His sightless eyes 'looked' in the same direction as his crew.

His companion gripped the captain by the arm. *We are under attack.*

A sudden rasping hum filled the air and beyond the wire perimeter fence of the dockyard thick dust rose in a fog bank.

A harsh growl from Blake jerked his crew into action.

The smell Tyrone detected, but did not understand, grew stronger and plumed into the acrid stench of decaying flesh, but the rancid odor of putrefying meat would not have been a new experience to Blake.

As a penitentiary governor in a high security facility when human, he saw a lot of hard men cry like babies, *and* a lot of hard men who were too tough to break. There were some who killed more inmates in prison than the acts of murder which had earned them their sentences, and as a vampire, before the rise, he took pleasure in redressing the balance – death row with a twist, and the blood-drained victims he hid beneath sewer covers had an aroma no one ever forgot.

If he had been able to smell, Blake would have already known – death floated on the night breeze, but now, it was too late.

The concrete beneath the containers sitting on the dockside began to crackle until fragments spat into the air like bubbles exploding on the surface. The vibrations increased and cracks crawled across the quay.

Nomads onshore moved faster, focused on reversing the unloading, re-securing lifting gear and disengaging mooring chains.

The containers which were still airborne swung in alarming jerking arcs as the crane pilots reversed the winch action and whipped them back to the ship at a reckless speed. Vocal clicks and barks broke the air as, for once, the rattled nomads' emotions transcended their telepathic communication and they urged their brethren to hurry.

What are they? Tyrone clamped his head in his hands as the clatter of thoughts inside his mind became a tangled mass of noise.

Ferals. Get the humans locked away, go. Blake thumped Tyrone on the shoulder, urging him into action.

Tyrone suddenly realized that some of the noise he heard was the swelling tide of panicked human heartbeats, and if he could feel them vibrating through the hull beneath his feet, then so could the enemy. He swung away, leaving his captain to his fate.

Rushing up the gangplanks from the storage area, a tall wiry vampire grabbed Tyrone's arm. His skin was less squid-like than the nomad cargo crew and the eyes of the Reverend glinted with steely determination. *Where's the captain?*

On the bridge. Tyrone felt relieved that Blake would have back-up.

The metal skin of the tanker whined as it vibrated beneath the shockwave of the incoming attack.

Out on the causeway, the glass windows in the Port Authority building shattered as if a bomb tore it apart, and bodies poured through every aperture. The approaching horde were like heat-seeking missiles, and their target was the container ship.

As if to herald the incoming storm, a rolling wall of gritty air whipped over the faces of the nomad crew like sandpaper. The ones still on the ground rushed inside part-unloaded containers to hitch a ride back across to the ship, slamming the doors shut behind them. A keening sound, akin to hyenas or wounded dogs barking, rode the gusting storm like wailing specters.

The metal fence rattled until the wire strands snapped like raw spaghetti, the fragments bursting into the air as the barrier collapsed beneath the boiling sea of writhing bodies. The ferals rushed onward, their mouths hanging open, the dried blood on the stained faces so thick it was a crust-like mask.

With a groan, the crumbling walls of the Port Authority building finally collapsed. The angular glass cloud sculpture hovering above it exploded in a cascade of splinters, embedding dart-like shards into the skin and clothes of the rolling tide of invading bodies.

The tightly packed army rose and fell like swells in an ocean, the whites of the eyes and gaping mouths creating a patchwork of distorted faces.

When four containers crunched heavily back down onto the deck, a swarm of nomad climbers jerked forward to unlatch the winch chains.

Abandon the cargo. Get back to the ship.

The last container to become airborne swayed and jerked.

Like strings of scuttling beetles, the ferals scaled the crane.

The cabin windows shattered beneath the hammer-like blows of feral skulls. The first wave poured inside, their flailing legs thrashing. The nomad pilot lashed out and a few feral bodies fell, hit the ground below and lay in broken heaps, twitching. But then the crane driver emitted a screech that sliced through his nomad kin like an electric shock. The crunch of shattering bone and snapping sinews cut the telepathic feed, and the tanker crew surged into renewed action.

The container suspended over the vessel shuddered and one end dropped. Crashing down, it slammed into the deck, buckling the guard rail and gouging a dent in the riveted steel plates.

The string of black bodies scuttled from the crane cabin, heading upwards, to where they could climb down the chains still attached to the crash-landed container. Nomads leapt up to detach the hooks and prepared to repel the attack. The crew swung the hefty metal clamps in desperate driving arcs, and four ferals fell overboard onto the concrete far below, their skulls exploding like watermelons.

The members of the mooring crew still on the quayside who had not yet been torn apart, lunged up and clung onto the anchor chains being wound in through hatchways in the hull, and the huge tanker began to inch away from the port.

Nomads lined the side of the vessel, armed with harpoons and flare guns. The seething mass of ferals snarling up at the ship writhed like bubbling oil, shrieking faces rising to the top before sinking under to be replaced by others. A discharged flare exploded inside a tight knot of packed bodies and made a hole in the onslaught, but only for a nanosecond.

Dull clangs rang out when the front-lines of the horde flung themselves against the hull, latching onto rivets and appearing to stick to the ship like barnacles before starting to climb. Harpoon arrows aimed over the side whistled through the air, the nomads reeling in impaled ferals like thrashing carp and scything off their heads with whatever hefty blades or fire-axes were close to hand. The distance between the vessel and the mindless predators on land grew wider until, finally, it was too far for them to make the leap, but then the front lines poured off the edge of the causeway and disappeared below the inky depths.

The ferals coming up behind, still pouring into the dockland courtyard, crunching over the shattered glass and crushing their fallen comrades underfoot, lost focus and began to circle aimlessly.

Blake sent orders to sweep the vessel. Some crew set about securing containers which began to slide on the greasy deck as the wide river tributary became choppy in the faster flowing currents.

A thick silence descended. The organism of shared consciousness ramped up speed, as if an electric current arced from one nomad to another. The search of the ship became a silent dance of perpetual movement. Guarding the human stock – emergency rations which were crucial now a blood delivery had been missed – became the primary concern.

Blake stood on the bridge absorbing the stream of information from the ceaseless wave of nomad activity, the Reverend and Tyrone at his side, until a flurry of telepathic communication jolted all three into action. The vampires skimmed down the metal stairway and strode to the stern of the vessel. Crewmen gathered there had a feral harpooned to the deck. Scrabbling noises onboard were clear signs the invader was not alone.

How?

A short stout nomad stepped forward. *They dropped into the river in Antwerp and scaled the hull below the water line before it was too deep. They broke inside through the anchor hatch.*

Blake's head jolted around, firing a thought-bolt to the crewman who 'spoke'.

The nomad shook his head. *No, they did not find the humans. The heartbeats thrumming through the metal confused them. Only ten crew were lost.*

Tyrone's grim expression reflected what Blake was saying. *We need to sail up the coast to Denmark and find out how extensive this invading army is.*

The five-mile sail back out to the Schelde estuary was accomplished in eerie silence, and the nomad brethren heaved a collective sigh when they were heading out into open sea.

Chapter 2

High up on the maintenance walkway that connected the towers of the 'H' shaped structure of the suspension bridge, Connor savored the exhilaration of a howling wind snatching at his shirt. His vampire cold skin tightened under the onslaught as the salt-laden gales clumped his jet-black hair into spikes.

The Severn Bridge was a brief way-stop, and he made the most of this moment of freedom before he faced the difficult process of pressuring the Cardiff Hive Council into accepting the new order of things. *Telling vampires they would be fed like invalids, and convincing humans that their 'rights' are now protected by the vampire councils.* Connor almost laughed at the prospect.

The journey from London had taken a mere twenty minutes, and that was only because Connor needed thinking time. Brynmor, his wingman and laboratory assistant, had continued on ahead into Cardiff to take charge of the blood substitute delivery which would arrive by more conventional means – by the truckload.

Vaulting over the rail of the platform, Connor clung to the steel cords of the suspension bridge and watched strings of white lace erupt on the fast-moving surface of the cobalt river below. Darkness had pressed the sun down, until its death throes bled across the horizon. Reluctantly, he slid down the thick steel cable and leapt into the middle of the tarmac road. The surface felt slimy underfoot. Very few cars had crossed the bridge in recent years. Humans still lived in prison camps and vampires had little use for even the fastest cars.

Mother Nature had done her best to reclaim the manmade derelict structures which now lay empty and, after more than twenty years of vampire dominance, she was winning the battle. The stunted weeds growing through cracks they had forced in the asphalt, creating a patchwork of green and gray across the magnificent span of the estuary bridge, were only kept in check by the storm force gales which did their best to tear down the structure.

Connor sucked in a deep cleansing breath and airborne salt granules made breathing feel like licking sandpaper. Swinging around, he turned his attention back to the Welsh side of the estuary and set off at a swift run for the coal-black structures ranging along the opposite shore.

At Newport, vessels were moored at the docks, where the docklands revitalization program formed part of the new order – it was an obvious choice. The North and South Docks, excavated at the mouth of the River Usk, created the largest expanse of dockland waterways in 1917, accessed by the largest lock in the world at that time.

Resurrecting the site was a fitting tribute to the past.

Silver glints of polished steel bore witness to newly constructed boat sheds and the smell of sulphur meant that vampires were inside the structures welding boats to reboot a new trade – luxury imports to make the human population feel more human and less like the cattle they had been reduced to. Vampires still possessed skills from when they were alive, and from when being cold, hungry, and needing shelter from the elements were important.

The only thing that truly drove Connor and his vampire brethren to find shelter, was the sun. It remained enemy number one, but not in the Hollywood movies Dracula-bursting-into-flames way. Dehydration, or rather, staying hydrated was the constant battle. Connor unconsciously rubbed a hand around the nape of his neck, his fingertips tracing the line of gouges in his flesh, put there by Captain Laurence of the Council Guard. The lethal adversary had died at Connor's hand and, even though it was kill or be killed, Connor regretted the loss of a great combatant. He had discovered the captain had served in the British S.A.S. as a human. *He would have been a valuable asset, if things had turned out differently.*

Connor had sustained many war wounds over the last hundred years, but skills honed along the way forged him into a warrior of magnificence. Very few vampires challenged his authority. *Which is just as well. I'll need that respect when they hear the news.*

Pushing aside his reminiscing and scanning the route ahead, Connor realized he had passed through Newport and arrived in Cardiff. The streets were wet with pools of rain and the glistening sidewalks were burnished to silver by the full moon overhead. The castle in the center of the city was to become the designated 'refueling station' when the blood substitute was ready to be rolled out – 'refueling' was meant to make humans feel more secure, safer.

But as Julian once said, let's hope we aren't finally fixing a car just as the wheels fall off.

The human farm in London had tripled its guard duty after a feral risked death and scaled the fences in broad daylight. His hair had ignited and his shrunken face burned until his eyelids released his eyeballs to slip down onto his cheeks, but he kept on coming. Human blood was all that stood between vampire sanity and feral dementia, and many still refused to face the fact that humans in captivity would die and make that fate inevitable. *The most important thing now, is to agree on the change from human to synthesized blood.* They would worry about the rest down the line.

"Doctor Connor." The owner of the voice stepped out from a shop doorway.

Even with his face shrouded in shadow, the ramrod straight gait and copper-toned hair of the new arrival were unmistakable.

"Captain Hugh, it's good to see you again."

"You too, sir." Pride resonated through his tone. His promotion to a captain in the London Hive was well earned, but the man remained modest.

Even in the dark, Connor sensed Hugh scrutinizing his disheveled appearance.

"I know. I look a mess and stink of salt."

Hugh smiled. "How do you think I knew you were coming? Although, you look more like a ghost."

Puzzled, Connor frowned and heard the crust of salt on his face crack. Touching his cheek, he discovered the spray of seawater had become a frozen mask, and he laughed.

"Come, I'll take you to the castle."

Moving swiftly along the narrow streets and past the many shopping arcades that were a feature of the old city, Connor wondered what the place had been like before vampires literally sucked all the life out of it. *Would humans return to their homes here, to begin again, or is the city ruined by the horrors they suffered?*

Moments later, the wide road running alongside the imposing boundary wall of the castle came into view. The fortification dominated the Cardiff skyline with its gilded Gothic clock tower and the breathtaking architecture of the Victorian apartments wing. The outer wall, crested by a castellation of broken teeth, loomed overhead.

For 2000 years the structure had weathered the passing of time, erected long before the first brick was laid to build the city which now sat at its feet. The castle grounds covered many acres in a more or less square formation, all enclosed beyond the granite block wall.

Both vampires passed beneath the wide archway of the North Gate – built in Roman times, its broad square turrets flanked the entrance.

Once inside, a breeze eddied around the enclosed space and the lush expanse of grass rippled like an obsidian sea in the moonlit night. In the distance, on the opposite side of the lawn was the irregular shaped wide fortification of the main entrance. To their right, a steep stone stairway rose sharply, cut into the side of a huge mound on top of which squatted the wide turret of a Norman keep. Bearing witness to the superbly strong construction, the curved walls, punctured by many arrow slits, had survived more than 800 years.

Connor had done his homework. Although the Roman fort dated from 50s AD, the Norman keep, first built in wood, had been the first of many medieval fortifications. But it was the castle lodgings that he longed to see.

The living quarters were beyond the keep. The central spire of the castle apartments wing jutted high into the velvet blanket of sky, the pinprick of stars could almost have been where the needle point tip had left its mark. It resembled an image seen in fairytales.

The 18th Century square clock tower commanded the site where two walls met in one corner. The gilded intricate details created an awe-inspiring blend of horological precision and artistic flair. The latticed clock face, marked out in Roman numerals, appeared to float on a sea of cerulean blue tiles in an arched alcove. Gilded statues on pedestals filled the neighboring arches, and coats of arms on shields in rich vibrant reds, blues, and gold, were displayed above their heads.

If Connor needed a reminder of what a tragedy the demise of mankind would be, then this display of human creativity in splendid glory did that with blinding clarity.

This was the first time Connor had seen Cardiff Castle, and he took a moment to soak up the eerie feeling that greater men than he could possibly imagine had walked along the path stretched out before him.

It was tempting to flirt with a world where men of genius could *choose* the immortal path, and their true capacity would not be dictated by a human lifespan. *What a world that could be.*

"Many battles have been won and lost here, sir. You can feel it."

"You can indeed, Hugh. You can almost touch the fabric of history."

Now, the castle acted as the council chambers for the Welsh vampire hive.

"Come. I'll show you to your apartment." Hugh set off across the slick, perfectly groomed field of grass. It was easily large enough to host a tourney in medieval times. Connor could imagine magnificent destriers thundering down the lines, the colors of their riders flowing out behind them.

Sweeping around the base of the mound from where the Norman keep glowered down, Connor fell into step beside Hugh and set his sights on the castle walls up ahead.

The companionable silence shifted, and a sense of unease brushed over Connor's skin, as though specters stalked him. He shivered and felt the dead heart in his chest plummet. Connor frowned. He was not given to flights of fancy, but the weight of foreboding would not be ignored. *No more dramas, please.*

Rebekah planned to follow him west, from London. She had stayed out of trouble this last year, so Connor had forgotten what worrying about impending disaster felt like. *This is nonsense.* Deciding it had been a long day, he plunged into the distraction of talking.

"How are you enjoying Wales? It is very different from the London Hive."

Connor glanced at Hugh's stark profile. The damp hair swept back from his companion's brow exposed sharp cheekbones and a hawkish nose. The captain of the vampire guard exuded fierce hostility, until he turned Connor's way to answer. The intelligence in his eyes wiped out the ruthless air, making it evaporate like mist.

"It's getting more interesting, I'd say, now you're here to stir things up."

Connor's burst of laughter echoed from the stone walls. "That's a good thing, I hope."

"I'll let you know tomorrow," replied Hugh.

Stepping through the door into the castle apartments was an Alice in Wonderland moment. The interior of the lodgings within the Gothic towers were a feast of lavish opulence. There were murals, stained-glass windows, marble, gilding and elaborate wood carvings. Each room Connor walked through had its own theme, ranging from Mediterranean and on to Arabian embellishment.

"1866, William Burgess," said Captain Hugh, reading Connor's mind as he wondered who was the architect of such splendor.

The castle had been modified by its vampire inhabitants over the last twenty years, but the battlement walkways remained largely untouched; the hidden tunnels beneath had provided refuge for more than 1800 people during the Second World War whenever the air-raid sirens sounded. Vampires now used the same space to take grave sleep. Crypts had been carved into the thick walls and metal doors fitted so each 'sleeper' could be isolated. Muscle relaxant was used as part of the process here; to damage such illustrious surroundings was unthinkable.

After passing through the labyrinth of rooms – which Connor suspected was for his benefit – they stopped outside a blackened wooden door four-inches thick and studded with brass rivets. Hugh pulled out a chunky metal key from within the folds of his cape and handed it to Connor.

"Mortice locks *and* medieval keys?"

They both knew the wooden door was symbolic. A vampire took little notice of doors, windows, holy water, stakes, or priests. These were all things that gave humans hope. In truth, a dead heart doesn't beat and a wooden stake driven into it did nothing but make a hole in dead flesh.

"Tradition. If it's open, then the councilors will know you are available. If it's locked, they'll leave you alone."

"Tell me about the councilors."

"Principal Glynn is a hard liner who only gave up on the practice of keeping a human pet when Sentinel Marcel of Spain sent a warning."

"Warning?" Connor's brows rose. The European hives rarely interfered with what went on in Great Britain. It was the beauty of being an island.

"He sent an envoy. It was years ago. A decade or so, but that's only a drop in the ocean when you're a hundred and seventy years old, as Principal Glynn is."

"Ah, yes, I remember Julian mentioning it. You think he's my target audience? Someone to win over?" asked Connor.

"Him and Councilor Eugene. Get them on your side and you're half way home."

"Thanks for the advice. Can you tell Brynmor I'm here and watch out for Rebekah."

"She's coming here?" Hugh sounded surprised.

"She's my secret weapon. Smoke and mirrors. Only a year ago, she was human. When we talk to the humans in the compound, she'll understand their fears better than we can."

"I'll wait for her myself," said Hugh.

"She will appreciate a friendly face, thank you, Captain."

When Hugh turned away, Connor closed the door, locked it and slipped the key into his pants pocket. Skimming up the spiral stone steps, he entered a large room with a high-ceiling. A chandelier overhead winked like a thousand stars, scattering coins of light over every surface. A plaque on the wall gave a potted history of the Clock Tower. The room Connor stood in had been known as the Summer Smoking Room.

Looking out of a small window over the darkened sprawling city reminded Connor how far from home he had come. He felt weary and all of his one hundred and plus some years. Being around Rebekah made him feel younger and the challenges of bringing up Seren, a journey into the unknown, kept him on his toes. He missed his family.

Turning back into the room, he contemplated what he should do next.

The bedstead was a dark walnut piece of impressive proportions, fit for a king.

A large desk was piled high with files on the Welsh Hive inhabitants: one for each hive member of standing, a dossier providing an overview of the health of the Welsh human herd, and files on human candidates suitable to sitting on a 'human council'. Vampire memory was limitless, but the fastest way to 'learn' all the information he needed was to simply read it. Each council file contained a photograph. *I'll get to those later.*

On another desk sat the hefty volume outlining the reason he was here; a set of manuals and 'instruction for dummies' troubleshooting crib sheets. Connor had handwritten the master copy of the darn thing – thankfully his call for scribes had turned up a team of six hive members who jumped at the chance to exchange their physical chores for a cerebral endeavor. He grinned. It reminded him of the era when monks in monasteries recorded history from the biased ecclesiastical viewpoint of their era. This time, the vampire scribes had created the 'Theory of Survival' according to the word of Connor Sanderson.

Printing presses could not have performed the task faster, and they only needed four sets now the Midland Hive had collapsed: The London Hive, whose territory now encompassed the entire South West peninsular beyond the Dartmoor Safari Hunting Park, Loch Glascarnoch in Scotland which extended down to Hadrian's Wall, The York Hive controlled the midlands, and The Cardiff Hive extended over the Welsh border to include the area from Bristol up to Manchester.

This visit marked the start of the transition to an age of vampire/human parity. *It won't be easy, but it will all be worth it.*

Connor ran a hand through his salt crusted hair and grimaced. Noticing an ornate brass handle set into a wooden panel in the wall for the first time, he grinned in a spontaneous expression of happiness. He could smell the hot water in the pipes in the room beyond. Going through to the bathroom, he caught sight of himself in the mirror and almost laughed. His jet-black hair was gunmetal gray and sticking up like iron filings being pulled by a magnet. The cracks in the crusted mask of salt left deep crevices in his skin.

Shrugging out of his shirt and pants, he stepped under the shower and blasted his body with boiling water. Being pummeled by the spray, like a thousand hammers beating him back into shape, felt invigorating. He shampooed his hair, scrubbed soap over hard abdominals, eased the tightness from his shoulders, and stepped out onto the bath mat a new man. His skin felt warm, like stone which had absorbed the sun's heat. He missed that sometimes, even now. The sun on his skin.

Toweling his hair dry, he walked back into the bedroom naked. His luggage had already been unpacked – presumably by the principal's household staff – and inside a polished wooden armoire with carvings covering every square inch, Connor found clean clothes, crisply pressed and hanging in order of garment type. He pulled on underwear, black pants, and a gray shirt.

Detouring to replace the towel on the heated rail to dry, he finally sat down at the desk.

Assessing the size of both piles of 'research', he picked up the manila folder on the top of the 'vampire' heap and read the label. 'Principal Glynn, Cardiff Hive Indent number: CA58391.' The picture inside gave little away. The principal looked about thirty-five human years. Scanning the text, Connor found the principal had been turned 177 years ago, and so, would have values instilled into him from that time, circa 1840. Julian, principal of the London Hive, was turned in 1810. *I understand how Julian works, so hopefully that's a good thing.* A small voice inside his head laughed. *'You must be joking.'* It sounded remarkably like something Rebekah would say, and Connor smiled. She had quickly become his voice of reason, but more so this last year.

He remembered what Hugh had told him about the Welsh hive principal keeping a human pet until he was ordered to desist. With humans in short supply, the practice was outlawed and carried a life sentence of confinement inside a storage facility. He was looking forward to meeting the man.

Flicking through the pages as though they were the flip animation books children played with, Connor worked his way through the hive personnel files. Each one took him a minute or so. He pulled out three of particular interest. Rolling out his 'human blood substitute' was a difficult prospect. There would be resistance, he knew that.

A juror named Cedric Hawkes possessed surgical skills Connor felt would be useful. A trained physician would be appointed at each refueling site. A vampire called Graeme Jones had been a university lecturer when human. The final dossier had more to do with curiosity; Baron Archibald. Connor had never met a vampire who was a member of aristocracy. *Interesting that he still uses his human title.*

Easing out the muscles in his neck with one hand, he pushed the files aside and made a start on the human candidates. Being held captive on a farm to be syphoned for blood each day would have caused deep physiological trauma in most of the inhabitants.

Setting them free required careful handling and a human panel to ease the transition.

After rifling through each dossier, he selected twelve candidates; the criterium was loosely based on representing the range of ages from thirty through to eighty – very few children, or even teenagers, existed. Trying to breed humans in captivity had limited success, and Connor had never been comfortable with the breeding program in any event. The other consideration focused on trades and skills that could ultimately make the human community self-supporting.

Vampires had farmed crops, herds of cattle, sheep, and pigs, and kept chickens, with which to feed the humans, and for the time being, that would continue. But human beings were fiercely independent. He could still remember his own pride and stubbornness when he was a young man. Even though he deplored the senseless waste of life when mankind waged war, when he became a vampire and hid in plain sight on the battlefields, he understood why men were driven to it; amongst the death and decay, there was a strong sense of honor and camaraderie – in the face of death, they felt alive.

The occupations Connor pulled from the pile were stonemason, carpenter, chemist, architect, dairy farmer, engineer, electrician, plumber, and teacher. The pool of human knowledge would require nurturing. He tapped a finger on his chin, lost in thought. *Academic text books.* He'd bring that up with Principal Glynn – the humans would need to refresh skills so long neglected.

His head jerked around when he heard a distant knock from down below. "Damn. I forgot to lock the door." He really didn't want to entertain strangers, yet, but he got to his feet, ran his hands through his still damp hair and smoothed it back into a sleek black cap. Returning to the armoire, he yanked a jacket from a hanger and pulled it on.

He headed down the stairs, scowling until a voice inside his head whispered, *"Aren't you glad to see me?"* Rebekah's smile appeared in his mind, as though printed inside his skull, and he whipped open the door, wanting to see the real thing.

There she stood, looking up at him. Her blond hair, damp from the evening fog, framed her face in curls. Her brown eyes shone with humor and a smile tugged at her red lips. Her translucent skin glittered like frost on a winter morning. Connor still felt entranced by her, as a newly blossoming vampire. She was the only person he had turned, and if he thought he loved her when she was human – when he had tortured himself for three years, trying not to injure her – he now found her the most fascinating sight on the planet.

"Hi honey, I'm home," she whispered, her smile full of mischief.

"Stop stealing my lines," Connor replied quietly. Reaching for her hand, he pulled her roughly into his chest, his arm around her waist lifting her feet from the floor. Pushing his fingers into her silken hair, he kissed her. Tasting the droplets of cold rain on her lips, Connor sighed. Her tongue tasted his and she ran her hands over his tight shoulders. When he lifted her and she wrapped her thighs around his hips, he turned and started back up the spiral staircase.

Tearing his mouth away, he muttered, "Damn."

"What is it?"

"The door. I don't want any interruptions."

"I should hope not. Give me a second."

Connor's hair fluttered with the breeze of her fast movement. The tornado of whipping air had just registered, when she was back, brandishing the key in her hand.

"Now, where were we?"

His smile faded as he reached for her again and scooped her up. His kiss more demanding as he resumed the climb up the stairs, holding Rebekah, breathless and laughing in his arms.

Once inside the room, kicking the door carefully shut, Connor headed for the bed. Laying her gently down, with intense concentration he unbuttoned Rebekah's black coat.

He frowned. "Hey, this is my coat."

"So, it is." Rebekah's brows rose in fake innocence.

It was Connor's prize possession, a scuffed and well-worn greatcoat from the Second World War.

"I was looking after it for you." The laughter dancing in her eyes faded and she shrugged. "It smells of you. Fresh, lemony." Lifting her head to run a tongue along his bottom lip, she murmured, "Yes, definitely citrus."

Gently stroking stray curls back from her brow Connor said, "I miss you, too."

He shrugged out of his jacket and shirt and lay on his side looking down into her face. He traced his fingertips along the row of pearly buttons on her deep red blouse, undoing them one by one. In moments, he was running his hands over her cool skin.

She noticed the muscle ticking in his tense jawline and laid a hand on his smooth cheek. "You don't need to worry. I don't bruise anymore, remember?"

Connor ran his tongue from the hollow in her throat down between her breasts and dipped it into her tummy button. She dug her nails into his back and he stopped teasing her. Stripping off her clothes as he moved, his mouth drifted further down until he tasted the sweet honeyed scent between her thighs, making her shudder beneath his hands. When he entered her, his gray eyes drank in the beauty of her face as though he might never see it again.

Rebekah gripped his hair and pressed her body closer, moving with him and savoring the building tension, until his muscles tightened and his breath growled in his throat. Together, they tumbled into the abyss, their bodies melting and, for a moment, time stayed still. Minutes ticked by as they lay in a sated embrace, in a tangle of limbs.

Reaching for a blanket, Connor pulled it up to cover them both. He settled on his side facing Rebekah, lifted her thigh over his hip, and wrapped his arms around her. She rested her head on his shoulder and sighed.

"I'm glad you're here," he said, simply.

"Me, too."

The moonlight bathed them in a silver glow. The night time noises were comforting and familiar, and it felt easy to just hold each other and be still.

An hour passed before Rebekah stirred and said, "Have you seen the 'blood substitute' panel yet?"

"I've chosen the candidates. But how well this will go, I can't say."

"You've asked Brynmor to stay behind. And there's Captain Hugh. I'm sure they'll come around."

Connor dropped a kiss on her nose. "Easy for you to say. You never drank blood from a live human. It's pretty addictive you know. Most vampires miss the thrill and already feel cheated that their blood is now doled out in glass vials."

Rebekah chewed her lip. "I guess you're right. I'm a vegan vampire."

He chuckled.

The loud thud of someone banging on the door below cut short his laughter and he frowned in annoyance. "Who the Hell is that?" It was difficult to decipher; it could be a vampire of standing being polite, but demanding an audience, or a low-ranking vampire expressing urgency as loudly as he dared.

Connor hoped it was the former. He was in no mood to deal with an emergency, but taking a vampire with a superiority complex down a peg or two would feel quite good, about now.

They were both up and dressed in seconds, and Rebekah sat in an armchair to wait.

Connor took his time walking down the spiral stairs and opening the door. He recognized the white face staring back at him, but only from the photograph in his file. Swallowing his annoyance, realizing a measured approach would serve him better, Connor smiled stiffly and tried to inject warmth into his ice-gray gaze.

"Principal Glynn, this is a pleasant surprise." Connor extended a hand, but blocked the doorway.

"The infamous, Doctor Connor, I presume?"

33

Connor nodded in acknowledgment. "I'll take 'infamous' over 'notorious'. How can I help you?" He glanced at his watch, making the point that a meeting in the Welsh council chambers had already been set for four a.m., in two hours' time. "Something urgent, I take it?"

The principal appeared to swell in size. "I preferred to meet you first in private. There are some things I want to make clear."

And, there it was. *Superiority complex.* Meeting the blue-flecked eyes of his host, assessing the outthrust chiseled chin and thin-lipped smile, Connor prepared for a battle of wits that he must win. For the blood substitute to be accepted within the hive, the principal's support would be vital.

Still blocking the doorway, Connor opened his mind, and, as though he were already upstairs with Rebekah, he warned her of the intrusion. *I think I'll need your help, honey. Principal Glynn has ruffled feathers to soothe.* To his visitor, he said, "Please, come inside, you'll have the opportunity to meet Rebekah, too."

Glynn's gaze sharpened. "And Seren?" His teeth flashed diamond white as keen interest pulled his face tight.

The hairs prickled on Connor's nape, but he hung onto a façade of calm, answering slowly. "I'm afraid not, Seren is still in London."

The principal looked disappointed. "My apologies. The chance of meeting the hybrid child, I'm sure you understand the curiosity."

Connor forced a laugh. "Perhaps, but my daughter is not a circus act to be wheeled out." Softening his disapproval as he recognized a chink in the principal's armor, he added, "I'm sure you'll meet her in the fullness of time."

Turning, Connor led the way upstairs, opened the bedroom door and stepped aside to let Glynn enter the chamber first.

Rebekah rose from her seat and smiled warmly. "Good evening, Principal Glynn. So good to meet you."

Introductions made, Connor leaned back against the desk, legs crossed at the ankles, and waited for Glynn to open the discussion.

"Before the BRP meets tomorrow, I wanted to make you aware of a condition I require."

"Require?" Connor's brows rose. The acronym for the Blood Resources Panel somehow sounded harsher and more confrontational when used by this Welsh leader.

"Indeed, *require.*"

"Go on." Connor folded his arms, fixing a probing look on Glynn.

"The vampire council – that is the jurors and the councilors – will not use this 'blood substitute'. The hive herd is eighteen hundred strong. The human cattle will be rehoused into their own 'village' and become freemen, and you have my support in setting up a manufacturing plant to feed our vampire population, however, myself and the council will each choose two human pets from who we will feed. They will live in the residences of those who own them."

Principal Glynn's defiant gaze remained locked on Connor's face as he laid down the demands.

Connor was grateful the principal had not dropped this bombshell at the official panel meeting; he would have been confined by council protocol when making his reply. Right now, the gloves were off.

"I have heard about you, Principal Glynn."

Glynn's ramrod straight posture jerked as if Connor had punched him in the chest.

"From Sentinel Marcel of Spain. Your notion of hospitality unsettled him," said Connor, quietly. Glynn had clearly forgotten that Julian, as a principal, would get to hear about the warning.

The muscles twitched in Glynn's quartz white face. The impeccably-tailored ruby silk jacket tightened across his broad chest.

As though thinking aloud, Connor mused, "Why would a vampire who refused to see that immortality became a bad joke when our human food supply is dying, be any less stupid, now?"

Venom ran from the corner of the principal's mouth and his hands pumped into fists. His glance darted to Rebekah and back, and Connor knew it was only her presence that kept Glynn glued to the spot.

"You disappoint me, *Doctor*." Glynn's frozen features barely moved.

"Principal Glynn, it seems to me, we have two ways to go. Either we forget this conversation ever happened, or I call Captain Hugh in here and you tell him your demands. A hive principal has never been stripped of his position and condemned to a life sentence in a storage facility before, but I'm willing to give you the opportunity to go down in history as the first, if you wish."

Time stood still for what seemed like endless seconds, and then the red blur of Glynn darted across the room, his clawed hands reaching for Connor's throat. The principal's snarl rose to the screeching pitch of nails dragging down a blackboard and the air reverberated with a sickening crack as one of his wrists snapped, his hand left hanging at an angle from an upraised forearm. His mouth dropped open, confusion in his face as he stared at Connor, who had not moved. From behind, a female hand eased the grip still clamped on the unbroken wrist and slid up over the silk sleeve of his jacket. Scented breath brushed over his cheek as Rebekah whispered, "I'm sorry, Principal, I don't know my own strength."

Pushing away from the desk, Connor took the step that brought him close enough for the principal to touch him.

Cradling his bent arm at the elbow, the stunned vampire stared at his lifeless hand, willing it to move. "Guards!" The bellowed command summoned the clattering noise of boots grating over stone, and four guardsmen wearing Regal purple uniforms swarmed into the room.

"Arrest them." Glynn waved the broken limb in Rebekah's direction, then jerked it across to jab Connor in the chest.

Connor held up a halting hand to the closest guard. The group of four became statues, except for the flashing whites of their eyes as their gazes darted around the chamber.

"Gentlemen, please," said Captain Hugh, pausing in the doorway before weaving a path through the standing stones of guardsmen and taking in the absurd scenario. With a speculative look at Connor, Hugh obeyed the chain of command. "Principal Glynn, what has happened here?"

"The woman attacked me." He swung the injured arm in front of Hugh, and the cracks in the chalk white skin covering the shattered joint began spewing gritty powder down over the front of his jacket.

Rebekah's brown eyes glowed with golden flecks. The network of silver threads beneath her skin shimmered as she smothered a sneer.

Connor moved to her side and took her hand. "I'm afraid Principal Glynn became aggressive in his argument. Rebekah defended me. Unnecessary, as you know, Captain, but she is a youngling. It is Principal Glynn who should know better."

"Principal, sir, I think we should get you to the hospital. You'll need attention to save your hand."

Glynn looked at the crevices opening up in the wrist joint and slumped, as if the air was sucked from his lungs. He slowly walked from the room, his guardsmen stepping aside as though repelled by his presence.

The door swung shut behind them, and Connor took Rebekah in his arms.

"Tomorrow will be interesting," she said.

Connor laughed. "I don't think he will argue when I suggest you chair a meeting with the human candidates I've chosen."

Chapter 3

The one armed figure stood inside the tunnel which extended out to the lighthouse at Roker Pier. The frail looking vampire brushed at the grit ingrained into his coat, twisting at an awkward angle to reach around the empty sleeve hanging on his 'armless' side. Checking his watch, he took a fast walk along the hundred yards of the dank pier tunnel to the far end and cocked his head, listening. His yellow-toothed smile crinkled his paper-thin skin as he grunted in frustration, executed a U-turn and returned to where the steps led up into the towering lighthouse structure.

The journey to Sunderland, skirting Newcastle and the vampire hunting grounds, had gone smoothly, but his present surroundings were a long way from the comfort of his London home. Running water had stained the tunnel walls ochre and soaked into the brickwork, creating dark patches where the off-white paint had flaked away. The rise of vampires had put paid to the pier renovation works set to begin in 2012.

Back at the spot in the tunnel from where he started, muttering, he pulled an I.V. bag from its resting place on top of the thick rusty pipe running along the wall, popped open the valve at the top, and guzzled half the contents. It was a blend of animal and human blood – a cocktail which slid down his gullet and trickled through his veins like warm honey. For a moment, a glazed expression softened his features and the old vampire's slack jaw dropped open. A stream of precious blood ran down his chin until he wiped it away with the back of his hand.

Closing the cap on the sagging bag, he set it back in its place in the center of the row. To the left, six empty oily-skinned pouches glistened in the dim light, and three still-full bulging bags sat side by side like ruby-red potbellied creatures.

"Three left." He felt like an inmate on death row waiting for an appeal hearing. "How much longer am I here?"

He had lost count of how many weeks the pier tunnel had been his prison.

The first crop of I.V. bags were already in place when he first arrived, and had been replenished by silent messengers countless times. It seemed a lifetime ago, which was ironic given the expected lifespan of a vampire.

He froze at the mournful clang of a bell out in the harbor. Reacting at speed, he pulled a thick linen sack from a hole in the brickwork and shook off the cement dust. He scuttled along the tunnel, faced the wall at a designated spot thirty feet away from his food supply, and pulled the sack over his head. It was a relief that his wardens would not let him starve. His coat flapped in the gusting breeze made by his fast-moving vampire visitors and the urge to look was compelling. But the sergeant's orders were crystal clear – if you look, you are on your own. He could hear the slapping noises the new full I.V. bags made when handled, slipping efficiently through fast-moving fingers. The whispering retreat of footsteps merely confirmed that more than one vampire had entered the tunnel, nothing more. Once the delivery of his food supply was accomplished, the bell sounded again and he was free to move.

Pulling off the hood and pushing it back into its crevice, his feelings were mixed when he counted a dozen dull-ruby pouches lined up against the cold damp wall. It meant he could expect to be here a few more weeks, at least.

Ten minutes elapsed, and when he dared to venture up the steps and peer out across the landscape, the lone building at the edge of the beach, which seemed a far more comfortable hiding place, taunted him. The fresh air rushing over the tight mask of his skin and whipping his hair into a gray cloud felt exhilarating.

One stormy night, when cabin fever had driven him out of hiding, he had climbed the cracked stairs and stood out on the pier itself – the exposed cobbled pathway was crumbling and the metal railings rusted. On the distant raised platform out in the bay, stood the sentinel guard of the lighthouse, its red and white masonry faded into blended bands of color rather than the stripes they once were. The glazed panels at the summit were frosted gray. Even with preternatural sight, he could not decide if the panes were cracked, crusted with salt, or if spiders had set up residence and filled the lamp chamber with cobwebs. Beneath the lead-gray stormy sky, the crashing waves collided with the seawall and rose as high as the towering lighthouse. The billowing mass of snowy white spray resembled a sea monster rearing up to consume the edifice. The gale force winds tore at his skin and clothes but the seventy-year old vampire remained rock still. He had stood unmoving for the hour it took for the squalling wind to die down before he descended into the pier tunnel once more.

That storm had been a month ago, and still he waited for instructions.

Today, the choppy sea glittered in the moonlight like a carpet of shattered glass.

A mist of sea spray rose as the buffeting wind picked up until he could no longer see the row of houses on the mainland. A shudder rattled through him, he closed his eyes and took an inventory of his own body. *I need grave sleep.* He snorted. His time as a vampire had been brutal and grueling, and far from the indestructible super being of legend. The human form he preserved was not so much 'prime beef' as 'emaciated goat'. He was a weak immortal.

All three types of vampire sleep replenished a brain-center, and rendered a vampire unaware and vulnerable. He had discovered the only grain of truth in vampire myth was that they needed to hide inside coffins or crypts for their own protection.

If he was unleashing the mellow traits of revival sleep, or even the aggressive drunken inclinations of rap-sleep, he could have avoided incarceration. With a resentful grumble, he returned to his subterranean prison, crossed to the metal hatch plate in the floor and with his one hand, pushed bony fingers under the edge and slid it aside. The foam padded pit beneath was 'man-sized', or rather 'elderly vampire-sized'. With a sigh of resignation, he stepped down into the hole, laid out flat, and used the handle welded inside to slide the metal lid back into place. The profound darkness made the psychopath of grave sleep rattle louder at the cell door. The human blood component in the I.V. bag meal would unlock his brainstem and allow rehydration and, as shudders racked his body, he would soon lose control; self-awareness would fade until hunger became the driving force.

When vampires had wandered through the human occupied London streets, in grave sleep, they would attack anything warm blooded that moved, taking the risk of exposing their kind as *real* monsters.

Luckily, here in the pier tunnel there was no such lure for the vampire to resist. Pulling on the handle and bedding the lid into place, he engaged the chain and padlock which anchored the steel panel to the concrete block sunk into the ground on his left side.

Did they make this sleeping pit just for me? He took a deep breath and the aged musty smell made him think not. This was the resting place used by an ancient, long before he arrived here as the latest resident.

As the cell door of his brain center opened and a ghostly screech reverberated inside his skull, he closed his eyes and unleashed the blood thirsty killer. He clenched every muscle tight but his body rattled and his teeth clattered – at his advanced human age, his muscle tone could not achieve the corpse-like stillness easily maintained by Connor, Julian and other younger men. The tendons in his neck bulged as pink tinted saliva dribbled from the corners of his mouth.

As the fuse-wire of heat raced through every nerve ending, he tried very hard to think of other things. The padded sides of the pit crushed his shoulders and he was reminded of the last time he was strapped down in a coffin.

When imprisoned in a steel coffin shell in the London hospital chapel, incapacitated by a dose of muscle relaxant, he had had a lot of time to think and to dread the 'ending' he would be sentenced to suffer. Staring at the chapel ceiling in the dimly lit and fragrant chamber, the last face that he expected to see peering down at him, was the sergeant who had escorted him here and arranged for his incarceration.

The vampire frowned in his sleep and ground his teeth.

If the help had come from Juror Alexander, he would have felt more in control. He knew how to manipulate the juror. The youngster had a conscience and that was a good thing – easily exploited. But the sergeant, and what was clearly his close-knit squad, were a different proposition. He remembered when one of the soldiers pulled a knitted skull cap on and just as quickly, at a hiss from the sergeant, whipped it off again. The gold thread of an emblem had glinted for a nanosecond and the vampire had the uncomfortable feeling that the unit were concealing their identity. *Why are they helping me?* He sensed he was part of a bigger plot and that was all the more threatening.

All these months later, he still knew next to nothing about the sergeant and that rattled him. Even when the sergeant provided the vampire with a disguise, and the squad of four guardsmen who escorted him through the London streets delivered him into the custody of a surgeon near Reading, he could get no more than five words out of the commander and his men.

The moment he arrived at the premises of the 'mad surgeon' – no longer allowed to operate when still human because of his scalpel happy attitude, he became a vampire who specialized in 'improving' his compatriots who 'wanted a change' – the squad of guards left the surgery. When the door shut behind them, the doctor folded his arms and inspected his next project.

The rattled vampire shifted his shoulders, feeling the weight of the surgeon's analytical stare as if it was pressing into his skin.

Seconds ticked away before the surgeon said, "Spending decades looking the same can drive you nuts and I ask no questions." His voice held a static crackle of disused vocal chords and his fixed grin was not reassuring.

Finally, recognizing a standoff he could not win, the vampire pushed back the cowl hood of his thick twill coat, revealing iron gray hair and a sagging face. Age devastated humans over time, but because of a bitter resentful nature, the aging process had accelerated far beyond his seventy mortal years for the vampire. Another bitter pill; there was no rejuvenation to youth in becoming immortal.

The surgeon circled the patient, inspecting the subject's skull from every angle. "We will see," he said, as he laid out instruments and then poured white powder into a bowl. "Sit."

The vampire did as he was told. Shedding the thick coat, he reclined in the padded examination chair.

The surgeon appeared in his vision with a scalpel in his hand and before the patient could even swallow, pushed back lank damp hair and made an incision through the yellowed aged skin of the forehead. Unlike living tissue, the stiff parchment crackled. The surgeon flooded the area with something wet, slid the skin across the lubricated bone, and in a similar sensation to the shriveling of dehydration, the vampire felt tightness pull his face rigid.

He tugged on the surgeon's sleeve with bony fingers, letting go quickly when he realized how dangerous that might be.

The small wiry figure stared down into the eyes of the patient and the cold black abyss of his gaze was chilling. He grinned.

"Not too tight," the helpless vampire pleaded, remembering the faces of celebrities he'd seen in newspapers, when the media still existed, of women apparently caught in wind tunnels.

The surgeon's hands started moving again, and the old vampire surrendered to fate. He felt relief when he saw a tube of glue in his tormentor's hand and a slug-like trail of adhesive oozed across his hairline and down either side to his jaw.

More liquid was wiped over the completed mask and, just when he thought it was over, the needle came out. The syringe barrel glistened red with blood and he felt the needle tip moving in a regimented pattern across his face, like a sewing machine.

"Hydration of the derma," muttered the surgeon.

The syringe clattered when it was replaced onto the instrument trolley, and the physician stood back and pressed a button which moved the couch from reclined to sitting up.

The vampire was not sure he wanted to see, but a mirror was thrust in front of him before he could close his eyes. He inspected the tauter and plumped up hydrated 'skin disguise' which made him look fifty instead of seventy. Thinking of the movie 'Death

Becomes Her' forced a dry chuckle from deep inside him. The last laugh was that the farce had become the new reality. When you wanted to live forever and your body let you down... *what are you gonna do?*

The plan was for the 'new face' to get the vampire through the towns between Reading and Sunderland – Principal Julian had posted an APB out on him the moment he was discovered as missing from the London hospital chapel.

Tilting his head as he, too, surveyed the result of his work, the surgeon whispered hoarsely, "Stay out of daylight for a month, at least. Feed often. I'd advise you to double your daily blood diet."

Still staring at the face that was his own, and yet not, the vampire merely nodded.

"You'll remain here in my basement for the first three days."

"Thank you," he said, and found that he meant it. As he swung his feet to the floor, it hit him that his body remained that of a wasted seventy-year-old, but that was the reality of smoke and mirrors.

When it was finally time to leave, standing on the sidewalk in a back alley which led out between two tall buildings, the mad surgeon handed over a piece of paper printed with a vampire Ident number.

"Memorize it. This is who you are now, if you are stopped. Jacob Pearce."

"Where is the real Jacob Pearce?"

"He resembled the younger version of you, so he no longer exists." The answer was stark and pragmatic.

Shuffling his feet, the vampire read the number and mumbled it under his breath. He was on the right side of the 'mad surgeon', but a cold feeling ran down his spine, a reminder that if that changed, he could suffer the fate of the *other* Jacob Pearce.

"Travel only between the hours of midnight and three a.m." said his companion.

He wanted to ask why, but the need to get away swamped any curiosity he felt. He did not know the name of this lunatic and that was deliberate.

The vampire returned the scrap of paper for the surgeon to destroy, stepped back out of arm's reach, and flapped his hand in a feeble farewell. He scuttled away and the cackle of laughter floating on the air behind him made his pace accelerate.

"Jacob Pearce. That's who I am, for now."

Wearing a mannequin's arm, reclaimed from a derelict department store and strapped to his shoulder by the surgeon as part of the disguise, he tried to swing it in time with his stride, but his rolling gait looked ridiculous. In the end, he opted for speed and hoped for the best. He couldn't imagine being spotted this far north west of London, but a one armed vampire was not a common sight, so he had submitted to the embarrassing subterfuge. The end result was good enough to dupe fools. He grinned. *And it turns out that a lot of hive members are fools.* As long as he avoided bumping into guardsmen, he would be safe.

Getting used to his new face had the unexpected effect of making him feel like a phoenix rising from the fire.

Who would move into his London home didn't matter anymore. Pausing on the corner of an intersection, he pulled the photo of his wife in his human past-life from his overcoat pocket and stared at it. Saliva ran down his chin as the photo lost focus. He tore it into tiny pieces and let the wind snatch them from his fingers. Doctor Connor's fate was all that mattered now. He scanned the streets before accelerating away as fast as the false arm would allow.

Traveling for three hours, only in the dead of night, he stopped at agreed waypoints where he found food and a secure place to hide from both the sun and the vampires who could be looking for him.

Roker Pier became his final destination, although he didn't know that until he arrived and found strict instructions to 'stay put' written on the wall in mud.

But 'staying put' became more difficult as each month passed.

When he surfaced from the knotted tension of grave sleep, after wrestling the psychopathic traits of his own nature back into the cell inside his head, the vampire opened his eyes and felt each grain of dirt sitting on his skin, as if they were specks of hot ash. He wallowed in the blazing clarity of a fully hydrated brain center, wishing he could stay in this moment forever.

Finally, accepting the inevitable, he emerged from the pit and replaced the hatch, flexed his hand and stretched out muscles to ease out cramp.

Still enjoying the renewed vigor of being fully alert and well-fed, the vampire was jolted back to his current predicament when a loud thud sent a shower of grit scuttling down the walls inside the pier tunnel, covering his shoulders in gray powder. Fear gripped the back of his neck and he pressed into the wall and stood stone still. *Who is there?*

Sidestepping towards the concrete stairway where moonlight plumed into the tunnel like mist, the vampire's preternatural sight made out the darker blot of a tall shadow on the ground. He had two choices, well three, call out, stay and wait, or run away.

The glisten of slouched I.V. bags sitting on the pipe mocked him and, resigning himself to a lung full of grit, he took a deep breath so he could talk, walked out into the open, and said firmly, "Who's there?"

A deep voice said, "You can come out, now. It is time."

"Time for what?" His voice quavered.

As boots scraped on the causeway overhead, the vampire jerked into action. The confined space was claustrophobic and the idea of facing the sergeant beneath ground drove him up the steps.

The tall stout figure dominated the eerily quiet night. The wind flipped at the sergeant's cloak like a mischievous child and the silver threads in his coal black hair gleamed in the moonlight. From where he stood, shadows on his face created ghoulish ink black pools over his eye sockets.

"Councilor." The officer dipped his head.

"Where am I going?"

"More to the point, are you ready to play your part?"

"I'll play my part." His new younger face allowed him to grin with fervor he did not feel.

Stepping closer, the sergeant tilted his head and inspected the mad surgeon's handiwork. "Our friend did a good job. You are you, but not you. Were you pleased?"

"Pleased? I had no choice." He drew up to his moderate height and glared. "Why did you get me out of the chapel just to leave me here?" He sounded like a spoiled child, and knew it.

The sergeant glowered and the old vampire shrank back, keeping his eyes glued to the hard planes of the taller man's face, even though he really wanted to close them and wait for the sky to fall in.

His irritation dying like a snuffed flame in a puff of wind, the sergeant unclenched his fists, lifted his chin and bellowed with laughter. "Here, make a hole in the lining of your coat and poke this inside it." He handed over a folded note in a sealed plastic bag. "You will share this with the captain only when the time is right."

"Captain?"

"Come."

The vampire found walking harder than he expected, as if terror had sucked the strength from his legs, and he staggered.

The sergeant gripped his charge by the elbow and pulled him back on track. "I can't tell you everything you want to know. A boat is here to take you onboard a ship." The sergeant held up a hand to ward off interruptions. "As I told you at the chapel, the plan is complicated, but it is time."

The vampire glanced at the triumphant grin on the handsome strong profile of his captor and did not doubt the truth of that. "I stay onboard the ship?" He settled for an easy question, or so he thought.

The silence stretched as the pair made their way along the length of the pier.

"Do I-?"

"I heard you."

"Well?"

"You'll be docked in London, for a while at least. Be ready to move against Doctor Connor when things hot up."

"You need me as much as I need you," The old vampire jerked his chin up to a defiant angle.

"You are right, we need each other to get what we both want." The sergeant smiled but his eyes gleamed with spite.

The vampire had no idea what motivated his companion and, during the months abandoned beneath Roker Pier, he began to think he had made a pact with the Devil. Fear of the unknown made his skin crawl. The knot in his stomach felt like it would tear a hole in his flesh so he clamped his one arm around his middle and dropped his chin to his chest, but he kept walking. Like a man on death row, he had nowhere else to go.

When the pair reached the stone steps which led from the pier down to a concrete ledge, the vampire saw a large tender bobbing on the water.

A glance at the sergeant confirmed this was his transportation. He instantly recognized the salt-encrusted garb worn by the pilot and crew. He didn't want to think about why *they* were here.

"You will be looked after and fed. We are pieces in the same game and when the time comes for you to play your part, you will know."

"At least tell me what made you choose me as a pawn." Ignorance weighing down on the old vampire felt like worms gnawing at his gut. "Give me something."

The sergeant tapped a long white finger on his chin, dropped his hand abruptly and, with a sharp nod, said, "You hate Doctor Connor almost as much as I do."

"Hate Doctor Connor?" A tight smile bared his teeth. "No one could despise him more than me, but it is good to know I have a partner in crime."

"Don't confuse a common goal with friendship." The old vampire's wrist creaked when the sergeant gripped it and yanked him closer. "Your instructions remain the same. Sit tight until the time comes."

Down below, one occupant of the boat stood up and reached out for his new passenger.

"They are right, it's time to go."

The vampire turned his attention to the waiting boat, watching a crewman leap nimbly ashore. The vessel rocked gently when a tall forbidding vampire rose, his black cloak glistening as if an oil slick poured over his shoulders. He turned to face the pier, and the metal mask he wore glinted in the moonlight.

The old vampire fell back a step to make room for the visitors.

A crewman braced his feet on the concrete steps and held out an arm until the metal mask wearing figure gripped his sleeve.

Is he blind? The vampire kept the question to himself.

The pair ascended to the cobblestoned causeway and the small escort led his master over to the sergeant.

"Things are moving fast," the smaller vampire said, his croaking voice jarring with the whispering lullaby of the waves lapping against the pier.

"Not yet," said the sergeant. Turning to his charge, he waved a hand towards the tender. "This is your transport to the ship."

With a sharp nod, the vampire went down the steps and took a seat on the boat. Hearing Connor's name had ignited a fire in his belly and the kindling of old resentment and hatred became an inferno.

The trio of figures still standing on the pier faded quickly from view, and the vampire zoned out as he basked in the news that it was not over. *Doctor Connor is not yet out of reach.*

The boat rocked gently in the embrace of the harbor and, in the distance, the black hull of a container ship sat on the rippling deep blue silk.

The vampire inspected his companion more closely and when the boat pilot turned towards him, the puffed blue-veined complexion of his face confirmed his fears. *Super tanker nomads.*

The tender was soon dwarfed by the hull looming high above. The pilot expertly swung the boat around until the side bumped into the ship. Swaying in time with the waves, it bounced gently with each cresting swell.

A ladder clattered down from above and landed in the bottom of the boat. When the nomad pilot stood and held onto it, his coal black eyes focused on his passenger with piercing intensity. As if twin lasers pierced his brain, the vampire felt compelled to scale awkwardly to the top. Swinging his feet over onto the deck, he froze.

The wall of broad-chested bodies ranged before him prevented him from moving. The expression on each nomad face was identical, and when those standing the closest all smiled at the same moment, his cold heart almost shattered. The pressure in his chest made thinking difficult, but then the crew from the tender sprang over the guardrail, landed beside him, and the throng instantly parted.

With barely a glance over a shoulder, his nomad escort strode away, leaving the vampire scuttling to keep up. Winding a path between the containers anchored on the deck, he kept the moving figure in sight. At the metal-lined wall where the living quarters extended below deck, the nomad pulled open a riveted door panel and waited.

Following the waved gesture from his escort, the vampire headed into the dark interior. Three narrow gangways and two flights of metal stairs later, he was ushered into a windowless cabin.

It was essentially a metal cell with a coffin-shaped safe – for grave sleep – a closet for a change of clothes, which the prisoner did not have, and a metal box with 'blood' stenciled on it.

The rattle of chains made the vampire's head shoot round. He watched the nomad cross to the coffin and raise an eye-brow, the squid-like complexion glowing in the dim light of a bulkhead lamp. "Please, I don't need to be restrained." He flapped one arm to illustrate his handicap.

The nomad tilted his head, darted across the room, and grabbed the vampire by the forearm, wrenching the limb into a grotesque pose – the tendons creaked and, as if testing the bone density, the nomad tapped the twisted wrist with his knuckle. Locking eyes with the prisoner, a guttural rasp gurgled in the nomad's throat and a fine spray of spittle covered the vampire's new face. The glow of gray teeth flashed, before his escort let go and retreated to the doorway. Jabbing his fingers at the rear wall, the nomad shut the door.

The vampire released a deep sigh and wiped his face with the empty coat sleeve. Circling his new prison, it felt like things had gone downhill. *But I'm happy to be part of the game, if this sergeant knows what the Hell he is doing.* As long as he was on the winning side, he would be content.

Shrugging out of his coat, he poked his fingers in through the tear in the lining, pulled out the plastic bag with the folded paper inside, and studied it. It contained information about the London Hive hierarchy and the location of the newly built synthetic blood manufacturing plant. *Connor is the main target, so that makes sense.* Now, he was onboard, the sergeant's instructions became clearer. He was to use the paper to persuade the ship's captain that he was on his side and useful. Feeling more relaxed, he rolled the note into a cigar shape and fed it back in through the hole in the lining. He rested his backside on the lid of the metal blood box, crossed his ankles and descended into a state of meditation. Survival instinct dictated that conserving energy was his only course of action.

Tuning into the gentle creaking of the hull, he listened for the return of the captain and for the ship to be underway. The sergeant would not be here to watch over him, but he knew failure was not an option. He had a performance to deliver. The backstory the sergeant was giving Captain Blake made his passenger a refugee called Jacob Pearce, who had lost his memory. *The rest is up to me.*

Chapter 4

The bedroom inside which Julian lay on his back with Leizle tucked into his side could have belonged to a normal couple, except for the *two* stacked mattresses resting on a bed-base made of bricks – they had tried various bed frames, but none survived more than a week beneath Julian's dense vampire weight. The dawn light drifting in through a sash window created a pearly glow, and he took in a deep contented breath, brushing his chin over her hair to release the delicious scent that was just hers.

He felt her warm cheek resting on his chest move as she smiled. He knew she'd been drifting in and out of slumber for half an hour – the electrical impulses sparking through her brain created static energy he easily tuned into – but they both enjoyed this time of day too much to want to move. They were completely alone and could ignore the demands and friction which waited outside these walls.

"Good morning," he whispered.

As soon as he said the words, tension crept into her muscles. When she tried to wriggle up onto one elbow, he pinned her still with the iron band of his arm, not gripping, that would cause bruising, but not giving her room to move.

She huffed with annoyance.

"Stop stressing. Enjoy the moment."

Like an obedient child, after all, she didn't really have any choice, Leizle relaxed back into place, resting her cheek on his naked chest, again, and trailing her fingertips over his cool, stone-smooth flesh.

It didn't take long before his fingers moved to cover hers and hold them still, and she giggled.

The distant song of birds greeting the dawn filtered through the air.

Situated off the beaten track in the quiet suburban streets of South London, Rebekah and her eco-shelter group of refugees had established this safe-house, unaware of the role it would play on the fateful day when Connor discovered them. The acceleration towards chaos that collision course triggered still made Julian's head spin. After decades of stagnation, the chaos felt exhilarating.

But, the Victorian terraced house in Clapham was now a second home to the eco-community and the chosen retreat where Julian and Leizle stole time together. The glass windows were clean, the carpets new, and beside the bookcase in the sitting room, the cork-board with the survival map of the safe and unsafe boroughs of London was framed behind glass as a reminder of the old days.

The basement the humans had used as refuge now served its correct function as a store for candles, coal and kindling, oil for lamps and dried or tinned food. A family-sized larder had been built and fitted with marble shelves in a throw-back to the early 1900s, before refrigerators were affordable. In the chill of the basement, the cold marble kept perishable food edible for much longer.

Being in this house was the closest Leizle could experience to living in the pre-vampire era. Things her parents had taken for granted remained a source of joy. Today, Leizle was going shopping in London; another first in her lifetime.

Vampires were being forced to carve a space for humans in a world they had dominated for over twenty years and, as part of the agreement, the human population could come out of hiding and once more walk the streets.

Like any society, there were still dangers – human cities had had muggers, rapists and murderers in their midst, and now there would always be 'hungry vampire' to add to the list, so for now, human outings were limited to the hours between midday and three o'clock. But, as it was a special occasion, Leizle had the joy of shopping for an entire day.

Shifting so he could look down into her eyes, Julian gently released Leizle from his embrace. "I suppose I'd better let you go. You have a busy schedule ahead."

They both knew that he was the one with responsibilities pressing down, but she grinned up at him anyway. "So, I do. Lots of things to plan."

As she hitched up onto an elbow, slipped her naked thigh over his and eased her body closer, her smile dimmed.

With a glint of mischief in his eye, he stroked a hand around her waist and ran it down to cover the swell of her backside, enjoying the silken warmth of her skin. Her breasts burned his chest and his gaze dropped to study the pulse throbbing in her throat. "Oh, delicious torture," he murmured.

She frowned, her gaze searching his face.

He didn't smile, not yet, he could see the worries chasing through her mind like wind-blown clouds. "I will not change my mind," he said gently, stroking a long white fingertip over her flushed cheek and hooking a strand of copper-bright hair behind her ear.

"Are you sure?"

He deliberately rumbled a growl through his chest. "Women," he groaned, and pressed his lips to hers. But, he couldn't blame her, not really. Julian's 19th Century repression had made him a reluctant suitor, at best, a rigid iceberg, at worst. But now, his mind was made up. "You have a wedding to plan, young lady."

In a weird role reversal, having spent two years desperately wanting Julian to give in and say he loved her, now he was committed and had asked her to marry him, all she could think of was giving him his freedom.

"But, you've been alive for hundreds of years, how can you know this – us – is forever?"

Julian looked into her eyes and said simply, "Eva."

Leizle knew of his wife when he was alive. She knew how much he had loved her, too. She faltered for one more second and then grinned. "I have shopping to do."

Rolling away and throwing back the bedcovers, Leizle leapt up and headed for the bathroom, but before she reached the doorway, Julian blocked her path, fully dressed for his day in council, with every mid-length blond hair in place. Slipping an arm around her waist, he nuzzled her shoulder and inhaled her scent.

With a smile, she wound her arms around his neck and pressed her lips to his, welcoming his kiss and letting him in. When she gently bit his lip as he withdrew, he coughed to clear his suddenly constricted throat. Resting his forehead on hers, he grumbled gently, "That should keep me going until I get home."

"Home. That sounds good." She reached up and dropped a kiss on the end of his nose.

Her hair flapped around her face as he disappeared – they *never* said 'goodbye'. Their world had been a rollercoaster ride and being together was all they wanted, forever. *And now...*

Standing beneath the warm spray of water, Leizle allowed the cocoon of happiness to warm her heart. She hummed tunelessly as she stepped out of the shower and grabbed a towel. Shopping for her wedding dress should feel surreal, but her entire existence had felt surreal for many years.

Returning to the bedroom wrapped in the towel, she yelped and jumped back when she spotted Seren sitting cross-legged on the bed, waiting.

"Good grief, you scared the bejeezus out of me. It's like a vampire turnstile," chuckled Leizle.

Seren beamed and leapt from the bed to rush over and grab her by the hand. "Come on. Hurry up, I've found some amazing dresses for you to try." Seren visibly preened, exuding triumph.

Leizle scowled playfully. "Now I know how your mother felt. Did Rebekah get to make *any* choices?"

"Mama will look amazing, and so will you. But a double wedding is a delicate balancing act, you know. I've been reading up on it. You both have to shine, and *that* is my job."

The hand Seren waved with a flourish almost made Leizle laugh, but she knew the young girl would be hurt, so she bit her cheek and turned her attention to locating clean underwear and clothes.

"How are we getting there?" Leizle threw over her shoulder as she pulled on a shirt.

"A motorbike is parked up outside." The young girl grinned.

Ten minutes later, Leizle hurtled along the eerily deserted suburbs following Seren, who was running. Inside the crash helmet which Julian insisted she wore, Leizle grinned widely.

Exhilaration at pushing the machine to its limit was only part of the reason. The twin engine of the bike whined like an angry wasp, and still Seren looked back at intervals and slowed her pace to let Leizle keep up. *What is it like to be able to run like that?* She would know, quite soon, and that was the reason she felt like an addict on a high. Her wedding night would be her last night as a human, Julian had promised.

As Leizle followed Seren's fleeting figure over Vauxhall Bridge, the spray splattered her visor and she automatically wiped it away with her glove, but, when she looked up again, Seren had vanished. *Shit. Where did she go?* At first, she wasn't concerned, but as she twisted open the throttle and darted forward, her nape tightened with unease. The darker days were not so far removed and crossing the bridge had always been the risky, exposed part of any foraging expedition into the City. Once they were over the river and headed towards Piccadilly Circus, there was plenty of shelter to dive into if a vampire appeared.

Slowing down so the engine note felt less like a siren shouting 'come and get me', Leizle scanned the street. Options ran through her head. *Do I pull over and wait? Go to Oxford Circus and hope Seren is there, or go back to the safe house… or find Julian?* She laughed wryly. She didn't think Julian would enjoy the diversion her appearance at the council building would cause. *Okay…*

Out of nowhere, up ahead, a dark figure appeared, and Leizle's body jolted with fear. The bike bucked, surging forward, and her feet scrabbled to keep it from falling, and then suddenly, a black-gloved hand gripped the handle bars and the drama was over.

"Anthony," she blurted, "you scared the crap out of me."

The tall brown-haired vampire quirked a crooked smile from beneath the hood he wore to shield him from the sun. "Sorry, Seren is waiting and I offered to come find you."

Leizle huffed. "That girl needs to slow down a bit."

Anthony kept pace beside Leizle as she trundled forward at a modest speed in a mark of protest. The miles to Oxford Circus were covered in a companionable silence. Anthony was a friend, and she began to smell a rat. He was very jittery. *But why?*

When they rounded the final corner, Leizle stopped dead. Anthony caught the bike as she scrambled off and let it fall, pulled off her helmet, and ran full tilt towards the corner where the gleamingly clean plate glass windows of Selfridges glowed with dramatic lighting. The tall Georgian pillars were bathed lilac by spotlights, and the scene resembled a fairytale castle, but it was towards the pair of figures standing in the doorway with huge grins pinned on their faces that Leizle pelted.

Rebekah stepped forward and held out her arms. "Surprise," she said, a wide smile lighting up her glittering brown eyes.

"You're back, I thought you were still in Cardiff. I'm so pleased to see you." Leizle grabbed Rebekah and squeezed her solid frame as hard as her human arms could manage.

"Hey, I couldn't miss the wedding dress shopping. What kind of sister would that make me?"

Leizle frowned at Seren. "You. You had me fooled."

"Sorry, Aunt Leizle, I couldn't resist."

It was then that Leizle peered in through the wall of glass behind her welcoming party. "Wow, Selfridges. I've never seen it 'open'."

Rebekah laughed. "It's amazing what the principal of the hive can accomplish with a working party of vampires at his disposal."

As a group, they pushed open the hefty glass door and walked inside. Every surface gleamed. The floor was like a marble mirror, the brass and crystal fittings glittered, and the rails of clothes smelled fresh and crisp.

"Julian did all this?"

Rebekah laid a hand on Leizle's arm. "Let's shop, hmm? Let's try on dresses and feel pretty."

Leizle peered into Rebekah's preternatural features and stroked her fingers down over the pearl tinted skin of her cheek. "Thank you for coming back. Is Connor-?"

"Connor will be away another day or two, but don't worry about him, *this* is girl time."

The three held hands and let Seren drag them along to the bridal department which Julian had resurrected.

Glancing back over her shoulder, Leizle noticed Anthony was the middle figure in a wall of five vampires out on the sidewalk. It was clear that no one would disturb their day.

Chapter 5

Feeling like a mischievous school kid, Julian took up a position in the rank of vampires guarding the front of Selfridges. Anthony caught his eye after the women had gone inside and said, "Happy, now?"

"Almost," replied Julian. He had told Anthony that he wanted to make sure the arrangements had been executed correctly and that the route through the City was cleared of vampires for Leizle's safety, but they both knew he wanted to see her face when she discovered the surprise shopping destination.

Julian tuned into the conversation unfolding beyond the glass doors. "He did all this? When did he get the time?"

Leizle would know he had directed proceedings because her favorite flowers were arranged in huge splashes of color throughout the store, a display stand had a selection of all the perfumes she had sighed over in old magazines, and Julian had combed the stock rooms of the high-end boutiques in London for an Alexander McQueen dress she coveted – embellished with sheer lace, ladder frills, and a tiered skirt. He felt certain he had found the dream dress.

His love and devotion was clear in every detail of the Selfridges 'renovation'.

Wishing he could stay, but knowing that duty called and he could not eavesdrop any longer, Julian finally grinned and gave a smart salute. "I'm going." He chuckled when Anthony raised an eyebrow in a look that said, 'really?' and folded his arms.

Leaving the shelter of the shady side of the street, Julian pulled on leather gloves and turned up his collar to shield the lower part of his face.

A golden lake bled over the horizon, the glowing bright orb swelling in the center warning Julian that the shadows he needed would disappear fast. *Leizle is worth it.* Spending time lying by her side and listening to her deep breathing as she slept was one of those 'being in the moment' experiences. He was not principal of the London Hive in that instant, he was just a man who felt at peace. It never lasted. Duty called. This morning, after watching her wake, while she was still warm and flushed from sleep, he found leaving her harder than usual. He smiled slowly. He had spent the night making love to her and left barely a bruise on her skin; that was a cause to celebrate.

But as he accelerated forcefully into his own arena of influence, he could not shake a heavy feeling in the pit of his stomach. To be fair, nothing had gone smoothly these last three years. *If I was human, I'd put it down to having an ulcer.*

Taking a route where the jagged, irregular, and, at times, graceful architecture of the London skyline provided adequate cover, within minutes, he had entered the jaw like embrace of the tall marble buildings which lined the final approach to the vampire council offices, where even the mid-day sun could not penetrate. He forced himself to relax and headed onwards to what they now called 'the blood district', where the newly built laboratory and manufacturing plant churned out synthetic blood. Trucks rumbled in and out beneath an imposing archway of brick. There were two sets of gates and security was tight as the trucks shuttled between the loading bay and the nearby vampire hospital dispensary, each day. Charles – the blood dispensary attendant – supervised the team of technicians working under him. With an additional industry to run, vampires were busier than they had ever been, but then, they did have unlimited wakeful hours to fill.

Skimming up the steps to the main entrance of the 'Synthetic Blood Factory', Julian scanned his I.D. card and went inside. The brightly lit interior always caught him out. Vampires could see perfectly well in near darkness, but Connor wanted every vampire to 'feel' the importance of their work here. He *wanted* it to be a jolt to their senses.

At the end of a corridor, Julian pushed through swing doors and walked slowly through the cavernous space. The acrylic panels covering the walls acted like milk-white mirrors, reflecting and refracting images and making the dozens of lab assistants appear to be a throng. The polished benches were crowded with stainless-steel machinery: agitators, centrifuges, dosing pumps –

all of which hummed and clunked in a musical a-cappella inspired rhythm.

Connor's worker ants, as Julian thought of them, kept the production line running in their mentor's absence. Julian's innards would remain knotted with tension until Doctor Connor returned from the Cardiff Hive. He felt as though he was babysitting Frankenstein's monster. He knew the theory, of course he did, but his side of the operation was the building of 'Human Town'. *I must find a better name for it, than that.* The engineering and town planning department being run by human foremen and the donkey work executed by vampire drones was a perfect example of irony.

The hive members might have lost touch with the luxuries humans needed to be happy, but with a whole town and its infrastructure to be built, they made an excellent workforce who could keep going for twenty-four hours straight – unless it was a baking hot day.

Covering their skin against the sun for too many hours had debilitating effects – vampire skin needed 'air-flow' to temper the surface to its ideal granite-like texture. Spongy skin made them vulnerable to harm. Not a problem in 'peace time', but battles rarely announced their arrival, and being ready for anything made sense in these strange times.

Julian nodded to the lab assistants who registered his presence, and headed up a flight of open metal stairs. Inside the shift supervisor's office, the hive mortuary attendant from the hospital was checking the inventory.

"Good morning, Isaac. How are things going? Are the targets being met?" asked Julian.

The master of multi-tasking and organization, Isaac didn't hesitate to reply, "Four trucks will head out in three minutes. Charles has a group waiting to go hunting on Dartmoor, they will be fed first. The cadaver drawers are full but-" Isaac glanced at his watch. "Twenty will wake up from grave-sleep in ten minutes, and by then Charles will have the supplies sent through for the next shift of sleepers I'm expecting.

The pair made a good team.

"It seems you have everything under control. Sound the siren if you need backup."

"Yes, sir," Isaac said. His relaxed demeanor was reassuring, and Julian skipped lightly back down the steps.

The crisp breeze whistling through the London streets when Julian resumed his journey lifted his spirits further. The battle to win over the hive members had been brutal at times. The blood substitute, perfected on apes and monkeys, was met with skepticism and hostility, in equal measure. The vampires who refused to bend were given stark choices: comply, stand trial for endangering the blood supply, or exile. *And then there were those who went off-piste and forced us to kill them in combat.* For Julian, the ones he felt most concerned about were the exiles. They were choosing a one-way ticket to dementia and, without human blood to rehydrate their brain, could become feral.

Arriving back at the council buildings, Julian pushed open the twelve-foot-tall oak doors, and felt the familiar blanket of security settle around his shoulders. *Home.* He had been the principal of the hive since the days of Jack the Ripper; vampires had been an underground fraternity then, of course, beneath the radar of the human race. Within these walls, Julian ran the show.

He whisked along the polished parquet flooring to enter his chambers, closed the door and assessed his surroundings. The plush carpet and solid wood furniture had not changed in decades. The wooden panels covering the walls, as usual, smelled of linseed oil. Connor often teased him, but Julian enjoyed tradition and, even though Connor had persuaded him to stop wearing a cravat, he still kept his blond hair 19th century long and always would.

He pulled his black principal's gown from the wardrobe and shrugged into it. After checking that it was sitting right in the mirror above the marble mantelpiece, he turned and rested a foot on the fire-grate in the open hearth to wait for Juror Marius and Juror Daniel. Anthony had filled the gap on the jury for a while, but then he stepped down to focus on where he was needed more, manning the surgical ward in Connor's absence. His medical expertise was where his value lay, now that the blood substitute was stable.

Juror Daniel had seemed a natural choice.

Julian smiled. He had only recently persuaded Daniel to leave his longbow in his own chamber. Some defendants found it unsettling when he brought it into the courtroom. He had only been a juror for a year, since Alexander's betrayal and death at Marius' hand.

Thinking of Marius made Julian's smile fade and his green eyes lose their luster.

Of course, his friend could never be the same again. Scars carried inside were one thing, but this time, Marius had paid the physical price in the battle at St Michael's Mount of severed vocal chords. In fending off Marius' latest request to 'die', Connor had fitted a whistle into the elder juror's windpipe. Vampires did not need to 'breathe' so now, whenever Marius wanted attention, he could literally 'whistle for it'.

Killing Alexander for betraying Connor, Rebekah, and Julian, may have been just, but the tall dark juror carried around the guilt as though he dragged Alexander's body behind him. Nothing Julian said made any difference. *He needs to make amends, but only he can say what that means.*

At the knock on the door, Julian called out, "Come."

Daniel entered first, his black hair, messy with curls, made him appear younger than his twenty human years, but the sharp edge of maturity in his slate gray eyes exceeded his vampire span of fifty. He had proven himself in battle against Birgitta and shown the capacity for justice over blind revenge. That made him the perfect candidate for the vacated juror position.

"Gentlemen," said Julian, with a slight nod. "Shall we begin?"

Going through the door in an adjacent wall, Julian led the way, with Marius and Daniel following closely, as though tethered to their principal.

Julian took the central throne chair on the bench, the jurors settling in their places on either side. The dais upon which the trio sat looked down over the square courtroom, the remaining three sides sloping upwards to the gallery, where row upon row of seats were occupied by hive members who had an interest in the 'defendants' who would be brought up from the cells.

There were more spectators than usual, but then, it was a sunny day and this was a good place to shelter.

Banging a gavel on a leather bag of sand, Julian called the court to order.

As the spectators shuffled in their seats and paid attention, the smell of freshly laundered clothes drowned out the other odors in the crowded room. Sunday best was the order of the day, it appeared. The pale faces staring at Julian and his black robed companions ranged in pallor from bleached white, to a disconcerting custard yellow, and onwards down the spectrum to ochre. Without the ruby flush of blood beneath the epidermis, even darker skins became clouded with a frost-like appearance, rendering their complexions dull. Only the newly-fed glowed briefly, like a shooting star across a blushing sky.

The session would last as long as Julian decided, and after dozens of vampire detainees entered, were pardoned or punished, and left again, it began to feel like Groundhog Day.

Julian watched the courtroom door close behind the latest defendant, and told his companions, "Two more."

Both jurors nodded.

"The court will hear 'Sampson verses The Council'," announced Julian.

The side door opened and a tall, harassed looking vampire wearing a torn bloodstained shirt shuffled into the room. The heavy chain between his ankles dragged over the parquet floor. The bowed posture radiated defeat, but Julian knew it was drug induced. A small dose of muscle relaxant slowed a vampire's reaction time and sapped their strength. A full dose was used under two sets of circumstances: to perform surgery, during which the patient would technically be 'awake', or following a sentencing which condemned them to Storage Facility Eight. During the initial stage of paralysis, blood feeds were withheld, accelerating dehydration until the vampire flesh became solid as granite. When the muscle relaxant wore off, the inmate could no longer move, even if he wanted to.

The blood on the accused shirt concerned Julian. "Escort the prisoner to the dock."

The two guardsmen, their purple robes flowing behind them, complied. One opened the wooden gate and the other gripped the prisoner's elbow to guide him up the steps.

Once Sampson could hold onto the brass rail, he seemed to stand taller.

"Sampson, you are accused of assaulting a guard at the human farm, and breaking through three perimeter fences? How do you plead?"

"Not guilty." Sampson jerked his chin up, the glint in his mud-colored eyes defiant.

Julian cut to the chase. "Whose blood is on your shirt?"

"A wolf's."

The gallery shuffled and many sets of eyes turned to stare at the defendant.

Julian smothered his own surprise, undeniably curious. "Please, go on-"

"I wasn't attacking the humans. Ask my friend, Peter. There was a wolf inside the compound. I tried to tell Supervisor Edmund, it had dug a hole and squeezed under the fence. It was skin and bone. Clearly starving. I tried to tell these clowns. They are such ass-."

Julian raised a hand, cutting short the vampire's building tirade.

"Your *human friend*, Peter?" Julian glanced at Marius.

His fellow juror had also sat up ramrod straight when the vampire's explanation spilled out. No words were needed. Marius' impassive face could still radiate curiosity with the merest twitch of a muscle.

Inspecting the distraught figure in the dock, with his grip clamped onto the brass rail as if his life depended upon it, Julian waited.

"I help him, Peter. He is strong and smart. I 'train' with him. Getting him fit enough for the new challenges ahead. Fending for themselves will open up a can of worms."

"What do you mean?" Julian stroked a long finger over his jaw.

Samson looked confused, but then decided the hive principal really wanted to know. "Peter is a leader. He's protected a lot of younger men and girls from the shitty elements. The rapists, thieves, and thugs who are waiting for the chance to act out urges the presence of vampire wardens keep in check."

"I see." And Julian realized, he did. *There will always be the strong who feed on the weak.* "It sounds as though Peter is a man of good morals, an association to nurture."

Sampson locked eyes with Julian. "He's my friend."

The defiant expression on Sampson's face blurred out of focus as Julian digested the information, playing out a scene in his mind of this odd pairing. The derision he would have felt a decade ago became a warm glow of hope. *A vampire/human friendship; a natural, organic occurrence.* This was not something to dismiss.

Concentrating once again on the vampire before him, Julian smiled.

Sampson exuded relief in almost visible waves, his jaw dropping open.

"You will be granted full access to the human compound to visit Peter. Supervisor Edmund will issue you with a pass ident number," Julian announced.

Nonplussed by his rapid change in fortune, Sampson remained frozen to the spot.

As though the jurors shared the same pool of thought, Marius whistled gently, before his long fingers, moving in the emphatic flow of sign language, took up the thread of the debate – his thoughtful features provided the tone he wanted to convey. 'Looking forward, to when all humans are living in their own villages, bonding called 'friendship' could make or break the success of vampires and humans living in harmony.'

Julian nodded slowly. "Sampson, you may continue to spend time with Peter, and extend the offer of physical training to any other humans who want to join you." Letting his attention range across the stiff faces in the gallery, he said, "This is a development that gives me hope."

At the principal's nod, two guardsmen walked forward, helped Sampson down from the dock, and supported his shuffling progress to the exit door. The only sound in the courtroom was that of his shoes scraping over the polished wood.

A shroud of stillness settled over the spectators and Julian let it lay like a drift of snow, hoping the importance of what had just happened sank in.

Finally, clearing his throat, Julian said, "The court will hear 'Joshua verses The Co-'."

But then, the door behind him whipped open. Instantly alert, his hefty throne juddered backwards as the principal jolted to his feet and spun round.

"Principal, I have urgent news," blurted Captain Gerrard, his agitation evident as he rocked from one foot to the other as if unable to stay still. His black-gloved hands repeated a succession of beckoning gestures.

Gerrard turned and disappeared as Julian stepped around his chair to follow.

Marius and Daniel moved as one to head out through the door.

The assembled vampires in the court would wait. Some would descend in to the meditative state familiar in ancient times – when food was scarce, energy must be conserved. Some would converse in low tones. Even though it was late afternoon, all would wait until dusk before giving up on the chance that the court session would resume.

Julian waited for both jurors to arrive in his chamber before closing the door with a firm click and turning an enquiring glance on Gerrard.

"Captain Blake. He requests an audience with you. No, he *demands* an audience."

'He has no authority to make demands,' Marius signed flatly.

Julian's reaction was less measured. "This can't be good. Blake couldn't care less about vampires outside of his crew. If he has something to say, we better hear it. Where is he? Onboard the tanker?"

"No, he's here."

"Here?" Daniel's fingers twitched, as if they searched for the longbow usually slung over his shoulder.

"Waiting in the blood dispensary at the hospital," clarified Gerrard.

Marius got the young juror's attention with a hand on his shoulder. 'Easy, Daniel. Blake is not our ally, but he has more sense than to become our enemy. He needs to barter for blood; his crew need us more than we need them.'

"Captain, have Blake escorted here and show him in," said Julian.

When Gerrard left, the three vampires lined up on the far side of the room. Julian took up his preferred position in front of the fireplace. Marius and Daniel, in the same formation as the courtroom, stood either side of him.

Reacting to the summons at vampire speed, it was only a couple of minutes before the door opened and Captain Blake walked slowly through it, his gloved-hand resting on the arm of his companion. Pushing back the cowl hood of his sweeping cape, Blake unerringly detected where in the room Julian was, despite the slick shiny pool of flesh which replaced his face. His empty eye sockets were damp pools in the translucent blue-veined skin. His mouth had a pink crust where lips had once been, and the charred lump of his tongue glistened like a slug under a rock.

The nomad at the captain's side was nodding, as though answering an imaginary question.

Blake's talking to him. Julian had firsthand experience of how the super tanker community worked. Their blueish flesh resembled jellyfish, or a bloated human corpse pulled from a river. In the two decades since the rise of vampires, Julian had gleaned from past encounters that the nomads were telepathically connected to their maker – Blake – and they lived onboard their

68

vessel. He had witnessed the self-sufficient existence of the entity, with their own herd of humans which got them through long stretches at sea. Blake owed allegiance to no-one and, until his encounter with Connor, had possessed a fully functioning face. A flare discharged at short range had altered all that.

Blake has no love lost with the London Hive, so why is he here?

Impatient with the silent discussion unfolding in front of him, Julian cleared his throat and said, "How can we help you, Captain Blake? My guardsman tells me you requested an audience."

A wet gurgle emitted from Blake's slack mouth, pus-colored saliva dribbled down his chin.

The captain blotted his face with a stained linen cloth while his companion spoke in a voice which crackled like a radio transmission with poor reception. "Principal Julian, as gracious as ever."

The pauses in the speech were as frustrating as listening to a stammer, but Julian gritted his teeth and waited, knowing that the smaller vampire was a puppet under Blake's control.

"I need your help. Medical help. You'll send a doctor to my ship. If you save my first mate, then you will have my information."

Julian glared, even though the captain wouldn't see it.

Blake's wet laugh sprayed phlegm onto the plush carpet this time. The bloated face of his companion bulged as he grinned widely – as though he was ordered to do it. "If my first mate dies, you'll regret it. One hour."

Blake's cape flared as he spun on his heel, the heavy fabric slapping against the captain's legs and settling into greasy folds; ingrained grime was visible beneath a crust of salt. At lightning speed, Blake disappeared like a master magician.

A saline-cloud stung his nostrils when Julian sighed heavily. Staring at the blank space, and then at the globule of greenish slime sitting on the carpet, he said, "Thoughts."

"Send a platoon of guardsmen to the docks. Send him packing," said Daniel. "I'll get my bow and join them."

69

The younger vampire started to move, but Julian held up a hand. Daniel's prowess with a longbow made him deadly at what he did. The flight of his steel arrows had caused many aggressors to turn tail, but Julian felt uneasy.

"Marius?"

'You have to hear him out.' Marius' granite face beneath the sleek cap of coal-black hair radiated certainty as he signed. 'If Blake has information we need, we win. If he is bluffing, *then* Daniel can demonstrate our displeasure.' His eloquent shrug said 'win/win'.

Julian nodded sharply. "All we have to do then, is get Connor back here within the hour."

"How about Anthony?" asked Daniel.

"He is good, very good. But I have a feeling we will need great."

Anthony dealt with the clinics in the hospital – routine amputations and removing graveling tissue from the wounds of sun-scorched vampires – and even the odd emergency, but not this.

"Daniel, go to Cardiff." Slipping the gold hive insignia ring from his middle finger, Julian dropped it into the young juror's palm. "If Principal Glynn has anything to say about it, send him to London. I don't enjoy pulling rank, but I will." Twenty years ago, there were ten hives on the mainland, but now, with only four remaining, although Julian avoided taking the title of 'Sentinel', he commanded the largest and longest running hive in Great Britain. In any dispute, *he* had the deciding vote.

Daniel wrapped the lump of gold in a handkerchief, pushed it into his pants pocket, and left the room.

Marius relaxed into a rare smile, emitting a long gentle whistle of laughter. 'Blake in the same room as Connor? We better have the fire extinguishers ready. Sparks will fly.'

"If Blake needs a good doctor, he'll have to bury the hatchet."

'Let's hope it's not in Connor's head,' replied Marius.

Chapter 6

Standing on the exposed quayside, Julian pulled his coat tighter around his body against the whipping wind. The container ship loomed overhead, the mirror-shine surface of the smooth black hull gleaming in the setting sun reminding Julian of a gigantic scarab. It caused the same trepidation inside his chest, too. The knots in his gut worsened as the sands of time trickled away.

For what felt like the hundredth time, he scraped aside hanks of blond hair that had blown across his face, and peered round to scan the dockyard entrance. *Where is Connor?*

When, twenty minutes later, the gate in the perimeter fence inched open and three figures appeared on the concrete walkway, Julian whacked Marius on the arm with the back of his hand. "They are here," he said.

'You don't say.' Marius whistled, drily.

Connor's driving stride was easy to pick out. He arrived first, and Julian held out a hand in greeting.

"Julian," Connor said, "what the Hell is Blake after?"

"It's something big. For him to come asking for help, it has to be."

Connor smirked. "Not exactly 'asking' from what Daniel says."

Julian glared at the youngster standing beside Connor, and then noticed Rebekah. He opened his mouth, then snapped it shut again and merely smiled. He still had trouble remembering she was no longer a fragile human in need of protection. *Will I have the guts to turn Leizle on our wedding night? I don't know.* Julian almost hoped he would be pushed into it, like Connor had been; Rebekah lying dead in his arms had made the choice a simple one. Drastic, but simple.

"Don't underestimate Blake, Connor. He's still the will that controls the nomads, the spider at the center of the web."

"Don't worry, I won't, but first, how's he going to take it? Seeing me again? Well, not seeing exactly, but you know."

"He needs a great doctor and you're the best there is. The only way to find out is to get on with it." Touching Rebekah's arm, Julian said casually, "Where is Leizle? Did the shopping trip go well?"

Rebekah smiled. "It went very well. I left Seren and Leizle trying out hairstyles. Julian, what you did was perfect."

His fleeting tight grin radiated the love-struck man inside for a moment, before the cloak of principal smothered all emotion. "She is safe, then. Let's get down to business."

The group of four walked towards the vessel and, as though by magic, a metal linked ladder shimmied down the side of the ship, making a musical chiming noise as it bounced against the metal hull.

Without pausing, Connor leapt up onto the ladder and quickly scaled to the top. Rebekah went to follow, her hand already gripping a rung, when Julian stopped her. "Be careful up there."

"I'll be careful, if you promise to keep Seren and Osiris away," Rebekah replied with a smile, but she was deadly serious.

Now full grown, Seren was as headstrong as her mother, she also tended to forget that, as a hybrid, she wasn't as indestructible as she'd like to think. There was no chance of keeping Seren in the dark. She shared a psychic connection with Connor which he could never completely block out. Although, Seren respected Connor's 'do not disturb sign' when he and Rebekah wanted privacy, the girl would sense that her father was primed for danger.

"If she takes Leizle back to the eco-shelter and turns up here, send her home, Julian. *Order* her home."

As if on cue, a slightly built figure scaled the boundary fence and approached in a run which transformed her into a blur.

"Good luck," said Rebekah, swinging up onto the ladder and going after Connor.

Julian faced Seren, held up his hands and said firmly, "Stand down. If you want to stay, you'll behave yourself."

The concern on her pale face tugged at Julian's heartstrings. Reaching out to smooth a strand of black silken hair behind her ear, he held her silver gray gaze, silently asking for her agreement.

"Okay, Uncle Julian, let me stay, and I'll be good."

"All we can do is wait, and no, you must go *home*. I need you to keep Leizle company." The noise of clinking metal rang out, and Julian peered up the sheer face of the ship to watch the ladder slither up the hull. "Your mama and papa will be fine. You know that." *I hope so, anyway.*

Seren folded her arms and made no sign of moving.

With a frown, Julian said, "Daniel, stay with Seren. If she does anything foolish, paddle her backside."

It was a hollow threat, but Seren demurely walked to Daniel's side and exuded meekness.

Julian turned back to the vessel, flanked by Marius and Gerrard, he froze with every tendon in his body pulled tight.

Powering to the top of the ladder, Connor vaulted over the rail and onto the greasy surface of the deck. Ranging a glance over his surroundings, he discovered little had changed since his last visit. The rows of shipping containers anchored to the deck brought back bad memories. Connor wondered if the actual container inside which he had fought for his life, and punched a hole through the back wall of when he escaped, was still in use.

The ship appeared deserted, and Connor frowned.

When Rebekah swung her legs over the rail and dropped silently down beside him, without looking around, Connor reached for her hand.

What now? Her thoughts were a whisper inside his head.

He did look at her then, raised an eyebrow and shrugged.

A tall nomad emerged through a door in the wall of metal panels opposite, which Connor remembered led down to the living quarters of the nomad community.

Silently moving past them, the crewman set about winding a handle to retract the ladder. While the clinking and whirring noises echoed across the deck, Connor and Rebekah held their ground as dozens of vampires swarmed out into the moonlight. The hostility on their faces bared their teeth, a growl rumbling deep in their throats.

"I think they recognize me," said Connor.

A nomad picked up a hefty coil of chain lying on the deck, and took a step towards him, swinging the clanging steel back and forth in the space between them.

Connor shielded Rebekah, baring his teeth in a 'bring it on' smile, but she refused to be protected. Shaking off the restraining hand, she side-stepped out into the open and inspected the row of puffed white faces with open curiosity.

The closest nomads exchanged looks – and no doubt thoughts – and the threatening attitude faded. One of the crew reached out and touched Rebekah's blond streaked hair, recoiling when Connor snarled. Female vampires were rare, and Connor reminded himself of the plan. *Rebekah is here to keep them guessing.*

The nomads, like an ebbing wave pulled back into the ocean, suddenly retreated. A tall dark figure approached and loomed over them. His chin lifted, bathing the pitted surface of his face in moonlight as he scented the air.

Blake. Connor swallowed, waiting for the first move in the game.

"You are the Doctor?" Blake looked towards his companion as he gave voice to the captain's question.

The youngster was a stranger to Connor. They had never met, but he knew others in the group would be falling over themselves to send news of his identity to their captain.

Sure enough, Blake, as if he could suddenly see, faced Connor squarely.

"Should I be impressed that you dare to set foot on my ship again?" his mouthpiece said, haltingly.

Connor dipped his chin, acknowledging Blake's challenge, but realized the ruined face could not see the gesture. "I'm here to treat your casualty." Nothing he could say would change the damage Blake lived with.

The seconds ticked away and Blake stayed frozen, like an ice carving.

Connor scanned the crewmen. They were one organism, if Blake decided to attack, it could come from any quarter, although none of the stares locked onto his face sharpened with intent. Taking a deep breath, Connor sampled the cloud of grit and salt the group exuded. His boots scraped over the deck as he moved back and gripped the guardrail behind. He was one moment away from giving Rebekah the signal to free-fall over the side.

"Who is the girl?" The guide pointed at Rebekah. Blake himself grinned.

"Rebekah is a newling."

A low hum grew into a wave of resonance, until the dam burst and sounds poured from the nomads. Blue-veined faces jostled for position, each trying to gain a better view.

When Blake extended a hand, Connor couldn't be sure who he wanted to connect with, but Rebekah unhesitatingly placed her hand in his. The nomad flesh squelched as his grip tightened around her fingers, testing her strength.

"We are wasting time, Captain Blake. Take us to your patient."

Lank hair fell forward to cover the burned section of Blake's scalp when he nodded sharply and swung around.

Abruptly, the sea of bodies parted as Blake's presence drove them apart, and Connor and Rebekah followed in his wake. Connor caught her hand in his as they stepped through a metal door and their footfalls echoed down the gangways. After turning two corners, Blake stopped beside an open hatchway to wave Connor through.

Inside the small room, on the thin mattress of a mortuary trolley lay a vampire. He stared at the ceiling, and the tattered strips of the black shirt he wore hung from a blood-stained white collar.

"A priest?" asked Connor.

Blake had followed them in, his shadow spreading over the walls.

"The Reverend. That's what we call him. He joined the ship in Africa. He was a missionary."

Moving closer, Connor assessed the chunks of flesh missing from his upper arm, but more worryingly, from his left side. "What happened? Who attacked him?"

"You treat him first, then you'll be told," said Blake's companion.

I don't know if I can repair the damage. Rebekah, be ready to slip away. Connor stared into her glittering brown eyes.

Her nod was barely perceptible, but it let him breathe easier.

"Now," Connor said. "You'll tell me now, or I'm leaving."

The dull groan of metal as the hull shifted beneath their feet filled the tense silence.

"Okay." Blake's dried slug of a tongue grated over his tight flesh when the small nomad said, "Ferals."

Connor frowned. Turning back to the patient and examining the torn vampire tissue more closely, he saw the imprints of human teeth. Decaying meat darkened the holes in places, even though the Reverend's flesh was chalk white and crumbling like shattered quartz. Without looking up, he said, "What does Captain Blake want? The Reverend repaired even if I can't restore the blood-network and he's just a head on a stick? Or do I put him out of his misery?"

Connor slammed into the wall when Blake unleashed a blind punch. Rubbing his jaw, he said, "I guess I owe you that one."

The stout figure turned away and left the room. His mouthpiece hung back a few seconds to say, "The reverend must live." And a moment later, Connor and Rebekah were alone.

Joining him at the examination table, Rebekah winced.

In silence, Connor ran his hands none too gently over the patient's skeleton, locating breaks and hard lumps where graveling was setting in. Without pausing, he said, "Go up on deck and tell Julian we need muscle relaxant, two pounds of chalk mortar, latex and wire gauze, pliers and a chisel."

"It might be quicker if you send the message through Seren," Rebekah said quietly.

Connor chuckled. "Of course, she's here. She's her mother's daughter." Frown lines marred his perfect complexion as he concentrated, sending his thoughts along the psychic zip-wire and into Seren's head.

By the time Connor had stripped the dirty clothes from the body and tested the Reverend's pupil reactions to confirm there was something worth saving, a suitcase sized toolbox was carried into the room by their newest best friend, Blake's companion.

Connor put on Perspex glasses and set about chiseling out the dehydrated flesh in areas where the blood network had been severed.

Rebekah made it her goal to charm Blake's companion, and by association, Blake, himself.

"Do you have a name?" she asked, raising her voice above the sound of Connor's hammer slamming against the chisel.

"Blake." The reply crackled in his dried throat. The vampire stood still as a statue, his attention glued on Connor's fast-moving hands as he used surgical tweezers to clean fetid flesh from the holes drilled into the Reverend's side by the feral's teeth.

The fist-sized crater was stuffed with nylon wadding – which was lighter than mortar – covered in wire gauze, and then rendered with a 'vampire flesh mix' of mortar, silicone, and latex. Like all 'building renovations', it would need re-pointing at some time.

The left forearm was shredded, so Connor had a decision to make. Let the patient drag around graveled flesh, or amputate the arm at the elbow.

"How much muscle relaxant have you given to keep him still?"

"None," replied the trancelike emissary.

Connor shot a sharp glance across the room. "None?"

Vampires didn't feel pain, but fear, that was another matter. Muscle relaxant prevented the panic which rattled around inside their minds like rats clawing to escape from being acted upon. Patients exuded blissful peace but, in Connor's experience, if it wore off too soon, the terrified subject would rampage through the operating theatre, crushing everything in his path.

"What is keeping him still?"

The bloated face of their Blake conduit, grinned, showing gums as milk white as his teeth. "The Reverend. He controls himself."

"Take the arm. I can manage without it." The voice came from the table, and sure enough, when Connor looked at the patient, his eyes were alert and filled with compelling confidence.

With a nod, Connor got on with the task. He checked the Reverend's face every few seconds, fascinated that the glazed expression had returned as quickly as steaming up a pane of glass with warm breath. *Remarkable man.*

While Connor packed away the toolbox, and a nomad arrived to sweep up the stone chips covering the floor, the patient sat up, flexed his good arm and inspected the newly glued latex patch on his side. "I was lucky. By the grace of God," said the Reverend.

Connor laughed. "More by the grace of 'your spine being intact'. Cut that super-highway, and you are just a talking head."

When the Reverend dropped down from the trestle table, the wiry figure only reached to Connor's jawline. With Rebekah's help, he pulled on a fresh black shirt and clipped the starched white collar around his throat. "Thank you, Doctor."

"I wish I could have saved the arm." Indicating the repair in his side, Connor said, "I'll return and repack that tomorrow. The filler will settle. I'll need to add more."

"Same time tomorrow, then," replied the Reverend. He shook Connor's hand, then pushed back a fall of thick brown hair. When he walked from the room, the half arm still swung with his stride as if the lower part was merely invisible.

Connor went to follow, but Blake's six-foot broad frame appeared, blocking the hatchway.

Falling back, Connor said, "He's a remarkable fellow. I'd like to know more, if I could."

The charred clump of his tongue protruded from Blake's mouth as he wheezed with laughter. "Like you wanted to know more about Hera?" said his interpreter.

Connor hadn't thought of Hera in a long while. "Is she still onboard?" *Of course, she is.* His fascination stemmed from her being a hybrid, the first he had seen since Seren's birth.

The slick flesh covering Blake's skull rippled. The lumps of muscle where eyebrows once were puckered as, reaching out to where Connor's voice came from, the captain made a grab for his shirt.

Connor danced out of reach. Moving the conversation onto safer ground, he asked, "Principal Julian upheld his part of the bargain. What information from Europe do you have? Does it concern ferals and what happened to the Reverend?" Having met the man, Connor could not imagine a feral stalking him and getting close enough to attack. *There is more.*

"As you say, the agreement is with Principal Julian. You will be escorted from the ship."

"I could remain onboard as a goodwill gesture while you have an audience with the principal."

As much as Connor wanted to hear Blake's news first hand, he also had another curiosity burning through him. *Will I even be able to find her?* When he first met Blake, and the captain possessed a functioning face, Hera had held the place at his side. Connor was worried about her.

"You will both wait in the loading bay until I return."

Rebekah, her leather coat buttoned up to her throat in readiness to leave, stood calmly by.

Flanked by two nomads, Connor and Rebekah were walked along the metal-lined corridors. Passing through a door, they found themselves at the top of a flight of metal stairs, with a handrail on one side. The cavernous loading bay below was filled with containers: some made of metal, some plastic, and some wood.

This is where Greg and I hid. Connor sent his thoughts to Rebekah.

As the nomads retreated, after giving Connor a hard shove which said 'down you go', the marine, jellyfish-tainted odor receded. Blake's loss of senses suddenly struck Connor as a blessing as he wrinkled his nose.

Rebekah walked down the steps ahead of him. When the door above slammed, even in the darkness, he could see lights in her blond hair glistening like gold.

We are down here alone. If they were still here we'd smell them. Rebekah's words oozed with the adventurous spirit which Connor had dreaded when she was a fragile human, but adored now she was his equal. Being a female vampire came with limitations – female humans generally had less muscle bulk than their male counterparts, and so did female vampires. Once the first decade passed, the spike of strength caused by the 'fuel injection' of human blood that filled each vein when she was turned, would fade. But, until then, Rebekah's prowess exceeded even Connor's.

Why did you want to stay on the ship? She peered at Connor expectantly.

He chuckled. *Hera. I hoped I could slip the leash and locate her.* He shrugged. *It was worth a try.*

Reaching the level below, the peeling paint on the metal floor crunching underfoot, Connor led Rebekah by the hand, heading to the huge laundry container inside which Greg had hidden. *Greg would enjoy this trip down memory lane.* He squeezed her fingers and smiled.

~*I knew you'd come.*~

Connor's head jerked around. This new voice had a husky quality; exotic, and with a musical lilt. *Hera!* It had never occurred to him that she would find him.

Rebekah looked confused at Connor blurting the name.

~*It has been a long time.*~ Hera appeared from between a row of wooden crates. She was running her hand over the warm wood as though it gave her comfort. Her footsteps dragged across the floor as if the boots she wore were made of lead. The nymph-like Hera of Connor's memory had faded, crumpling to this lackluster slip of a girl.

"Hera?" Connor whispered, for Rebekah's benefit, knowing she couldn't hear the girl's thoughts.

~*I'm glad to see you, Doctor Connor. You are my last chance.*~

A scene unfolded inside Connor's mind. The steel walls around him shimmered and the metal became molten, and then frosted, like ice. Blake lay on a wooden pallet in a small cabin, his face oozing lava-colored detritus which stank of burning. The aftermath I left behind, thought Connor. As if becoming an actor in the movie, he witnessed the scene through Hera's eyes. He felt the rough fabric of Blake's coat on his face when the girl laid her cheek on the captain's chest, and the tears which trickled down her face blurred his vision. The pain inside his own chest had the burn of a blade twisting – grief.

Blake lay inert. His arms didn't close around her, no matter how much she pulled on the sleeve of his coat. Her ebony hair hung over her face and the vision faded as she fell into exhausted sleep.

~*Everything changed on that day. I live below now, with the other cattle.*~

"I'm sorry, Hera." *Your gift has grown stronger, though.*

Hera smiled. ~*I surf the ship by hopping from the mind of each nomad. It is a way I can see my master. That has had its compensations.*~

Connor could feel Rebekah's curiosity burning a hole in his skull where she stared at him. "Hera's psychic abilities from when she was human were magnified when Blake created her hybrid state. Hypothermia interrupted the 'change', preserving human DNA in her bone marrow."

"I'm happy to meet you at last, Hera." Rebekah reached for the girl's hand, her face tight as she concentrated on not crushing fragile bone. "I have a hybrid daughter. She is much like you."

Not wanting to cut Rebekah out of the communication, he said, "What do you need me to do?"

"Take me with you. I want to live." Hera stepped closer and looked from Connor to Rebekah. Her deep brown eyes gleamed and, for a moment, the vibrant graceful creature she had once been emerged. This time, her smile shone from within like a beacon.

"I promise, I will get you off this ship."

"I believe you. He is coming back. I'll wait for you to return." Pulling her hand from Rebekah's, Hera retreated and disappeared between the wooden crates, once more.

The door at the top of the metal stairs whipped open and in the blade of moonlight, two nomads appeared. One of them was Blake. "It is time to go," said the companion, his hoarse whisper echoing through the chamber.

Regret that they could not take Hera with them made Connor slow to move.

"It is time to go, *now*." The crackling voice strained its owner's vocal chords.

Connor mounted the steps, with Rebekah following close behind, and asked, "What happened?"

Blake vibrated with annoyance while his sidekick said, "Principal Julian insists you are present at the meeting. Come."

If Julian had the leverage to pull Connor off the ship, that was a bad sign. It meant the Reverend was just the tip of the iceberg of the dangers Blake had faced. The captain *needed* Julian.

The party of four skimmed down the side of the ship and began the run into London.

A small detail of nomads accompanied them as far as the suburbs before peeling away to head back towards the Docklands and assume positions as lookouts on the return route.

The council guard took up the baton and the grim-faced purple-clad escort forced the pace until the party ran as fast as Blake and his escort could manage. The captain's clawed grip on his guide's shoulder riveted the pair together into one entity.

What on earth is going on? Rebekah maintained a bland expression, showing nothing of the worry tightening her gut.

I don't know, yet. Connor grinned. *It must be something big, but there's no point second guessing.*

As they entered the City, Rebekah said, "I'll find Seren and head back. We promised to spend the evening trying out wedding hair with Leizle, but I'll get everyone together for an update when you know more."

Connor caught Rebekah's fingers and squeezed them without breaking stride. "I'll be along when I've heard what Blake has to say."

Chapter 7

Julian and Marius waited in the council ante-chamber. The gleam cast by wall-mounted lamps refracted off the black glass surface of the conference table in the center of the floor, making it shimmer like a glacier. From where they were seated, the stony pale faces of both vampires reflected in the glass.

"Where the Hell are they?" muttered Julian, his green eyes glinting with annoyance. The four empty chairs opposite taunted him, until the knock on the door heralded the arrival of the entourage from the super tanker.

"Come," barked Julian, his chair skidding backwards as he jumped to his feet.

Captain Gerrard entered first, closely followed by Blake and his guide, and then Connor.

Once the newcomers were seated, Connor updated Julian on the condition of the patient. "I can confirm our part in the agreement has been fulfilled."

The attention turned to Captain Blake who now wore the steel mask which resembled a frozen approximation of how he used to look.

"It is time. What do you know?" asked Julian.

"I can't say I know everything." Blake gurgled as his aide grinned.

Julian rested back in his seat. "I meant what I said. I will rescind feeding rights and cease trading with the tanker nomads if this has all just been a tap-dance to demand Connor treat your crewman."

They all knew that even Blake would not be foolish enough to risk being blacklisted from a hive.

The captain's guide stood up and took a position front and center of the jury desk. He cleared his throat and Blake's hand gesture indicated the gravity of what he was about to say.

"Europe is collapsing. Ferals have always been a minor problem, but from what we are seeing in Europe, the number has spiked and now they outnumber vampires in the hive populations.

Their guardsmen are losing the battle to enforce the perimeter walls of syphoning farms and the human stocks are being killed."

Julian, Connor, and even Marius, turned to stare at the impassive steel mask of Blake, but the way his fingertips brushed the table, constantly moving, portrayed agitation.

The companion blurted into speech again. "We have been attacked twice, now, when leaving our ship to take onboard human blood. The English Channel is not so wide. Once the ferals reach the French coast, if they detect you are here, they will walk across the seabed. Your survival depends on moving your humans west and fortifying the south and east coastlines."

"Why are you telling us this, now?" snapped Julian, interpreting Marius' aggressive jabbing sign.

"This can't have just happened. You must have seen it building," Connor chipped in.

Blake inclined his head. "We are not welcome inside the hive boundaries in Europe. The time when we collected our blood from the human farm facilities ended long ago. For some reason, we make people uncomfortable." Blake cackled. "If we had, then perhaps our crossings would have given us more warning, but no, we didn't see it building. For us, and you, it has been a sudden uprising."

"Malachi did warn us, Julian," mused Connor. "When he had a cry for help from Egypt – it is why he returned there. To support Imhotep and the Earth Walker tribe."

"I remember, but the unrest was 5000 miles east of Egypt."

"Not anymore," said Connor, simply.

Turning back to Blake, Julian asked, "Are you seeking sanctuary here in England?"

"Not at all. We are seafarers." Blake shrugged. "True, the container ship is a safe enough place, but we still need a port to dry dock and make repairs. We are not entirely self-sufficient. Africa and Australia are still safe, as are South America, but if Western Europe goes the way the East has gone, for how long? We need to stick together, and deal with this, now."

Blake's air rattled through phlegm as his interpreter said, "Two days ago, in Rotterdam, we abandoned an attempt at docking when the lookouts saw fighting in the port.

We barely survived an attack in Antwerp last month, and only a fool heads into a war zone. These insane vampires are becoming more aggressive. We thought we had their measure, but some still managed to board us within the harbor walls at Rotterdam. That was when the Reverend got injured. He exposed himself to risk to block the route to the human cattle. The heartbeats resound through the ship, so misdirecting them was possible using Hera as bait, and the Reverend would never let harm come to her. I owe him a lot."

It made sense now. Blake would come cap in hand to Julian to help a man who saved Hera. As much as he could love anyone, Blake loved the hybrid girl.

"You weren't moored up, then?"

Blake shook his head. "No, we were anchored offshore, and ferals walked across the harbor beneath the water and scaled the mooring chains of both the stern and bow anchors. They saw the vessel and could smell our human herd. We lost five humans and forty crew."

"How did you get the ferals off the ship?" Julian asked.

"We used flare guns, harpoons, and the water cannons we fitted after the close call in Antwerp, then we set sail as fast as the engines could take us. The ship is slow to get moving, but once we were at sea, we swept the vessel, decapitated the ferals we found and threw the parts overboard."

The room fell silent as all those present pictured the scene. It sounded like something out of a pirate movie.

Julian lay his hands flat on the slick table top. "It seems we owe you our thanks. If Europe falls, we need to prepare for an invasion."

Blake rose slowly to his feet, his interpreter seamlessly continuing to provide his master's voice. "We leave at sunset tomorrow, after Doctor Connor has finished patching up the

Reverend." The tall figure half turned away, then stopped. "I hear you have a blood substitute in production?"

Ah, thought Connor, and now we get to the truth.

"It's in the early stages of distribution, but yes," replied Julian.

"I imagine that makes us worth protecting?" mused Connor. "We will be able to live without humans, eventually, as would you. Without the bait of a human herd, the ferals would have no reason to attack."

"I will continue to patrol the coast and keep you informed of events in Europe." Blake inclined his head and turned to leave, with Captain Gerrard preparing to act as an escort.

When the aide reached the door and opened it for his master, Connor said, "Can you get a message to Malachi? He's still in Egypt – the port of Alexandria. Citadel of Qaitbay near the harbor." Connor knew Malachi had not survived two thousand years without being clever, but these were extreme times. His mentor's abode was easily defended, with an escape vessel moored at what used to be the 'El Sayd Club'. Even if Malachi was with the Earth Walker tribe, the messenger based at his Alexandria dwelling could get word to the elder vampire – in Connor, Rebekah, Seren and Osiris, he had family, now, so he stayed in touch. *The ferals are on the rise and forewarned is forearmed.*

"I'll pay him a visit next time we are in those waters," Blake's nomad replied, as Gerrard escorted them from the room.

The three remaining vampires settled back in their seats to wait for Gerrard's return.

'Thank the Lord we have a few hundred castles in Britain,' signed Marius, without cracking a smile.

"Blake's advice is sound. There are only four hives left on the mainland, now. A few thousand humans, at most. Relocating them in the northwest would be wise," said Connor.

"We have Principal Glynn in Wales. He might be persuaded to oversee the transport," Julian said thoughtfully.

Connor cleared his throat. "About that." His last view of the principal, his hand swinging uselessly at the wrist, came to mind.

"We might have a few apologies to make – a few bridges to build."

After listening to how badly the encounter had gone, and Rebekah's part in it, Julian slammed his fist down on the table. The shockwave caused cracks to crawl over its brittle surface and curiously delicate music accompanied the violent act. "Damn it all, Connor, we have to pull together." Julian dragged a hand down over his face, easing the tension. More calmly, he said, "Principal Glynn is a dinosaur, and we don't have room for them. We have two level-headed principals to appeal to. I'll set up a summit meeting in York."

Edward of the York Hive controlled the midlands with quiet efficiency, and although Julian had not seen the Principal in a decade, on each occasion they had met, the seam of kindred spirits fused them together like long lost brothers. "Principal Edward will be onside."

Principal Tavish of Loch Glascarnoch – his domain situated over 600 miles away – had become more like a king of Scotland. Very little of the politics of the southern hives bothered him. The Cairngorms reindeer park and surrounding hunting ground were all north of Hadrian's and the Antonine walls. The Glascarnoch Hive was a self-contained fiefdom. *But not anymore.*

"I'll travel north and meet with the three hive principals tomorrow night. As Blake says, we are an island, and safe, for now, but let's not be complacent."

When Captain Gerrard re-entered the room, he brought along with him the twelve strong 'Council Elite Guard'. The men lined up at attention, their purple surcoats immaculate.

Marius lifted an eyebrow.

"If I may, Principal Julian, I have an interim plan we can implement immediately."

"Proceed, Captain."

"Until we can determine the level of threat, each of the council guardsmen will lead a platoon of men to outposts along the coast, focusing on the English Channel. They will hold the line, but be close enough to come together as a stronger force if one outpost is attacked." Gerrard stood at attention and waited.

Marius whistled to get everyone's attention, his fluid hand signs having a hypnotic calming effect. 'We'll take Blake at his word, for now. But once we have the humans relocated, we can send a scout ship of our own south and see for ourselves. We can assess the level of risk by docking at the Spanish port of Vigo. The ferals have nowhere to go if they detect us and come into the sea there. Even *they* can't walk across the Atlantic without feeding or sleeping; those waters spell death.'

"We have to launch a plan of action, gentlemen. Captain, post a squad of guardsmen at the docks to make sure Blake remains on his ship, dispatch the Elite Guard along the coast, and report back."

After Gerrard had left, Julian turned to Connor. "Blake sets sail at dusk tomorrow. When you follow up on your patient, see if you can build bridges there. I never thought I'd say this, but we need to be able to trust him."

Connor stood up and began pacing the floor. He ran his hands through his cobalt hair, inhaled deeply and squared his shoulders.

Julian watched his friend whipping back and forth, pulled a shard from the glittering fractured surface of the cracked table and rolled it between his fingertips, crumbling away the sharp edges to create a needle-sharp dart. "You have something to say, Connor?" Julian bared his teeth in a wry grin. *And I'm not going to like it.*

"Hera," said Connor, ducking as the glass icicle whipped across the room.

But, Julian had anticipated the move and the glass spike made a satisfying crunch when it smashed into Connor's left cheekbone and left a patch of glittering specks on his skin.

"Very mature," muttered Connor, brushing the glass fragments from his cheek, and checking automatically for a puncture wound.

Unperturbed, Julian said, "What about Hera?"

"She asked for sanctuary. I promised I would help her."

Marius whistled. 'It was not your place, Doctor Connor.' His pragmatic view of the world had shifted in the months since

Rebekah and Greg had joined their ranks; the first humans to be turned in three decades. One hundred and fifty vampire years, and spending time in the Middle East witnessing how cheap human life was to mankind, gave Marius a firm grounding. 'One hybrid asking for help is not a reason to alienate Captain Blake. You made a mistake.'

"I gave my word."

'That is unfortunate, but it does not matter, in this case-' Marius' dark gaze glimmered like the luminescent current in an oil slick. 'You lied.'

Connor visibly recoiled, even though he maintained a frozen mask of respect.

Julian knew Marius was waving a red rag at a bull. *Does he know that, too?* A glance at his fellow juror left him still wondering. The principal sighed and poured oil on stormy waters. "Maybe after, when we have battened down our hatches, but now is not the moment to stir up mud."

Connor inclined his head. "Perhaps you're right."

"One step at a time. If Hera needs sanctuary, she shall have it, but not yet."

"There is no *if*, Julian, but I will wait. If you'll excuse me. I have work to do." Connor took in Marius with his courteous nod and went to leave the room.

"Connor, once Gerrard confirms Blake is safely back on his vessel, he'll return here. We need a strategy meeting to protect London and our cattle before I leave for York."

"I can be back before nightfall."

"Better to meet tomorrow. I have a few avenues of my own to explore and I want all the players at the meeting."

When Connor had disappeared from view, both jurors stared at the closed door.

"Did we do the right thing?" asked Julian.

Marius' throat whistled quietly. 'We did the only thing. Blake already has enough reason to want Connor dead.'

"You really shouldn't take your irritation out on him. We should be working together, if things turn out to be as bad as Blake says."

Taking a deep breath, Julian commanded the dark juror's full attention. He felt as if he trod on eggshells opening the subject, but Marius struggled to communicate in formal situations. The only reason his views were not 'ignored' was because his companions made sure he was given the platform to contribute.

"Marius, now that the 'whistle and sign' option has bedded in, have you considered expanding your communication abilities?" After the meeting with Blake, an obvious solution stared them in the face.

Marius played dumb. A flap of a hand was his short response. 'Such as?'

Julian cleared his throat. "Well, turning a human? The psychic connection would give you a 'voice' again." Faced with the thundercloud of Marius' expression, Julian tried out a chuckle. "You wouldn't sound like you, but at least you could get your point across…"

Julian's grin became fixed as his voice faded.

Marius jerked to his feet, turned on his heel, and left the room, slamming the door behind him.

"Well, that went better than I expected," Julian murmured.

Chapter 8

Smothering his anger, Connor took care to close the door of the jurors' anteroom quietly and then whipped away down the corridor. His dash back from Cardiff had disrupted his feeding pattern and his tendons grated when he moved. Just like in humans, spikes in physical exertion caused dehydration, and Connor was beginning to feel like a hamster on a treadmill.

When he burst out through the doors of the council building main entrance, Connor barely noticed the needle points of rain driving into his face as he dashed through the London streets. Turning the corner and out onto the embankment, his favored route through the city, the whirling wind dumped buckets full of rain onto his head, or so it felt. Thoughts of getting to the dispensary and logging in with Isaac at the morgue for the secure lock down of grave sleep was the driving force, but his emotions were high and Marius' rebuke made him want to hit something. His greatcoat became soaked through and the thick fabric cloying to his thighs irritated him for the first time, ever. *I let Hera down.*

Shedding the coat, he bundled it up and left it in a shop doorway to collect later, but for now, he needed to outrun his rage and burn off the anger pulling his tendons tight. *Sleep.* The cell mate inside his brain was on the rampage. *Grave sleep.* The safety valve was close to blowing. Shoving a hand into his pants pocket, he pulled out a gel pellet while running, its dark center glistening like a ruby. The capsule of blood substitute would be enough to unlock his brainstem. Tossing the gel-cased sphere into his mouth, he ground it between his teeth and swallowed down the thick syrup. It lingered in his throat, coating his tonsils and vocal chords until his thirsty flesh absorbed the fluid like a dried-out sponge, and the liquid hitched a ride along his spinal cord. The starburst of heat at the base of his skull drove Connor's pumping stride harder until he hit top speed.

The rolling mass of the River Thames loomed closer and the turbulent water became a siren call. The deserted span of Vauxhall Bridge vibrated underfoot as Connor accelerated, veered to one side, and vaulted gracefully over the high wall. The weightless airborne moment filled him with exhilaration. The deep blue water beneath him shimmered, threads of frothy white lace rolling over the choppy surface as though tying the blue silk into knots. As his body twisted in the air, his arms extending into a diver's pose, Connor squinted into the depths and locked onto his prey. *Seals.*

From the vantage point of London's skyscrapers, Connor often found peace watching the sleek, oil-colored creatures playing in the waters. The sightings of seals, dolphins, and even whales, were occasionally reported in the early 2000s, but now, with mankind no longer polluting the River Thames, marine life flourished. Today, some would flourish no more.

The icy water parted as Connor tore a path through it, his streamlined shape spewing a comet tail of churning bubbles. The world under the rippling surface resembled indigo velvet, cut through with silver blades of light. The torpedo-shaped mammals dancing and darting around him exuded slick grace. Connor salivated at the alluring sound of thrumming heartbeats. He closed his eyes and savored the musical banquet, his primal instincts tracking each one and deciding which heart would beat no longer. The deeper the resonance, the larger the animal. Staying still, and allowing his body to spiral downwards, Connor plotted the trajectory of his prey overhead. The moment his boots touched the moss-covered rocks cluttering the riverbed, he pushed upwards, focused on a three-meter-long bull seal passing across his vision. The blubber covering the smooth body rippled when the seal convulsed in shock and writhed in Connor's clawed grasp. Its teeth scraped over its captor's shoulder, the powerful flippers and tail thrashing. Gripping the seal by the muzzle, Connor clenched his fist until he felt the jaws grind together and crumble. He clamped his legs around the creature, mimicking a cowboy riding a bucking bronco. Air bubbles raced to the surface as Connor wrapped his arms around the bull's ribcage and squeezed. Electrical impulses in the animal's brain sizzled in a firework display that Connor felt like a static charge. Biting into the fleshy neck, he tore away the blubber, exposing the veins and arteries beneath. The rush of tepid blood hit the back of his throat. In a macabre lovers' embrace, both bodies, still entwined, pirouetted gracefully down into the depths and, for a moment, lay together on the riverbed as though they were spent. Connor lifted his face away and the merest puff of blood stained the water as it rushed into the gaping wound in the sleek pelt, as if it could soothe the pain. The seal's black-beaded stare glinted with quick-silver each time the current gently rocked the limp carcass. Connor clamped his throat shut to keep the blood inside and the river water out, his meal filling his mouth with a metallic taste. Powering through the water like a bolt from a crossbow, he headed to the riverbank and climbed up the boulders at the edge. Walking along the uneven craggy surface, he found the gaping mouth of a rainwater sewer and, crouching, he went inside.

Hera's anxious face flooded his mind and the impotent anger he had pushed down inside when Marius had said his piece threatened to break its banks. The psychopath living inside him, and every vampire, demanded to be fed. Digging into the silt and grime caked into the floor of the conduit, Connor laid down. He clamped his muscles into a rigid cocoon that kept him still, opened the cell inside his mind, and descended into grave sleep.

Rebekah, and Greg, with their reservoir of human blood still locked inside their tissue, had not yet had to feed this monster. *The Mr. Hyde to our Dr. Jekyll.* The purpose behind Connor's research with apes and monkey blood cells, and perfluorocarbons used in crush injuries, was to manage the blood lust that threatened the human stock. Only human blood could hydrate the vampire brain, until now.

In the hours Connor lay with the synapses in his brain burning like an ignited fuse wire, rats ran over the mud encrusted mound of his body. If found by a passerby – indeed, in the decades when vampires were still in hiding, it had happened – his taught white flesh and rigid muscles would be mistaken for the rigor mortise in a corpse. But then, as Connor himself had experienced in 1910, a corpse could leap into animation and inflict a mortal wound.

As he surfaced from grave sleep, the brain center that controlled rage and hunger refreshed, Connor focused on what needed to be done, next. *Osiris can help*. Like a sleep walker, he scraped fetid mulch from his eye sockets and sat up. Crouching low, he walked out of the concrete conduit and submerged himself in the river. Running his hands through his hair as he emerged, he sluiced the water from his cleansed skin.

The gray light of a new day dawning was a stark reminder of the hours he had lost, and he needed to get moving.

Rushing up the steep bank of the river and vaulting over the wall onto the wide walkway running along the embankment, Connor accepted the inevitable. *Hera has to wait*. With a wry grin, he let go of his resentment. Marius and Julian were right, but he didn't like it. *I need to get cleaned up*.

The clock was ticking, Blake was expecting him to attend to his patient before dusk. He had wasted enough time, although, he knew it was not truly wasted. His freshly-hydrated brain buzzed with ideas, and the solutions to each problem snapped into sharp focus.

Swerving along the sidewalk and diving down backstreets, Connor shadow hopped until he entered the hospital via the side door. A vampire porter wheeled human blood along the corridor on a trolley and Connor waved him to a halt.

"Surgical assistant Anthony. Where is he?"

"He left the hospital, Doctor. A meeting with the jurors, I believe."

Damn it. The rebellion of taking sleep in the river instead of using a cadaver drawer in the morgue had robbed him of a chance to talk with Anthony. Connor frowned and powered his way along to his surgical wing. In a whirlwind of perpetual movement, he stripped off his wet clothes, pulled on fresh ones stored in a wooden chest inside his office, and headed out again.

Chapter 9

Julian returned to his chambers to remove his principal's robe. Having brought the day's court-list to an early close, he listened to the crowds leaving the courtroom gallery. The footfalls of one hundred vampires created a whispering crescendo of movement. He could not imagine his brethren ever being raucous, it was not in their nature, or at least, being quiet and staying below the radar was ingrained behavior.

He checked his watch, finished dressing in a cream tailored shirt and ran a comb through his hair, his frown reflecting eagerness to get the strategy meeting underway. Thrashing out a plan of action would kick up problems he hadn't yet figured out.

He strode down the corridor and entered the jurors' anteroom, hoping all the players would be in place. He was not disappointed. With his hand still on the door handle, Julian surveyed the gathering, gauging attitudes and feeling confident that everyone would come through. In his mind, he had a tick list of the skill set each team member brought to the table.

Captain Gerrard knew the hive forces and the 'talents' of the guardsmen at his disposal. They had all been trained by him, and he only retained the best. The surprise in Gerrard's crackerjack box turned out to be Greg – the Marine could crawl inside the skin of the enemy and offer up scenarios that even Gerrard missed.

"Greg," Julian said, with a serious nod. He was pleased to see the newest vampire here. Fresh blood was rare, and Greg provided a current and insightful perspective on how to get through to the human inmates; he had experienced being a human under vampire rule.

Not surprisingly, at the Marine's shoulder stood Anthony. The two were friends, and had the symbiotic relationship that came from being maker and fledgling. Malachi had 'helped' by feeding Greg when he was dying, so the two did not share the usual exclusive mind-link, but it didn't stop them seemingly being two halves of the whole. Anthony had been a bare-knuckle fighter before he paid the ultimate price – death, so as a front line in a physical battle, they made a formidable team.

Connor flashed a grin which said 'childish tantrum over', and Julian threw him a lazy salute before addressing the room.

"Welcome, Sampson. For those of you who do not know him, Sampson is an expert in hand-to-hand combat and, more important to our cause, he is a *friend* of a human in the town, called Peter.

"Nice to meet you, Sampson." Greg shook the newcomer's hand and nodded in approval.

The six-foot-tall vampire had an open friendly face and a ready smile, and looked a million miles away from having hands which were lethal weapons, but his strong grip told a different story.

Marius unfolded his arms and his dark brows lifted in speculation. Julian did not need the flurry of sign language to know what the dark juror was thinking. 'Why is he here? Can you trust him?'

Signing back, Julian replied, 'Gerrard checked him out.'

"Well, if that's all the introductions made..." Connor called everyone's attention back to the reason they were there. "Let's break this down. First, protect the humans."

Julian nodded. "That's where Greg, and Sampson with Peter come in. The humans need to be ready to move west, but that journey will have to wait until I meet with the other hive principals. In the short term, the siphoning sheds will make the best refuge in an emergency. Drill it into the community that if the siren sounds, they get inside the sheds."

Marius nodded.

"That works," said Connor. "It will be easier to guard them inside the human farm perimeter fences.

"That's the short-term plan, but what if Blake is right about the ferals?" Gerrard asked.

Julian took his seat at the conference table and rested his chin on steepled fingers. "It is as well to treat the feral threat as serious. I'll head north to the summit meeting of the hive principals when we finish here. I'll stress we are safe, for now, but must plan for the worst. Principals Tavish and Edward are reasonable leaders, and I'm sure we can bring pressure to bear on Glynn."

"Brynmor is still in Cardiff. The manufacturing plant construction is well underway, and rolling out the blood substitute is not far off. It makes Wales a good location to explore as a human settlement, down the line. Brynmor can be persuasive," said Connor. "But first thing first, I'll head to the eco-shelter and get Leizle, Oscar, Evie and Thomas up to speed to plan the evacuation."

"What about Seth's group? Do you think they'll come in?" asked Greg with a frown.

Connor laughed wryly. "You'd know more about that than us. I'm not hopeful, to be honest."

"He's a stubborn old buzzard," muttered Greg.

Anthony laid a hand on his friend's arm. "I'm sure Rebekah can talk Seth and Adam round when the time comes. After all, she has some say, Uncle Harry is her family."

"If she can't, then *I'll* knock some sense into his thick skull." Greg grinned widely as if picturing the encounter.

"We'll need to be ready to act, and fast," said Julian firmly. "Charles and Isaac are preparing a blood delivery for Blake's ship. After Connor checks on the Reverend, then we can focus on making sure all hive members are fed and at full strength for battle."

"Are ferals able to execute a strategy? Can they think?" asked Greg.

Connor laughed. "They are feeding machines, but they have weaknesses. They neglect exercise and air exposure."

"Exercise? Really? So, they have the same weakness as unfit humans?" asked Greg, his brows raised in surprise.

"Think of us as an engine. Blood is the oil that lubricates and gravity is a force which even vampires can't resist." Connor grinned. "Have you heard of lividity?"

"Everyone who loved a good cop show has heard of lividity. In death the blood settles at the lowest point of the body. It's how they can tell if someone moves a murder victim and fakes the scene," said Greg.

Connor nodded. "Sunlight is our primary threat, but weakness comes in other, more subtle forms. As vampires, we fight lividity everyday. Luckily, bursts of movement reset the blood network, but now we don't need to pretend anymore, the instinct is to do away with mimicking human movement and gestures. Standing too still for long periods can cause tissue damage, and *ferals* stay still until triggered by external stimuli. It seems likely they will have developed mobility issues."

"The tanker nomads don't look too healthy, either, in my book," said Greg.

"The super tanker nomads get enough exercise loading and unloading the containers. Don't underestimate them just because they look like decaying squid."

"Even if the ferals have an Achilles heel, if the numbers Blake is implying turns out to be correct, we'll have our hands full." Julian frowned fiercely, shaking his head like a dog breaking a rabbit's neck. "I wish I trusted Blake. I can't see what he has to gain in lying, but is he telling us the *whole* truth?"

"That, we will never know, but I have my own theory." Connor gave a derisive snort. "We need to watch our backs. Blake will be on the lookout for an opportunity to take his revenge. He has good reason to hate me."

Marius' throat whistled to get Julian's attention. 'What do you need me and Daniel to do? Keep the hive running?'

"Captain Gerrard can manage the hive members. You and Daniel guard the Synthetic Blood Manufacturing Plant. Blake knows about it, so it could become a target for a nomad raid."

Connor's brows lifted. "London Zoo and the simian blood donors should be guarded, too."

"Gerrard, see to it the Elite Guard are on alert in the London Royal Parks. Stop any strangers crossing through the City, with deadly force, if necessary."

"Anthony, man the hospital. Business as usual for as long as possible, but when battle commences, you'll triage casualties as they come in."

Anthony nodded. "Will do."

The vampires began to circle the room as contemplating the tasks ahead created urgency.

All that remained was for Julian to release them. "You all know what to do."

Connor shuffled into line and slotted in behind Anthony as they emerged into the corridor. Bumping his surgical assistant on the shoulder, before they moved towards the main exit, Connor muttered, "Anthony, can I have a word?"

Slowing to let the others rush into the distance, Anthony assessed Connor's tense expression. "Is something wrong?"

"Not exactly, but I need you to do something for me."

Half an hour later, Connor paused beneath the shelter of the porch outside the main doors of the hospital. He stood gazing out over the puddles of rainwater – he focused on each falling water droplet, reconnecting with the wonder of vampire senses as they appeared to fall from the sky in slow motion. When he flexed his jaw and ground his teeth together, fragments of dental cement gathered under his tongue and he spat them onto the ground.

Anthony had turned out to be almost as good at dentistry as he was at gluing war wounds, but then, over the decades, Connor had single-handedly provided many opportunities for him to perfect that skill. *I plan to stick around for hundreds of years, and I want to keep all my teeth, no matter how amusing Anthony finds it.* Connor chuckled.

In the dull overcast late afternoon, not bothering to pull up his collar, Connor leapt the flight of marble steps, creating a claymore splatter of water when he landed, and set off to accomplish the next task on his list. Update Rebekah and prepare the humans to move.

In a burst of acceleration, he ran across the Kent countryside, passing over fields and along deserted roads. The sun would soon be setting and the deadline for the visit to Blake's super tanker and the Reverend loomed.

The familiar rolling hill which marked the subterranean location of the eco-shelter soon came into sight. The entrance no longer resembled a dark fissure worn into an escarpment – it was framed by a permanent brick-built archway. The rough cavern beyond had become an entrance hall with plaster-rendered walls in this new 'human friendly' era.

Connor's boots scraped over the concrete floor which had replaced packed mud, and found Seth, Oscar, and Thomas waiting for him. Seth grunted as he pushed away from where he leaned against the wall, the suspension of the closest motorbike creaked when Oscar shifted his hefty bulk and stopped using it as a perch, and the youngster scrabbled up from the floor. Their heartbeats played over his senses like a drum tattoo, and Connor felt relief that he had already fed.

"If you are waiting, then Rebekah must be here." Connor grinned, and it felt good when the smile came from within. This was his family.

He inhaled gently, washing the odor of human sweat over his palate and appreciating the cocktail of different pH factors and pheromones. Other smells of earth, grass, the fumes of a wood burning stove, and the static of the electric lamps lining the tunnels beyond his view, all faded into the background as he homed in on the individual honey sweet scent of Rebekah. Connor latched onto the paler smudge of her face, deep inside the dark recess of the access tunnel. Her laughter rippled over his senses like silk and, without pausing, he crossed the cavern, took her into his arms, and kissed her.

"Get a room," muttered Seth, hoisting a large bore rifle higher onto his shoulder. The weapon could knock a vampire off his feet, or stop him dead, if Seth got the shot into an eye socket where the bullet could rattle around inside the brain cavity – game over.

"I would, Seth," Connor murmured, looking into Rebekah's eyes, "but it will have to wait."

"The meeting hall is full of volunteers," said Oscar. "I've laid on food. They were pretty hungry after the hike over here." Humans still preferred to travel on foot than be driven by a vampire chauffeur. Keeping control was important to them.

"Hiked over from where?" Connor looked confused.

"The human town. A vampire called Sampson and their group leader, Peter, said you were on your way here to talk about an evacuation," said Oscar, his usually jovial face set in a stern expression.

"I had hoped to get here first, Oscar. I would say there's nothing to worry about, but I'd be lying. But all we need to do is stick to the plan."

"Oh, there *is* a plan, eh, lad?" Oscar thumped Connor on the arm. "That's okay, then."

"Are Seren and Osiris here, too?" Connor asked.

"Yes," said Leizle, as she emerged from the darkened access tunnel to join the group.

Even in the dim light, Connor could see the emerald glint in her eyes. The girl had become a strong young woman; her love for Julian radiated warmth when his name was mentioned, but her impatience to see him was tempered with mature anticipation and security. Gone was the fear Julian would run from his feelings. The principal, for want of a better word, had surrendered to his fate. Now, of course, Leizle's curiosity in Rebekah's new-found vampirism meant she was always there, asking questions and watching how Rebekah managed the transformation. But, calm emanated from the younger girl. She knew her time would come.

"We better not keep everyone waiting, then." Connor reached for Rebekah's hand, and took off down the tunnel at speed. The humans, using flashlights, ran after them, the blast of air in the wake of their preternatural friends plastering their clothes to their bodies.

The meeting hall held sixty men and women of all ages, seated on wooden benches and muttering under their breath. Many were from the newly constructed 'human town' and had never seen the eco-shelter before. The buzz of excitement was tinged with anxiety.

Both vampires waited outside the doorway to eavesdrop. Tuning into each human conversation with ease, Connor said, "They are all nervous. Not surprising. Are you ready to be my wingman?"

"Or wing-girl." Rebekah grinned. "Lead on."

Connor was under no illusion that this would be easy. Rebekah and Seren had been busy preparing the ground, but only he could answer their questions.

Seth, Oscar, Thomas and Leizle arrived, all breathing heavily, and their accelerated heart rates and gushing pulse made Rebekah retreat behind Connor. She was caught off guard sometimes, and still learning self-control.

As a group, they entered the hall, and very quickly, a murmur of questions rose in a swell.

Connor held up a hand. "The bottom line is that Europe is under threat by vampires who have become dehydrated – ferals. We are safe, at the moment, but must plan for the worst case scenario."

"And that's an attack by demented vampires?" asked Sandy.

Connor remembered the harmonica playing eco-shelter dweller. "We can't rule out an attack."

"So, what is the grand plan, lad?" asked Oscar.

"The council have met. There are guardsmen and defenses in place, but we need you all to prepare emergency rations and move out to the human farm."

Mumbles of dissent became shrill. Seth had taken up a position lounging against a wall, and his clenched jaw radiated his personal feelings of 'not a chance, buster'. Connor knew he could talk to Seth and Adam alone, later. *They are soldiers. They know the score.*

"Why?" Finally, a question was shouted out. "Why can't we stay here?"

"I'm not saying you won't come back, but the safest place for humans is *inside* a perimeter fence that vampires can patrol. And more important, the siphoning sheds-" *Shit.* Connor saw the way they reared in aggression at his words.

Rebekah jumped in. "C'mon guys. You know me, Greg, and Julian, too." She paused as the humans she had grown up with fixed their attention on her glowing preternatural features. "You know I love you all. Becoming a vampire hasn't changed that."

Connor felt the agitation in the humans ease, slowing the rate of their pumping bloodstream and settling their heart beats into a steady adrenaline-soaked rhythm.

Clearing his throat, Connor said, "The *sheds* are steel barns where you'll be safer *if* there is an attack. That's all. We can't protect you here, if ferals cross The Channel, the South Downs of Kent will be the first region to be over run. We need to protect you until the danger has passed."

Rebekah caught Connor's eye. *The danger will pass?* Her smile became set.

I don't know. He took her hand and squeezed it. "Oscar, food. Choose a team and get the supplies organized. Sandy, Leizle, Evie, clothes. Make sure everyone has what they need to camp out overnight. It will be a two day hike."

From the corner of his eye, Connor saw Thomas' shoulders slump. He zeroed in on the youngster and added with renewed vigor, "Thomas, how's your maths coming along? I need you to keep count of supplies and to know where everyone is, got it?"

"Yes, sir." The youth jerked to attention and tried to smother his smile with an intent frown.

Rebekah shot Connor a 'thank you' look before he plowed onwards.

"Sampson and Peter know the shortest route to the compound. Talk to each other." Connor ran his eye over the party of unknown faces – they looked tired but determined. These humans had come across country prepared to take on whatever threat came at them. "Stick together and you'll all get through this."

The sudden swell of voices all talking at once promised to rumble on for a long time. Connor attracted Rebekah's attention, tapped his watch, and jerked his head. *I have to go, but bring Seth outside. I need to talk to him.*

Tuning into his thoughts, Rebekah nodded.

She drifted across the cavern to where the Marine glared out over the room, as if the crowd of faces were invisible. Rebekah smiled and within a second, Seth stood up, yanked his combats straight and strode towards the entrance.

Outside in the tunnel, Connor waited, resting his shoulder on the wall.

"Connor," Seth said.

"You know what I'm going to say?"

Seth removed the twig he had gnawed to strings of bark from between his lips. "No. We'll head back into the woods and take our chances."

Connor sighed. "The tree-dwellers won't be safe. Even using the shelters in the treetops. You've got to come in, Seth. You, Adam, and how many able-bodied men? Eight? Ten? You can't fight the ferals."

Seth's jaw muscle twitched. "I'm heading home."

"Greg would beat your ass if he was here," grumbled Connor.

"Well, he ain't here."

"He didn't *want* to become one of us. You know that."

Seth froze in the act of turning away. "'Oorah. I know that. Okay, we'll come in."

"I'll go with you. It will give me a chance to catch up with Uncle Harry," Rebekah said quietly from where she had crept up on them, still framed in the arched doorway of the meeting cavern.

Seth's raised eyebrows showed his thoughts clearly. "It's not a babysitting mission, then? What with you being a vampire, now?"

"I wouldn't say that." Rebekah maintained a straight-face.

"I would," grunted Seth, before his tight features relaxed into an accepting smile.

"We'll head out within the hour," said Rebekah.

"I'll tell Adam."

Connor rested a hand on the Marine's shoulder. "Be ready for anything."

Chewing on the twig he poked back into the corner of his mouth, Seth gave a final salute and left.

With Rebekah matching his stride, Connor walked away, pausing ten yards along the tunnel.

Idly plucking on the sleeve of his shirt, she asked, "When you said 'the danger will pass', do you believe that?"

"I believe we can win, but it won't be easy." Connor glanced towards the entrance leading up from the sleeping quarters of the eco-shelter and, as he hoped they would, Seren and Osiris arrived.

Seren's gray gaze, so much like Connor's, studied his serious face.

I need to borrow Osiris for a while. Help your Mama, hmm?

With a smile, Seren laid a hand on Connor's shoulder and reached up to kiss his cheek. *Stay safe, Papa.*

Touching Osiris' hand in farewell, she joined Rebekah, and the two women headed towards the meeting cavern where hushed voices murmured and human heart rates pounded as the nervousness of planning an escape kicked in.

Connor waited until they were alone.

Silently, Osiris tied back the obsidian curtain of his hair, exposing his strong bone structure. Standing as tall as Connor, he met his father-in-law's gaze with quiet confidence.

Osiris' Egyptian dress had barely altered, even after living a year in the English habitat. When inside his new home, his caramel-colored chest remained bare, his skin glistening with the aromatic oils he bathed in. Osiris did, however, now wear combat pants. He carried his tribal dagger on his belt, and silver armlets fitted around his bulging biceps still covered the bamboo catheter with which his hybrid blood had fed Malachi when the pair were master and servant.

Connor knew that since Malachi's return to Egypt, Osiris had missed him, as did he.

"Come," said Connor, "I need your help."

106

◇◇◇

Curiosity about what Connor and Osiris were discussing distracted Rebekah from the focus of reassuring her friends. She felt detached and remained near the meeting cavern doorway.

When Oscar stopped in front of her, his broad chest blocking her view, Rebekah started breathing again, tapped into the human gestures she knew he found reassuring, and smiled up into his unusually serious face.

"Well, lass," Oscar smiled back, but it was a mere movement of muscles and the twinkle in his gaze remained absent. His look showed concern. "You're setting out to warn the tree-dwellers, I hear."

Rebekah nodded absently. "We are going to bring them in, Oscar… hopefully." She turned her head as a sudden breeze whipped her hair forward over her face. *Connor's leaving.* Her hands clenched into fists, and then unclenched, again. "I'm sorry, Oscar, I'll be right back, I just have something I need to do."

In a blur of movement, Rebekah left Oscar staring open mouthed at an empty space.

Emerging from the access tunnel and crossing the entrance cavern, Rebekah paused to stare out over the meadow. Rays of dying sunlight transformed the rain-soaked grass into a carpet of diamonds to her new vampire sight.

In a burst of determined movement, she catapulted out across the slick grass, kicking a spray of raindrops into a comet trail of mist. She sped through the woods until she caught sight of Connor and Osiris flitting between the trees.

As she accelerated to close the gap, taking in a breath to call out, Connor wheeled around and opened his arms to catch her. Grinning widely, she rushed forward and collided with him at full tilt.

Osiris, ever the gentlemen carried on until he was out of view, but the thrum of his steady heartbeat revealed where he was waiting.

A chuckle rumbled through Connor's chest as he held her tightly and kissed her.

Pushing her hands into his hair, she tasted his kiss, biting on his lip.

Lifting her until her thighs framed his hips, Connor turned to press her back into a tree and deepened the kiss until a growl of frustration rasped in his throat. Pulling back, he rested his forehead against hers and closed his eyes. "I miss you, too, honey, but I'll be back soon, I promise."

"You better damn well stay safe." Rebekah pulled his head back to glare at him. "I've not waited three years to be with you to have Blake finish you off."

They both knew it was a harsh take on reality, but Connor quirked a crooked grin. "He'd have to find me first and I was always good at 'blind man's bluff'."

"Ha-ha," said Rebekah, the tension draining from her body as she dropped her feet to the ground. "Can I ask why Osiris is going?"

Connor's gray gaze clouded and she snorted. "I thought not. Go, and then get your ass back home."

Gripping her jaw, Connor said, "Getting the tree-dwellers to come here will be tough. If they won't come, then leave them and look out for Leizle and Thomas, okay?"

"Uncle Harry might be stubborn, but he isn't stupid. I'm sure I can persuade him, after all, vampire or not, we are still blood."

With a gentle kiss, Connor held her gaze for a moment before stepping back and saying, "See you soon, my love. It's better not to keep Blake waiting, the sooner he sails into the sunset the better. I must go."

With a wave, Rebekah remained resting against the tree trunk and watched him disappear. She heard the distant sound of splintering bark, and knew he was carving an arrow-straight path through the woods. Only the oldest trees would be safe.

Chapter 10

The black hulk of the container ship blotted out the view across the river and appeared to suck in light rays like a hungry predator. The water around the hull barely rippled, as though even the river was trying to slip by unnoticed.

With Osiris at his side, Connor stood high on the embankment and studied the menacing craft. Piercing the dull afternoon gloom, a light appeared onboard, the sudden yellow tinted glow pouring out through the windows of the bridge – the beast had woken.

"They have seen us," said Osiris.

"I have to go in alone. Captain Blake has agreed to a truce, for now."

"It is safe for you, then?" Osiris lifted his chin, his curtain of hair flaring out behind him in the breeze rushing across the estuary. His onyx gaze passed along the vessel from bow to stern, where figures wove in seamless patterns along the deck as the crew stowed equipment and battened down hatches in preparation for departure.

"Time is running out." Connor laid a heavy hand on the warrior's solid shoulder. "Thank you, Osiris, and be careful."

Skidding down the slope, sending an explosive shower of gravel and stones ricocheting out in front of him, Connor dropped down onto the blacktop of the access road to the Dockyard. The asphalt gleamed with iridescent beads of oil, the glittering display picking out the path Connor had to tread. Akin to a yellow brick road, he knew where it led, just as Dorothy had, but whether he would get to return home, he was not so certain.

Glancing back up the steep escarpment confirmed, as he expected, that Osiris had gone.

Passing through the sturdy iron-barred gate, Connor found an empty tender already moored at the quayside. In case there was any doubt it was meant for him, Blake had left a calling card; a flare gun, although it was not loaded.

Unease uncoiled inside Connor, a knot the size of a fist churned in his stomach and the hairs on his nape rose. The balance of power had shifted. The Reverend was out of danger, and Connor had the feeling he was being lured into a trap. *I could just go home*. But he knew he couldn't do that.

Jumping down into the small craft, he sat on the wooden bench and inspected the flare gun. Was it the *actual* gun? He couldn't tell but, like a bullet with your name on it, or finding a severed horse head in your bed, the message was chilling. In this case, it implied the hatchet was not buried.

Putting the gun down and picking up the oars, Connor stopped speculating and started rowing. *If Blake wants revenge, then it's going to be a hard day at the office.*

As he drew closer, the shadow oozed around the huge vessel like an oil slick crushing the water into submission. Connor knew the science – a spoonful of oil could calm a lake. Seeping engine oil provided the likeliest cause, but it still felt like an alchemist's spell. He rowed up to the wall of blackened steel and heard the skittering noise of a ladder falling from the heavens, sounding like a giant cockroach scrabbling downward. The metal rungs swayed slowly to and fro, as if daring Connor to touch them. *Get a grip.* His fanciful imaginings were irritating even him. *Rebekah would give me a hefty thump and say man-up.* Squaring his shoulders, he did just that. He reached out to grab the ladder, leapt across onto the lowest rung, and then climbed as fast as his pumping muscles would allow. Scaling the side like a missile shot from the depths, he vaulted smoothly over the rail and landed silently on the deck.

The constant stream of nomads passing back and forth froze as though his arrival cut the power. Each turned a pale, blue-veined face in his direction, and then drifted towards him like iron filings being dragged towards a magnet. The glances they exchanged exuded 'communication'.

Knowing their interlinked consciousness was controlled by Blake, Connor scanned the upper levels and the metal stairway leading to the bridge. Sure enough, the nomad commander's silhouette blotted out a jagged lump in the gray sky.

"Captain." Connor raised a hand in greeting. "How is the patient?"

Blake's gurgling laughter stuttered on the breeze, and the captain's companion appeared on the deck, stepping through a space in the closely-packed line of bodies in front of Connor.

The rows of watching eyes glinted.

The bloated face of his guide split into a puffy grin. "Come this way."

The wall of grime-encrusted coats parted, creating a channel which Connor had no choice but to walk down. Even though many of the nomads were shorter than Connor's six foot two inches, they were intimidating.

The guide disappeared through a door in the metal wall, and Connor followed. He expected to head down towards the infirmary but was led through the storage hold and into the corridor beyond, which he remembered as the route leading to the human quarters of the vessel. Between the two self-contained areas, the feeding lounge was located. *Why would Blake meet there?*

It was the venue in which Connor had killed Viktor and won a place on the crew. Even though, engaging in another fight for survival was a long-shot, Connor scanned shadows for an ambush. *Maybe Blake has more sick humans to treat?* He held his tongue while his curiosity ran riot.

Spinning the metal wheel on an airlock door, Blake's guide opened the hatch and waved Connor through. The red Perspex covers over the bulkhead lamps lining the corridor dyed the walls blood red, as if to scream 'warning' to humans, but Connor suspected it stemmed from Blake's black sense of humor. Going through the door at the other end, he entered the feeding chamber and, sitting in the throne chair at the midpoint of the curving arc of benches, was Blake.

At last. He just wanted the suspense to be over.

"Doctor Connor, welcome." Blake inclined his sleek black head, acknowledging the words spoken by his guide.

"Captain Blake, how fares the Reverend?" Connor asked, mildly.

111

Blake waved to indicate a seat to his left, and Connor took the hint and sat down.

Taking up a position behind his master, the guide placed a hand on Blake's shoulder and, like a strange ventriloquist act, he spoke, but Blake provided the gestures.

Connor studied the metal mask the captain wore, trying to gauge his host's intent.

"I am grateful to you for saving the Reverend." Blake waved a hand. "Oh, I know he could have been fed and survived like a man in an iron lung, but living and being treated like a babe in arms – that is no life, so, thank you."

"But-?" Connor said bluntly.

"But, now you must pay." Blake reached up and pulled the mask away from his face. "For this." The concave expanse of gristle and bone glistened in the dim light. The seared surface was still stained blood red and looked wet.

"What we do in battle has a code of honor, Captain," said Connor quietly, "You were trying to kill me."

"Perhaps. But you will still pay. An eye for an eye."

Faint shuffling sounds behind Connor grew louder. The rustle of dried leather moving over hardened bodies surrounded him, and then an arm snaked around his throat, and the vampire who had appeared behind yanked sharply until Connor's head was crushed back against his rock-hard torso.

Blake stood then, the muscles in his face rippling in what Connor imagined was a smile, exposing the black stump of his tongue.

His hands outstretched, Blake's seeking grasp only stopped when his fingertips brushed Connor's jaw. A pair of nomads each gripped an arm, so even though Connor jerked back, he could barely move.

"Any last words," Blake's guide said, in a strident gloating tone, which Connor felt sure reflected his master's voice inside his head.

"Blake, you know Principal Julian will hunt you down and condemn you to death for this." The iron bar of the forearm pressed into Connor's neck reduced his voice to a hoarse whisper.

Dribble ran freely down Blake's chin as his fingertips crawled over Connor's stiff features. "Oh, I think Principal Julian has more important things on his mind. The rampaging enemy across the water. He needs me more than I need him, for the moment."

"So, it was a lie? The ferals?" Connor's mouth formed the words, but the sound didn't come.

The pads of Blake's thumbs dug into Connor's eyes. He kept them open and watched the eclipse of sight, the captain's calloused skin feeling like broken glass grinding into the slick surface of his retina. A rainbow burst into flame as the optic nerves compressed. *He suckered us in.* Connor remained still with shock, waiting for his eyeballs to pop and for the glutinous vitreous fluid to ooze down his cheeks.

Blake enjoyed prolonging the agony. "How will you manage, I wonder, without sight?"

The pressure built inside Connor's head, until a booming sound reverberated around the room, like a clanger hammering a steel bell.

Everyone in the chamber froze. The vibrations faded, but still rang inside nomad skulls like a struck tuning fork. Before silence reasserted itself, the noise swelled again. Louder this time. Blake's thumbs lost their downward force and Connor ripped an arm from the grip of a distracted nomad and punched the captain in the chest, sending Blake sprawling. His arms flailed as he collided with the curved bench, fell backwards over it and thumped onto the floor. The nomads lunged into a synchronized attack, grabbed Connor by arms, boots, coat, hair and anything that offered a grip, and tore at his struggling frame. He dislodged a leg hold with a jerking kick and punched another attacker in the pale flaccid face, before he felt a lump of his hair being torn out by the roots.

113

Another clanging beat on the hull brought instant order. The nomads darted puzzled glances around, clearly rattled. In a thrash of movement, Connor rolled off the wooden bench and gained his feet in a clear space, his back pressed to the wall.

"You want to know what that sound is?" asked Connor, with a grim smile. He straightened his coat and ran his hands through his hair, confirming the presence of a square inch of torn scalp. The fiery orange orbs dancing in his vision gradually faded until the assembled vampires slowly came into focus from the outside edges inwards.

Blake surged back to his feet and nodded sharply.

"Hera. She has been taken off the ship." Connor tensed, the metal rivets he dug out of the panel behind him protruding from his clenched fists like stiletto blades.

Blake's jaw dropped open and a roar erupted from deep inside him.

Raising his voice, Connor bellowed, "She will stay in London as our guest, until you return with proof." In Connor's mind, if Blake had lied about the feral attacks, that secured Hera's freedom, permanently. "Unless you were lying, of course." While speaking, Connor worked his way around the room, the nomads all twisting on the spot as though their feet were nailed in place. *Blake has told them not to touch me.*

Connor reached the door, dropped one rivet spike, and touched the door handle. Suddenly, the blinding colors behind his eyes returned, but this time clear images came rushing in to replace them. An azure blue sea, gleaming like a mirror, expanded across his horizon. Shadows mottled the surface, the patches growing darker as something rose from beneath the waves. Hundreds of domed heads emerged slowly, water streaming down over ice-colored stiff faces as an army walked out of the surf. The rotting flesh dislodged from their clothing by rolling waves turned the sea brown. They waded forward and clambered up rocks, their heads swinging left and right as though seeking by smell. Water poured from the hanks of wet hair obscuring their faces, dripping from their chins. Their teeth bared, a constant growling sound rose and fell as they moved. *Ferals.*

'You must come Connor. I cannot escape.' The voice inside his head belonged to Malachi.

The picture panned around until Connor was looking at his friend's face. The wizened features were the same, the putty-colored skin and sparse covering of silver hair remained. But Malachi's fish scale-tinted gaze reflected fear – *no, not fear, terror.* The robes Malachi wore were blood-stained. A gash in his cheek oozed chalky pink fluid and his eyes were sunken deep into his sockets. *He is starving.*

'I cannot last much longer. They are breaking through the citadel wall. You must come.'

The door handle buckled in Connor's grip and he dropped to his knees. Aloud, he said, "I'll come for you, Malachi. Barricade yourself in and wait for me."

The steel walls around him came back into focus, the images of Alexandria fading into wisps of smoke, and Connor became aware of the profound silence in the room. When he staggered back to his feet and leaned against the door, fifty nomads watched him and waited. Even Blake appeared to have been turned to stone.

"The ferals are on the move," whispered Connor. "In the east. They are coming out of the sea."

"You know then, that I spoke the truth. Return Hera to my herd."

Connor looked at Blake's ruined face and felt sadness. *He still loves her.*

"She is miserable, Blake. Why have you cut her out? Leaving her to live in silence was cruel."

"Why would she want to look upon this?" Blake spat on the floor and held out a hand until a nomad placed his steel mask into it. Pressing it over his skull, a sucking sound created a seal which held it in place. "I want her back," his guide said, heavily.

"What happens when the ferals have overtaken North Africa, then the USA, Canada? There are no safe places, not forever. You'll starve, in the end. Let's help each other?"

"Go on." Blake waited.

"Help me rescue Malachi. When we return, you'll be provided with synthetic blood, enough to keep you alive while Julian, Marius, and I figure out a way to kill the ferals. We have time. They don't know we are here, so we have some time."

"And you'll return Hera?"

Connor nodded slowly. "If she wants to return, then yes."

"We set sail tonight," blurted Blake's guide.

"Perfect. I'll be back within the hour. I need to tell Julian what I've seen."

No one tried to stop him as Connor pulled open the door, rushed along the gangways, and out into the gusting winds cutting across the deck. A thick shroud of cloud covered the sky. The sun could not puncture the canopy, but he knew it was up there. He felt that way about the ferals, now. *We can't see them, but they are there, and like an infestation, they are flourishing.*

Swinging over the side of the ship, Connor scaled down the hull until the tender was beneath him, dropped down into the boat, and set off for the quayside.

Chapter 11

Buttoned up against the dying light of the blustery afternoon, Connor ramped up speed and, even though the wind-chill encased his features in a mask of ice, he was frustrated that he didn't have more acceleration to call upon. His world was rotating on an axis, the gyroscope becoming dangerously close to crashing. *Malachi is in danger.* He knew that everyone he cared about in London would soon be under threat, too. He felt like a magician trying to juggle exploding bombs. *I can do this.* He made himself factor in Julian, Daniel, Anthony, Marius, Gerrard and Greg. *Quit with the God complex. There are others who can hold the fort.*

Focusing on one step at a time, Connor shuffled the errands he had to complete into order. The two tasks at the top of the list pulled him in different directions – he made a choice and hoped it was the right one.

Approaching the City from the south made the safe house the first destination to tick off the list. Connor took a few seconds break from his hurtling run to survey his surroundings and make sure no one had followed him. The only source of danger would come from a nomad crewman, but the odor of salt and fetid skin could easily be detected.

Happy that Blake must be focused on setting sail, and would do that without him onboard if Connor wasted too much time, he headed straight to the row of Victorian houses, leapt the flight of stone steps and, in a nod to letting humans have some control, used a key to unlock the door of the safe house. He swept through the ground floor and found it empty. Lifting his chin, he listened to the faint creaks of wood. Julian and Leizle had a bedroom upstairs, but Osiris would be hiding. Homing in on two muted hearts beating in a steady calm rhythm, Connor pulled open the trap door in the wooden floorboards in the lounge.

It was almost pitch-black down below, and Connor grinned as the memory of his very first encounter with Rebekah came to mind. The humans had slept in the small enclosed cell of a basement for many years, until he had discovered them.

The barest rays of gray light seeped in through a high window set at the outside street level, the glass caked in grit-encrusted cobwebs. When Connor swung down without using the stairs, the two occupants sitting as still as statues down below didn't seem rattled by his arrival.

"Glad you made it," Osiris said quietly.

"Well done, Osiris." Connor crossed the dust-covered floor and laid a hand on the Egyptian warrior's shoulder. The plan they hatched had been sketchy at best, but Connor never doubted the outcome. His own fate had been a different matter. Locking gazes for a moment, Connor received an assurance that how close he came to dying would remain between them.

"How did you do it?"

Osiris shrugged. "I used the humans' heartbeats as cover. They are all in the same part of the ship."

Connor knew it was his own projected image of Hera that Osiris had been tracking, but until he saw the slight girl with her bronzed skin and lustrous black hair for himself, he could not quite accept they had succeeded.

Rising gracefully from a cross-legged pose, Hera emerged from a deep shadow in the corner. She gripped both Connor's hands and laid her forehead against them in thanks. *~You are a man of your word.~*

Connor's smile was tight. "We have a way to go before we can say that, Hera, but you are safe, for now." Turning to Osiris, he said, "Anthony will know where to take her. It is the safest place until I return. Wait here, I'll send him to you. We can't risk Hera being discovered."

"Seren won't know, I promise."

"When the time is right, but not now." Connor nodded his thanks.

Osiris knew how to keep Seren at bay. His Earth Walker meditative skills created a wall that even she could not break through.

"Stay safe." Whisking up a storm of dirt, Connor spun on his heel and disappeared back up the steps to the room above. Just seeing Osiris had put his mind at rest. The secret would remain between them and Anthony. *I just hope he's not in surgery.*

Minutes later, when he burst through the glass doors of the hospital, Connor made the vampires waiting inside jump. He pulled off black gloves as he whipped past the four open-mouthed faces. Flipping down his collar, he headed for the operating theater, wishing for the hundredth time that he shared a psychic link with his surgical assistant.

Connor entered the scrub room and peered through the small square window into the theater beyond. Anthony was frowning and had a bovine syringe buried deep in the eye socket of his patient – trying to rehydrate an eyeball and restore vision.

Shit. Connor inched the swing door open carefully. Making Anthony jump would blind the patient for good.

Circling the room until he was in full view, Connor spoke quietly. "Anthony, can I have a word, please?"

An irritated sneer curled his assistant's lip. "In about ninety seconds, yes."

Connor cocked his head. *I can do ninety seconds.* With an apologetic wave, he slipped back into the scrub room and waited with his hands locked behind his back, rocking back and forth from heel to toe.

Anthony was as good as his word. Eighty seconds later, he swung in through the door, wiping his hands on a linen square.

Connor launched straight into his dilemma. "I've had a vision. Malachi is in trouble." He raised a hand and silenced the flood of questions. "It's a long story. I'm going aboard the container ship with Blake – yes, Blake. I know, I have no choice but to trust him."

Anthony's face radiated curiosity, so reading his mind was not an issue, right now.

"I have two things I need you to do, and one of them must be kept from Julian. Are you game?"

Anthony folded his arms across his chest and gave a crooked grin. "Nothing can be any worse than what we've already done together this last five years."

"Okay, first, go to the safe house – Osiris is there and... Hera."

"What." Anthony dropped his arms and jerked to attention.

"Yes, I know, but you can see why I want Julian kept out of this. Deniability could be crucial if Blake cuts up rough."

"Is there any way Blake won't be after blood, *your* blood?" Anthony said heavily.

"The mission to save Malachi is the focus, right now. Who knows what that will turn up? Just take Hera to the soundproof room, okay?"

"Julian will be over the moon about that." Anthony snorted.

"Which is why you won't tell him. Next, go to Cardiff and bring Brynmor back to London. Things are getting hot here and I'll need him." Connor's arched brow said 'got it?' before he whipped around and disappeared from view.

Step one achieved, Connor raced through the wet streets to the council buildings. He composed his features and rehearsed his speech. A lot was about to land on Julian's plate.

But, the eerily deserted corridors didn't bode well, and Connor felt like the world was against him. He checked his watch. Blake would wait another half an hour, and after that, Connor would face a treacherous run along the Thames estuary to catch up with a ship that would be heading out at top speed.

A court session was not what Connor needed, but the muted rustle of moving fabric and the smells of damp dog were clues that made his heart sink. *Julian is not going to like it, but it's an emergency.* Connor grinned and punched a hole in the glass window on the square red fire alarm trigger – left over from when 'fire evacuation' was part of the human world of 'health and safety'. The alarm bleated like an annoyed goat, but then, as the seized mechanism loosened up, the bleat became a shrieking banshee wail.

The comet tail blur of a hundred hive members pouring out through the door of the courtroom struck Connor as amusing. He grinned as clusters of hurrying vampires bumped into each other, bouncing from the walls as they progressed along the wide corridor. But, the brittle sound of splintering wood made Connor wince.

A result he hadn't considered was damage to the aged and finely carved panels. *Julian will not be happy.* The court building, with its gravitas and intricately tooled décor, was the principal's pride and joy.

When Julian, Marius and Daniel burst out through the 'jurors only' exit, Connor tried out an apologetic shrug. But, Julian took the wind out of Connor's sails by reversing back into the anteroom, beckoning Connor to follow. The principal showed no sign of irritation, and when Connor caught sight of his reflection in a large mirror hanging on the left wall, he realized why. *I'd never make a good poker player.* The worry carved into his face said it all.

Julian shut the door and said, "Tell me."

"You need to scrap the siphoning shed shelter plan."

"Why?"

"Malachi sent an update. The ferals are rising. Humans won't be safe there if ferals make it to England. We need to revisit the Cardiff Castle option down the line, but for now, we must find a more secure location closer by."

Marius whistled. 'Is Malachi in danger?' The elder Egyptian vampire had become the father figure of the London Hive council.

Connor nodded. "I'm heading out with Blake to rescue him. I need you, Julian, to find a safer place to keep the humans."

"And the tree-dwellers *must* come in," muttered Julian.

"Rebekah is heading out with Seth and Adam to persuade them. Greg could help there. It might take a day or two, but then, at least all the humans will be in one place, on the siphoning farm."

"Where should we move them to after that?" asked Daniel.

"We can't move the eco-shelter group across country until Rebekah returns," Julian chipped in.

"I know you'll think of something, but find somewhere easy to defend. I have to go, Blake said he'd leave on the hour and I'm sure he's hoping I won't make it back in time."

Marius burst into a flurry of aggressive sign and Connor averted his gaze. He needed to let go and trust they'd work it out. Rebekah and Greg would be on hand, too.

"I'll know more when I get back- *We* get back," said Connor with a determined nod.

Chapter 12

Emerging from the access tunnel, Rebekah crossed the entrance cavern and stared out over the meadow. At times like this, when dusk was falling, the muted rays of sunset gleamed like a fan of silver thread to her new vampire sight.

She leaned carefully against one wall of the sweeping entrance arch, took in a deep cleansing breath and held it. Crossing her legs at the ankle, she hitched a thumb into her utility belt – she had put on the combat gear she had always worn when she was human. It was a way of saying 'hey, I'm still the same girl'.

With a deflating sigh, she stopped blinking and became as still as a dummy in a shop window. But her cheeks were flushed from a recent blood feed and the frown on her face was not an expression a mannequin would wear.

She tuned into the heartbeats in the underground chambers and willed Adam and Seth to hurry. Even for Marines, it would take four hours to reach the outer perimeter where the tree-dwellers patrolled daily on foot. *If we miss the patrol at the oak glade we'll have to go in unannounced.* She had been human the last time she saw Uncle Harry. They were bringing enough bad news, so revealing that his niece was now a vampire would be better done gently.

Her frozen statue twitched in a knee jerk reaction to guilt. Rebekah hadn't thought of Harry in many months. *He chose the tree-dwellers to get away from me. Well... from my relationship with Connor.* But she knew that was harsh. Harry chose humans over vampires – a community he could understand over the one that scared him. *I did that to him. Brought a vampire into the eco-shelter.*

She couldn't turn back time, and didn't really want to, but she could take responsibility and say 'sorry' to Harry.

Seth and Adam finally emerged out of the gloom.

"Are we taking the bikes?" Seth asked, hefting his backpack higher and tightening the webbing straps.

"The ground is too wet for bikes," she replied, and both men grunted. "But Connor's sending Greg out to join us,"

"Whoopidy doo, we better hang out the bunting," Seth drawled past the twig he was chewing on.

Rebekah grinned widely. "You can't fool me, it'll be good to see him, but he'll have to catch us up, we can't wait any longer.

With a final glance at Adam, Seth took off across the moonlit meadow at a forced run, taking the direct path uphill to the shelter of the trees at the top of the rise. Rebekah accelerated past the pair of men, heading quickly into the woods on a scouting mission. She didn't expect to find any hive vampires within the twenty-mile exclusion zone, and her mind was already racing ahead to the meeting with Uncle Harry. She enjoyed the feeling of being at the top of the food chain. Even another vampire would think twice before challenging a 'newling', unless they were alpha males when turned. Being a female vampire was rare, but the residue of her human blood put her at the top of the 'strength' curve.

Reeling around, she headed back to where Seth and Adam powered their way through the trees, thick brambles and tangled undergrowth forcing a change in their direction every few hundred yards or so. The ground was boggy and the mud reached half way to their knees at times, but neither men complained. They tucked their chins down and forged on.

I could carry them both. Rebekah clamped her lips tight on a bark of laughter. *As if these two would allow that.* Father and son were a formidable team.

The sound of rain splattering on the thick canopy overhead created a curiously cocooned feeling. The musty smell and dank atmosphere in the woods were challenging for humans – breathing and seeing clearly were no picnic – but at least they would not be soaked through.

A sharp crack made Rebekah's head shoot round. Dashing forward and catching Seth's eye, she held up a clenched fist and both men dropped to the ground on their bellies. Moving fast to rest against a nearby tree and blend into the landscape, she peered out with a narrowed gaze.

The leaves shuffled in the undergrowth and the smell of crushed moss and bark plumed into the air. Rebekah intently scanned the spaces between tree trunks, looking for a glimmer of movement.

When an owl call floated on the breeze, Rebekah huffed noisily.

Seth and Adam heard it too and clambered to their feet. The mud caked onto their combat jackets had splattered over their white faces. Tension remained etched into their tight expressions, but it was tinged with annoyance, now.

"I'll bloody kill him," muttered Seth, pulling a mace from his belt.

"Now, now, boys," replied Rebekah with a chuckle.

Seconds later, a face peered around a tree trunk. Greg took one look at Seth's soaked clothes and said, "Sorry?" When the hefty vampire stepped forward, his sober expression was genuine.

One look at Seth confirmed that jumping in on Greg's side would not help, so Rebekah folded her arms, leaned back and propped her boot on the tree behind, and waited.

Seth swung his mace in a threatening arc and darted forward. But, Greg easily caught the spiked ball in his hand, pulled on the chain and yanked Seth off balance.

The pissed off Marine glared into Greg's face from only ten inches away.

Tension radiated in waves from the pair, and then, Seth thumped Greg on the shoulder with all the force he had, and muttered, "Asshole."

"Agreed," said Greg.

Rebekah pushed away from the tree and grinned. "C'mere you."

Greg walked over and she greeted him with a hug. Entering that preternatural world where Seth and Adam became frozen, like posed clay figures in time lapse photography, Rebekah said, "What were you thinking, leaving the owl call so late? You scared the life out of them."

"I got much closer than I realized." Switching gear, Greg said, "Who's left at the eco-shelter?"

"Oscar and Leizle are in charge. A vampire called Sampson-" Rebekah stopped to give Greg a probing look.

Greg nodded. "He's a good guy, don't worry about that."

"-and Peter from the human farm. This negotiation is going to be tricky. I hope you have your wits about you."

"We'll get them to come in."

"I'm glad you're here. Do you think Seth will let you take him on ahead? Time is ticking and we need to catch the tree-dweller patrol at the big oak clearing."

"Well, here goes nothing."

Both vampires turned and closed the gap to where Seth and his son had sat down on a fallen log, and both men jumped to their feet as if stung by a wasp.

Adam cleared his throat and said, "It's like watching time travel when you just appear like that. Never gonna get used to it."

"We need to get moving. Seth, it will be quicker if we run on ahead." Greg lifted one eyebrow.

Seth shot a sideways look at Adam and gripped his boy's shoulder. "Greg's right. I'll see you there, son."

Both the Marines, their strides in perfect harmony, jogged away and disappeared between the trees. Rebekah could hear them pushing through the undergrowth, and then there was silence.

"Greg's carrying him, isn't he?" said Adam with a grin.

"Yes, but that's our secret. You know how proud your dad is. Greg was the same when he was human. Marine macho is hard to shake off."

"Are you going to give me a lift?"

Rebekah stared hard into Adam's dark brown eyes. This was more than she could hope for. "Would you mind?"

"If dad can swallow his pride, then I guess I can, too."

"It would be better," said Rebekah, "the mud bath has soaked you through, so getting there quickly makes sense."

Not giving Adam time to change his mind, Rebekah circled round, caught hold of his hand and ducked beneath his arm. Using his utility belt, she effortlessly lifted his mud-caked boots off the ground and started running. With his free hand, Adam hurriedly pulled his beanie hat lower and flipped up his collar as Rebekah smoothly accelerated.

Passing through a densely packed area, a straggling end of a tree branch whipped Adam across the chest and he winced.

"Sorry," said Rebekah, "This is a first for me, too."

The miles of forest swept by in swathes of green and brown silk until the air cooled and became fresher. *Almost there.* Giving Adam a reassuring glance, Rebekah let her speed die away.

Setting Adam down near the edge of the clearing, the pair walked to where Greg and Seth were sitting side-by-side beneath the canopy of an ancient oak tree. Visibility across the glade was poor in the mist of drizzling rain, but the hollowed-out chamber inside the tree trunk beside them still held the morning patrol's carved twigs, used as a crude means of communication. *We got here in time.*

Adam headed away across the field towards the path the tree-dwellers would use. He had been out on vampire patrol a hundred times, before Connor and Rebekah came into his life and all the rules had shifted. His stout figure disappeared and Rebekah took a seat beside Greg.

They sat in companionable silence. Adam was a good choice to meet the patrol – he'd grown up with the community and they were his friends.

Whispering voices hissed on the breeze and then a harsh grunt. Moments later Adam reappeared accompanied by five tall men. One carried a staff and Seth stood up and grinned. The tall wiry sandy-haired man loped across the field but stopped ten yards out, his hair color turning to caramel when the rain soaked it.

Seth went over, threw his arms around the man's shoulders, and thumped his back in a resounding rhythm. "Old friend. It's been awhile. Too long."

Over Seth's shoulder, the taller man fixed his attention on the pair of vampires and his hold on the staff tightened to a white-knuckled grip.

Rebekah and Greg sighed in unison. *This is not going to be easy.*

The other men joined the tall man, Seth and Adam, and huddled together, their harsh whispers of protest stuttering through the air.

"Times are changing. If you want to stay alive, you need to hear them out," said Adam.

"We don't need them," a gruff voice replied.

"Think, man. Not all vampires are the same." Seth grunted and staggered backwards when someone in the knot of bodies shoved him.

"Is this going to get ugly?" Greg ground a lump of bark to dust as he watched anxiously.

"We can't let it get ugly." Rebekah left the shadow of the trees and walked slowly across the open expanse of clumped grass. "If I can just interrupt."

The group turned sharply in her direction, and Seth and Adam moved to one side, both wearing a tight grin,

They probably have their fingers crossed behind their backs. She focused on each tree-dweller, in turn. They were all sweaty, with dirt-streaked faces. Their hearts thudded loudly, and Rebekah carefully swallowed down the saliva that flooded her mouth. Three of the men were older and weather-beaten. She chose the one with the steadiest heart rate and said, "You don't know me, but I'm Rebekah. Harry is my uncle."

He shot a glance at his companions and when the man looked back, his brows rose in surprise. "Your uncle has told us all about you."

Rebekah nodded. "I hope that's a good thing."

"But he didn't say you were a…"

"No, he wouldn't have." Rebekah met the tall man's probing look with a gentle smile. "Seth and Adam brought us here because it's a matter of life or dea-. Sorry, bad choice of words, I meant a matter of survival. Please, let me talk with Uncle Harry. You can't make the choice for him."

The youngest man in the scouting party coughed. "You'll only visit Harry?"

The group jolted with agitation when Greg appeared beside Rebekah. "Seth is on your council. We need to talk with them and then, whatever you decide, we'll know we did our best and will leave."

His voice gruff with emotion, Seth said, "Hear them out. It's bad. If we thought we were in danger before, that is nothing compared to what is coming."

Even beneath the masks of dirt, the tree-dwellers faces noticeably drained of color.

"Lead the way, time is short and we must get going," said Greg, and to Rebekah, at vampire speed, he added, "If they refuse, we'll just follow on behind."

Seth and Adam struck out, making the decision for the tree-dweller party, and Rebekah and Greg buried their frustration as they matched the human pace on the trek through the woods.

The patrol group stayed in close formation and kept the vampires in their sights.

Rebekah felt better when the adrenaline levels in the odor of human blood drifting in the air dropped. *They are ready to trust us.*

The tree trunks became broader in the oldest part of the forest and Rebekah looked up with keen interest. Sturdy platforms built into the highest branches overhead blended in. The habitats fashioned from canvas and woven branches could only be seen, even by her vampire vision, from some angles. There were newer planks in places. Proof that, although the hiding chambers were not needed so often, now, thanks to Julian and the London Hive moving towards humans and vampires living in harmony, the tree-dwellers remained alert.

It would take time for the newly constructed 'human town' to evolve into a community, and the tree-dwellers and eco-shelter families were like stubborn relatives who preferred to fend for themselves. They planned to watch, wait and see, and perhaps come into the fold when they felt safe. *But now, we'll just have to bully them into it.*

The tall man made a high-pitched bird call as they drew closer. Humans appeared between trees from every angle and Rebekah assumed it was a code for red alert. Each tree-dweller was armed with spears, swords, darts, but one held a gun – the last resort.

Both Greg and Rebekah stopped walking and surveyed the camp. Undulations in the ground marked locations of large Anderson-shelter type buildings. Smaller ones served as storage sheds. Other higher mounds had front facing doors and windows set into stone walls. But rolls of camouflage fabric anchored above the gutters on the roofs, if dropped down, would mimic the surrounding branches, vines and moss.

A small man appeared in the doorway of a nearby habitat and blinked like a mole emerging into the sunshine.

"Uncle Harry," said Rebekah, impulsively walking forward and extending her arms in greeting.

Harry squinted up at her and his features pinched tight.

Is he angry? Her steps faltered and her dead heart suddenly felt so heavy she could not walk.

A keening noise came from the old man and he wiped his eyes with the back of his hand.

He's crying. "It's okay, Uncle Harry," she whispered and inched closer, taking his thin bony fingers in hers.

"It's really you," he finally croaked.

"It's been a long time. Too long. I'm sorry." She gently took his arm and guided him back inside. Greg, Seth and Adam knew what to do, and she hoped they would win the negotiation.

Inside a surprisingly cozy sitting room, Harry sank into a deep armchair. "You are well?" he asked.

Sitting opposite, cringing inside when the chair creaked mournfully, she leaned forward to take his shaking hands again. He looked so much older than she remembered, but of course, the last few years had been tough. "Much more importantly, are *you* well?"

The old man nodded, but Rebekah's vampire senses revealed the truth. An irregular heartbeat thudded through her skull, and washing his scent over her palate, she found his iron levels were low. Getting him to come into the human farm where food and medicines were on hand became vital.

"Uncle Harry, do you trust me?"

His watery eyes met hers and she sat very still as he absorbed her new vampire appearance. "How is Connor?"

It was not the question she expected, but she smiled. "The same. Driven, dynamic, and carrying the world on his shoulders."

Harry nodded slowly. "He is a good... man."

"You are a good man, too." She would never forget that he had taken in the six-year-old Rebekah when the pandemic wiped out most of the human population. He, too, was driven, dynamic and carrying the world on his shoulders, back then. He saw the rise of vampires coming, and gathered supplies and moved the group of human refugees out of London. Rebekah felt a burst of pride warm her chest. *Harry and Connor are not so different.*

"I've come to get you, Harry. All of you. You are in danger if you stay here."

"We've always been in danger." Harry smiled gently.

"For me, please. Come in to where I can protect you." Rebekah stared into his eyes. "Please."

"Something worse is coming?" Harry asked quietly.

"Yes."

He suddenly nodded and eased himself up out of his chair. "We'll need to take the blockers and spray with us. I've accumulated a stock pile." Walking to the rear of the curved roofed shelter, He disappeared through another door Rebekah hadn't noticed.

Following him, she stopped on the threshold and whistled. The space was a laboratory. Red rubber tubes connected gas canisters to Bunsen burners, and glass jars, funnels, pipettes, syringes, etc. ranged across the bench-top. Rebekah's vampire sight detected the particles of dust which had settled on the surface, and she guessed that Harry had not been 'working' in the lab so much in recent weeks.

Transparent plastic crates stacked high along one wall were loaded with containers of pills and I.V. bags filled with clear fluid.

"This is amazing." Rebekah remembered the laboratory Harry had in the London house, and the scaled down version inside the eco-shelter. The production of the modified beta-blockers and pheromone suppressant sprays had made the difference between life and death for her and all the humans in their group.

"I won't leave my medicines behind." Harry's voice rang with conviction.

"No, we won't leave them behind. You'll need to come now, but the crates will be transported, I promise."

Returning to his living area, Harry opened a chest and began pulling out waterproof oilskins and woolen jumpers.

On impulse, Rebekah touched his shoulder and when he looked round, she kissed his cheek. "Dress warmly. I'll be right back."

As she stepped out into the night, she scanned the encampment for signs of Greg. He was sitting on a log seat around a huge pit where the embers of last night's fire were now piles of black ash. She sat down beside him. "How did it go?"

Greg grinned. "They are packing up, now."

"How many are there?"

"Eighteen."

"That's not many."

Greg nodded. "They had a flu outbreak last winter."

Rebekah followed the direction of his gaze. Through a gap between the trees, she made out a gray standing stone.

As confirmation, Greg said, "A grave yard."

"Should we have come earlier? Made them move to the eco-shelter. We had the exclusion zone and vampire protectors."

"They wouldn't have budged. Seth and Adam visited often enough. Don't you think they tried?"

"I guess you're right. What changed their minds?"

"Straight talking and luck."

"Luck?"

"They saw a feral in the woods six months ago. Coming across *one* was a terrifying event, so telling them hundreds might be heading our way – interestingly they saw reason pretty fast."

Rebekah chuckled. "Hundreds?"

"Well, who knows? And it did the trick."

"I'll go and help Harry, oh, and we need to send out a party of vampires to bring in Harry's supply of beta-blockers and spray to the human farm. It could be useful." Rebekah got to her feet and returned to Harry's shelter.

Just before she passed through the doorway, she heard the mumble of human voices and the scuffing sounds of boots crunching across the woodland floor towards the fire pit.

They are ready, just Harry to prepare. I wonder if he'll let me carry him?

Chapter 13

As Connor expected, Blake set sail without him. The container ship slid smoothly out of the docks under power and, without pause, Connor stepped off the quayside and plummeted into the river. Landing on the jagged carpet of rocks and moss-stained boulders beneath the water, he leapt from one to another, gaining on the wide swathe of churning wake spewing out behind the huge torpedo-shaped hull. Although he would never know if the captain's constant companion acted alone or as Blake's mouthpiece, when Connor drew close, a length of chain 'fell overboard'. Ducking as the fast-moving string of metal links whipped past his head, he grabbed hold of the end as it whisked by. He was dragged along behind the vessel until he pulled himself up, found a foothold and managed to climb the row of rusted links. With unexpected assistance from Blake's guide, who reached over the top rail and hauled him up by his elbow, Connor finally launched himself over onto the deck.

Within the hour, a dried out and freshly clothed Connor joined Captain Blake on the bridge. Gazing out over the moonlit waters of the English Channel, he felt an unspoken truce pervade the silence.

Blake stared ahead through the salt stained window, and Connor speculated on how many senses the captain still possessed. *How well can he hear?* He knew taste and sight were destroyed, but only in the traditional sense. The captain's quiet companion scanned the horizon, and Connor noticed that each time the guide paused, Blake's throat gurgled. *Maybe their connection includes 'vision' of some sort.* It was frustrating, being too wary to talk with the nomad who seemed to be hard-wired into Blake's mind, somehow. *Does Blake trust me? Does he believe Hera will be returned to him?* Refocusing on the first brick in the wall of obstacles, Connor turned his attention to Malachi's rescue.

The ship powered on through the night, slipping smoothly out of the Thames estuary and setting course for Alexandria, Egypt. The nomad lookouts on the deck resembled a row of sentinels scouring the distant shoreline. Like wolves howling at the moon, every now and again a mournful feral cry drifted out across the water.

Once the vessel reached the open sea, the vampire occupants became statues, sinking into the meditative state which conserved energy.

Connor tuned into the faint thrum of human heartbeats deep in the bowels of the ship and, moving for the first time in many hours, he eased the tightness cramping his neck and shoulders. The silence on the bridge smothered him and the need for action trembled through his muscles. Looking out over the rolling black expanse of the ocean, Connor tried yet again to assert himself – take back control.

"Put me ashore on the coast of Libya. I'll get to Alexandria faster than the ship can sail."

Blake snorted and, as if nudged out of a deep sleep, the guide jolted to attention and in a robotic voice, said, "The ship is slower but safer. You will become a victim of the ferals if things are as bad as your maker, Malachi, says. You will stay onboard."

Sinking down into the leather embrace of a chair, Connor accepted his fate, turning his mind instead to the plan of attack once they arrived. Recalling Malachi's vision of how the surf boiled with emerging ferals, it seemed likely that the 'sane vampires' onboard would be vastly outnumbered.

"Have you got firearms on the ship?" asked Connor.

Blake grunted, and his guide didn't waste his breath.

"I know. You have wide bore rifles which can stop an elephant, but there are too many of them." Connor folded his arms, closed his eyes, and tried to make contact with Malachi again.

They sailed for a day and a night, and the nomad lookouts reported the North Africa coastline appeared deserted.

With the destination drawing closer, Connor relaxed, opening the door inside his mind and, as he hoped it would, Malachi's voice cut a path into his brain. *'I have cattle tethered along the sea wall. It is working as a distraction, but I don't know for how much longer.'*

135

'We are on our way', Connor projected the thought. 'Just pack everything you need and get ready to meet us on the sea wall when I say'. He darted a look at Blake's still figure; it would be easy to assume the captain was oblivious to the world around him. *Would he let on, if he could read my mind?* With Rebekah, Seren and Malachi, and surprisingly, Hera, he felt he had enough voices to contend with. Hera's skills had become stronger. It appeared she was learning to communicate with Osiris without words, too.

Blake remained frozen in the attitude of a captain piloting his vessel, standing behind the console and facing out across the water as though he could see.

"If the ferals boarded your ship in Rotterdam, we can't take the tanker too close to the shore." Connor tried sucking Blake's interpreter into sharing something. Going into battle wearing a blindfold might be something Blake was accustomed to, but the pressure was making Connor jittery.

"As you know, we have fitted water cannons around the deck, like the ones humans used on container ships to prevent pirates boarding. We have hand held versions, too, which are more effective when targeting isolated invaders. But no, we don't want to get close enough for ferals to attack the vessel en-masse."

Connor ran a hand over his nape. *That is better than no strategy at all.*

As the ship forged on through the choppy sea, Connor pulled a vial from his pocket, flipped the lid and downed the dose of human blood needed to calm him. He felt the guide's eyes slide across his relaxed features and then dart over to Blake. Connor didn't care. Sinking into revival sleep clarified his mind – the battle plans he was forced to make in isolation came into crisp focus and he achieved a sense of satisfaction. His only real concern was that he and Malachi make it out alive.

Like a man waking from a trance, following a train of thought no one else shared, Connor mused aloud, "How is Malachi staying alive? Feeding, I mean?"

"When you see him, you can ask," was the blunt reply Blake relayed through his guide.

136

Connor inspected the still features of the nomad who spent his time tethered to Blake like a shadow and curiosity got the better of him. "Do you have a name?"

The seconds stretched, and just when Connor thought the nomad would not answer, he said, "Tyrone." He frowned, the veins beneath his flesh bunching into blue tram-lines.

Trying to make sense of the worried look on Tyrone's face, Connor watched the nomad's hands twitch and tug at his coat. *He's nervous.*

After a number of facial contortions, Tyrone said slowly, "I am not used to finding my own words."

Connor guessed Tyrone meant, 'not used to *thinking* for himself'. He had become an echo chamber for Blake's thoughts. "What is it like being connected?" Connor jerked his head, indicating the places outside this room. "Can you hear all of them, all the time?"

"I can choose. We stay in touch with our captain, but the rest, we cho-" Tyrone jolted to attention as Blake spluttered. "No more talking," the guide said flatly.

"Thank you, Tyrone."

The silence filtered through the cracks inside the room, the creaking of shifting joists and rivets onboard were the only sounds. The clouds were dyed black by the setting of the sun, their rolling jagged fabric descending onto the horizon like the jaws of a beast swallowing them whole. The eerie glow of the ships lantern found no answering specks of hope shining back on the passing coastline.

Deep in thought, Connor turned over the merits of each plan he had come up with, and hoped he'd know which one to use, when the moment came.

Dawn was breaking by the time the tanker stopped off the coast of Egypt. Down each anchor line, a squad of nomads descended until the sea swallowed them up; their job was to scan the sea floor for ferals, and yank on the anchor chains in an early warning of an attack.

The distant shoreline seethed with the distorted black mass of feral bodies, forming a roiling mountain of moving flesh. The ones clambering over others to reach the top of the pile, had reached the crest of the sea wall and were punching holes in the masonry, transforming the run of smooth coping stones into a row of sharp broken teeth.

Scanning the windows in the stone walls of the immense citadel, Connor, even from hundreds of yards out, picked out Malachi's face framed in an opening, looking out to sea.

"The harbor is around the back. Will the ferals have found their way around? We could try taking the tender out into the bay."

"Too risky," came Tyrone's stoic reply.

"A helpful suggestion would be good," snapped Connor.

"We arm ourselves for hand-to-hand combat and force a way through," Tyrone said, his face a mismatch of uncertainty at what he was being forced to say.

Connor detected a crack in the nomad's shell and realized for the first time that the nomads weren't just one consciousness; they had their own will locked inside, where the ego cowered in isolation.

"If we all want to die, that's an excellent plan," Connor said drily. "I'll talk to Malachi." *Malachi, has the fort got a jetty? A cellar? Basement? Any hidden access at all?*

Staring across the rippling water at his mentor, Connor willed a response.

Access to the cellar is inside the hallway, so no, just the main entrance.

Connor watched the ferals mindlessly punching their way through the boulders of the sea wall. A spray of red paint plumed into the sky – no, not paint, blood – and the nearby mound of ferals erupted into jerking movement as they lunged towards the unfortunate animals tethered in place. Lumps of flesh flew up into the air, one larger clump causing another roiling jerk of movement as dozens of ferals threw themselves after it. Those who got there first were soon swamped by another wave. One limb spiraling through the air had a hand attached. Guttural snarls rode on the breeze.

Keeping his attention glued to the mindless carnage onshore, Connor began to think Blake could be right. Clubbing defenseless seals came to mind. "Okay, if the plan is to force our way through, we have to work together. Tyrone, what weapons have we got?"

Without a backward glance, the guide burst into movement and led the captain from the bridge.

Glad to be doing something, at last, Connor followed them down to the deck. He hung onto his place as third in line when the nomad pair dived through a metal door and headed downward to the lower levels of the ship. *How does Blake know where he is?* Speculating on sonar, or having an internal map so precisely embedded that the captain never faltered, occupied a small part of his attention. He quickly tracked them through the network of gangways and storage holds down into the bowels of the vessel.

Connor tried not to second guess what he might find. Hoping for grenades and claymore mines would lead to disappointment.

At their destination, Blake pulled a set of keys from his pocket and opened up the armory.

Without hesitation, Connor dodged past, entered first, and scanned the wooden crates lining the walls. Sitting on metal shelves were nylon kit bags bulging with irregular shaped jutting objects.

Blake crossed the room, grabbed a bound handle and dragged a bag to the front of a shelf. Opening the zipper released an avalanche of metal blades and hatchets.

Not a good start.

Next, using a crowbar, Blake jimmied open three wooden crates.

Connor peered inside.

They contained crossbows and flare guns, but, another strange type of gun he had never seen before caught his eye. Picking up the weapon, holding it by the thick black-rubber grip, he turned it over and inspected the barrel. It was blocked by something. "What's this?"

"It's a bolt gun. Used to kill cattle in an abattoir," said Tyrone, from the doorway. "Standard issue for the crew at battle-stations… we learn from our mistakes." The guide's steady look at Connor said it all. It was the lesson learned from *his* personal attack on the captain.

With a wry grin, Connor pointed it into the air and pulled the trigger. The metal bolt shot out and almost yanked the gun from his hand.

"When put against the head of an animal, it punched a hole through the skull. It was a clean and humane method to slaughter cattle," said Tyrone.

With a nod at the guide, Connor shoved the weapon into the waistband of his pants. "Anything else?"

Tyrone moved into the room, and Blake handed over the crowbar. The next two crates revealed fire extinguishers and aerosol cans.

Connor pulled one out. "Lighter fuel." The canisters had rust spots eaten into the gloss-painted surface. When he removed the plastic cap, the trigger reed looked free of corrosion. Using his thumb nail on the edge to press it down in a sharp stab, a plume of gas hissed into the air.

"Have you got any lighters?" Connor tried to keep a lid on his excitement.

Blake shook his head and Connor swore under his breath.

When the captain erupted into his peculiar brand of wet laughter, Tyrone said clearly, "Not here, no. But the Reverend is a collector of cigars, pipes, and lighters."

With a grin, Connor resisted the urge to kiss the blue-veined guide on the putrid looking forehead. "Okay," he muttered, "now we are cooking." Giving in to sudden euphoria, he slapped Tyrone on the shoulder. "Let's see if the Reverend will part with his goodies."

Blake gave Tyrone silent instructions, and, with a 'this way' jerk of his head, the nomad set off down another network of corridors.

The Reverend opened his hatch door while Tyrone was still approaching and turned away so his visitors could pour seamlessly into the room.

Protecting his recovering wound, the Reverend awkwardly dug around in a cubbyhole and then swung back with a thick clear plastic sack clenched in his fist. He held out a haul of thirty or so lighters.

Telepathy certainly speeds things up, thought Connor. "Thank you," he blurted, grabbing the bag and returning the way they had come.

Back on the bridge, Connor filled all the lighters with gas and tested each one. Ten would not ignite, so he put them aside, the flip lids of the remaining twenty he sealed with candle wax and separated them into four plastic bags. He, Tyrone, and two other nomads, both of whom were built like brick outhouses, loaded up utility belts with lighter fluid canisters. The plastic caps of which had again been sealed with wax.

"Okay, we are all set," Connor said. The group of four headed out onto the deck. Blake appeared in his usual vantage point, outside the angular structure of the bridge.

As though crawling from between cracks, other nomads poured out from unseen exits, and soon, they were twelve men deep in all directions. The wind whistling in from the sea made the silent throng appear more eerie. It felt like standing shoulder to shoulder inside a church. Connor wanted to whisper and ask Tyrone what was happening, but he felt bound by the invisible force passing through the ranks.

Finally, the nomads shifted in one fluid movement, slipped over the side of the ship, and disappeared from view. Only Connor, Tyrone, and the nameless pair of brothers-in-arms remained.

"The crew will wait on the seabed," said Tyrone, "to ride shotgun."

Connor searched for a glint of humor in his new-found ally, but found none. The larger of the nameless mountains of flesh shoved Connor and, with a quick check that the bolt-gun was still there, he took the hint and swung his legs over the rail. Shinnying down the almost vertical wall of black steel, Connor descended smoothly into the water.

Dropping down into the murky depths, he closed off his vocal chords to keep his chest cavity dry and scanned the field of nomad-shaped standing stones. Silt plumed up from the seabed when Tyrone and the terrible twosome dropped down beside Connor, and, as though the power had been switched on, the platoon of nomads began to march slowly forward. Visibility was poor in the pea green murky depths, but looking down, Connor saw evidence of the ferals' progress. He was trampling over chewed hunks of undigested meat, the fibrous fronds of torn flesh waving to and fro. They could only have fallen from the encrusted clothes of the carnivorous horde. The trail of crushed stones covering the seabed created a surreal pathway between the larger, moss-covered boulders in the distance on either side. The feral army had literally ground bedrock to dust.

Connor rubbed his eyes, hoping to clear his vision, but it made no difference to the haze of silt churned up by the nomad forces moving up ahead. The bolt upright stance of the shifting wall of bodies might have been reassuring, except he couldn't see beyond them. The rush of cold water wafting over his skin made him shiver, but there was something more. Thudding sounds hammered against Connor's eardrums. Over to his left a nomad swung his clenched fist upward and the 'whoomph' of an explosion shunted a wave of gritty water into Connor's face. Raising his own weapon, he waded faster through the velvet depths to where black shadows up ahead swayed and turned in graceful forceful arcs. Pairs collided as though dancing, but the sickening cracking noises that rang out, the water amplifying the sounds, told a different story. *Feral stragglers are dying.*

Connor ran to where the steadily marching force of nomads advanced towards the beach in an arrowhead formation, closing in on the throng of ferals.

The water churned with bubbles and then, briefly, his head broke the surface, before the swell of the rushing waves submerged him again. Like freeze frame photography, every time the undertow dragged at his powerful thighs, the water level sank, and he captured a shifting scene.

The ferals at the rear of the pack fell into the boiling surf as the nomads, like automatons – terminators come to life – picked them off one-by-one.

Connor watched a nomad grab the foe by their greasy hair, put a bolt gun to their temple, and a crack rang out. The victim's head jerked sideways and glutinous jellylike-fluid poured from the hole, washing fragments of skull away with it. When the nomad let go, the feral dropped into the surf, not dead, but thrashing around with no coordination left. By the time Connor passed over the bodies, the thrashing had faded to seizures; violent twitches of tendons which dislocated or fractured bones.

The reportage of dozens of bolts cracking open skulls became the soundtrack of death. The ruthlessly efficient guns couldn't run out of ammo.

On dry land, the gyrating mass of ferals clambering over their own kind to get to the tethered cattle herded on the walkway beyond the wall rose like a swell of black oil. Connor, Tyrone and the 'Two', as Connor now thought of them, waded hip-deep in the sea, water streaming from their hair and clothes, and many snarling demented faces, stained ochre and brown with dried blood, turned towards them. The gaping caverns of their mouths hung open as they began to bellow. Like an enraged beast with many heads, the undulating mass reared around as one, and ran towards the line of nomads.

"This is it," shouted Connor.

The crashing noise of the surf, the cracking beat of a few bolt guns killing more ferals continued, and then the guttural roar of attacking ferals rushed into every space where rational thought could have lived. Connor broke open the pack of lighters and put one between his teeth. With deliberate speed, talking himself through it calmly and not letting panic screw things up, he pulled out a gas canister and broke the wax seal, letting the plastic lid he flipped away with his thumb fall into the surf.

A quick sideways look along the line of four confirmed his hopes. *We are ready.*

"Wait," Connor yelled. The intense faces of his small team didn't shift their focus. The ferals jostled for space, shouldering each other aside to make room to run faster and faster.

The forward line of the company of nomads stood perfectly still, their dragging coats billowing in the water and slapping around their knees. They resembled onyx pillars. Their weapons hung down at their sides.

"Wait," Connor yelled at Tyrone, knowing the other nomads were included in the loop. "Wait until we see the whites of their eyes."

The stampeding figures kept coming, their clawed hands reaching out, as though anticipating tearing their prey open.

A spray of water erupted into the air when the ferals hit the tideline.

Connor shouted, "Down."

In that split second, the nomad barrier ranging across in front of him dropped to their knees and fell onto their stomachs beneath the water. Connor spun the flint wheel on his lighter and pressed the reed on the canister at the same moment, igniting the gas. A flame rushed out, fire leaping from one airborne gas droplet to the next, until it found more fuel; the greasy hair and clothes of the barraging ferals.

As a line of four, Connor and his team advanced, directing flames into individual faces. The constant roar of fire drowned out the soundtrack of death. Like watching a silent movie, Connor and the others saw the ferals shriveling open-mouthed faces cry flames, as the blaze melted eyeballs and the fluid charred their skin. When the searing heat registered in the demented brain, they circled away, slapping at their burning clothes and spreading the fire through the packed mass of bodies following on behind.

Connor used up both his canisters and all the lighters, and when the whispered whoosh of his flame died, he scanned the charred figures ricocheting into other members of the ghoulish army. Eventually, the ferals who had not fallen staggered down the coastline as though, stunned, they had forgotten why they were there.

A thick scum of charred debris turned the sea water around Connor's ankles jet black. The glow of dawn rendered the scene stark and eerie as the only sound became the rhythmic lullaby of the waves. Even the cattle in the distance made no noise. When Connor took a breath, the warm air stank of carbon.

"Let's go," Connor pulled his bolt gun from his belt as the submerged nomads rose like monsters from the shallows. The crew fanned out along the beach. Connor heard the crack of metal on bone shattering the quiet whenever a nomad found a feral still moving.

The top of the sea wall was covered in broken lumps of masonry and a river of blood ran over the path beyond, congealing in pools where cattle had been pulled apart and their lifeblood had pumped out over the rocks. Connor felt deep sadness, not just because of the suffering of dumb animals, but the failure of vampire kind to work together. Just as humans waged war upon each other, vampires had turned out to be no better at working as one species.

Connor swallowed down his hunger as the blood fumes cut through the taste of soot coating his mouth. The nomads were less focused. Their bead-black eyes homed in on the remaining cattle as the spoils of war. As he strode away, the keening cries of the terrified beasts became wet gurgles as the nomads drank their fill.

The battle had been easier than he feared, and instinctively he scanned the landscape. Connor frowned. The haze rising like a fog bank in the distance struck dread into him. *There are more?* The faint sound of distant fighting rang out, like the percussion section of an orchestra in a frenzy. He didn't need his mentor's thoughts to tell him what was happening. *A war on two fronts.*

Leaping up onto a wall and scaling to the highest point, Connor tracked the bursts of movement. Craters opened up in the ground, swallowed ferals, and puffs of grit created a mini sandstorm. The surface of the sand seemed to boil and shift as bronzed figures erupted like sea creatures who instantly dived into the depths once more. *Earth Walkers.* The blades the warriors wielded flashed in the dim light of breaking dawn. Red pearl drops of blood scattered into the air and drew clumps of ferals in, isolating them from the horde, and the long, curved blades flashed again. Connor realized that Earth Walkers were using their own blood as a lure, cutting their flesh to use their weakness as their strength. Of course, they were far from mere mortals. Connor felt an urge to join the battle and see the warriors' devastating skill at close quarters, but Malachi's plight called him back.

He returned to where the pale stone construction of the citadel reared up, but holes in the outer walls and scuffling noises beyond the boundary meant the enemy was within.

Torn, Connor stared at the conflict playing out on the horizon for one final moment and saw the movements fade. As if it had been a mirage, the dust in the air slowly cleared. He felt frustrated, sure that Imhotep had been within touching distance and he had missed his chance, again.

When he ducked in through a hole in the citadel wall, a figure lunged out from the left. The sleeve of his coat tore as a clawed grip gained purchase. With cold precision, Connor drew his bolt gun. He let the feral's open mouth latch onto his shoulder for a nanosecond, but before the jaws could close, he rammed the gun against the temple of his attacker and pulled the trigger. The feral's head jerked sideways and Connor heard the neck snap before the vampire hit the ground.

Turning away and refocusing, Connor raced towards the thick-walled tower sitting out near the harbor wall. He reached out to Malachi. *Where are you? Why aren't you coming out?* Connor would not rest easy until the landing party were back onboard the tanker.

Ascending the spiraling stone staircase inside the tower three steps at a time, Connor shoved open the doors on each landing before dashing upwards again. *Trust Malachi, he would be on the top floor.* Connor's tight expression showed his irritation.

"Of course, I'm up here," Malachi said calmly when Connor burst into the room. "Where else would I be?"

The thick oak door slammed back against the wall and a shower of plaster hit the bare floorboards. The walls were covered in Egyptian tapestries and, in places, hieroglyphics adorned in gold-leaf glinted in the glow cast by lanterns placed around the turret-like chamber.

Connor froze on the spot and stared. His mentor's bony countenance had not changed; the gray putty-toned complexion had the sheen of frosted glass, as always. Other things, though, were surreal.

Inspecting the room more closely, sensing that things were not as they appeared, Connor impulsively flipped back the corner of a hanging tapestry, and sure enough, the surface below gleamed with beaten metal. Connor quirked a brow at his mentor.

"I reinforced it. The old building was too flimsy for these uncertain times," said Malachi, with a flap of his hand.

Hit by a wave of relief that the wily vampire had survived, his shoulders sagged and, shaking his head, Connor burst into laughter. Acknowledging another piece in the surreal jigsaw puzzle he faced, he said, "And the monkeys?"

"Ah. Meet Silas and his mother Portia." Malachi stroked the glistening jet-black fur of the young chimpanzee who was clamped around his body as though the chimp thought the floor of the room was a bear trap. Portia stayed close, but had reared up at Connor's intrusion and her sharp brown gaze remained pinned to his face, even though her soft leathery palm rested on Malachi's shoulder.

Connor sensed a very long story lay behind the startling scene. Holding out his own hands and showing his palms in an 'I come in peace' gesture, Connor resorted to telepathy.

I can't imagine you'd be holed up here with two monkeys unless they are important.

Malachi's smile exuded mystery.

Checking the alcoves and window apertures, Connor asked, "No vampire friends or Earth Walkers?" Assessing the tight grip of Silas and the stare Portia still bored into his face, Connor had no idea what to do next. *Will they board the ship quietly? Or do I need to drug them?*

Malachi's jaw lifted, affront exuding from him in waves. *They aren't savages. They will come quietly.*

Scanning the snarl rolling Portia's lip and the way her son shoved his face into the security of Malachi's neck, Connor raised a brow. *If you say so, but we must go, now. As you said, metal sheets on the walls can't protect us.*

The mother held out her arms, and the youngster swung from Malachi and into her embrace. Malachi turned, made eye contact with Portia, and his hands erupted into movement. The rapid exchange of sign language between the two was as graceful as it was surprising.

With a sharp nod of his head which made his sparse hair flutter, Malachi walked towards the door.

Connor moved quickly ahead, down the stairs, keeping the elderly vampire between himself and the chimpanzees. Always expect the unexpected with Malachi had long been Connor's mindset. *But this is bizarre, even by Malachi's standards.*

The sharp jab of a bony finger in his back reminded Connor that there were no secrets where Malachi was concerned. As Connor's maker, the older vampire could read his protégé's thoughts at will.

I've missed you, too, old man. Connor grinned as his thought earned another needle point jab in the shoulder blade. Needing to say the words out loud, he said, "I'm glad we got here in time, but, was that the Earth Walker tribe out in the desert?"

Malachi nodded. "Imhotep divided the feral herd. They will hunt the ones fleeing inland. It cut the numbers storming the harbor and gave us a fighting chance."

"I wish I could have met him." Connor frowned.

"You will, when the time is right. The Earth Walker tribe are protecting their own. If they win, we will come back together."

"And if they lose?"

Malachi blinked slowly, his pearl-tinted gaze became clouded and Connor felt a door close in his face. His mentor was not ready to talk about the worst case scenario, not yet.

With a brisk nod, Connor said gently, "Let's go."

Running quickly to the bottom of the stairwell, the group stepped out into the weak dawn light.

Tyrone and the 'Two' emerged from the gloom in an instant. If they were shocked at Malachi's odd company, it didn't show.

Malachi darted left, away from the scene of the feral onslaught and down a wooden ramp to where a jetty of boulders jutted out into the harbor. Skimming effortlessly to the end of the rocky pathway, Malachi stopped at a sturdy wooden post. His black cloak flared like crows wings in the gale rushing across the bay. His shimmering skin and taloned grasp created a stark illusion any film maker would have killed to capture on celluloid. He reached down to where a slack rope sagged from the post and snaked out across the surface of the water. The other end disappeared into the mouth of a cavern carved into the cliff.

The tendons in his arms bulged as, with an efficient hand over hand action, he wound in the rope. The creak of wooden planks grating against rock made it easy to guess what was on the end of the tether.

The large rowing boat rocked from side to side, the oars lying in the bottom rolling back and forth. With five yards of rippling oily water still to go, Portia leapt across into the craft, settled Silas at her feet in the bottom of the boat and, with expert ease, set up the oars.

I'll see you onboard the container ship. Malachi grinned.

Connor gave a thumbs up sign and left to round up the nomad crew and head back into the rolling surf. Tramping across the boney carpet of fallen feral corpses took all Connor's attention, until the seawater suddenly became an impenetrable curtain of black velvet when the tanker loomed overhead. A thump echoed through the water as the lookouts on the anchor chains gave the signal and a wall of ladders dropped over the side.

149

Once safely back on deck, Connor dripped water as he gripped the handrail and scanned the distant beach. The next wave of ferals could emerge at any time. They moved in herds, but how many rampaged over Europe no one knew. *Malachi may know more.* And hearing the story behind Silas and Portia was bound to be fascinating.

As the sea became a glimmering golden pond in the breaking dawn, Connor leaned back against the metal panels, taking shelter in a band of shade on the deck. Watching the vigor with which Malachi rowed the boat across the divide reminded him that the paper-thin skin and gnarled joints of his mentor were an illusion – the sinews were like wire cables.

Chapter 14

After an hour of discussion, exploring the possible places to where they could relocate the humans, Julian left the council building, with Anthony, Marius and Daniel traveling in his wake. Each vampire was focused on their own mission, knowing that failure was not an option.

Julian himself was heading off-piste on a quest of his own. If the evacuation and protection of the human community was to succeed, he needed the support of men he could trust. The newly promoted Captain Hugh remained in Cardiff and Gerrard could do with a second in command in the City.

In recent months, he often speculated about the crossbow wielding sergeant in charge of guarding Serge, when the councilor was detained inside his London home. *If I had left Serge there, and not moved him to the chapel, perhaps he would not have escaped.* He felt certain the sergeant would not have taken his eye off the ball.

All Julian had to do was track him down.

Checking his watch, Julian took up a position beneath the trees in Hyde Park with a clear view of the parade ground outside Wellington Barracks on Birdcage Walk. The previous inhabitants were The Grenadier, Coldstream and Scots Guards, now, it was the Vampire Hive Council Guard.

Four in the afternoon was the witching hour. Julian surveyed the wide sand-colored yard where, before the 'vampire uprising' mounted platoons would have gathered before heading out to Buckingham Palace for the Changing of the Guard. The regimental uniform of black bearskin headdress and blood red tunics was the image most tourists associated with the Queen.

Julian felt relieved that being of noble descent had not gifted immunity to the pandemic which wiped out eighty percent of the population. Just the thought of having members of the British Royal family imprisoned on the human farm did not bear thinking about. Fortunately, he had not had to face that difficult decision.

Imagine the fight which might have broken out over 'blue blood' – Royal blood. That would have been a massive headache.

Impatiently, he waited for the apparently deserted white marble façade to erupt with activity. At 'promenade', platoons of vampire guardsmen would pour out of the barracks and into the space enclosed behind twelve-foot tall black metal wrought-iron railings. It was the time of day when vampires felt safe to expose their skin and use airflow to harden the surface – the survival tool neglected by the super tanker nomads. *And thankfully, ferals neglect it too.* Hefty swords stored in the basement of the Victoria and Albert museum could come into their own. Being wielded by guardsmen with preternatural strength would make them a devastating weapon. Julian made a note to bring up the topic with Gerrard, Connor and Marius.

When the expected flow of vampires began to appear, Julian checked the face of each arrival.

He had a feeling this sergeant would have another angle to bring to the table. *Sergeant Frank.* Gerrard couldn't shed light on why his 'best man' showed no interest in being promoted to a position inside the Council Elite Guard. Julian shivered, his bronze-colored hair lifting in the stiff afternoon breeze, but that wasn't the reason. Was he making a mistake? He felt sure he would know once he spoke with Frank, but for now, he just hoped his recollections rang true.

The yard filled with vampires walking in seemingly predetermined circular tracks around the huge parade ground. They peered at the dull afternoon sky to check that the sun was reassuringly smothered by cloud cover and, after a few moments, shed their surcoats, dropping them into crates which had been wheeled out into the yard.

Very soon, shirt sleeves were rolled up and the vampires lifted their chins to feel the breeze the rapidly increasing pace of promenade moved over their skin.

The sergeant did not appear in the first three hundred or so walkers. *Maybe Gerrard got the wrong barracks. Maybe the sergeant is based at Hyde Park.* Julian frowned, resigning himself to having wasted an afternoon, when he spotted a face he recognized – one of the two guards in the detail, who had stood guard in Councilor Serge's back garden.

His coat flared out behind as Julian burst into movement. Slipping in through the gate, he cut a path through the flowing crowd until he matched the pace of the familiar guardsman. The vampire had his eyes half-closed and was basking in the chilled breeze as though sunbathing.

"Good afternoon," said Julian, quietly.

The vampire shot a glance sideways and froze mid-step.

With lightning reflexes, Julian stopped, too.

"Principal Julian?" the guardsman murmured, his brow creasing in confusion.

"And you are?"

"Harold."

"I'm looking for Sergeant Frank, your squad leader on the Councilor Serge mission."

The guardsman grinned. "Ah, Sergeant *Frank.* He left earlier to lock down for grave sleep."

Julian took in a deep breath. There seemed a cruel irony that he was trying to stay under the radar and vet the sergeant in person before enlisting his help, only to find that the guardsman was in the morgue under Isaac's care in grave sleep. "Ah, I see, thank you."

As Julian went to swing away, the guard reached out and touched his arm. "Not at the hospital." He hesitated, as if weighing options, then in a very low voice, said, "Sergeant Frank prefers Smithfield Market."

The good thing was that the meat market was within London's Square Mile, so at least Julian would not have far to go – although locating the sergeant would be another matter.

"I don't suppose you know *where* in Smithfield?"

The guardsman grinned, the muscle in his jaw ticking. "The cold store."

"Thank you,' replied Julian, and wove a path back to the gate to set off for North London. He had never been to Smithfield

Market, but knew it was on Charterhouse Street and that it was built in the 1860s. As he approached the main entrance, he admired the Grade II listed buildings. The East and West Market sites were separated by the Grand Avenue – a wide road beneath a sweeping arch fashioned in cast iron.

The cavernous spaces enclosed within were gutted now, but Julian knew the cold store was not at the street level and searched the dust-filled concrete halls for the elevator. The doors were wedged open and the buckled elevator carcass lay at the bottom of the shaft. Peering down, Julian could see broken cables haphazardly coiled like silver boa constrictors on the roof of the square metal box.

Dropping down the shaft, he landed on the metal roof and waited for the rattling vibrations to die away before he swung down through the hatchway in the ceiling, walked out of the elevator car and scanned the dark corridors.

The infrastructure showed evidence of the days when trains were used to transport the meat to market, before the underground space had been converted into a parking area.

He skimmed purposefully along the walls, until finally, he located a hefty stainless-steel panel on a wide runner – the cold store room.

Listening at the door, Julian heard faint scratching sounds. 'A vampire in grave sleep' type of sounds. *But only one?* Stepping back, he calculated the potential size of the cold store – or freezer – and wondered at the standing of Sergeant Frank that he could commandeer such a large facility for personal use. Thinking back to their first encounter, when the sergeant had crept up on Julian and leveled a cross bow at his chest from the upper branches of a tree, the officer clearly possessed finely-honed combat skills. *Perhaps others are scared.*

For a nanosecond, Julian wondered if that was a good thing or a bad one, but his gut instinct said that dark times were coming and he needed a ruthless and powerful vampire on his side.

Leaving and trying to catch up with the sergeant another time was a waste of effort, so he settled down to wait.

He sank into a meditative state and closed his eyes. Every grinding of teeth and scrape of fingernails made by the entombed grave-sleeping vampire beyond became the focus of his attention. The frenetic activity faded and, finally, when Julian heard measured sane movement, he pushed away from his resting place on the wall and took up a position ten yards from the steel doorway, in full view. It would not do to surprise the sergeant and put his back up.

The door slid aside smoothly, even though the stuttering groaning noise revealed that the action required a lot of force.

With one foot over the threshold, Julian was not surprised when the sergeant abandoned the door, and leveled a crossbow bolt at Julian's face, going for the kill shot of an eye socket.

"Sergeant, sorry to intrude," Julian said, in a much smoother tone than his tight muscles betrayed.

With a low chuckle, Frank lowered the weapon, finished sliding the door shut and clicked the hasp on an industrial sized padlock. It screamed 'keep out'. It could not actually stop a vampire from entering, but the sergeant was clearly used to being obeyed.

Turning around and cradling the crossbow in the crook of his arm, Frank said, "Principal, to what do I owe this pleasure?"

Julian inhaled deeply, washing the scent of Frank over his palate and making a final assessment before taking the plunge. The sergeant exuded calm control – the vampire clearly balanced his brain centers well. Which was more than could be said for Julian, at times. The principal's lip curled as he recalled an occasion when only Connor's order to take revival sleep had avoided the stress pulling at his muscles from becoming a full-blown seizure.

Frank raised his eyebrows and waited. Another promising sign in Julian's mind – he wanted a strategist onboard and Frank gave all the signs of using his head and not his heart.

"I'm looking for a commander I can trust." Julian waved a hand towards the crossbow. "But, not only to fight. A protector for the human herd."

155

Frank's dark eyes glowed as if a flame ignited in his brain. "Protector from who?" he said, his tone low with curiosity.

"Let's just say, dark days are coming and we should all be ready to fight."

Frank gripped his crossbow tighter and snorted. "Cut the crap, Principal. If you want me to join ranks with the Council Elite Guard and protect the human herd, I want to know who's coming at me."

"Ferals," said Julian, grinning at the sergeant's straight talking.

Frank frowned. "Ferals have been around for decades."

"They are overtaking 'sane vampires' in the Far East, and I expect the same to happen in Europe. We need to be ready to move our humans to safety. We'll know more soon." Before Frank could ask, knowing he would not get away with anything less than the whole truth, Julian said, "Doctor Connor has left our waters on a rescue mission. I can't say anymore than that."

Drumming his fingertips on the shaft of his weapon, Frank appeared to weigh up the options. Finally, he nodded sharply. "Fair enough, but I prefer to work alone, to have a freehand, so to speak. Rest assured, I'll carry out my orders. Who should I report to?"

"Me," Julian replied, "or Captain Gerrard."

"Yes, sir. I'll do a recce of the human farm facility and get the lay of the land. Supervisor Edmund has the herd numbers and emergency relocation plan?"

"Yes." Julian's expression remained blank and Frank laughed.

"You haven't got a relocation plan?"

"The siphoning sheds were the safe place we decided on, but Connor has left us to come up with something more... robust."

"Such as?"

"Juror Daniel and Gerrard are checking maps for fortifications and castles in the area. Somewhere easy to defend."

"It is a life or death situation, yes?"

Julian nodded.

"And the living are more important than the dead?"

"Of course."

"In which case, use Storage Facility Eight."

Julian's knee-jerk reaction was a bark of laughter, but then, visualizing the setting and logistics, his features relaxed. "It could work."

"It will work as a stop gap, until you know the true level of the threat."

"But-"

"Terminate the inhabitants. Send a death squad, or do it yourselves, but clear the inmates out."

Julian shook Frank's hand. "Welcome aboard, Sergeant, something tells me you have a lot to contribute. I'll get the ball rolling."

"I'll be at the human farm."

"Remember to feed first and-"

Frank's raised eyebrow stopped Julian in his tracks. The sergeant reached behind his back and pulled a gel mask from his belt. "I'm always prepared."

Julian laughed as he swung away and headed for the elevator shaft. When he glanced back, Frank was standing in the same spot, watching.

With a final wave, Julian swung in through the open door and back up onto the roof of the elevator car. While automatically scaling the brick wall, he grinned. *I was right. He came up with something we hadn't even thought of.*

Chapter 15

Being hosed down like a dog that had swum in a stagnant lake was the quickest way to remove the stains of battle from Connor and his fellow combatants.

Adjusting the collar of a clean shirt and running his hands through almost dry hair, Connor followed the captain and Tyrone as they skimmed along the metal-lined corridors in the bowels of the ship. Blake unlocked a hatchway and waved Connor through it.

Tyrone stepped in over the high threshold and stopped. "Doctor Connor?"

Turning around, Connor said, "Yes, Captain." He had become used to talking with Tyrone as though Blake inhabited the younger vampire.

"You must use only this corridor. Your mentor is in the fifth cabin after the next airlock. Do you understand?"

"Understood. Anyone would think you have secrets to hide," said Connor lightly.

As Tyrone went back through the hatchway to rejoin Blake, he forced an artificial laugh, sounding like the puppet he was. "Just make sure to knock loudly when you return."

"Tyrone?"

"Yes?" His serious face reappeared around the edge of the metal door he was about to swing shut.

"Why is Malachi so far away? Surely it makes it harder for the captain to keep tabs on him."

"Maybe." Tyrone nodded. "But the chimps are an unusual odor best kept at a distance."

"Of course."

The door swung shut with a muffled thump and the floor clanged beneath the deliberate drumbeat of Connor's fast-moving stride.

Spinning the airlock wheel and ducking through the gap, he closed it quickly behind him. Inhaling, he detected the sweeter aroma of simian blood cells. *I see what Tyrone means.*

Nomads led a sheltered existence, although Connor understood them better now having shared this voyage. The single cell analogy held true, but there *were* personalities in the background of some crewmen, at least.

Whispering, Connor said, "Malachi, it's me."

His mentor's dry laugh echoing inside Connor's skull made him realize the ridiculousness of the action. *Smart arse, Malachi.* He grinned and opened the cabin door, knowing Malachi listened to his thoughts and his arrival was no surprise.

Closing the hatchway, Connor took a seat opposite the elder Egyptian. The young chimp remained pressed into Malachi's side, as before, and his mentor's flushed complexion shifted Connor's curiosity up a notch.

The floor beneath their feet vibrated slightly as the tanker powered its way out into open waters and headed for London.

Connor opened with the question he knew would come as soon as they landed. "Do you know where Imhotep is? Is Osiris' father and the Earth Walker tribe safe? Can you see?" He waited with clasped hands as if in prayer, because he needed the news to be good.

"Imhotep and the Earth Walkers headed deeper into the desert, away from the Nile. He has his ways, Connor." Malachi shook his head, cutting off any more questions. "Even I can't explain. He is descended from the human deity of the same name, and his tribe seem to thrive like satellites around a sun. They live long. But don't ask me how."

Connor stared into space, frustration gleaming like frost in his gray gaze. *One day, I will meet him and I'll ask.*

Malachi laughed at Connor's stubborn childlike declaration. *Perhaps. I will certainly want to witness it.*

With a wry grin, Connor said aloud, "So, what's the story." His tone was quiet and reassuring, or so he hoped, as he could feel Portia's stare boring a hole into his skull. "You've had a busy year."

Malachi arranged the thick silk of his robe over his bony knees.

Going home has led me along a new pathway. Osiris will be proud of what his Earth Walker brothers have achieved.

Connor settled back into his seat. "Tell me," he said, and closed his eyes.

The barely detectable sound of the ocean swell faded. The metal walls inside the cabin grew texture and shone with a different sheen. *Polished marble.* Connor gave himself over to Malachi's memories and relived the experiences through the elder vampire's eyes.

The earthy smells of wet reeds and the black soil of the Nile filtered into his sinuses, and the Earth Walker warriors, each dressed in white linen skirts and wearing belts of gold, populated the ceremonial chamber Connor looked in on. A new Wenuty priest stood in Osiris' place – although his young companion's parting from the tribe had left a deeper scar in Malachi's world.

The young warrior placed the golden hourglass onto the altar shelf and the fine white sand began to flow. It was only then Connor, seeing through Malachi's eyes, looked at the glass vials of blood being warmed in a brass bowl sitting on hot coals. A heavily pregnant chimpanzee Connor recognized as Portia had pride of place on a plinth in the center of the chamber. She rested back upon a bed of straw, her eyes half closed from the effects of a sleeping draft.

Whose blood is that? Connor wanted to understand what was happening.

My own and Mahood's, the Earth Walker priest. Malachi eased himself down from the elaborately carved throne and slowly descended the steps from the dais. Drawing closer, Connor felt the waft of cold air emanating from Portia and her 'bed'. The chimp's fur appeared fluffed up and she shivered. The more exposed skin around her muzzle had a blue tinge and the fine down was stiff with frost. The drowsiness was more than drugs, it was the onset of hypothermia. Connor understood and his interest sharpened.

160

Portia's chest rose and fell with shallow breathing and her hands gripped the edge of the altar stone each time her rounded stomach jerked into a tight ball. *Labor.*

The Wenuty priest passed behind Malachi, carrying the brass bowl, and the musical chime of glass vials clinking together filled the air. Malachi placed his palm on the mother's cheek and her drowsy eyes opened for a moment.

The next contraction tightened every muscle in her body. Malachi spread his palm over the distorted abdomen and said, "It will be soon, Mahood. Prepare the blood infusion."

The warrior bent over the vials, each one glinting with the clarity of polished rubies. The sleek black curtain of hair which fell forward and obscured his features could not hide the tension the priest felt. His biceps bulged and the tendons in his forearms stood out like thick twine under the skin. His fingers shook a little as he removed the stoppers of each vial in turn, filled four syringes with the warm blood, and placed them on a bronze platter which rested in the embers of the fire.

Connor knew the Earth Walker tribe's longevity defied the laws of nature. Their meditative ceremonies and herbal infusions had effects that science could not explain, but how would their blood and Malachi's help Portia?

The other warriors watched from the perimeter of the room, each one held either a lantern or swung an incense orb slowly back and forth from a heavy gilt chain. A calming incantation swelled to fill the air, and the minutes slipped by with Malachi frozen in place as a reassuring presence beside Portia.

When the waves of tension cramping her swollen belly became unrelenting, and the chimp made keening noises through clenched teeth, four hand maidens entered. Steam rose from the pails of water each one carried.

Silently, Malachi took Portia's hand in his and raised it to his mouth. In a sudden violent act, he bit into the chimpanzee's tender wrist. Her blood gushed and a glazed expression of bliss tightened Malachi's face. He swallowed down the pumping nectar until Portia's body went slack, the heartbeat inside her chest stuttered, and the chimp's head fell backwards. Mahood rushed forward with the tray of syringes, but Malachi held up a hand and the Wenuty priest froze.

Tearing his lips away from the wet blood-soaked fur of his victim's arm, blood gurgled in his throat as Malachi said, "Not yet."

The Earth Walker warriors continued chanting. Their certainty felt compelling. Malachi, and Connor, watched and listened to Portia's heartbeat fading; the whispering current passing through the chambers becoming slower and slower until the muscle clenched and stopped.

"Now," Malachi said, as calmly as though he were asking for a weather report.

In an efficient flow of movement, Mahood carried the copper tray over, injected the four syringes of blood into the vein in Portia's arm, and the fifth, containing clear liquid, he injected into her lower body. Connor instinctively knew the final syringe contained syntocinon – a drug used to accelerate the detachment of the placenta after birth. *But usually administered after the baby is born, not now.* Portia's eyes shot open and, at that moment, as though a shock to her system triggered it, the birth happened in a rush.

The sparse wet down of the infant resembled a slick seal-like pelt. The tiny face was perfect. Beneath the smears of blood, in places where it showed through the fine fur, the newborn's skin was so much paler than the mother. A mewling sound accompanied the jerky limb movements of the infant, the scrunched-up face turning to seek out the warmth of its mother. The frost on Portia's lip melted as the warmed blood rushed around her system.

Reaching down between her legs, Portia lifted her baby onto her slackened stomach and latched him on to suckle. Malachi exuded calm as with a wave of a hand, he directed Mahood to administer another dose of warm vampire/Earth Walker blood into the still cold child via the trailing umbilical cord.

The images around Connor began to flake away like old paint burning from a wall. He closed his eyes tightly and digested the information.

"The baby is Silas," said Connor, stating the obvious.

Malachi inclined his head.

"Did it work?" Connor asked.

"Yes, it did, up to a point. Silas is a hybrid. A unique one. The low temperature shielded his bone marrow from the 'transformation' my vampire blood caused. As for the Earth Walker, Mahood, his blood was taken after he fed from me." Malachi's thin eyebrows lifted. "No, he wasn't dead and being turned, it was part of another experiment in the sequence we trialed. Desperate measures, Connor. A hybrid food supply liberates me from staying near humans and as the feral horde became larger, them hunting out blood and killing humans becomes more inevitable. It's a numbers game."

"What is happening in Europe? How many hives have secured their herds?" The idea that humans could become extinct shocked Connor to the core.

"From what I've seen, the end is coming. The area inside perimeter fences around the humans has become smaller; easier to defend. Many humans are locked away, where they are safer. The human stock is dying from old-age, over siphoning and infection. And of course, at such close quarters, illness is hard to control. Viruses spread like wildfire."

Both vampires sat in silence staring into space.

"The end is coming," Malachi said again, slowly. "The pandemic twenty years ago might have left a human race capable of starting again, had it not been for the existence of vampires. Survival of the fittest has become an ironic parody. Humans are dying and vampires without a standing in the hives are being cut out first. They are starving and surviving on animal blood alone – so they are descending into a state of dementia and swelling the feral numbers. The hive councils' ruthless starvation policy is literally feeding the fire of our demise. The horde are on the move, searching constantly for food, and they can't be stopped.

"So, the ferals will inherit the earth?" Connor said, with a wry grin. "Over my dead body."

"That is always possible," responded Malachi.

Connor looked across to where Portia and Silas were now huddled together in the far corner – no, not huddled, the entwined posture exuded comfort and relaxation. Even though he was a juvenile and much bigger than in the 'vision', the young chimp nestled into his mother's body, his head resting beneath her chin. The expression on Portia's face was one of bliss.

For the first time, Connor noticed the feeding catheter implanted into Silas' arm. Absently, he mused, "Osiris still has his syphoning tube. I've offered to remove it, but I think it connects him to the time when you and he were traveling companions. You brought him into the world, so you're his father."

"I did what I needed to do, and he served me well as a food supply. But he has found happiness with Seren and that is as it should be."

Malachi's matter-of-fact tone did not fool Connor. Vampires aren't supposed to *care,* but Osiris mattered to the ancient Egyptian.

"Is Portia a hybrid, too?" Connor changed tack.

"No. I hoped she would be. The ceremony and the hypothermia. It was worth a try." Malachi shrugged. "Maybe the injections of warm blood didn't have enough vampire venom in them. Or the dosage was wrong, but her simian blood didn't succumb to a transformation."

"You are on the right track, though. Creating a hybrid or a blood substitute are the only avenues left."

Malachi laughed. "Don't reveal my secrets, Connor. If you do, then simians could become the next species we wipe out."

"From what we know of ferals, they won't stop until everything that moves is dead." The worst kind of zombie horror movie was unfolding. The final curtain would see the ferals turning on each other. "Perhaps birds, reptiles, and small mammals will survive."

"Don't be arrogant, Connor. If you believe that every human on earth bought into your version of civilization, you are wrong." Malachi's absent tone robbed the words of censure. "There are hundreds of small islands throughout the globe. Not every human is within the grasp of ferals."

"They'd have to be far out in the ocean to guarantee ferals would die if they tried to walk there."

"Indeed. But it's worth considering. All you'd need is transportation."

"Blake?" asked Connor. "I sincerely hope we'll never be that desperate. Talking of islands. That is what Julian is working on. Protecting the humans in Britain, and winning the battle if the ferals invade."

"When," said Malachi.

Connor shot a glance at Malachi's bony profile. "When?" he repeated.

The old Egyptian chuckled. "Not *if* they invade, but *when*. They are coming, of that you can be certain."

"When. Of course," said Connor, getting to his feet.

Malachi waved him away with a sweeping hand. "I'm sure you have a lot to do. We'll talk again, soon."

Connor was half way through the hatchway when he paused. "I'll get a nomad posted outside the door... or 'Two' in particular," said Connor, thinking of his new-found crack team. "You feed and take revival sleep. No one will disturb you."

As he shut the hatch door, he heard cackling laughter. "You hear that Silas? I must look pretty bad."

Connor strode back along the corridor, but before he could bang on the airlock in the agreed signal, it whipped open and he stared at Tyrone.

"Captain Blake is waiting for your report and to discuss terms for Hera's return." Tyrone turned on his heel to lead the way back to the bridge.

Hera was a problem Connor would rather not think about. He and Blake were tolerating each other quite well at the moment. *Why spoil it?* But perhaps Malachi had a point. *I might need Blake's ship, down the line.* Keeping Blake onside would be prudent. *But will that mean betraying Hera's trust?* Connor hoped not.

Chapter 16

Julian led the way through the wet London streets. It was only mid-afternoon, but the sun had given up the fight to break through the gray blanket of cloud. Even though the rain had stopped, the party of four, under Gerrard's command, kicked up a comet trail of fine spray.

It was not a squad of guardsmen, as Gerrard was used to, but these were strange times. The act they were about to perform could divide the hive – only Connor knew the intricacies of 'stage three skull crushing'. It was merely a concept to most and being at the sharp end, to see it up close and personal, was a lot to ask of a guardsman.

Julian had chosen the members of the 'death squad' party from Connor's medical team.

It felt strange to be visiting Storage Facility Eight mob handed, but the complex was at eighty percent capacity and the detainees ran into hundreds. *Time is of the essence.* Despite the pressure to get the job done, Julian was determined to give each vampire inmate a humane ending. When Gerrard suggested they use a flame thrower, Julian, for the first time, had blasted his commanding officer for being crass and insensitive.

Connor had once been imprisoned in the facility, lying in a steel coffin in a pitch-black tomb, and for weeks afterwards, Julian could sense the vein of despair that had marked his friend.

Glancing at the medical team, Julian felt a sense of satisfaction.

Surgical assistant Anthony had come a long way since Connor and Julian had dragged him into their world of subterfuge – his expressive brown eyes radiated calm certainty. Charles, Isaac and Brynmor were used to managing rattled vampires who needed to feed or were struggling to balance their sleep centers. *This is different, they all have to die, but this team can make it quick and painless.*

The colossal gray granite structure positioned on the banks of the River Thames loomed up ahead, the lower few feet of the towering walls wreathed in the mist of rain. It dominated the embankment like a squatting gargoyle staring out over the water. Eighty percent of the facility was below ground, and the inmates were moved down through the storage levels as they drew closer to their 'death date'. Although Connor, as the surgeon of record and medical officer of the hive, was authorized to oversee skull crush ceremonies, it was always at Julian's command. *I sentenced them to storage, so it seems right that I am here for this. What Connor will say when he finds out –*

Julian didn't want to go there. What was about to happen made nausea swill in his gut. Glancing over his shoulder at Isaac, Charles and Brynmor, his pace stuttered as his muscles pulled tight. Their faces, beneath the layer of frost the wind-chill of a fast run had laid down over their skin, wore fierce frowns. To say the three companions were anxious about what was to come was an understatement.

But protecting the human stock was at stake and everyone knew there was no choice.

Julian slowed as the 'termination party' reached the twelve-foot-high metal fence marking the boundary of the storage facility enclosure. The tall gate was locked in a 'keep out' message. It was impossible to construct a vampire-proof fence-line and the notice was more a declaration that interlopers would be executed. Julian punched in his access code and the lock disengaged with a sharp click.

Gerrard and the team filed into the compound and waited on the concrete pathway in an uncertain cluster.

Julian relocked the gate and when he cleared his throat, every face turned in his direction. "This is a sad day, but remember, we are putting an end to the suffering." Julian paused to let the words sink in. "Every vampire here is already dead. All are past the point of rehydration, so this will be a relief."

The hive vampires were well aware of the stages of dehydration. They had all been escorted around the facility when the hive council first erected the storage building over two decades ago. It was the ultimate deterrent at a time when the food supply of human blood became as precious as liquid gold.

The medical team squared their shoulders and Captain Gerrard added his piece. "Time is of the essence, so let's complete the task as painlessly as possible."

They paired up and ran to the base of the towering gray walls and into the cool damp purple shade which covered the concrete walkway. Charles and Isaac brought up the rear. Anthony and Brynmor kept pace with Julian and the captain as they whipped along the pathway. Swinging left, the group headed around the building to where the main entrance faced out over the turbulent river. It was high tide and the roiling iron-gray swells were crowned by strings of frothy lace. The breaking waves crashed against the concrete plinth of the storage facility, cascading water high into the air.

All six faced the tall door and, as Julian thumped on the thick steel portal three times, droplets of water, like a deluge of pelted pearls, splattered over their shoulders. Charles' spiky rust-colored hair became a waterlogged pelt and he shook his drenched head like a dog.

"Remember, the warden doesn't know why we are here, so wait for my signal," said Julian.

Protocol demanded that the warden be given notice of scheduled visits, but there was no way to prepare him for the drastic event about to happen.

The tall door eased slowly open and, with only one eye visible, a gray face peered out through the narrow space. The door moved faster when the vampire recognized the sopping wet hive principal.

Although, Gerrard and the team stepped inside out of the splattering assault of the surf, they hung back while Julian disappeared down a tunnel. The door swung shut behind them and the rush of fresh air that had whipped in through the entrance was smothered by the stale musty atmosphere inside the tomb-like chamber. Before the stagnant air could crawl into their lungs, they all stopped breathing. Brynmor silently removed his salt-streaked glasses, cleaned them on a handkerchief and then pushed them back into place.

The doorkeeper had vanished. His role was to notify the warden of visitors and his whispering footfalls were already distant and fading.

In the pitch-black entrance chamber, Anthony ran his fingertips along the wall and collected a flashlight from the alcove he knew to be there. The burst of dim light triggered by the flick of a switch drove the thick darkness back by a mere few feet, but activated vampire sight which could see hundreds of feet beyond that.

Seconds later, Julian returned and took charge of the flashlight.

Following the weak yellow glow pooling on the floor ahead, the group strode along the gentle descending slope of the square cut stone tunnel. The flashlight beam swung in time with Julian's stride. Their footfalls echoed louder when they reached the end of the corridor and entered the reception chamber.

As expected, the warden was waiting, his hands clasped behind his back. His staring owl-like eyes blinked slowly.

"Warden." Julian nodded in greeting.

"Principal Julian and-"

"Doctor Connor's medical team." Julian decided names were superfluous, given the task ahead.

At Connor's name, the warden blinked and his lips twitched in a smile. "Doctor Connor is here?" The man latched onto the comfort of familiarity, and the doctor was the only visitor the warden ever expected. The vampires sentenced in court by Julian, immobilized by muscle relaxant, were transported in open coffin shells. Doctor Connor always attended twenty-four hours later to move them from the stage one reception ward, down to the stage two storage chamber.

"Not today. We have a unique set of circumstances."

"But, he will be joining us?" The warden frowned, clearly unable to comprehend the situation. Like cloistered monks, the warden and his vampire attendants lived inside the storage facility. Their gray air-deprived skin was soft and they only became animated when administering the prescribed daily dose of blood required to hydrate the brain of the inmates – a process designed to retain cognitive thought. How long the detainees lay confined in steel coffin shells, left to consider their crimes, was Julian's decision.

"Doctor Connor cannot be here." Taking a deep breath filled Julian's lungs with dust, which made his nose wrinkle, but he had a lot of talking to do.

The warden was ignorant of anything going on outside these walls and, in that sense, he and his attendants were incorruptible cogs in the prison process. They had no friends and were oblivious of the identity or standing of any vampire sent into their care. *Except The Butcher, of course.*

"We are moving all the inmates to 'Stage three: Skull crush' status immediately," said Captain Gerrard.

The warden reared. "*All* of them? That's hundreds of inmates. I really think Doctor Con-"

"I know this is shocking, but the facility is needed as a secure refuge for our human herd," said Isaac, quietly.

The warden looked up at the tall thin vampire whose shock of black hair made his skin appear to glow in the dim light. "I work in the morgue." His sweeping gesture took in Charles, Brynmor and Anthony. "We all work for Doctor Connor and he sent us."

"The human cattle have to survive this attack or we *all* die." Julian didn't feel bad lying. The warden had no idea of Connor's success in finding a blood substitute and now was not the time to muddy the waters by sharing that information.

"We are under attack?" The warden jerked as if a slap sharpened his focus. "I see. So, how will this be accomplished?"

Gerrard's flame thrower idea drifted into Julian's mind – standing here brought home the enormity of the task. *They may be condemned, but they deserve respect as vampire brethren.*

"Captain Gerrard will coordinate the moving of the inmates." Julian laid a hand on the warden's thick set shoulder – the bulk he had achieved as a human remained, despite the sedentary debilitating vampire years which followed. "Gather the facility attendants. All the inmates will be moved down through the levels as the terminations progress."

The shudder Julian felt run through the warden made him freeze. *These are his charges. It's a terrible thing we are doing.* Julian had only shared the solution suggested by Sergeant Frank with Gerrard, Marius and Daniel when all other avenues were exhausted. Even castles or forts in the South East of England would not be defendable against the enemy numbers they could be faced with.

"Warden, this is a sad day, but this *is* a release for them," the principal said, quietly.

The vampire nodded. "I'll gather the attendants."

At Julian's signal, Isaac took the flashlight.

"If you can show us around before we go down to the death chamber." Julian raised a brow when the warden coughed.

"Is *every* inmate being terminated?"

Julian knew which inmate the warden was thinking of. "Yes, *all* the inmates."

Turning away, the warden led them along another granite-lined corridor to the 'stage one' holding area. In an odd parody of a real-estate agent, he opened the door and waved a hand in a sweeping gesture.

"This one is empty. A sign of the times, I assume?" The warden looked at Julian.

"If by that you mean vampires are not coming before me in court, then you'd be wrong. But their crimes are less violent and the storage facility has become a 'three strikes and they are out' prospect."

The warden chuckled, his dry vocal-chords stuttering like a jumping stylus on a vinyl record. "Next level," he muttered.

At the bottom of a spiraling slope, stage two inmates filled three chambers. Ducking his head inside each packed room and scanning the rows of reclining figures, Julian began to share the warden's sadness.

As if Brynmor read his mind, the tall bespectacled vampire said, "They are already dead. Granite bodies. If they could talk, they'd welcome the relief."

Julian knew the laboratory assistant had accompanied Connor on 'Stage three: Skull crush' ceremonies a couple of times. He was a young vampire of sixty years but his human age could be anywhere around thirty. His curtain of black hair and glasses exuded a diffidence which was deceptive; Julian had seen Brynmor fight.

The Principal was grateful for Brynmor's pragmatic approach, after all, he would share the responsibility of giving the termination signal, when the time came. "You're right. Isaac, count the stage two inmates on this level and catch us up."

On a further three descending levels were more chambers filled with vampires in the suspended existence of 'stage two'.

Isaac rejoined the team and gave Julian a thumbs up signal. "Captain, you can take it from here."

"Charles." Gerrard stroked his jaw. "Help Isaac to organize the inmates on the upper levels into groups of twelve. Brynmor will let you know when the death chamber complex has been cleared and you can start bringing them down."

The whispering sound of movement echoed along the ascending tunnel as Charles disappeared.

Julian beckoned to Brynmor and Anthony and they followed the warden down another slope. At the bottom, the warden pulled a card from his pocket and swiped it through a slot. When a green light blinked, the rubber-edged steel door sighed as he pushed it open. It marked the air-tight boundary of the death chamber wing.

The stainless-steel walls beyond glistened with condensation and the air temperature plummeted with each step they took. The rushing current of the River Thames thrummed through the metal. At high tide, this level was below the water line, as its design intended.

"Stage three," said the warden, as he opened the first of four doors on one side of the corridor. "Two of the wards are empty," he added.

Julian felt relieved, which was ridiculous, because essentially, *every* vampire here had just been fast tracked to stage three.

Going inside a side ward, Brynmor, Anthony and Julian walked the rows. As expected, the inmates resembled wasted corpses carved in stone. Desiccation reduced preternatural flesh to pitted marble and the stature of each figure had shrunk. Julian stopped abruptly when a face he thought he recognized caught his eye. The skull looked abnormally large above thin wasted arms and angular shoulders. Julian remembered the vampire as being broad-chested and thick-necked, but no longer. *I have to start somewhere.* He leaned over the inmate and pressed a thumb onto his eyeball, sliding back the crinkled paper-thin eyelid. The pupils he stared into were sluggish, but they contracted, and then, as if they were shocked at what they saw, they blew wide open.

"Have they all been fed today?" asked Anthony.

"Yes," said the warden, "I didn't know-"

Without looking up, Julian said, "Of course you didn't, that's okay."

When Julian withdrew his hand, the one eye remained half open, as if trying to keep the principal in its sight. Pressing his thumb to the vampire's temples and cradling his skull, Julian closed his eyes. The electrical brain activity tingled beneath his fingertips, and the pictures he tried to decipher were like wisps of smoke.

Withdrawing, Julian heaved a sigh. "It will be a kindness, Brynmor."

"Yes, sir," the younger vampire replied solemnly.

Walking briskly back to the doorway, Julian said, "Bring the first twelve through to the death chamber." About to exit the room, he froze in mid-step. "Has The Butcher been fed today?"

The warden nodded, his nails tapping against the metal rim on one of the coffins betraying his unease.

"It is time to let The Butcher go, so let him be the first, after all, he has waited the longest."

As Connor's assistant, Anthony jolted into movement, but Julian held up a hand. "I will do this, it is only right."

The warden led the way past the row of closed doors, until he stopped at the last one, pushed it open and stepped aside. "Principal," he said.

Julian crossed the threshold and surveyed the small stagnant cell and the trolley in the corner upon which sat an empty syringe. Dregs of blood lined the glass barrel. Crossing to the coffin shell resting on a platform in the center of the floor, he stared down at the wizened skin-covered skull of The Butcher. The network of cracks in the dry parchment resembled a dried-out mud pack. The blood the warden had earlier syringed into The Butcher's mouth glistened on the compressed line of the shriveled lips.

Taking a deep breath, Julian pressed a thumb on the nearest eye socket and crumpled back the dry lid until he could see the eyeball. It too had a dry cracked surface and was covered with a frost-like cataract. Still, Julian looked into the misted pupil and said, "It is time."

The pupil contracted and a gleam ignited deep inside the orb. Curiosity drove Julian to grip the skull and press his thumbs to The Butcher's temple. Preparing himself for the worst, he expected blood red images of the carnage The Butcher had left in his wake – the acts the inmate chose to relive on a loop in defiance at being kept a prisoner.

No, not relive, enjoy. Julian's gut clenched in revulsion and he steeled himself against the urge to snatch his hands away, closing his own eyes to block out The Butcher's frosted stare, still visible beneath the shriveled eyelid yet to creep back into place.

His fingertips tingled as he tapped into the erratic electrical impulses firing inside The Butcher's skull. The pink-tinted mist parted like a curtain being drawn aside, and Julian jerked back. As if he was there, in a London back alley, in 1915, he followed a thin girl dressed in rags. The greasy hair hanging down her back rushed closer. *Shit, he's showing me a killing.* Julian wanted to end the session and pull the curtain shut but couldn't look away.

A gloved hand reached out and gripped the girl by the shoulder.

"Oi, gerroff," she blurted, trying to pull away. The fingers dug in hard and pulled her back.

"Ouch." Twisting around, the girl looked over her shoulder this time. Her eyes lifted to stare into Julian's and her mouth fell open. The face he saw reflected in the glossy black mirror of her pupils was that of The Butcher. The girl took in a breath to scream, but a drowning gurgle erupted as hot blood spurted from a tear in her throat. Julian flinched as if the spray of blood had hit him in the face. Suddenly, like a light going out, the picture went black. The darkness crept into his skull and, as though carved by a knife in black silk, the words 'let me go' floated behind Julian's eyes.

Withdrawing his hands from the dry bald skull, Julian rocked back on his heels. "It is time." He recognized the warmth in his chest as relief. When he looked around, the warden nodded in agreement.

The Butcher, the first resident of the storage facility, had first been imprisoned in a mausoleum in London's Kensal Green Cemetery in 1919. Back then, humans remained blissfully ignorant of vampires living in their midst. The Butcher's killing spree threatened to expose the vampire brethren, and Julian had sentenced him to an eternity of locked-in syndrome and used him as a deterrent. Any vampires who needed a reminder to disguise their kills as 'human crimes' were taken to the cemetery and shown the fate which waited for them.

The value of The Butcher as a threat had not diminished in the new vampire-led world. His annual outing from the storage facility to lie in state at St Paul's Cathedral, and the viewing procession all hive members had to attend, rammed home the penalty for killing a human during these times of food shortage. *But, it is time to let him go.*

"I'll get an attendant to take him to the death chamber." The warden turned towards the door.

"No," said Julian, "let's do it here, now, just us."

The warden's raised eyebrow made Julian laugh wryly.

"Foolish, I know, but I feel we owe him the right to die in private. He has been imprisoned for a hundred years. We can give him a dignified ending."

"Very well." The warden slipped from the room and returned seconds later with a deep tray containing a skull vise. "What do we do with his remains?"

"Wheel him through to the death chamber for disposal when the storage terminations are complete."

Julian watched the warden lift the clamp, lean into the coffin shell and fit the C-shaped metal band over the crown of The Butcher's head. Winding the screw thread on one side, he took up the slack until the vise pressed circular plates of metal onto the temples of the condemned vampire. As if he sensed his moment had arrived, The Butcher's eyes creaked open and he stared at the ceiling.

The warden took up a position with his hand poised on the T-bar handle of the thick screw.

Julian stood on the opposite side, his face solemn, as he whispered, "Cleanse your heart, ease your soul, and find peace." He raised a hand and when he closed it into a fist, the warden struck the T-bar handle with force, the screw thread shushed with an oiled whisper, stuttering when it met the resistance of curved bone. At another forceful twist, a shriek vibrated through the chamber, the skull fractured and the plates slammed together. The dried-out features crumbled as the facial structure imploded and gray jelly oozed out – the only moisture remaining in The Butcher's brain soaked into the pile of bone-dust.

Clouds of bone fragments spat into the air and both vampires stopped breathing to avoid filling their mouths, noses and throats with the grit. They stood in silence for a full minute, before Julian finally turned to leave.

The warden joined him in the corridor outside, led the way to the death chamber, and hit the button which activated hydraulics and a metal shutter slid up with a sigh of soft rubber; the seal around the entrance made the room watertight when closed.

The usual row of six stone plinths had been supplemented by steel gurneys, so the chamber could accommodate twelve 'stage three skull crush' candidates in one ceremony. The first dozen facility inmates were already in place, lying on the plinths and trolleys, with the C-clamps fitted over their heads. Their eyes were open. The stainless-steel ceiling reflected the expression frozen on their stiff faces back at them. *They won't miss a moment of their own death.*

The practice of 'connecting' with each prisoner on death row to let the condemned express regret and ask forgiveness had been abandoned a decade ago, when Connor's sanity began to suffer and the visions of the inmates stained his soul and would not let him rest easy. Now, the ceremony comprised of the inspection – a badly fitted vise would not crush the brain – and the final blessing.

Brynmor and Anthony stood inside the entrance, waiting for Julian to give the order for the terminations to begin.

The dozen death chamber attendants stood in a line against the wall like statues in an Egyptian tomb. Bone dust plumed from their clothes when a gesture from Julian jerked them into action. In a blur of movement, each took up a position beside a prone inmate. At Julian's nod, Brynmor and Anthony, starting at opposite ends, walked the line, checking the C-clamp settings, until they met in the middle and gave nods of confirmation.

In a crisp tone, Julian said, "Cleanse your heart, ease your soul, and find peace." His upheld hand clenched into a fist, and the twelve attendants, without the obstacle of a coffin shell to hamper them, hit the T-bar handle and set the screw rotating at such speed that the shriek and snap of bone collapsing was almost immediate. The condemned would not have had time to feel anything and that was a blessing.

As the attendants filed across the room preparing to exit by a side door, Julian said, "No. There are hundreds of inmates to terminate, we cannot purge the chamber after every ceremony."

If the warden and his team were fazed, they hid it well. The attendants returned to their charges and, as if the condemned were still aware, slipped their arms beneath the shoulders and knees of the headless bodies and lifted them with care. They laid each one down on the floor against the back wall. The bone fragments and wet paste cocktail of their brains were scraped into specimen bags and reunited with their owners, placed on to the chest of the bodies.

The sound of the rushing river water could be heard behind the outer walls, and it reminded Julian that they were working against the clock.

Condensation trickled down the polished steel at the back of the death chamber; it was the sluice gate which held back the fast-flowing river current when the tide was high. Disposing of vampire remains had evolved into an event of clinical precision. Terminated inmates remained sealed inside the death chamber. Once the metal shutter locked down, the sluice gate was opened and the rush of thousands of gallons of water purged the stone-like bodies from the chamber and out into the river. *But only at high tide.*

The rumble of wheels trundling down the slope outside marked the arrival of the next dozen inmates, and Julian beckoned Brynmor and Anthony to his side.

"The tide is still coming in. We have three hours to clear as many inmates as you can. Charles will send the stage two prisoners down through the levels. We have maybe two days to get through them all." Turning to Anthony, who exuded calm, his arms folded across his broad chest, Julian said, "You'll come with me. I need you to keep the dispensary and the morgue running while Isaac and Charles are here."

Brynmor blinked behind his glasses when Julian looked at him.

"Captain Gerrard will report back when it is over. I should be the one to tell Connor what we have done. Once the tree-dwellers are on the farm, we can move the humans across country. Brynmor, when you return to the hospital, stock-pile blood supplies for the Elite Guard."

"Yes, sir."

Julian patted the laboratory assistant heavily on a shoulder and followed the warden from the death chamber wing, with Anthony falling in behind.

As the trio started up the slope to the upper levels, they pressed into the wall to let a line of attendants pushing inmates loaded onto trolleys trundle past. The motionless vampires appeared accepting, but Julian knew that dehydration may have turned their flesh to granite, but their minds were doubtless in a state of panic – locked-in syndrome was indeed a living Hell. *It is a kindness to let them die.* Aloud, he asked, "How many exits does the facility have?"

"Just the main entrance," replied the warden. "It is impossible for inmates to escape. The main entrance is the only way in or out."

Julian nodded. "That makes it easy to keep the humans safe from attack. Good."

Charles and Captain Gerrard stood in the doorway of a stage two storage chamber up ahead and waited for Julian to reach them.

"Has it begun?" asked Charles.

Julian could detect the faint telltale aroma of bone-dust drifting in the air. "Yes."

"And-" Charles shuffled his feet.

"The Butcher has found peace, but let's keep it to ourselves for now." Julian frowned.

Connor had often pleaded for Julian to show clemency and let their longest serving prisoner rest in peace but, by the same token, he would have wanted to be there when it happened.

"I'm glad. A hundred years was enough suffering, even for him," said Charles.

"I agree." Julian nodded. "When it is over, you and Isaac get back to the hospital and send blood rations out to the barracks. We need our forces fed and at full strength."

Anthony fell into step as Julian waved farewell and carried on up through the levels.

Julian felt lighter. The vampire/human relationship was evolving and, even though his hand had been forced, he believed that letting the storage facility inmates find peace was part of that process.

When they arrived back at the reception chamber, Julian shook the warden's hand. "Prepare the storage room for human occupation. Food supplies, mattresses, blankets and warm clothes will arrive late tomorrow." Humans were adaptable creatures. The practice of using The London Underground tunnels as sleeping quarters during bombing raids in the Second World War proved that. Being entombed in air raid shelters was not so different from the scenario they now faced. *They will make the best of it in times of danger.* "Do what you can to make it comfortable."

"Yes, sir." With a salute, the warden left Julian and Anthony to make the final ascent alone.

The doorkeeper appeared like a skilled magician, grated a key in the lock, and opened the door.

Julian stepped out into the sea breeze where the buffeting wind tore at his hair and clothes. He closed his eyes, lifted his chin and took a moment to gather his thoughts. One piece in the puzzle of the escape plan was underway, but there was still much to do.

Accelerating around the building, Julian hit top vampire speed and focused on the tall fence-line rushing towards him. Anthony kept pace and, in effortless coordination, both vampires scaled the fence and vaulted over the top. Sharing a brief grin as they landed, they set a direct path back into the City.

When they were approaching the Square Mile, Julian called a halt. "You head back to the hospital. I have an errand to run and then I'll be in the council building."

Julian wheeled away and headed west at a powerful run.

On the road out of London, he passed Supervisor Matthew's home. The front door was boarded up and the hedge lining the sidewalk was overgrown and strangled with ground elder. The last time Julian visited the house, he and Gerrard had exhumed the supervisor's body.

Julian remained thankful that before Marius executed Alexander, the young juror had revealed the details of Matthew's fate. In a parody of a human murder/mystery novel, Alexander had *buried* his victim in the supervisor's own back garden, breaking Matthew's neck before putting him into the pit which became his grave. Even though Supervisor Matthew was a co-conspirator in Alexander's crimes, exhumation brought the skull crushing of true death and he was not left to feel beetles and ants eating away flesh which had not yet desiccated.

The disgraced supervisor had become a rarity; a vampire criminal given a gravestone to mark his resting place. *It stands as a reminder.*

Carrying on, Julian cut across countryside that was shrouded in ink-black shadows. The clear night sky was littered with stars and a gusting breeze transformed fields of grass into a rippling sea. The floodlights surrounding the human farm emitted starbursts of brightness which reached to the heavens and lifted the dark inside the compound to a permanent state of dusk.

We must switch them off. Even though ferals were beyond rational thought, Julian could not rule out the remnants of survival instinct – lights could act as a dinner bell. *Vampires don't need light.* Blocking off the doors and the few windows in the steel walls of the siphoning sheds was an easy fix. The humans could have light inside, but not out in the compound.

Reaching the outer perimeter, where the razor-wire running along the top glittered like a string of lethal diamonds, Julian felt pleased when half a dozen guards appeared in an instant. The alert gleam in their narrowed eyes gave him confidence.

"Principal." The head guard punched in a code which opened the gate in the wire metal fence.

"Where is Supervisor Edmund?" asked Julian, directing his gaze across the divide towards the inner fence-line. The tall figure he saw standing in the no-mans' land between the boundaries made Julian grin – the cape he wore flapped in the breeze, offering glimpses of the crossbow cradled across his chest.

Julian powered across the rough meadow to the sergeant's side. "It's good to see you."

The sergeant nodded slowly. "I have a vested interest in protecting the humans. After all, if anything happens to Doctor Connor then the old tried and tested methods could be all we have to fall back on."

Julian shot a sharp glance at Frank's stiff profile.

Frank shrugged. "It's no secret that the good doctor has had some close calls in the last few years."

Julian did a mental run through of the dangers Connor had survived since Rebekah entered his life and couldn't fault the sergeant's logic. "True, but I've known Doctor Connor many decades. His survival instinct is finely honed."

"I'm sure you're right," replied Frank.

"How are things progressing here?" Julian moved the conversation onto the reason he came. "Are the humans in the siphoning sheds?"

Both vampires turned and walked towards the inner fence. A warden opened the gate and Julian went through it first.

"Things are well underway," said Frank, falling into step beside Julian again.

The row of siphoning sheds rose into the night sky, the polished steel walls gleaming in the floodlit glare.

"We must power down the lights once they are all inside," Julian murmured thoughtfully.

"Agreed. Let me show you the preparations." Frank changed direction to go up the concrete ramp of the nearest shed.

The double doors, through which resistant humans were wheeled in on gurneys and blood filled I.V. bags were transported out in carts, were propped open. The constant stream of traffic over the years had worn track marks into the sloping surface.

Inside, they were faced with three other sets of doors. To the left was the blood storage room, the right door led to the isolation ward where humans who needed new catheters, siphoning tubes, or those who had infections received treatment. The one straight ahead entered the siphoning hall of the shed.

The scent of blood tainted the air as though it had seeped into the fabric of the building, and Julian dived into the blood storage area to collect a thin plastic face mask. When he returned, Frank was already wearing his own.

"Play it safe until we see what's inside," was the sergeant's muffled explanation as he pushed in through the door.

In the hall, Supervisor Edmund was standing with hands clasped behind his back.

Scanning the surroundings, with a nod, Julian removed his mask and tucked it into his belt. "Where are the siphoning beds?" he asked, shaking the hand the supervisor offered.

"Moved out and stacked in siphoning shed number 6."

Julian surveyed the transformation of the space which used to be filled with rows of steel 'autopsy type' beds – each one had a channel running around the outer rim to catch any blood spillage, and hooks from which to hang the I.V. bags used in the siphoning process were welded to the side. Restraints held the donor in place.

Before, the vast shed had barely enough light for humans to see anything other than passing shadows of the vampire monitoring the siphoning, but brighter lightbulbs had been fitted. Wooden panels divided the cavernous hall into cubicles. Edmund led the way to where Julian could view the spartan accommodation which housed a pair of single beds, made up with pillows, sheets and blankets, and a cupboard occupying the space between.

"The humans in the compound are packing a few personal items." Edmund waved a hand to indicate a door at the far end. "The siphoning recovery room has been converted into a kitchen and dining area."

"Good to see things are underway. When are the first groups being moved in?"

Frank replied, "First thing, just before dawn."

"That's good." Julian spun on his heel and headed back to the main entrance. He tossed his face mask into a crate in the vestibule before stepping back out to where the floodlights created the false dawn. "From what Captain Blake told us, this is the biggest threat we've faced since 'the rise'." He took a deep cleansing breath. "We better be ready."

Frank nodded. "Being at the top of the food chain, complacency is a risk. The siphon shed porters have counted the human stock and allocated each one a cubicle. If needed, they can all be moved in quickly."

Julian inhaled to relay instructions for the next step in the plan, but Frank was there ahead of him. "The crop reapers are bringing in the trucks. We'll use those to transport the humans to the storage facility when you give the order."

"That will be soon. Gerrard and the medical team have things underway there."

Frank ran a firm hand over his jaw and his dark eyes narrowed as if he weighed his words.

"Go on, Sergeant, permission to speak."

"I know, the entire hive knows, there are refugee humans out there under yours and Doctor Connor's protection. Where do they stand in the framework of this emergency plan?"

"It's complicated, but Rebekah is out bringing the tree-dwellers to the eco-shelter. The next step will be to get them all here." Julian's clipped tone betrayed tension.

"If I can make a suggestion."

"Yes?" He straightened and pinned the sergeant with a curious look.

"If the feral attack could move fast, then the eco-shelter group should come in *now*. Is there a vampire who can wait there for Rebekah and these others to arrive? If you delay the evacuation, it could be too late."

Julian tugged his shirt collar and cuffs into place as he sank into thought. *Anthony could do it.* But Anthony had the hospital to run. Peter and Sampson were at the eco-shelter, but they would both be needed to guide the community to the farm. *I can't let anything happen to Leizle, Oscar, Evie and the rest.* Julian peered at Frank's neutral matter-of-fact expression. "You're right. Go to the eco-shelter and wait for Rebekah. You know the location?"

Frank nodded. "All guardsmen know the location, we enforce the exclusion zone."

"What you won't know about, is Leizle." Julian said her name in a hoarse whisper.

"Who?"

"You'll know her when you see her. A small red-head, and she'll put up a fight. She won't like leaving without Rebekah. She forgets that she and Rebekah are different now, so will kick up a fuss. Don't let her stay behind."

Frank chuckled. "Yes, sir. Understood. Leizle."

Chapter 17

Beneath ground, the low hum of the generator provided a comforting soundtrack to the eco-shelter living chambers – like a maternal heartbeat that reassured a fetus. Seren and Leizle sat cross-legged on large beanbag cushions, both pretending to read. Wooden bookcases covered three sides of the stone-encrusted walls of this cave, creating the illusion of flat surfaces and homeliness.

Leizle's hair gleamed in the light of the bulkhead lamp. Copper-colored curls framed her face, still damp from the bath Oscar had insisted she take, to ease her aching muscles after shifting evacuation supplies all day. The rest was piled on top of her head in a messy knot. Her complexion was paler than her usual alabaster and dark rings stained her eye sockets a bruised purple.

The bath was meant to relax her, but Seren could sense the tension pulling her companion's shoulders tight. She peered from the corner of her eye, pretending to read, and from her fixed expression, Seren guessed that Leizle was faking it, too.

She took a deep breath. *What do I have to do to make the girl relax?* Bring Julian back, popped into her head, and she snorted, knowing that was not on the cards.

"What?" asked Leizle, her words a whisper.

"Nothing," said Seren, "I'm just wondering where Osiris has gone." It was not entirely untrue. She was frustrated that she couldn't make contact with him, psychically. Thinking aloud, she added, "Either, he's too far away or blocking me out because he doesn't want me to know what he's up to. Both options are worrying."

Leizle smiled weakly. "He's okay. He's a warrior. He can look after himself."

"I know, and so can Julian," replied Seren softly, reaching out to take Leizle's hand.

The young girl sighed. "I wish I had a 'connection' with someone. You and Osiris are lucky, you're the same, both hybrids."

"The same but different." Seren gently squeezed Leizle's fingers. "Earth Walkers are a breed apart." Suddenly shaking her head and sitting straighter, she added, "But, you are right. Osiris is a warrior and I should let him do what is needed and not worry. I'll cheer-up if you will?" Seren's gray eyes glittered in the dim light as she peeped through the jet-black curtain of her glossy hair.

As if she hadn't heard, Leizle ran her gaze around the makeshift library.

The thick tarpaulin covers the girls had pulled down to expose the book cases lay in gray heaps on the floor like slain ghosts. When vampires first rose, Uncle Harry had created this temple of thought and meditation. The group of refugees would gather every evening and one of the adults would read a few chapters, but that routine had lapsed.

"I remember when my father first met Harry and we settled here. I was only three, and Rebekah was six years old." Leizle sighed. "We were partners in crime, but the thing we learned first was to be quiet and hold in our emotions. Now, I'm a grown woman and don't know what to do with the fears eating at me."

Slipping her fingers from Seren's light grip, Leizle snapped her book shut, rolled to her feet, and deliberately slid the leather-bound volume of Romeo and Juliette back into a slot on the shelf. "I should find something more uplifting to read." A bark of laughter grated through her throat. Leizle returned to her beanbag, dropped down into it and rested both elbows on her knees. "Do you trust Sampson and Peter?"

"Papa and Julian trust them. That's good enough for me, but yes, I do." Seren frowned at the swift change of topic.

"Isn't it odd? A vampire and human being friends?" Hearing Seren chuckle, Leizle rushed on. "No, I know, Rebekah and Connor, me and Julian, and even Anthony and Greg, well *human* Greg – he's a vampire now but..." Leizle shrugged. "It feels odd."

"Uncle Julian says it's a good sign that maybe humans and vampires can co-exist once Papa has perfected the blood substitute. Sampson and Peter *chose* to be friends."

Leizle smiled. "I get that. I'm glad the world is changing." She rested her chin on her hand, and her breathing soon became slow and steady.

"Hey," Seren said gently, "get some sleep. We don't know when Mama, Seth and Greg will get back, and we need to be ready to move, so sleep while you can."

'You're right." Standing up and stretching out the kinks, Leizle headed towards the doorway. "Night, Seren."

Waiting out the seconds it took for Leizle to take the left turn towards the sleeping dens and disappear, Seren whipped smoothly to her feet, left the chamber and went right, heading back to the dining and meeting caverns. Even before she reached the approach tunnel, she could hear the bustle of activity and smell the odors of the evening meal Oscar and Evie were preparing.

Her rumbling stomach caught her by surprise. Doing a quick calculation, Seren worked out her last meal of human food was three days ago. *And I'm preaching to Leizle.*

Being a hybrid meant juggling the needs of both species, and her human side was rebelling.

Seren swung around into the meeting cavern. Sandy and most of the men were dotted around the room, hunkered down doing last minute checks. Thomas was resting back against a pile of sleeping bags, his chin nodding down to his chest and then jerking up sharply as he fought sleep. The young man looked up as Seren entered and struggled to get to his feet, toppling back onto his backside twice before she offered a steadying hand.

Wearing combat gear made him look younger than his eighteen years. His fine-boned features and wiry stature betrayed the gentle and sensitive man he would become.

"I'm hungry, you hungry?" asked Seren, clapping him on the shoulder when he nodded. "Let's go."

In theory, Seren was younger than Thomas but she had reached five foot six inches in less than four years. Her permanent physiological age of 'young adult' made her ageless in every sense of the word.

Walking along the aisle between the piles of crated food and canvas camping equipment, the pair waved at Sandy, who wiped the sweat from his forehead with the back of a gloved hand and waved back.

"Chow time?" He grinned. "Good idea."

Shoving a canvas bag into a space in the pile, Sandy pulled off the work gloves, stuck them in his utility belt and dusted off his hands. Patting Thomas on the shoulder, he said, "Smells good. Oscar's worked his magic again."

The three crossed the threshold together. In the dining cavern, Oscar was wheeling in the last of six trolleys. Two were loaded with bread, potatoes, and bean stew, the next with fruit, salad, vegetables, and from the last, steam rose from joints of roasted meat. Oscar's repertoire had expanded, thanks to the food delivery made by vampire farmers – another advantage to being a protected community.

Stopping to wash-up in a bowl of warm water, Sandy queued up behind a suddenly ravenous Seren. Even though she loaded up her plate with meat carved from the bone – being a hybrid, her body cried out for protein only – Seren felt jittery. She shot a glance at the men sitting at wooden tables, scooping food into their mouths. The murmur of uninterrupted conversation stuttered through the air. Setting down her piled plate to claim the seat beside Thomas, with a half wave at the youngster, Seren sidled over to where Sampson leaned against the wall. He wore a plastic mask and his eyes were closed, as if in meditation. *He's in revival sleep.*

Seren coughed and the vampire's hazel-colored eyes shot open.

"Can you hear that?" she asked.

Sampson pulled his mask away and listened for a second. "Hear what?"

"Something..." Seren knew it wasn't her imagination. "Someone is coming."

"I hear it. Wha-"

Sampson jolted upright as a sudden ear-piercing shriek filled the air.

Cutlery clattered down onto plates, benches shunted back with a scrape, and boots hit the packed-earth floor as every human leapt up and rushed from the dining cavern into the kitchen.

Peter appeared beside Seren. "What's happening?"

"Warning siren. Vampire inside the exclusion zone. Take cover," said Sampson.

Seren stood firm even when the tall vampire nudged her shoulder. She had been here before, and once the humans were inside the panic room with the soundproof door shut, there was nothing to do but wait. "Is it an attack?" she asked. Her black hair swung as she shook her head to ward off another shove from Sampson. "I'll go in last. Oscar and Sandy will get everyone inside safely, but Peter, you should go, now."

A visitor to the eco-shelter, Peter didn't know the emergency drill.

"Just follow the others. We'll let you know when it's safe to come out." Seren pointed to the doorway where the others had disappeared and gave the man a push. "Go."

As Peter rushed out of sight, Seren turned back to Sampson. "What, now?"

"I'll go and find out what's happening." But before he could move, the siren stopped.

In the sudden silence, Seren's steel gray eyes remained glued to the vampire's face.

Sampson cocked his head. "False alarm," he muttered, "but we do have a visitor."

Tuning into a distant rushing noise, Seren frowned. *It's not Osiris, there's no heartbeat, and I'd know if it was Papa, Mama or Uncle Julian.* "Who is it?"

Hearing another louder 'rushing human' noise, Seren swung around and slapped a hand on her forehead. "Shit," she spat, using her mother's favorite expletive.

Footsteps pounded up the slope of the tunnel outside and Leizle burst in through the arched doorway. Struggling to breathe from

191

the fast sprint, with the 'alarm' call silenced, she doubled over and braced her hands on her knees to recover.

Resting an arm around the girl's hunched shoulders, Seren whispered, "Sorry, I should've come for you."

Leizle gasped a laugh. "I'm an old hand, I've got odd boots on and didn't button my pants up right, but I'm fast enough." Straightening and putting her hands on her hips to expand her lungs, she said, "So, crisis over?" Her relief ramped up to alarm when a sudden gusting blast plastered her shirt to her back and her copper hair flapped wildly around her face.

The air rushed in from the tunnel outside as if an express train was entering a station, and all three turned, primed and ready, standing shoulder to shoulder.

The plum colored uniform worn by an Elite Guardsman made them relax a little.

The squad leader's white face was grim, his mouth crimped in a straight line. He relaxed his features long enough to say, "We have a messenger. Principal Julian sent him."

When he stepped aside, a tall dark vampire walked into the meeting hall. He, too, was dressed in a guardsman uniform, but the bottom eight inches of his dark gray coat was splattered in mud.

Seren stared at the vampire, inhaling slowly to waft his aroma over her palate. She sensed that Sampson was doing the same and a glance at her companion's wary expression was far from reassuring. *He doesn't know him.*

"Can you prove Principal Julian sent you?" asked Sampson, stepping forward to block the visitor's progress.

The Elite Guard briefly laid a hand on the newcomer's shoulder. "I can vouch for his credentials. He is one of us, a sergeant."

Seren stared at the officer with keen interest. "And, what is the message?"

The comrades in arms shared a sharp look, then the sergeant said, "Please, this is for everyone to hear."

"That bad, eh?" muttered Leizle.

With an accusing frown, Seren said, "As luck would have it, you caused quite a stir, so *everyone* is assembled inside the panic room."

"The squad leader was on his mettle, I didn't realize I'd crossed into the twenty-mile exclusion zone until I was laid out on the ground." With a sheepish grin, the sergeant rotated on the spot to reveal that it was not just the hem of his coat covered in mud. A dried-out layer caking his back cracked and spat dirt every time he moved.

Seren and Leizle led the way through the dining chamber and into the kitchen.

Only Oscar had emerged from the reinforced hiding place, his white-knuckled grip on a carving knife easing when he spotted Leizle. "Thank God, I was just coming to find you." Switching his attention to Seren, he asked, "What's happening, lass?"

"False alarm, Oscar, but-" Waving a hand towards the sergeant, Seren continued, "Julian has sent news, so we need everyone out here."

Without missing a beat, Oscar returned to the large refrigerator, pressed the trigger and swung the four-inch-thick door wide.

Unable to contain his curiosity, the sergeant darted forward.

In a nanosecond, Sampson grabbed the visitor by the throat, swung him around and pinned him against the wall. But, in an explosion of movement, Sampson flew backwards across the room, skidded over the tiled floor and thumped into a wooden panel. The sound of splintering wood froze everyone to the spot.

When Seren glared at the sergeant, he held up his hands as if she pointed a revolver at his chest. "I'm sorry, it was a reflex."

Sampson rolled back to his feet and brushed himself down.

Leizle peered out from where Oscar had pulled her behind him to become a human shield.

The sergeant said quietly, "I won't make another move, I promise. This is all new to me."

His tentative smile was disarming.

The humans inched their way out of the padded panic-room of the converted refrigeration unit and lined up, like a choir jostling for a good view of their conductor. Each human scanned the three vampires, looking for reassurance, and then settled their attention on the sergeant.

"I think it best if you deliver your message and leave," said Seren, firmly.

"Very well. Principal Julian sent me here to wait for Rebekah and the away party to return with the human refugees." He raised a silencing finger when muttering started within the human ranks. "Sampson and Peter – those were the names he gave me – are to be your guides. The Elite Squad will arrive at dusk to escort *all* of you to the human farm."

"We *are* going to the human farm," said Oscar, "but only after Rebekah and Greg bring the others in." He folded his arms across his broad chest.

"I have my orders," the sergeant said flatly.

"I'm not going without Rebekah." Leizle lifted her chin, glaring up at the vampire.

"Leizle, I presume?" The sergeant chuckled. "Principal Julian told me to expect trouble from a fiery redhead."

Leizle snorted, but her shoulders slumped and her stare wavered. "Seren?"

"If Uncle Julian sent this order, the danger must have stepped up." Taking Leizle by the hand, she added, "Mama will be okay, it's *you* who is in danger. Julian is right to worry."

"By the looks of the supplies piled up in the other room, you are ready to go, yes?" asked the sergeant.

"They are ready," said Sampson.

Catching Leizle's eye and holding it, the sergeant said, "I know what it means to be a close-knit group, believe me. Principal Julian wouldn't ask you to leave here if there was another way."

Leizle's eyes brimmed with tears and she dashed them away with the back of her hand. "You're right, Sergeant-?"

He dipped his dark head. "Frank. Sergeant Frank, and please know, I have been entrusted with your safety and I will not let Principal Julian down."

Chapter 18

Muttering beneath his breath, Julian circled the room for the twentieth time, swinging around and barely avoiding a collision with the wardrobe where his Principal garb was hanging. The traveling coat he wore flared out and knocked a copper-veined pebble from a side table and onto the floor.

He scooped the polished stone up from where it nestled in the carpet like an amber eye.

Since Leizle first left it on his mantelpiece at his Richmond home, as a sign that she was being sensible and was hidden away in the soundproof room at the rear of the house, the pebble traveled with him as a talisman.

He slipped it into his coat pocket.

It would make the trip north to York with him. It was a reminder of their beginnings and how she had changed his life. *Will Sergeant Frank persuade Leizle to leave?*

He knew now how Connor felt, trying to juggle plates and stop everything from crashing down. *I should turn Leizle. Even as an impetuous foolish vampire her chance of survival would skyrocket.* With a firm nod, he acknowledged that this time, he meant it. This time, taking her human life from her did not fill him with fear. With his hand still dipped inside his pocket, he rubbed his thumb over the stone as if it were a genie's lamp giving him strength.

He jolted when a sharp rap on the door shattered the peace, instantly shouting out, "Come."

Even before his visitors stepped over the threshold, their scent revealed their identity.

"Juror Marius, Juror Daniel, what is the situation at the Synthetic Blood manufacturing plant?"

"No unrest in the technicians," replied Daniel, pausing to read the fast flow of Marius' sign gestures and nodding. "Marius agrees, he thinks that the success of the synthetic blood trials have ignited a sense of unity. Even the threat of feral attacks has not dented the focus of the workforce. The stockpile is building steadily."

"That is good news. We may need to feed an army in the coming weeks." A muscle ticking in his jaw, Julian said, "Or it may be only days away. We need to be ready."

"How are the other preparations going?" Daniel swung his bow down from where it lay against his back. Resting one end on the carpet and holding it like a staff, he made the weapon look like an extension of his body.

"Captain Gerrard is doing an inventory of the hive arsenal, allocating weapons to squads on the front line in case things happen fast. Anthony has prepared the surgical wing for casualties."

From where he had settled in the room, occupying Julian's favorite chair, Marius raised a brow and tapped a long finger on the intricately carved wooden armrest.

Julian laughed gently. "Yes, the termination of the storage facility inmates is underway."

Marius' sign came at a slower pace which matched the serious expression on his face.

"Yes," replied Julian, "I terminated The Butcher personally. He is at rest."

The rigid lines of the juror's body melted and he sank deeper into the chair, showing his approval with a nod and a gentle smile.

"What now?" asked Daniel.

"I've called a summit meeting of the remaining hives, in York."

"That's two hundred and thirty odd miles away." Daniel and Marius wore matching frowns.

"True," said Julian, "but it's still a mid-point. It's six hundred miles to the Glascarnoch Hive in Scotland. Principal Tavish is attending, and Sergeant Hugh is still in Cardiff, so I've enlisted his powers of persuasion to make sure Glynn attends."

Marius' throat whistled and his wide grin supplied the rest.

It was well documented that Principal Glynn allocated human blood rations by 'seniority'. In other words, as he held the highest rank, his blood quota was guaranteed while lower-level vampires would be left to starve if human cattle numbers became critical. He regarded the 'blood substitute' as contamination. Getting the principal to attend the meeting would take some doing.

Julian laughed, dryly. "York is a central location, now the Midland Hive has folded. And, yes, Glynn will be there, Marius, or he'll be replaced. I'm not in the mood to take his bullshit."

"How long will you be gone?" asked Daniel.

"I'll be as fast as I can and, in the meantime, all our humans are being moved into the siphoning sheds until I return. That's what I need you to manage. Court hearings are suspended." Julian buttoned up his coat as he spoke.

Daniel slung his steel longbow over his shoulder, and Marius rose to his feet, a flurry of his fingers relaying a last-minute message. 'Be careful, Julian.'

"I will, old friend." Pulling on black gloves and flipping up the collar of his thick coat, Julian gave a final nod and disappeared out through the door.

Marius and Daniel descended into stone-like stillness. The only noise was the ticking of a walnut grandfather clock, if you discounted the scuttling noise of ants, the hum of a fly and the whisper of the silken web a spider in the far corner patiently wove.

With a whistle through his vocal chords, Marius burst into an explosion of sign. 'Julian suggested I turn a human to act as my 'mouthpiece'.'

Daniel focused on the older vampire's intense features and the blackness of his gaze. With his oil black hair and ramrod straight posture, he epitomized the human notion of vampires, but it was more than that. Like the 'thousand-yard stare' of battle-weary soldiers, Marius exuded the despair of one who had seen too much.

I wonder what thoughts they would read, this chosen 'mouthpiece'. Instead, Daniel said, "You would have to choose carefully."

With a slow nod, Marius signed. 'I'll discuss the matter with Malachi, but persuading a human to volunteer could be hard.'

"Greg and Anthony are finding a way to manage the mentor/student connection. Maybe you should ask them? Perhaps, a human from the eco-shelter will be amenable to becoming immortal." Daniel grinned.

'It has to be someone I trust.' Marius became a stone sculpture once more, and Daniel sank into his own thoughts. The relaxation of revival sleep softened their expressions. Being fully refreshed was a crucial part of being around humans and resisting the gnawing hunger. Both vampires would visit the human farm once dusk had fallen.

◇◇◇

Fine drizzle laid a shroud of dew over Julian's still figure. His blond hair had darkened to caramel and the moonlight cast ghoulish shadows over his tight expression. He stood on a hill looking out over the ink-black cluster of buildings down below. *York.*

Vampire society had chosen the hive settlements carefully. Each hive location had two key factors; easy to defend and land nearby suitable as hunting grounds. London was an obvious choice, and the impressive fortification of the castle which formed the hub of the Cardiff Hive spoke for itself. York was a city with Roman roots and a Viking past and the ancient walls surrounding the city had been fortified by its latest occupants – vampires.

Julian had visited York during its human years and as his narrowed gaze ranged across the landscape, easily picking out the detail even in the misty rain, he felt sadness. *It has changed so much.*

One site cast rays of light into the night sky like a lighthouse beacon; the human compound was a vampire constructed facility within the fortified wall. In the center of the city, the impressive golden needlepoint spire of York Minster towered above its surroundings. The magnificent church was an easy choice as the hive council building. Constructed in the 7th century, medieval stained-glass windows told the story of Jesus Christ from the human Christian perspective, and the vampires now inhabiting the space could not help but admire the exquisite craftsmanship on display. Given the ominous agenda he had come to discuss, Julian hoped the inspirational setting might ignite a spark of unity.

He frowned fiercely, realizing that the British hives had become fragmented during the past decade and he had not spoken to Principal Edward in years. *Are native ferals a cause for concern this far north?*

With a deep sigh, Julian burst into movement, accelerating across the scrubland and down onto the asphalt of a crumbling disused main road. It was clear by the weeds and grass forcing its way through wide cracks in the surface that the road south was not a transport route the hive used. The north/south divide in human society was an even wider gulf in the immortal community. Finding common ground could be harder than Julian imagined, even with his standing as the highest-ranking principal in Britain. *They won't like it, but I'm pulling rank and they will do what's good for them.*

Following the road to where the vampire reinforced city boundary interrupted his progress, Julian stopped, raked his wet blond hair back from his face and called out, "Principal Julian at the gate."

Darker blots of shadow beyond the locked entrance shuffled silently and Julian clenched his teeth against a swell of irritation. *Play the game.* He already knew they had seen his approach – the Roman road was as straight as an arrow so, unless the checkpoint was deserted, vampires on duty in the upper level of the lookout tower had an eight-mile warning.

Resembling a statue which had erupted through the grainy asphalt, Julian remained silent.

A cough interrupted the still night air, metal grated as a key was inserted into the locked gate, and a high-pitched creak bore witness to how few times the gatekeepers had opened the portal in recent years.

Julian grinned. Connor would doubtless have leapt up onto the ramparts and taken on the York guardsmen, but Julian had a point to prove. Exuding power was a different kind of strength more suited to this occasion. Smoke and mirrors were the currency of council jurors and the rules of engagement formed part of the power play.

Julian remained still and maintained his silence until a gray-faced figure stepped out into the moonlight. After another cough, the guard said, "Principal Julian, welcome to the York Hive."

Reanimating smoothly, Julian pinned the guard in a cool green stare and replied, "I trust the portcullis and exit gates are already open, I don't have time to waste."

"Yes, sir, they are all open." The vampire spoke louder than necessary, given the distance of four yards.

Julian smothered a wry smile as he heard metal grinding on stone and another wailing creak, and knew the other guards in the squad were scuttling around to clear the way. The guardsmen had pushed their luck as far as they dared, even if the snub was a result of Principal Edward's orders.

Striding forward, Julian drove the waiting guard aside, went through the damp stone archway and along the deep access tunnel which passed beneath the lookout tower. The closed doors to left and right created a medieval aura – nails hammered into them embellished the thick, aged and pitted wood with half-inch square nubs of buckled iron. The portcullis at the midpoint of the tunnel allowed interrogation of visitors to take place inside the cave like space, out of the sun. A row of dull spikes protruding from a gap overhead were all Julian could see of the thick iron grid barrier. The dreary night spat rain into his face as he drew close to the exit gate beyond and Julian adjusted his thick damp coat in readiness. On the threshold he paused.

"Has Principal Tavish arrived?" asked Julian. It would be by the north gate, but the news would travel fast.

"Yes, sir, he arrived an hour ago." The lone escort bobbed his head. The glance he shot at the closed door beside him made Julian chuckle.

"Your squad have deserted you," said Julian with a smirk.

"It looks that way," replied the vampire, his half smile sharing the joke.

"Has Principal Glynn arrived?"

"Yes, sir." The guard squared his shoulders and stood straighter. "He came through here."

Julian narrowed his eyes. "Was he alone?"

"No, a captain was with him. One of yours, I believe. His Ident number was of the London Hive."

"Captain Hugh." *So, Principal Glynn is resisting, still.* "Thank you, guard," said Julian absently, already turning towards the blustering wind and powering forward into the city.

The closer he got to York Minster, the fewer structures remained from times of human habitation. Many shopping centers, restaurants and commercial districts had been leveled, but some derelict shells of houses and private human dwellings lined streets, a reminder of a way of life suddenly ended.

Coming across a wide avenue closed off with a barrier of rotting wood, its red hazard paint faded to pink speckles, piqued Julian's curiosity.

Vaulting the obstacle, he headed along the sidewalk.

The first dwelling he came to was set back from the road. An impressive house in its own grounds. Julian paused, gripped the rungs of the tall rusting metal railings and peered across the waist high wilderness of grass, weeds and creepers. Dark mold stained the cream paint of the rendered walls and the pillars supporting the portico were cracked; black holes where lumps had fallen out looked like teeth marks left by a demon. The grit-encrusted windows emanated horror movie menace. If the house and gardens had a joy-filled history, it had been eradicated.

He ran his tightly gripped fists down the iron rods dislodging a whispering shower of rust flakes. Tuning into the sounds beyond the stark façade, he could hear the scuttling of small creatures – rats, hedgehogs, mice – and their hearts fluttering inside their chests.

On impulse, Julian scaled the railings and dropped down onto the uneven gravel. Clumps of grass mottled the driveway with trip hazards, but he whipped across the surface, kicking up a trail of scattered stones. Within the musty shade beneath the portico, he pushed open the front door. The panel of splintered wood and broken leaded-glass groaned as the bottom edge scraped across the moldy wooden floor beyond.

Inhaling deeply, he detected the final piece to this particular puzzle.

The fortune of the human family who lived here had not been the horror of being imprisoned and siphoned for blood. *They died in the pandemic.* The odor of disease, desiccated remains and bacteria spores tainted the stagnant air. Julian didn't need to go any further to know the decaying husks of the human family were inside, along with many others.

When the dead had outnumbered the survivors, human communities could no longer keep up with the pace of burials and cremations. *Did the York vampires pile up the bodies in this district?* Although, it could have been the humans – death and decay brought with them more diseases to terrify the living.

Returning to the sidewalk, Julian peered along the row. In some houses further along the street, the windows were jagged holes in crumbling soot-stained walls. *Funeral pyres.* The dwellings had been burned to the ground. He frowned. It seemed logical that this last house was still waiting for a final load of corpses to fill it before being set alight, but that had not happened.

With a shake of his head, Julian turned away. *Enough.* He could not put off the summit meeting and time-wasting distractions did not alter the truth, disease may have wreaked havoc in the past, but the feral invasion could end *every* human life.

Leaping back over the rickety barrier closing off the street without touching it, he ramped up to top speed in seconds. The wet streets glistened in the moonlight, but it had stopped raining. The feeling of his muscles and sinews humming with exertion brought a wide grin to his face. He shed his damp coat and hitched it over his shoulder where it flapped and flared like a trapped bird for the last few miles of the trip.

Sunlight and air exposure were horses of a different color and vampire existence hinged on a very simple survival tool. Julian had no intention of fighting but instinct dictated that he take advantage of the air exposure which hardened the crystals in vampire skin to a tough shell. Always being prepared had got him this far in his over two-hundred-year undead span.

With a halo of moonshine glowing behind it, on the crest of a grassy mound, the silhouette of Clifford's Tower, the heart of which was an imposing castle turret of magnificent girth, dominated the skyline. The tower had twice been burned to the ground. The block stone structure now standing had been built in the 13th century by Henry III and had been crucial in subduing the rebellions in the north.

Passing around the base of the mound, Julian hit a wall. A tall imposing uniformed guardsman blocked the only gap in the brick-built obstruction.

Here we go again. Julian took a deep breath and prepared for another identity check.

The tall guard dipped his chin, stepping aside as he said, "Principal Julian."

Darting a look up into startling blue eyes, Julian grinned. "Guardsman Owen. It's been a long time. You traded London for York, I see."

"Two years ago, now. You recommending me for the Elite Guard started the journey. Thank you, sir."

The youngster had come close to disappearing down the rabbit hole that was 'Serge's household guard', as Julian remembered it. He clapped the guard on the shoulder. "My pleasure."

With a parting nod, Julian headed down the access path cutting through the eight feet deep boundary wall and out into the enclosure between Clifford's Tower and York Minster.

The vast flat lawned area housed the York Hive 'grave sleep center'. Set into a side wall was a squat windowless building. A plate riveted to the steel door had 'Blood Dispensary' engraved into it. The granite stone block was essentially a large cold store.

The dramatic embellished walls of the Gothic cathedral of York Minster rose majestically on the far side of the enclosure, its multi-colored stained-glass windows glinting in the distance.

In keeping with the ancient aura of the setting, the York Hive solution to confinement for grave sleep resembled an open gravesite, it was as if stone coffins had been exhumed and placed in rows across the field of grass.

Heading away from the blood dispensary, Julian tracked the sweeping arc of the rough-hewn wall until Owen called out. "Principal."

Swinging around and retracing his steps, Julian lifted a brow.

Shuffling his feet, Owen murmured, "I think you should know, Principal Glynn checked in for grave sleep."

"Principal Glynn?" The muscle in Julian's jaw ticked. "What time was that?"

"Not sure, sir."

"Thank you, Owen." Julian changed direction, headed to the granite blood dispensary building and banged on the door.

The door whipped open and cold air plumed into the night like dry ice. The vampire on duty remained inside the near pitch-black interior. In his left hand he held three vials of human blood and with the other, he thrust a clipboard under Julian's nose.

Without missing a beat, Julian plucked the clipboard from the attendant's grasp and inspected the top sheet of paper. "Paper? Really?" muttered Julian.

The attendant stepped out into the yard and stood bolt upright. "Principal Edward wanted a record of visitors using the facility."

Wanted to pick out troublemakers, more like. I could have told him Glynn would be one of those. Handing the clipboard back, Julian said, "Principal Glynn, where is he? Where is 'C8'?"

The glass vials clinked as the vampire dived back inside to set them and the clipboard down. Seconds later, he led the way across to one of three sectors filled with stone sarcophagi.

The regimented grid-like pattern of stone shells were numbered in one direction and allocated letters in the other. Understanding the system instantly, Julian slipped ahead of his guide. *C8. C8. C8.* Julian repeated the mantra as he walked the main access path, frustrated to find that in row 'C', the numbers on either side of him were forty and forty-one. Swinging left he whipped along the row, running his hand along the succession of pitted stone boxes as he counted down from forty to eight. Earth spat into the air as he dug in his heels and came to a halt.

The attendant appeared at his side, coughed politely, and Julian stepped back.

Sidling into the narrow space between two sarcophagi, the vampire wiped the dew from the metal plate hanging from hooks screwed into the stone and read the occupant's 'sleep plan'. Looking up, the attendant said, "He has another two hours before rehydration is complete."

Julian sighed. Even his authority as Chief Principal could not speed up the grave sleep process.

"Very well, thank you. Send word when Principal Glynn wakes." If Julian's clipped tone left any doubt, the erratic jerking action of his run as he took a shortcut through the field of coffins and disappeared into the oil-black shadow cast by the cathedral screamed his annoyance.

The ire consuming Julian evaporated the moment he rounded the final corner and mounted the wide stone steps leading to the cathedral. The exterior, with the soaring pillars and tall spines culminating in twin bell towers, was majestic, but inside, the cavernous gold-embellished vaulted space of the Gothic nave was breathtaking. The sense of awe pervaded the air and Julian stood still and soaked it all in. Raising his chin and taking a deep breath, he washed over seven hundred years of history over his palate.

Admiration for the human spirit anchored his boots to the floor. He became as still as the row of towering statues which formed the King's Screen – fifteen stone figures of English kings from William the Conqueror down to Henry VI, carved in the 15th

Century. Immortality of a different kind than becoming a vampire, but destined to stand many hundreds of years more.

A sense of calm sank into his bones and Julian stopped breathing. The dust motes in the air stroked over his skin and he enjoyed a moment of transcendent peace.

A distant noise echoed, bouncing from the stained-glass windows and Julian slowly reanimated. Renewed determination sat heavy in his chest and with a measured stride, he followed the noise, passed beneath the central tower and headed towards the chapter house – the venue of the summit meeting.

In the vestibule, Principal Tavish stood with his hands behind his back and his head cocked to one side. His red hair burnished in the candlelight and the ghoulish shadows cast over his face could not disguise the warmth in his wide grin. "I thought I heard you enter. Welcome." Inspecting Julian's dirt speckled shirt and the coat hanging over his arm, the principal said, "Preparing for battle, I see."

The raised eyebrow of the Scottish principal made Julian laugh. "I do hope words will be the only weapons I encounter, but a tough skin in a literal sense can only be a good thing."

Pulling the garment from his companion's arm, Tavish shook off the grit and held it out.

Julian obligingly shrugged into the coat and submitted to the dusting down Tavish moved on to.

"I hear the London Hive lost Councilor Serge." Tavish's lips twitched. "Och, laddie, that'll neh do."

"I can't deny Glascarnoch did a better job as custodian than we did, my friend." Julian wagged a finger. "Keep your eyes open for a one-armed seventy-year-old stowaway when you return. It could be he is missing his old lodgings."

Tavish shook his head. "I dinna ken, a cell in the coldest place on earth is not something to yen fer."

Sharing a chuckle, Julian slapped Tavish on the shoulder. "Into battle, my friend, let's go."

On the threshold, the pair paused and scanned the large octagonal chamber. The windows ranging across the upper level flooded the chapter with light in the daytime. It would act as a countdown clock for this meeting. If a whole night could not bring a consensus of opinion, then Julian's cause was lost. *No pressure, then.*

The vampires inside were dotted around the perimeter, alliances and grudges clearly defined. Just inside the doorway, the four strong party from the Cardiff Hive were deep in conversation, their dark heads bent as if studying a map laid out on the ground at their feet.

At a wary distance, the York Hive representatives clustered together; four vampires Julian knew only as a list of names, but could not put faces to. Principal Edward had rounded up his jurors and a core medical team.

In contrast, close beside them, both Tavish's jurors exuded patient relaxation. Two small figures beside the pair were strangers to Julian. He nudged Tavish who instantly supplied, "Our doctor, Jock, and blood clerk, Donal."

Just inside the door, Captain Hugh was a welcome sight. *I have a wingman, at least.*

"Have you seen Glynn?" asked Hugh in a clipped low tone.

"Not exactly, but you got him here, and that's what matters."

"The man is as slippery as a greased pig." Hugh growled deep inside his throat.

"He can't avoid us forever." With a grim smile, Julian inspected the gathering. "We need Principal Edward, and then we can start preparing the ground."

As if saying his name cast a spell, the towering principal of the north hive swept into the chamber. "Gentlemen, welcome, it's an honor to host the first hive summit in decades. Take a seat, and I shall yield the floor to Principal Julian." With an expansive wave of a large hand, he said, "Please, be seated."

The throng drifted forward, choosing places at the black oak table which reflected the octagonal shape of the chapter. Church councils had gathered here for centuries in human times, but Julian felt sure the table was Principal Edward's contribution.

A golden stake pierced the center of the polished surface and cradled in a cup at the top, sat a crystal orb the size of a tennis ball. It glinted whenever the moon broke through the clouds. The metal stalk cast a barely detectable shadow, but that would change when dawn approached.

Julian and Hugh chose their seats.

"Firstly, thank you for answering the call. Unfortunately, we have to wait until Principal Glynn graces us with his presence," said Julian, irritation showing in his fierce expression.

"He will be here, directly," said Edward.

Julian shot a sharp glance at his fellow principal, and Edward grinned. "I pulled rank on our friend. As principal of the York Hive, grave sleep hospitality is at my discretion. Glynn has slept long enough."

Hugh and Julian exchanged smug glances in the moments before clipped footsteps echoed through the cathedral and Glynn appeared in the doorway. Shadowed figures behind him hung back in the vestibule, but clearly, the principal had an escort.

"Excellent, gentlemen, we are all present." Edward waved at Glynn to join his seated jurors and medical representative. "Forgive the rudeness, but the night is passing so we will forgo introductions, save to say, all the hive principals are in attendance."

A motionless black clad vampire standing at a crook in the octagonal wall nodded when Edward looked his way. A scribe to document the exchanges elevated this to a summit meeting. The vampires would memorize every word and recall arguments, but if the meeting became unruly, the scribe's impartial interpretation held most weight.

"Where are the London jurors?" asked Glynn. His dilated pupils made his usual sharp blue gaze appear unhinged and the body tremors he couldn't quite suppress bore witness to the rude awakening from grave sleep.

Julian noticed dried pink fluid crusting along a line gouged into Glynn's neck and wondered about the fight that must have broken out. Vampires had been known to die if they disturbed a sleeper whose murdering psychopath was on the loose while refreshing that brain center. *The blood dispensary attendant must have had reinforcements.* Realizing Glynn was still waiting, Julian focused on the other principal's tight expression.

"I know it breaks with protocol, but urgent matters kept them in London. These are dark times."

"I don't see why the London Hive can play fast and loose with proto-"

"Your objection is noted Principal Glynn, but let us give Principal Julian some latitude and hear what he has to say."

"Britain is facing an attack."

Clothes rustled as members of the gathering shuffled in their seats.

"Attack? I find that hard to believe." Glynn's darkened gaze glowed like frost gray coal embers. His fingers shook as he scraped his dark hair back from his face. The gray pallor to his skin took on a jaundiced tinge in the near darkness.

Taking a deep breath, Julian rested back in his seat and asked in a conversational tone, "Ferals. When the Midland Hive collapsed, what happened?"

"Glascarnoch lost some big cats in the safari park north of Hadrian's Wall, but a hunting party sounded the alert. The ferals never reached the Antonine boundary."

"Midland Hive ferals slaughtered their human stock before they drifted across country," said Edward. As their nearest neighbor, Principal Edward had secured the area and offered the 'sane' vampires places within the York Hive.

"How long did it take to track and dispose of the ferals?" asked Julian. Detachment made the termination of their brethren less horrible, but the bottom line was, anyone sitting in this room could become feral if human blood dried up and their brain centers could not be hydrated. *They were a version of us.*

"Three days," said Edward.

"Two," said Tavish.

"And the Cardiff Hive? Did any ferals reach Wales?" asked Julian.

The Welsh principal sat stone still, despite Julian's probing glare, defiantly drumming the nails of one hand on the polished wood. His other hand was paler and shook minutely.

A Welsh juror cleared his throat. "We lost two guardsmen out on patrol before we realized the cause, but snipers took out the ferals roaming around the city walls with headshots. But this was over a year ago. Why does it matter?" The juror bravely ignored his principal, as Glynn's stare bored a hole into the side of his head.

"Juror-?" Julian waited.

"Cedric Hawkes, I'm a surgeon, too." The vampire nodded, his angular face softening with a smile.

"I've heard of you. Doctor Connor thinks-"

A harsh grunt from Glynn drew everyone's attention. "Why *is* Doctor Connor not here? Urgent matters keeping him, too?"

Julian was beginning to wish Glynn had stayed in the sarcophagus and he shot Tavish an eye-rolling look.

Laying his hands flat on the table top, Julian took a deep breath. "Ferals are coming. No," He silenced the rustle of activity with an upraised hand. "Not just the number of an imploded hive. Thousands, many thousands."

The mutter of voices shot a series of questions at once and Julian registered each one and shuffled them into order before answering. "They are already on the move across Europe. They came from the east but are headed our way. Malachi of Egypt sent word – it was simpler than saying he transmitted a cry of help – and the super tanker nomad commander confirmed it. If they discover our human herds, they *will* come for them."

The thick silence was satisfying.

"This is a war council. Tavish, you have the safari park between Hadrian's and Antonine Walls. Fortify them. Move the human herd into the Glascarnoch fortress and shift the vampires outside. You are far north, but the North Sea is not so wide as to make you safe." Turning to Edward, Julian said, "York is a walled city, use that fortification well. The London Hive is moving our humans to a secure and easily guarded location."

Juror Donal slowly raised a hand, his gaze skittering to Tavish and back again. "On the journey down here, we found feral bodies."

"Where?" Julian beat Tavish to the punch.

"Beauty Bay, East coast. They were smashed up on the rocks."

"How do you know they were ferals?" asked Glynn with a skeptical lift of an eyebrow.

"They were ferals. Rotten teeth. Tears in the flesh around the mouth. Rancid stink."

"Things are worse than I thought. Only stragglers, but how long before they cross The Channel from Europe en-masse." Julian stood up. "Principal Glynn, Cardiff Castle is well fortified, get your humans off the farm. Use the air raid tunnels inside the castle walls, and the keep, but get them to safety."

Glynn rose to his feet and rocked gently from side to side. "Do you know what your Doctor Connor and his bitch did to me?" He lifted the chalk white hand up and when he moved his fingers, the piercing sound of grating glass screeched through the air.

"You are lucky Juror Cedric saved the hand." Julian took a guess and knew he was right when the young vampire nodded. "Do your damn job and stop thinking about yourself." In a comet trail of blurred movement, Julian whipped around the table and grabbed Glynn by the shirtfront. "And if you call Rebekah a bitch again you'll lose the other hand."

Every vampire in the room froze, the sigh of expelled breath filling the chamber.

Glynn swallowed noisily and croaked, "Understood."

Julian withdrew slowly and unclenched his fist. "This is war, Principal Glynn, and we must all pull together. Forget old rivalries, they don't matter."

Principal Tavish made his way smoothly around the table and fixed a sober look on the Welsh principal.

"Blood allocations and rolling out the blood substitute program are issues for other days and other meetings, it is clear we have imminent danger to address, first." Looking at Julian, Tavish asked, "Is Doctor Connor on the front line?"

"Yes, he has sailed on a rescue mission and is checking out the enemy force. We are battening down the hatches and locking down our humans. To win the battle we need more information."

"I understand." Glynn adjusted his sleeve cuffs, his rescued hand less nimble and again making the crackle of grinding glass.

Julian had no idea what Glynn had done to provoke Rebekah, but then, Connor's return from Cardiff had been a call to arms. *Whatever happened, I bet she had just cause.* Refocusing on the task, he said, "I need to get back to London. If feral bodies are washing up on the south coast, I need to know about it."

Retracing his steps more slowly, Julian caught Sergeant Hugh's eye. "Feed yourself and collect vials for my use. We can make London before dawn, if we go now."

As Hugh raised his eyebrows, nodded and swung away to leave the room, a loud grunt from behind made Julian freeze. A shadow oozed over the floor at his feet, the hackles on the back of his neck rose and he whipped around.

In the mid-act of leaping up onto the table, Principal Glynn towered overhead. Tavish and Edward were both in full flight and the scene unfolded in slow motion.

Rushing forward, Glynn scooped the crystal stone from its cradle. Swinging his arm back, he stared down at Julian with crazed menace, a snarl distorting his features.

Tavish dived forward, tearing a hole in the cloak of the fast-moving Glynn. Edward, the tallest of the three, vaulted up onto the table behind the Welsh principal and made a grab for the hand wielding the stone.

Julian, calculating the force and time he had left before his skull would be cracked open, pulled the copper-colored pebble from his pocket. With a flick of the wrist, he launched the stone upward to where Glynn would be in two seconds time.

Glynn froze in a comic overarm bowling stance as the pebble lodged in his throat with a wet thump. He grunted, spat shattered tooth enamel into the air, and the crystal orb fell from his slack grasp onto the table with a crack and rolled away. Glynn dropped to his knees, the eyes in his shocked face fixed on Julian for a moment before his head flopped forward. From where he stood behind Glynn, Edward planted his feet wide, and yanked the fallen principal's head up by the hair.

"Are you okay, Julian?" asked Edward.

Julian stared into the dilated pupils of Glynn's eyes, noticed the tremor scuttling through the principal's body, and said, "Send him back for grave sleep. I think we must accept some of the blame for this."

Tavish raised an eyebrow. "Generous."

Leaping nimbly up onto the table beside Glynn, Julian thumped him on the back and caught the pebble as it shot out through the toothless gap in the principal's mouth. Drying it on his sleeve, he dropped it back into his coat pocket.

"Not that generous. Strip him of his title." Julian swung back down, scanned the row of stunned onlookers, and honed in on Juror Cedric Hawkes. "Doctor Connor thinks highly of you, Juror Cedric, you will be acting principal with immediate effect."

Catching sight of Hugh framed in the doorway, Julian laughed harshly. "Back to our original plan, Sergeant, let's get going."

As the pair ramped up speed and headed towards the blood dispensary, both pulled on thick gloves. "We might still make it back before dawn," said Hugh.

"We've played the shadow hopping game before, we'll *have* to get back. Moving the humans into Storage Facility Eight is the top priority."

Chapter 19

Rebekah smiled encouragingly at the line of trudging humans even though she felt impatient with the slow progress. The forest at night was alive with movement to her preternatural sight – the flapping wings of insects scattered a myriad of colors into the air, moths blending into tree trunks stood out like black spots on a Dalmatian's coat and the reflective eyes of rabbits flashed like car headlamps. There was plenty of light to see by, unless you were human, soaked through, and dog tired.

Along the line of eighteen humans, clusters formed, like knots in a string. The strongest in the group were armed and in single file, while the rest supported each other in huddles.

Uncle Harry was swamped by his wax jacket and even the thick sweaters beneath it couldn't hide the angular lines of his bony shoulders.

Rebekah stayed close to offer a helping hand whenever he struggled to pull his boots from swampy holes in the woodland floor.

The renewed downpour glistened on the bark as rain ran down the channels in the tree trunks. In a macabre reflection, rivulets of water also poured down over vampire faces as they traveled bare-headed and unbowed by the icy water. Greg and Rebekah scanned the undergrowth for danger and listened for their fast-moving brethren. No one would be allowed to get near without identifying themselves.

When Greg passed close by, he muttered, "If ferals are around, we'll smell them."

Rebekah nodded grimly, dashing forward to catch Harry by the elbow as he stumbled.

The old man hissed through clenched teeth and grimaced.

"Sorry," muttered Rebekah, easing her grip where the bone fibers creaked beneath her fingers. The smell of blood made her nasal lining tingle as bruising throbbed beneath the old man's skin.

Seth appeared out of the darkness like a silent specter. The whites of his eyes flashed in his camouflage painted features as he darted a look from Harry to Rebekah and back again. "I got you, old fella," Seth murmured, "The lass don't know her own strength, eh?"

As Harry shifted his weight onto Seth's solid arm, Rebekah mouthed a silent 'thank you', and watched the pair move away, swaying gently from side to side like drunken buddies returning from a pub crawl session. Harry's hawking cough fractured the night air and Rebekah closed her eyes. *He will make it.* But in the few hours she had been around him, the wheezing rattle deep inside his lungs had begun to haunt her.

The grim reality of the graveyard at the tree-dwellers camp played on her mind. *Would Harry have been the next inhabitant? When we get to the eco-shelter, I'll make sure he gets a physical and the medicines he needs.*

Satisfied that, no matter what, she would talk him into it, Rebekah doubled back to make sure there were no stragglers.

A keening noise erupted from up ahead and hoarse human shouts jerked both Rebekah and Greg into action. It sounded like an injured animal. The loud click of a weapon being cocked reverberated beneath the canopy and, taking the most direct path through the trees, Rebekah lost sight of Greg as she crashed into three solid trunks, grinding lumps of bark from the rough surface as her dense bulk won the battle of attrition.

A gunshot exploded and Rebekah swore. "Dammit, what the Hell is going on?"

Her vampire brain went into overdrive as the commotion came into view. Greg held the barrel of a gun which was pointed at his chest. The human on the trigger end was as white as a vampire, their wide-eyed stare framed pupils that had eaten away the iris to the thinnest thread of blue.

The human man, thin and grubby, but still one of the healthier in the group, muttered, "Sorry, sorry, sorry."

Rebekah skidded to a stop beside Greg and ran her hands quickly over his hunched shoulders and chest. Sure enough, she found a hole burned in the front of his combat jacket. The crater she felt crumbled beneath the pressure of her probing fingertips.

Absently, she said, "You know we're not indestructible, right?"

Greg laughed harshly. "It was either me or him."

Looking back over Greg's shoulder, she saw a young man sitting on his backside in the undergrowth, entangled in a patch of brambles. Pearls of blood running in lines down one cheek made the terrified expression on the white face peering up from the darkness more stark.

"What happened?"

A slight woman rushed into view, moving human fast, and Rebekah smiled. At times like these, she realized how futile human efforts to outwit vampires truly were.

"It was me or let the bullet hit the boy," grumbled Greg, gingerly taking in deeper breaths to feel where the bullet had lodged. Jerking a chin towards the thin man who still held the gun, but had aimed it towards the ground, Greg said, "Tension is getting to everyone. He thought it was an animal launching an attack."

"I didn't see Jeff down there. I'm sorry, sorry. I didn't..."

Greg straightened at last, approached the shocked man carefully and held out a hand. "No harm done, but I'll hold onto the gun, eh?"

The man sagged with relief as he laid the pistol in Greg's palm.

The slight woman struggled to release Jeff from where he had fallen into the hole beneath the brambles, and the odor of blood pluming into the air focused both vampires on their stumbling progress.

Uncle Harry appeared, shrugged out of a small backpack and dropped to his knee. He undid the zipper, flipped it open and pulled out a bundle of Band-Aid dressings and an antiseptic spray.

"The smell of blood could draw attention," muttered Greg as he shoved the pistol into his belt. He planted a boot beside the entangled Jeff, plunged his hands into the bank of brambles and pulled them aside. The thorns made white scratches over even Greg's hard flesh.

Both the humans bled from deep gouges, but the woman gripped Jeff's hand and pulled him to his feet. The hem of his combat pants tore as he got a foot hold on safer ground and dragged his other leg out.

Sitting side by side, the injured pair pushed up their jacket sleeves and submitted to Harry's efficient first aid session where fifteen Band-Aid strips covered the wounds and antiseptic masked the smell of human blood.

"Done," muttered Harry, quickly repacking and hoisting the medical kit onto his back. Pulling his woolen cap lower over his walnut shrunken features, Harry eyed the gathering as if to say, 'What are we waiting for?'

Impulsively landing a kiss on the old man's cheek, Rebekah grinned. "Let's go."

The rest of the humans had regrouped, following the survival instinct of sticking together.

Jeff, getting back to his feet, asked, "How much further?"

He and many of the others had never been outside the tree-dwellers hunting region, and some had never even left the encampment before.

Scanning the row of grubby faces, Rebekah tuned into the nervous tension vibrating through their muscle fibers like a plucked guitar string. Smiling, she answered, "About two more miles."

When Seth went to speak, Rebekah shot him a look that snapped his jaw shut. She was lying, but if it raised spirits, then that was the vibe she was after.

Seth nudged Adam and shared a rueful grin. In a low gruff voice, the Marine said, "Homeward stretch guys, load up."

The line formed again and Rebekah matched her step to Harry's, asking casually, "Can I carry that backpack?"

A sharp look from beneath gray bushy eyebrows gave his answer and she chuckled. *Same old Harry. Stubborn.* But that was the fighting spirit she owed her life to as a kid.

Jeff and his female companion limped less as they acclimatized to the soreness of their gashed skin, and the party settled into a trudging march. Slow and steady reduced the pheromone cloud of sweat, and made breathing a few notes quieter, so Rebekah relaxed.

◇◇◇

Frank stood on the asphalt watching the last of the trucks trundle away down the road. The vampire at the wheel took the 'drive with care' edict to the extreme, and Frank doubted the convoy would travel at more than twenty-five miles an hour. But that was still much faster than the humans could walk, not to mention safer.

The human community was close knit and after an initial tussle even Leizle caved, packed up her things, hiked out to the road, and settled beneath the tented canvas cover of the flatbed truck.

Phase one, complete. As if waving off relatives, Frank stood on the road, boots planted at hip distance, and followed their progress with a narrowed gaze until they were out of sight.

I think the girl trusts me. That thought made him grin. His orders were to stay at the eco-shelter and wait for the 'tree-dwellers' to arrive.

Whipping back across the meadow, he re-entered the gash in the hillside and inspected the supplies and equipment piled up ready to load onto the next wave of lorries. Poking out of a partly closed zipper was a threadbare stuffed toy. Pulling it through the gap, Frank put it to his nose and inhaled deeply. Shuffling through his catalogue of human scents, he laughed. The gray bear belonged to a stout, thick necked man. *Who would've thought?* Dropping the bear onto the packed earth floor, he ground it beneath his boot until white stuffing erupted.

Turning around and pulling two vials of human blood from his coat pocket, he flipped the lids and downed the contents. He settled against the curved upright wall at the entrance and sank into vampire stillness. Relaxation descended like a cloak, his eyelids drooping to half-mast as the meditative state of revival sleep crept through that brain center.

When he eventually stirred and raised his eyes to the heavens, where the palest pink wisps of dawn, although still many hours away, bled into the sky. Cocking his head, he listened, hoping to hear the heavy footed approach of humans. He was fed-up of waiting.

On impulse, from another rucksack, he pulled out a combat jacket and inspected the olive-green garment. Shedding his mud stiffened surcoat, he put on the camouflage jacket and grinned.

Back at the archway, he dropped low and scanned the feathery surface of the meadow. The path the human group had taken out to the trucks was a flattened swathe, but he was looking for the passing of two humans and two vampires – Rebekah's group.

He walked ten yards out and dropped to his haunches again. *Is that them? I've got nothing to lose.* Striding in a direction dotted with the odd clump of crushed grass, he quickly reached the tree-line of the forest. Scuff marks in the mulch beneath the thick canopy showed where the pair of humans had stopped. Scanning the undergrowth as he walked, Frank easily tracked the group deeper into the forest until he heard a gunshot. *What the Hell was that?* Turning slowly on his heel, he switched his attention to assessing for other dangers. *Did they see a feral?* But when he inhaled deeply, there was no telltale rancid rotting aroma to confirm that.

Undecided, Frank waited and stopped breathing when he saw the labored progress of two human men. Their faces were downturned as they picked out the safest path through the stony ground. Behind them, more appeared. Their dark clothing melded the group into a multi-headed creature which swayed left and right as they walked.

Frank counted fifteen, before he spotted a thick-set male vampire. *That must be Greg.* Principal Julian had told Frank to wait at the eco-shelter and surprising the group could mean trouble. For the first time, he wondered if he had made a mistake. Easing back into the shadows, he waited until they had passed him by, having decided to circle back and meet the group at the end of their journey.

A fair-haired female vampire strolled slowly into view, keeping pace with an elderly man, and Frank became mesmerized.

Her skin glowed like polished pearl and every angle of her body exuded grace.

As she walked past, he ran his hand over his jaw, a jolt of tension jerking his muscles tight when her head shot around and her dark brown eyes bored into his.

Damn.

She dived off the path towards him. Frank moved one foot, but she became a blur too fast to track and in a nanosecond had rammed him back against a tree trunk. The iron rod of her forearm crushed his windpipe until his neck creaked. The message was clear; if the newcomer made a move he would die. He managed a wry grin of surrender. Even if he could land a counter blow, her 'new vampire' strength was in full evidence. *I'm outgunned.*

"Greg," she hissed, above the spectrum of human hearing.

Frank remained stone still. His open hands framed his head in capitulation but his sharp gaze steadily inspected the female vampire.

"Who are you?" she asked, as Greg arrived at her side.

Even through a compressed windpipe, he croaked, "Sergeant Frank."

"That means nothing to us. *Who* are you?" Greg surveyed the intruder's clothing. "Not a guardsman, so, you're not here as a friend."

Frank flapped his hands, begging for space to speak.

Rebekah eased the pressure and glared into his face. "Start talking."

"Principal Julian sent me." Frank was bending the truth, but only a little.

"Really?" Rebekah's lip curled. Her brown eyes melted to glittering jet as she shoved her arm back into Frank's neck and leaned in hard.

"Le-" he croaked.

She eased off again.

"Leizle,' he rasped. "The principal said look for a fiery redhead. Told me to make sure she went with the others. He said she'd not want to leave without Rebekah." Now he had their attention he barreled onward. "That's you, isn't it?"

"It looks like Julian did sent him," Greg murmured.

"There's been a change of plan. All human refugees must go to the siphoning sheds, now. I have to take you there. Your human habitat is empty."

Rebekah looked at Greg, and then both studied the huddled group of humans staring wide-eyed at the vampire standoff. Seth and Adam were at the front, and Seth swung his mace from side to side.

"That's over twenty miles. They won't make it," said Greg.

"The trucks are returning to the eco-shelter to load up the equipment and stores. If we go now, they can hitch a ride."

As if Frank wasn't right there listening, Rebekah said, "Do we trust him? We could snap his arms, just to make sure."

Frank's admiration grew. He wasn't worried. From what he knew of the morally upstanding Doctor Connor, his woman would be cut from the same cloth.

"Julian might be pissed. If he sent this guy, then he will expect to see him back in one piece." Greg looked Frank up and down. "He looks useful in a fight."

"Okay." Rebekah swung around and returned to where Harry waited. Offering her arm, she started walking as if Frank no longer existed.

"Nice," Frank muttered.

Grabbing the front of his jacket and pulling him away from the tree, Greg shoved Frank in the back until he started walking. "Think yourself lucky. Now, move it."

Chapter 20

Birdsong accompanied the rumbling noise of trucks trundling towards the approach road to the human farm. The dark green and black vehicles blended in with the mottled texture of the distant tree-line. Julian stood at the outer perimeter gate, shading his eyes with a hand as he watched them emerge and trickle across the open grassland like a line of box shaped ants.

The glow from the towering floodlights transformed Julian's blond hair into burnished gold. He projected the aura of an Emperor and every line of his tense body exuded contained power.

"I don't think they could drive any slower without stalling the damned engines," Julian muttered, casting a sarcastic look at Captain Hugh.

The suspension groaned as the vehicles rocked through potholes and bumped over the meadow until they reached the ribbon of cracking asphalt.

"That's a good sign," said Hugh, "it means there are humans inside and not just supplies."

"We must resurface this road," Julian said, absently. Focusing on something mundane felt good for a brief moment. "I'll be happier when I see they are safe, nonetheless."

On the concrete pathway behind him, the scuff of human footsteps had been drawing closer for the last ten minutes. When Julian knew their owner was only twenty yards away, he turned around. Her scent rode on the breeze and, if *his* hair was golden, Leizle's rich dark chestnut mane became molten copper as she moved out of the shadow and into the pool of light.

She ran forward and threw herself at Julian. His face lit up with joy as he caught her and spun her around, before setting her carefully back onto her feet. His long white finger tilted her chin and he kissed her chastely. Leizle wound her arms around his neck and dipped her tongue into his mouth, tasting him and smiling against his hard set features. He always froze when she surprised him, reining in his desire for fear of hurting her.

She released him and dropped from her tiptoes back down to the ground and batted her eyelashes.

"Minx," he murmured as he traced a finger along her cheek and looped a silken strand of titian hair behind her ear.

"Is she here? Is this them?" Leizle took the half dozen steps to where Hugh stood, politely gazing forward.

Julian took her hand and rubbed his thumb in circles over her skin. "Hopefully, it *is* them." The muscle in his jawline twitching betrayed the tension he felt. The clock was ticking. Without looking at Leizle, Julian said, "If it's not them, then you, Thomas and Oscar are leaving in the next convoy. No argument."

Her stubborn silence earned her a glowering look. "It *is* them," she said.

The floodlight glare glinting on the windshield of the vehicles turned the glass into mirrors, but suddenly, from a lowered side window, a female hand was raised in a salute.

Leizle hopped from foot to foot, bouncing more when the passenger door of the lead truck flew open, and Rebekah jumped from the moving vehicle to run the remaining hundred yards with a huge smile on her face.

"Thank God, you're here." Leizle's tearful relief as she gripped Rebekah in a tight hug brought it home to Julian that he wasn't the only one worrying.

When Leizle reluctantly released her, Rebekah fixed Julian with a probing look. "Who is this guy?" The glance she shot back at the slowly approaching truck was loaded with tension.

"Sergeant Frank? He was the squad leader on guard duty at Councilor Serge's house. Useful man."

"He's one of the good guys, then? Does Connor agree?" It was clear by her frown that Rebekah reserved judgement.

"Connor hasn't met him, yet, but he will agree, I'm sure, when he gets back to London."

Rebekah eased her shoulders and visibly relaxed. "Oscar, Evie, Thomas and the rest are all okay?" She smiled at Leizle as she spoke, but then the smile faltered. "What are you all doing here at the gates? Is something going down?"

Stepping aside as the trucks finally arrived in the yard, Julian drew Leizle with him. The convoy rumbled past and Hugh closed the gates and clicked the padlock shut. The group walked along on the grass verge, making their way to the inner perimeter entrance which Hugh had already darted ahead to open. Leizle pulled the neckline of her sweater up over her mouth and nose, coughing at the cloud of dust kicked up in the wake of the crawling vehicles.

With a casual smile at Leizle, Julian lowered his voice to where she couldn't hear, and with preternatural speed, said, "Things are moving fast. This is only a waypoint for the tree-dwellers. The siphoning sheds aren't robust enough for the danger we could be facing."

Struggling to move so slowly when the sense of danger urged her to react, Rebekah shot back. "The news from the north was bad?"

"Ferals are washing up on the Scottish coast. It is starting."

The group entered the human compound where the distant siphoning sheds glowed like gigantic silver boxes. The doors of four sheds were shut, the guards outside the entrances creating a solid wall of vampire flesh.

"How long have we got?"

"I don't know. Connor and Malachi will know more, but I don't think we should wait for them to return." Julian frowned, his green eyes were dim.

"They will return." Rebekah lifted her chin and glared at him until he chuckled.

"You're right. Connor has been a pain in the butt for a hundred years, he'll be back."

"What's the plan? I assume you have one?"

The line of guards outside siphoning shed number one parted as if Julian activated a force-field which drove them back. The hefty metal door groaned as he pulled it open, ushered Leizle in ahead, and let it clunk shut.

"I know you two are plotting," Leizle threw over her shoulder. "I might be human, but I'm not stupid."

Exchanging glances, Rebekah shrugged. "She's *your* girl."

"And your friend." Stopping suddenly, he waited for Rebekah to retrace the steps she had taken, then murmured, "Make sure she goes. Threaten her, bribe her, guilt trip her, but make sure she goes in the trucks."

Rebekah nodded slowly.

The outer door opened again and the tall dark figure of Frank filled the reception space as he moved a chunk of metal with his boot to wedge the door open. When he was done and met Julian's eye, the calm he exuded was like oil poured on choppy waters.

"Sergeant, well done on bringing them in, and evacuating the eco-shelter. I'm sure it was a challenge," said Julian.

"Yes, sir." Clasping his hands behind his back, the sergeant moved aside to stand against a wall.

The sound of human feet grew louder as the grimy, exhausted tree-dweller community shuffled into view. Uncle Harry walked in under his own steam, but with a steadying hand from Seth hovering nearby.

"Harry, it's good to see you," said Julian. The old man looked frailer than he expected. Three years in the tree-dwellers camp had aged him by a decade. Inhaling and running the human odor over his palette, Julian assessed the old man's pH and iron levels in his blood. Tuning into the weak heartbeat, he hid his sadness with a smile. *It is good Rebekah and Harry have made peace.* Harry had found it almost impossible to accept Connor – vampires were the enemy – but he was an intelligent man and Rebekah owed her life to Connor's protection. The old man was trying to make amends.

"I'm glad to see you, too." Holding out a thin veiny hand, Harry said, "Thank you. You didn't have to extend your protection to us, so, thank you."

Releasing Harry from a brief gentle handshake, Julian chuckled. "Rebekah and Connor would have strung me up if I forgot about you, you know that."

Harry pulled the knitted hat from his head and rubbed his fingers over sweat-stained white hair. "I don't suppose you have showers here?" he asked, inspecting his dirt ingrained nails and touching the visible grit dried into the folds of his neck.

The straggling line of humans slowed and the tired group stood silently waiting. Julian raised a hand to attract the attention of a vampire porter who appeared further down the hall. "Make sure they have everything they need." Looking down at Harry again, Julian said, "This is just a stepping stone, I'm afraid. Get cleaned up then assemble in the main shed. We're moving you all out."

"Where are we going?" Leizle's defiant expression did not bode well.

Rebekah raised an eyebrow. "Good question."

"The storage facility."

Rebekah's jaw dropped but she held back the flood of questions. Like parents not wanting to argue in front of the children, only her sharp look revealed the concerns racing around in her mind.

"Sergeant Frank will be with you." Julian stared at the tall motionless vampire, his half smile begging the sergeant to agree.

"I'll look after you, Leizle." With a rueful grin which showed ice white teeth, he said, "May I call you Leizle?"

"Okay."

"You, Oscar, Evie, Sandy, even Uncle Harry-" The sergeant paused, and Julian nodded. "You are all under my protection, so nothing will happen to you."

As Uncle Harry took small weary steps along the corridor, the sergeant followed, gathering up stragglers as he murmured reassurances and guided them to where hot water and showers waited.

"I wish I felt better," said Leizle. "With you, Rebekah and Connor all gone. Hell, we haven't seen Anthony in forever. I just wish someone we know could be looking out for us, but okay."

Slipping his arms around her and pulling her close until she looked up into his face, Julian dropped a kiss on her lips. "I'm sorry. Things will return to normal soon, but Frank will be there until they do." Locking eyes with Rebekah over the top of Leizle's fiery hair as she rested a cheek against his solid chest, he read the questions her clamped lips held back and nodded minutely.

The sound of truck tailgates clanging shut pierced the still air of early dawn.

"Go and reassure Uncle Harry, Red. There is no time to waste." With a calm smile, Julian stroked a fingertip down her cheek and turned her gently around.

When Leizle walked away, Rebekah frowned. "Storage Facility Eight? How will that work?"

Slowly, Julian said, "It has only one entrance and exit, has granite walls four feet thick and is easy to defend. It's the best place."

"And it's full of vampires, dehydrated ones, but still. And what happens if the vampires which aren't comatose get hungry?"

"The place is empty." Or should be, by now, thought Julian. Before Rebekah could ask, he said, "Brynmor, Isaac and Charles cleared it out with Captain Gerrard. The only vampires locked in with Harry, Leizle, and the rest will be Greg, the sergeant, Sampson, and you."

With a harsh laugh, Rebekah said, "Over my dead body. I'm waiting for Connor."

"It was worth a try," grinned Julian.

He headed out of the siphoning shed exit, and Rebekah kept pace. In the pearl gray light of dawn, the floodlights picked out the wisps of early morning mist rolling like toxic gas across the meadow.

A wailing sound made Julian freeze. Three pulsing bursts with a two second pause, on repeat, brought an end to the wait. "A ship in the estuary. It has to be Blake."

Sweeping over to the convoy of trucks, Julian put his head together with the knot of vampires dressed in the heavy cloaks, gloves, and thin leather face masks needed to continue working into the daylight hours.

Rebekah was already at the gate in the perimeter fence when he rejoined her. "What did you say," she asked as three vampires climbed up into the cabin of each waiting truck.

"They'll cut the engines and push the trucks when they near the storage facility. I don't want ferals to hear noise which will attract attention."

Scraping her hair back and flipping up the hood of her coat in readiness for the dash across country, Rebekah asked, "How long can they stay inside the storage facility?" She had been inside the tomb like structure, and for all that it was secure, clean air would be at a premium.

"The main door will be heavily guarded but remain open until the facility comes under attack, and the Elite Guard are patrolling the surrounding countryside. For now, we don't need to worry, so let's get going and find out if this is Connor returning."

Rushing through the gates side-by-side, the pair hit top vampire speed in harmony, skimming through the countryside and London streets as if the docks were magnets that pulled them in.

Chapter 21

The container ship rolled in the choppy water of the Thames Estuary and, even below deck in the cabin with Malachi, Connor knew they were no longer at sea.

Silas and Portia lay in an entangled embrace on a pile of cushions in one corner of the cabin. Portia snored gently, a sure sign that both chimpanzees no longer found Connor's presence stressful.

Mentor and protégé sat side by side on the hard metal floor. Their still faces and silence exuded relaxation, but each time a distant creak of a door opening echoed along the tunnel-like corridors, both vampires stopped breathing. Their telepathic exchange ebbed and flowed, and now the topic filling both their heads was the plan of action when the container ship berthed in London.

I'll head up on deck and commandeer a storage container to get you, Silas and Portia across to the quayside. Connor opened his eyes and muttered, "Once we pass through The Thames Barrier, I'll find Blake. He'll be on the bridge. "

Malachi nodded slowly.

It was clear that the chimps were the immediate problem. "Do you think Silas will let me carry him?"

Malachi glanced over to where the pair of chimps slept. Their deep breathing and slow thudding pulse rates made a relaxing soundtrack to the vampire conversation. "I'll feed from him when you go. That makes him drowsy."

A low rumble skittered through the shell of the massive hull, and Connor gracefully rose to his feet. "The Thames Barrier is being lowered." Holding Malachi's pearl-tinted cloudy gaze, he said, "If I'm not back within the hour, get yourselves up on deck and hide. When we get closer, you should be able to let Osiris and Seren know where to find you."

Without waiting for a reply, Connor removed the twisted hunk of metal braced against the door to hold it shut, and left. As he whipped away along the bulkhead compartment, he heard the metal piece clunk back into place. It was a crude early warning signal and in a last resort, a handy weapon. Connor had torn it from the metal panel he removed to create an escape route into the next cabin. The chaos would be like an Ealing comedy of revolving doors – nomads rushing in as Malachi rushed out through the hole in the wall.

Connor trusted Blake about as far as he could throw him and that would never change.

He found the captain up on the bridge. Closing the door against the squalling wind that tried to rip it from his hand, he nodded at Tyrone.

Blake faced out to sea, as if looking through the salt-streaked glass wall. He wore a long coat of thin supple leather and the hands he clasped behind his back were encased in gloves, already dressed for the daylight hours fast approaching.

Connor stopped beside him and scanned the lead-gray waters of the estuary.

The line of steel-shaped bonnets extended across the width of the river and the ship was lined up to pass between the central two, where vampire lookouts stood on top of the pair of massive arced shells. The barrier, built to control the tidal levels in the Thames, remained shut in times of conflict when the vampire hive was on 'red alert'.

"A feral attack is coming soon, I'm certain," muttered Connor.

Blake turned to face his visitor, the metal mask he wore glimmering in the early dawn light, and Connor wondered which artisan had fashioned the image – it was remarkably close to the striking features he remembered from before their fateful battle.

"I agree," said Tyrone.

"We'll be at the London Docklands soon. Malachi wants to move the chimps into a container for transport ashore before the nomads assemble on deck."

Phlegm in Blake's throat rattled and he turned away, as if to watch the Thames Barrier bonnets slide past. The calmer surface of the water beyond glittered as if strewn with splintered glass.

Connor looked at Tyrone. "What should I tell Malachi?"

"The Egyptian can take your chimps ashore, but we have a deal to conclude. Hera must be returned to me." Tyrone moved forward until Connor had to meet his eye as he relayed Blake's thoughts. "*You* will stay onboard until Principal Julian returns Hera." The interpreter frowned, his hard tone reflecting the force with which he received the telepathic communication.

Connor grinned, playing the game, focusing on Tyrone and resolutely ignoring the tall figure standing beside him. He couldn't tune out the saliva rattling in Blake's throat, but the captain couldn't know that. "I don't mean to be flippant, but you know where I live. It's not as though I'm going anywhere. I have a feral attack to defeat, and I'm afraid the principal doesn't know where Hera is. Only one person knows that, and he will only tell me. It is my life insurance policy, if you will."

Blake shrugged. "Very well. Go. As you say, I know where you can be found."

Frowning, Connor left the bridge. As he descended through the deck levels in the ship, his tight muscles made his stride jerky. *That was too easy.* But if Blake is hatching a plot, there was nothing he could do until the captain made his move.

When Connor opened the door to Malachi's cabin, the old Egyptian was dressed for travel. His flowing linen robes skimmed the floor, and his pearlescent gaze glowed from beneath his cowl hood. Portia sat on her haunches stroking Silas' fur. The adolescent chimp's eyes were half closed, as if his mother's touch hypnotized him. The spark of intellect in Portia's stare when she looked at Connor made him pause mid-step. It was as if she knew what was in store for her child, somehow, and was giving her permission. *Or am I being fanciful?*

Portia ambled over to Malachi's side, her padded knuckles making a soft whisper as they brushed the metal floor.

Malachi held out a cotton sheet. "Make a sling from this and wrap Silas up in it."

With quick fluid movements, Connor shrugged out of his greatcoat. He folded the fabric to make the sling, eased the dozing youngster into it and, with Malachi's help, tied the corners around his waist and over one shoulder until Silas was cradled snuggly into his chest, leaving both Connor's arms free. Slipping the coat back on, he shielded the sleepy chimp with the flaps of fabric, and jerked his chin at Malachi. "Let's go."

The short time Connor had spent onboard as a nomad crew member might be years ago, but he remembered the unloading drill very well. The crew assembled below deck in the mess hall – although it was now just an open space without tables, chairs or counters, as vampires did not 'dine'.

Once the ship docked, the crew would split into their teams of four and prepare containers for unloading.

Connor led the way through the lower storage compartments. Human sweat plumed from unwashed laundry stored in huge hampers. Others contained the dried food humans had to live on when at sea. Weaving a path through the stacked crates, Connor ran to the top of the open metal stairway to where daylight bled in around the edges of a riveted door panel. He brushed his hair forward to cover his forehead, tucked his chin down, opened the door with a gloved hand and walked out onto the deck. Running across to the nearest container, Connor stopped in the shade, with his back pressed to its ridged metal side until Malachi joined him.

The muscle in Connor's jaw ticked as he looked around at the seemingly endless run of metal boxes, each one dull with flaking paint.

The brisk wind whipping along the gap between the rows of containers whistled, but Malachi's thoughts came through loud and clear. *The container is not a good plan.*

Connor could not agree more. The last time he hitched a ride inside one, Blake lost his face. The container ship's engine cut, and the huge vessel drifted closer to the quayside.

Can you carry Portia? Connor stared hard at Malachi until he nodded. *Okay, head to the stern.* Connor set off at a silent run, crouching low so Silas felt safe. He powered on, knowing Malachi may look frail but had strength equal to his protégé. His paper-thin cracked skin was literally the wear and tear of sleeping below the Egyptian sands two thousand years ago.

The internal Malachi was a young man of twenty.

Connor reached the high metal wall at the stern and sidestepped around to the shore side of the vessel and peered along the gap between the containers, which extended a hundred yards or so, to confirm they were alone.

Portia clung to Malachi's side and the elderly vampire clamped his arm around the chimp's solid body. With his free hand, he tugged Connor's coat sleeve and jabbed a bony finger, to show he understood.

Putting his head above the guardrail, Connor studied the flotilla of small boats whipping across the divide between the tanker and the dock, as the London Hive crew guided the ship to its berthing point. He watched as the quayside slide into view. In the pink glow of dawn, he picked out the dark silhouettes of guardsmen lining the causeway and more, high up on the embankment from where they could launch an attack on the tanker crew, if needed.

At the top of the lookout tower, Julian, Gerrard and Rebekah stood. Even from the ship, Connor could read tension in Rebekah's stance. Her hands gripped the metal frame of the tower and her head scanned left and right along the length of the vessel, as she searched for him.

The clattering noise of hatch doors in the hull dropping open galvanized Connor into action. Grabbing the top rung of the side rail in one hand, holding Silas clamped tightly to his body with the other, he launched himself over the side and leapt across the divide. As he landed on the concrete below, to his left, he saw the scuttling beetle-like figures of the nomad mooring crew skitter down over the side of the vessel, intent on grabbing the mooring chains which fell out of the hatches. Waiting the nanosecond it took to hear Malachi land beside him, Connor took off at a crouched run towards the cover of the Docklands machinery graveyard – the resting place of outdated and rusted forklift trucks and contraptions vampires did not need.

Diving into a dark space between two trucks, Connor stopped. Portia arrived first, bounding into the gap and thudding into

Connor's shoulder. He rocked sideways to absorb the impact, for the chimp's sake. Malachi was close behind.

"We made it." Connor grinned. *Rebekah, we made it.* The joy he felt flood through him came from her thoughts as they rode the zip-wire of their psychic communication. Within seconds, she arrived beside him. Glancing past Connor at Malachi, she said, "I'm so glad you're-" When the chimp registered, Rebekah raised her eyebrows. "You have a tale to tell, I see."

Connor's bulky figure drew her eye and the gentle brown eyes of Silas blinked slowly as the young chimp peered out from beneath his coat.

"Let's get you to the council building," said Rebekah, landing a fleeting kiss on Connor's lips when he touched her cheek.

"We'll take them to the hospital. They'll be safe there for a while, and I might need my laboratory." Indicating Silas with a nod, Connor said, "This little chap is a hybrid. He could give us some answers. When Julian has finished here, tell him the feral threat is worse than I feared."

"Captain Hugh is back in London. He can act as an escort." Rebekah smiled. "But, Hell, I'm so damned happy to see you, my love."

Resting his forehead on hers, Connor ran his fingers into the silky blond hair at her nape. "I've missed you too, honey." He kissed her, running his tongue over her lip and sighing. When Silas' head nudged his chin, Connor chuckled against her mouth before releasing her, his gray eyes twinkling with relief and amusement.

"I'll send Hugh." Rebekah squeezed his fingers before reeling around and disappearing.

◇◇◇

Heading across the Kent countryside and back into London, Connor forced a direct path through the overgrown shrubs and hedges which had laid claim to the landscape, encroaching on the uncultivated rolling fields. Just as weeds and grass had shoved their way through the blacktop of roads and pathways like determined weightlifters, the peat and rich soil of the meadows and farmland were a breeding ground for thorny shrubs, tall hedges, and saplings.

With Silas clinging to her fur as if both chimps were fused together, Portia's ranging lope dictated the speed. Malachi brought up the rear.

Each time Connor made the journey in recent months, he noticed the undergrowth had grown denser as the expanding thickets choked the meadows. The world was changing. *I don't like it.* He had seen the rise of society – both human and vampire – throughout the 1900s, and seeing it all sink back into the primeval ooze made his flesh tighten with fear.

His usual reaction to feelings of impotence, was to leave a trail of devastation in his wake, but he had traveling companions to protect and even though the site of the attack at Port Siyad was thousands of miles away, he felt a shift in the atmosphere here in England, as if the sun was filtered through a shroud of menace. *The ferals are coming.* They could sweep across the country like a plague of locusts. Connor looked out over the green fields and tried not to imagine the horde crawling across the landscape.

Crashing through a dense patch of brambles, he tore his shirt and his hair became spiked with thorns and twigs, but he didn't care. The rescue mission to Egypt had done one thing; it brought the impending attack into sharp focus, but Great Britain's strength came from being an island nation. *And we have time to plan a defense.*

Captain Hugh swung in from the left, returning from another circuit of the surrounding area, scouting for *any* vampires, and his curt nod was a welcome signal. It was not only ferals who were dangerous, Councilor Serge had proved that. *And the wily fox is still out there somewhere... or dehydrating in a ditch.* Connor dared to hope.

Keeping Connor between himself and the mother chimpanzee, Hugh said, "All clear. I found Anthony and he's preparing a side ward in the surgical wing for the monkeys."

A grumble came from Malachi's throat, and Hugh said, "Sorry, chimpanzees."

"Well done, Captain." Connor brushed bark dust from his shoulders as Hugh slowed and matched his stride. "We'll use the side door of the hospital and keep their location a secret, for now."

The remainder of the journey was accomplished in silence. The fast breathing of a tiring Portia slowed the pace to a jog through the London suburbs. Connor scanned the darkened windows overlooking the streets, glad that Malachi had thought to give Portia his cape as a disguise as soon as the city buildings offered him enough shelter from the sun. Although, she resembled a distorted hunchback rather than a human or vampire.

The polished marble walls of the hospital reflected a grainy image of the oddly matched traveling companions.

Hugh sighed with relief when the black painted side door of the hospital drew closer.

Outside it, Connor knocked five times in the pattern shared with the vampires on his surgical team and the door opened.

Charles peered out of the dark interior. "Doctor Connor," said the short sandy-haired vampire. "It's so good to see you." He craned his neck to get a better look at the bundled up figure of Portia.

"Anthony has brought you up to speed, then?" Connor grinned.

"Oh, yes. These are strange times." Charles stepped back and ushered the group inside.

"Things will move too fast for explanations, so just trust me, hmm?" Connor fixed Charles with a probing stare.

"Understood." Charles nodded. "I'll take Malachi and the... refugees to the surgical ward."

"Malachi." Connor laid a hand on his old friend's shoulder. "Stay quiet, Charles will bring you some human blood so Silas can be rested." They both knew, when the time came, Connor would be taking samples from the young chimp to run tests.

Like scattered pebbles, the group rushed off in different directions. Hugh returned to update Julian and Gerrard at the council building. Charles escorted Malachi and the chimpanzees through a door which took them along a maintenance tunnel and into the surgical wing. Connor swung around and left by the door they had entered.

Running around to the front of the building and in through the thick glass doors of the hospital's main entrance, Connor jerked to a halt. *Where is everyone?* He scanned the slick waxed floor and the empty reception desk. The stagnant air carried no sign of recent movement; it tasted as thick as the smog he had experienced in his human youth. The Industrial Revolution was a time when coal fires burned in every home, belching pollution so dense that it earned the label 'pea soup fog'. It killed thousands of Londoners, but, in the velvet cloak of its darkness many other monsters thrived. Some human, but many were inhuman in every way. Jack the Ripper made one of the biggest dents in human consciousness, but he was a vampire who didn't just step over the line, he shattered the invisible wall between the species. As the London Principal, Julian had dealt out the sentence of death.

The human tabloids were left reporting his sudden disappearance, with all the confusion that had evoked. It took longer for working girls walking the streets to believe Jack had gone and his legend elevated him to notoriety.

When the pandemic hit, the humans destined for confinement on the farm discovered the true extent of vampire infiltration within their society with the speed of a hammer blow. *Although, we were always here in the shadows.*

Cocking his head, Connor pushed through the doors and into the corridor leading to the blood dispensary. Moving aside the stiff clear plastic sheet obscuring the entrance, he peered inside. The queues of vampires resembled a storage room full of dressed mannequins. There was no one on duty behind the counter at the front of the room. It made sense at last. They were waiting for Charles, Brynmor or Isaac to return.

Skimming along the corridors, Connor descended the stone staircase to the lowest level of the hospital. At the security door to his laboratory, he jabbed in the access code and entered. The decontamination chamber slowed his progress, but he exhaled deeply, clearing all the dust, pollen, and other contaminants from his lungs.

He stripped bare, entered the tiled airlock and hit the activation button. Mist plumed as scalding water was forced out of the holes in two walls and the ceiling, the force creating a smothering spray. Breathing in deeply, Connor felt the vapor tingle through his chest as it cleansed the inside of his airways.

The water stopped and when the door seals hissed as they released, Connor exited through the opposite door and dressed quickly in sterile green scrubs.

When he stepped into the laboratory, as expected, Brynmor was waiting, leaning back against the pristine white workbench, with his arms folded across his broad chest. The black wing of hair falling across his brow gleamed with blue-black highlights in the fluorescent light. In many ways, the two vampires could have been brothers.

Assessing the rows of simian blood samples, all labelled and arranged in date order, Connor grunted his appreciation. "News travels fast."

Running his fingertips along the row, Connor frowned.

"What is the plan? How can this fight the ferals?" asked Brynmor.

"Give me an inventory of our viral and bacterial samples. Find out how much Tetanus virus we have stockpiled."

Brynmor pushed his glasses up his nose, opened the refrigeration unit and began shuffling and sorting glass vials in an effortless flow of movement. "What are you thinking?"

"I'm just spitballing right now. But the endgame sign of Tetanus is lockjaw. Maybe we can use that?"

Connor walked around the central spur of the workbench to the human side of the laboratory where the vials glinted with the ruby nectar vampires craved. Samples taken from the siphoned farm stock were stacked upright in rows, inserted into holes in trays. Again, labels made the date of sampling clear, and those in one tray were labelled 'diagnosis required'. This was the one Connor pulled out first. Thrombosis in inactive humans began as a grainy texture which caused seizures in the vampires who drank it. *Will that work against the ferals?* Connor considered two avenues worth exploring – literally, cure or kill.

The medical practitioner in him focused on curing the ferals. Opening up the brainstem with a cocktail of hybrid/simian blood and perfluorocarbons. If their brains were beyond saving, then the kill option would be needed.

The thousands of snarling, crazed feral faces which gave Connor nightmares were too many to cull, but an infection, if he could find a delivery mechanism, could work.

Still moving without pause, Brynmor asked, "Was it as bad as you feared?"

"Meeting Blake again? Or seeing the rise of the ferals?" Connor laughed.

"I can see both would be scary," Brynmor replied, deadpan.

"There is one helluva storm headed our way," said Connor, frowning. "Are the latest supplies in from the siphoning sheds? Donations will be slow now the humans are using some of the sheds as living quarters."

Brynmor laid out a row of Petrie dishes and lined them up next to a high-powered microscope. Removing his glasses before starting to examine the samples, he squinted at Connor. "The human farm is empty."

Connor froze for a nanosecond, then smiled. "Principal Julian found a secure location, then. Where?"

"Storage Facility Eight." At Connor's stunned expression, Brynmor hurried on. "I know, you should have performed the stage three ceremonies, but Isaac and I showed the inmates due respect." The younger vampire clasped his hands together in an unconscious reverent gesture.

"I'm sure you did. So, all the inmates have gone?" Connor let out a long sigh. "What about The Butcher?"

"Principal Julian performed his skull crushing ceremony personally. He felt it was fitting."

Connor nodded slowly. "That's as it should be."

The Butcher's status as the hive deterrent had been unique. Connor understood Julian's determination to keep The Butcher alive, but, hundreds of years on, the sight of his hollowed-out husk invoked pity. I'm glad Julian let him die. You were all well occupied while I was away."

The muscle in Brynmor's jaw jerked as he clenched his teeth.

"What?" Connor asked.

"If this is a war, I'm not sure we'll be ready."

In a heavy tone, Connor said, "We *have* to be ready. Our humans are safe. The guardsmen are fed, and the rest is down to you and I." Waving a hand to indicate the array of agitators, centrifuges, and Petrie dishes, Connor added, "Break it down into one step at a time. Germ warfare is not new. This is what you are good at, so focus on growing the cultures we need."

"What are you going to do?" Brynmor asked as with vampire speed he loaded a stack of dishes with the cultivated gel and used a pipette to dose each one with samples, then placed them into temperature control chambers to optimize bacteria growth.

"If Captain Gerrard is at SF8, I'll head to London Zoo and collect ape and monkey blood to test for compatibility with Silas. If we can use the hybrid host blood to 'infuse' the zoo stock, they might become a delivery system to hydrate the feral brain. It will need to be tested…"

Absently, Brynmor muttered, "Gerrard is at the blood substitute manufacturing plant with Marius and Daniel, guarding the stockpiles of human blood."

"Who the Hell is guarding the humans? The eco-shelter group and tree-dwellers are there, too. We literally have all our eggs in one basket." Connor stopped loading human samples into the centrifuges and glared at Brynmor.

"Sergeant Frank."

"Who in God's name is *he*?"

"Principal Julian and Captain Gerrard appointed him to protect the humans."

"I don't give a shit, I don't know him from Adam," Connor scowled.

Brynmor laid a hand on Connor's arm. His firm tone reassuring. "The sergeant headed up the squad who held Serge under house arrest. Greg and Sampson are there too, not to mention Seth and Adam. As you said, there are a lot of bases to cover."

Connor relaxed slowly. "I see. Okay, I trust Julian's judgement."

The pair returned to the setting up process of the tests and culture preparation, occupying an hour of silent continuous movement.

Finally, Connor flicked on the last centrifuge machine, shut the glass door on the refrigeration unit and said, "Ask Charles to crate up all the human blood I.V. bags ready for distribution. Tell him to deliver phlebotomy kits, catheters and empty I.V. bags to London Zoo. I've got a few things to check up on, but I'll meet him there."

Chapter 22

The bricked-up windows should have made the room feel like a prison, but the furnishings – carpet, lamps and soft blankets – conveyed a message of thoughtful care. Running her fingertips over the table top left them clean, but Hera could see motes of dust dancing in the air and the room had the musty odor of a house closed up for winter. *Someone cleaned the room in a hurry.* That implied her comfort mattered and that felt good.

She picked up a blanket shot through with green and gold thread and pressed it to her nose. The feminine scent was unfamiliar, but it was human.

When Osiris brought her here under cover of darkness, she had had a fleeting glimpse of the exterior of the impressive Edwardian detached property. Some windows were bricked up, but the clean glass on the remainder showed that this was a home, not an abandoned human dwelling.

Following Osiris through the house to this room at the rear, Hera had detected the familiar smell of Principal Julian. *It is his home.*

She sat cross-legged on the carpet with her eyes closed. Osiris had been gone many hours, and even though she did not know when he would return, she felt at peace. The backs of her hands rested on her knees, and her chest rose and fell in a slow, easy rhythm.

The quarters inside which she usually spent many hours alone were very different to the plush silence of this room. The pipes running along the back wall of her cabin onboard ship generated heat, but her small bunk in a cramped space had provided meager comfort. Restful sleep had become a rare luxury, and these last few days, cocooned inside this safe environment, had been a revelation.

With her eyes closed, Hera listened to the whisper of approaching footfalls. They stopped outside the door. She delayed the moment of opening her eyes, choosing to remain in the place of hope – that Blake would demand her return was an inescapable truth she shied away from.

The day would come when the messenger brought news that the super tanker sat out in the estuary, and that she must return to Blake. *I understood him, felt connected as only a lost soul and a savior could be, but now...* The collision course with Connor, two years before, had ended that. The imperious, confident Blake who had saved her from drowning and changed her from human to something in-between no longer existed.

Her visitor was not breathing. *So, a vampire.* It was a game Hera enjoyed; living in the grim darkness of the tanker had honed her senses. It didn't smell like Rebekah. The upturned fingers of her hands trembled, she smiled and slowly breathed in his scent.

A draft sighed over her skin when the visitor pushed open the door with silent stealth.

Hera opened her eyes and looked into the serious face of Connor.

"Ah," she said quietly, "I can tell you and the principal apart, but you both exude the same energy."

Connor moved away from the doorway, looking for permission to sit, awhile.

"Please." Hera waved a hand in welcome.

Lifting a linen wrapped parcel into view, he set it down on the dining table and said, "Food, and vials of blood."

Watching Connor take a seat at the table, she asked, "Is it time for me to go home?"

He rested back in the sturdy wooden chair and it groaned beneath his solid weight. "Do you want to go back?"

"Maybe, at one time, but not anymore." Rising gracefully to her bare feet, Hera perched on the edge of the deep plump couch. Her long black hair framed her delicate face, as her almond shaped ebony eyes met Connor's steadily.

Without speaking, Hera gathered the unanswered questions rattling around inside Connor's mind.

~Meeting Osiris helped me, and so did finding out about Seren.

I understand more, now. I am not alone in being neither one thing nor the other. We are a new breed, species, call it what you will.~

Connor nodded. *And Blake? Does he treat you well?*

Unspoken communication flowed between them. Both remembering her elevated position on the super tanker, back then. In many ways, Tyrone now filled that place. Although, when Blake had been in possession of all his senses, he enjoyed the game of communicating with Hera telepathically.

Hera smiled through the thickest shroud of sadness Connor had ever felt. He could almost see the shadows oozing from her. He frowned and, in a firm measured tone, spoke aloud. "You don't have to go back. We just need to find a way of persuading the captain to let you go."

"That will be impossible," Hera whispered. Her shoulders dropped and she melted into the thick down of the cushions.

"Did you see the ferals in Europe?" Connor asked.

"I could not see them. I can feel them. They are empty vessels. I don't go into their minds. I might not get out again."

"They outnumber us, all of us. I need to find a way to capture one. At the same time, Britain needs to plan their defenses. Perhaps I can draw Blake into helping me. He must fear them, too." Gathering information was key. So far, it appeared that ferals behaved like zombies. If they heard or saw prey, they animated, becoming hunters focused on the kill. They were stone still and silent with no stimulus. It seemed as though, the killing instinct kicked in if they detected someone not part of their group. "The puzzle is far from complete."

Hera patiently watched Connor sink into deep contemplation, embodying the stillness of one who had fallen asleep with his eyes open, until he roused himself with a sheepish smile. "Can you help Osiris and Seren to practice the form of telepathy you have? Explore the possibility that it stems from being a hybrid. A new and better species."

She knew he was finding her a role, something to hold off Blake for a while. "I can try. It does seem to be like exercise, the more I visited the nomads' minds, the stronger the connection became, so I can try."

"Good." Connor stood up. "I'll send them to you."

"Where am I?"

Connor grinned. "You are in Principal Julian's private dwelling. His home." Gazing around the room, he said, "It is well soundproofed, but it's wise to remain quiet, and no one will find you."

"Principal Julian is very kind."

The twitch in Connor's smile gave the game away and Hera chuckled. "He doesn't know, does he?"

"There wasn't time, but he would have agreed if we had asked him."

"So, you will ask him, now?"

Connor's grin widened. "Probably not. He has enough to think about."

"Didn't it make his enemies suspicious, when Principal Julian blocked up the windows?"

Gathering enthusiasm for the topic, amusement lit his eyes as Connor said, "Oh, you don't know the half of it. This room is four inches smaller than it was. New plasterboard was added and soundproof wadding that fills the gap. But no, the windows were the least concern. There are many bricked up windows in houses built in the 18th and 19th centuries. It was a way to avoid the window tax imposed at that time." He shrugged. "It was a safe option."

"Was Principal Julian alive back then?" Hera's tone was soft with wonder.

"He became a vampire in 1810, and is a man you can trust with your life." Connor faltered on a coughing breath. "Although, I don't expect it to come to that."

Hera waved a graceful hand and nodded. "We both know that where Blake is concerned, anything can happen, but thank you. Your neck is on the block, too."

"My neck has been on the chopping block many times. Let *me* worry about Blake." Reaching the door, Connor waved farewell.

Left alone again, Hera eyed the parcel sitting on the table. When she flipped aside the linen cloth, a knife blade of vampire hunger seared through her gut. She scooped up both vials of human blood and downed them in quick succession. Running through the internal assessment which was second nature to those who juggled the rehydration of three brain centers, she felt relief that it was revival sleep she craved; it would wrap her in the blanket of relaxation she needed.

Rap-sleep, with its hunger for excess – resembling a drunkard looking for a fight – which vampires took in their stride, could be physically exhausting for a hybrid. And grave sleep, well, Hera hoped she wouldn't need to ask Connor to lock her in a cadaver drawer. Adopting the custom used in the London Hive represented a terrifying prospect. The metal cabins onboard the container vessel were less claustrophobic.

Returning to the plump invitation of the couch, Hera tried to recapture her calm meditative state but the tingle of excitement refused to fade. *Osiris and Seren. Are there more of us I wonder?* As if the realization unleashed a stream of consciousness, Hera cleared her mind and 'looked' for Blake. Their connection was strong and, as if viewing him through a misty window, she conjured his face. She pulled back sharply when a purple aura drifted closer, creating a vortex which tried to suck her in. *He is strong, I must be careful.* Casting her psychic net wider, she looked for Osiris and thought she found him. Pulling up her knees and settling into the cross-legged pose, she sighed gently. The colors of Egypt drifted across her mind like a halo of mist. *Osiris.*

Resting back, she let her head fall into the soft embrace of the padded cushions and studied the ceiling before closing her eyes and letting her consciousness follow the current which pulled her closer to Osiris. It created a floating sensation, like an astronaut drifting in space on an umbilical tether – she felt free, but safely connected.

The images of a glistening cerulean blue sea and bleached sand-colored stone of a harbor wall filled her vision. Blindingly white sails of boats in the bay flapped in a breeze. *Osiris was recently in Egypt?* Hera frowned. Her point of view rotated with dizzying speed, and an aged Egyptian face smiled at her. The thin parted lips revealed yellow stumps of teeth, and his eyes shimmered like fish scales. *Who is this?* Tightness gripped her chest, forcing her breathing to come in short pants. The consciousness she felt settling around her shoulders like a cloak was unclittered. An adult chimpanzee was the strongest memory of her host's mind. Eating fruit and hearing parrots screeching at dawn were the sounds of home. The room the old Egyptian stood in was a bare-walled turret like structure. Hera felt anxiety compressing her lungs, until an adult female chimp loped across and the eyes she saw through closed as the host burrowed into black fur. *I can't see.* As if her thought sent a command, the room came into view again. *Who is the man?* Vibration rattled through her and the picture shuddered as a string of whooping sounds filled her head. *I am inside a young chimp!*

Hera's eyes snapped open. She regained control of her own breathing in seconds. *This chimp must be here, in London.* Lifting her head to stare at the closed door of the padded room, impatience surged inside her. Realization hit with the force of a sledgehammer. *The chimp must be a hybrid.*

Being locked up without knowing what was happening outside became harder to bear with each passing hour. When, finally, she heard a soft sigh of naked feet brushing along the hallway beyond, Hera jumped up.

The door opened and she knew Osiris instantly by the curtain of jet black hair. He held the hand of a girl, and Hera felt warmth, as if a current of electricity connected her to the visitors.

"This is-"

~*Seren.*~ Hera smiled as she dipped into Osiris' mind and read the answer. ~*Our connection is strong.*~

Seren's serious gray gaze traveled down to Hera's bare feet and back to her warm olive-toned complexion and rich chocolate eyes, and then she smiled. *Hera, it is good to meet you, at last.*

Impulsively reaching for Seren's free hand, Hera pulled her across the room and sat down beside her on the couch.

Seren laughed, pushing back the black silk of her hair. *It is good if we use telepathy. Quieter, and good practice.*

With a smile, Osiris closed the door carefully and took up a position beside it, from where he could listen for noises outside. *We can't stay long, we will be missed.*

Hera nodded. ~*But please, tell me who the old Egyptian is? And he has a chimp?*~

The surprise Seren felt reverberated through all three, like welded links in a chain, and Hera grinned. ~*This is going to take some getting used to.*~

The Egyptian is Malachi, my maker. Osiris' expression filled the aura inside the room with calm affection. *Where do I start?*

Hera tucked her feet up and settled her chin on her hand. ~*At the beginning.*~

Happy to let Osiris take center stage, Seren watched his face as he did what Hera asked, and told their story.

Chapter 23

The one-armed vampire listened to the creaking sounds of the huge ship groaning to a halt. Its lazy rolling motion died away when the mooring chains tamed the hulking beast. He circled the bare metal cell for the hundredth time, following the track he had polished into the steel floor.

His internal clock told him that the next food delivery was imminent and his nerves were strung tight. *When do I get to see Blake?*

Joining the ship as a fugitive stripped him of power. Being at the mercy of others rankled and, each day, he tried the door in the hope that a careless nomad would give him the opportunity to explore the vessel, but no such luck. *Please, let it be the tall nomad.*

None of his captors were chatty, but a tall nomad, who had only one eye, seemed more amenable and had even answered a couple of questions when, four days ago, he had experienced a rare vampire moment of terror. The container ship had jolted so violently it threw him to the ground. With only one arm, he stayed down and rolled around like an unconscious drunk until the shrieking growls seeping through the seams in the walls faded.

The tall nomad who appeared from nowhere, had helped him up and dusted him down.

'What is happening?' had been a natural question he blurted at the time. It made him cringe, now, the memory of how he had clutched the nomad's arm and cowered.

That was a low point. *We were being attacked by ferals on a fool's errand to rescue the Egyptian bastard. And the fool responsible was Doctor Connor.* He spat on the floor. Inhaling and exhaling four times, slow and deep, he eased the tension knotting his muscles. *He was right here, onboard this ship.* The wasted opportunity stuck in his gullet. *I can't lose control, now. We are back in London and Frank will hand me over to Principal Julian if I fail.*

Just thinking of the sergeant caused sickness to roil in the old vampire's stomach. Frank had his own agenda, but he didn't ask – he felt safer not knowing.

The brushing sound of vampire footfalls jerked the old vampire back to the present. The door seal sighed when the vampire outside pushed it open. As he hoped, the tall nomad stepped into the room and closed the door.

Without looking at the prisoner, he held out three vials of human blood.

The vampire could smell the contents. The fumes were still warm, and nomads didn't siphon their humans, so they must be freshly drawn from the hive stock onboard. Instead of taking them, he rested a hand on the nomad's forearm. The flesh covering the cold limb was soggy beneath the fabric. It felt as though his fingertips were being sucked into it, so he let go again, fast.

The nomad turned a blank face towards the prisoner and, through creaking tight vocal chords, said, "Take your feed."

The old vampire smiled and bobbed his head. "Are we back in London?"

He took the nomad's grunt as agreement. When the vials of blood were poked into his chest, this time, he took them.

Taking the plunge before his jailer turned away, the vampire blurted, "I need to see Captain Blake. I have remembered something important."

The nomad's steps faltered, but then he walked to the door.

"Wait." Putting the vials of blood on the floor and wincing when they rolled away until they hit the wall, the vampire tore at the hole in the lining of his coat and pulled out the stained, greasy piece of paper. "Give this to Captain Blake."

The nomad returned to where his charge stood, took the paper and held it at arm's length as if it was an unexploded bomb. In seconds, he was gone.

Frozen to the spot and staring at the closed door, the vampire felt the knotted fist of tension inside him dissipate. Stooping to pick up the tubes of blood, he slid down the wall to the floor and pushed the cap off each one in turn.

The coffin-shaped box glinted in the dim flicker of a failing bulkhead lamp and the vampire laughed hoarsely. Only grave sleep would make him go that far. He couldn't be sure it was not a trap, so he stayed where he was.

Resting his head back, he savored the burn as the blood trickling down into his stomach unleashed a blaze of heat. The skin on his face pulled tight as, like a flame rushing along a fuse-wire, his spine tingled and his vampire brainstem felt like molten lead. He slowly toppled over sideways, his mask of newly tightened skin blanching white with tension, and gave himself up to rap-sleep. Locking his tendons and muscles down, he surrendered to fantasies where he looked into Doctor Connor's gray eyes, and saw the light in them die. His fingers twitched as he imagined how it would feel to grasp the cool hard flesh of Connor's neck and crush his windpipe, and the last glass vial still in his hand shattered.

His body shuddered in a seizure of ecstasy and saliva rattled in his throat, speckling his face in pink residue. *This time, I will end him.*

His hooded gaze studied the limited slice he could see of the oil-stained floor pressed into the side of his face and, like a human sated after the adrenaline rush of violence, his body became slack. He lay on the floor as motionless as a corpse.

The distant dull clangs vibrating through the ship were sure signs he was not alone, and when the note changed to the metronomic beat of footsteps, he sat up. He ran his hand over the cold flesh of his cheek where the hard floor had ironed the skin smooth and pushed a strand of gray lank hair back from his face.

By the time the door opened, the vampire was standing erect, ready to greet whoever appeared. His stern look became fixed when an unfamiliar nomad was framed in the doorway.

"Well?" The prisoner lifted his chin.

The nomad sank into stillness for fractions of a second, as if communicating with a 'higher power', then reanimated smoothly and said, "Come."

The vampire darted forward as the greasy coat of the nomad flared when he spun around and disappeared from view.

There was no time to think, so the vampire chased the flitting shadow, scuttling along in the wake of his escort. He ducked through an airlock door into a dark cavernous space, and his hesitant footsteps echoed through a huge storage compartment. A labyrinth of large crates obscured his view in every direction and he swore softly. "Where did he go?"

When he reached the corner of a wall created by stacked wooden boxes, the light of a distant bulkhead lamp set high on the opposite wall was eclipsed by a towering figure.

"How do you know Doctor Connor and the hive layout, *Jacob Pearce*?"

The vampire jerked his head to the left when the voice came from further away than the person blocking his path.

Saliva rattled in the throat of the stone-still form.

Darting his gaze from one figure to the other, the prisoner chose to keep the larger more menacing vampire in his view. "Captain Blake, can we talk somewhere more private?"

The captain gurgled with what sounded like laughter.

"This *is* a safe place." Tyrone moved closer until the captive could see his face.

Swinging around, the old vampire began retracing his steps, back towards the airlock door. When he reached the spot where the next pathway cut through the maze, Blake appeared, obstructing his progress again, his hand thumping down onto the vampire's shoulder, this time. From behind, from where he had followed, Tyrone said, "You will have a comfortable cabin and freedom to move around the ship, but only after you talk."

"I was a London Hive councilor."

Blake's head tilted and his glistening black lips gaped in a grin. "Your *memory* has returned?" Tyrone gave voice to Blake's sarcasm.

The vampire's bones creaked as Blake's grip tightened and he felt for his captive's other shoulder. He ran his hand down the empty coat sleeve and a harsh bark of laughter speckled the pinned vampire's face with putrid saliva.

"You're Councilor Serge. The *weak* councilor. Now, I see we share an enemy, but why do I need you when I already have an ally in London?"

"Did Doctor Connor return Hera? As he promised?" It was a shot in the dark, but when Blake's hands fell away, Serge grinned.

"Not yet."

"I *know* him. I know Principal Julian, and I know how they work." Serge waited for his words to sink in. "We can use the threat of a feral attack to take the London Hive human cattle. A death sentence for them and enough food to make the crossing to North America, if that's what you want."

"*We* can use the feral threat?"

"Yes, *we*." Serge lifted his chin and glared, even though the gesture was wasted on Blake. "I am part of the plan that will destroy them."

Finally, Blake nodded, and the black bulk blocking his way disappeared.

"Follow me," said Tyrone.

His legs shook as Serge started moving, he bounced off the wall of a crate and then used his good hand to steady himself. If Tyrone noticed, he gave no sign.

Once settled inside a cabin with the comparative luxury of a shore-facing porthole, Serge should have felt easier, but he ground his yellow teeth and peered out at the London Hive guardsmen standing in clear view high on the embankment and inside the Docklands compound itself. *I've done what the sergeant said, for what good it will do.* But the truth remained, the sergeant held all the cards and all Serge could do, yet again, was wait.

◇◇◇

Without confining the humans in the trucks, Frank doubted he could have persuaded them to enter the storage facility, but the windowless boxes hid the hulking granite structure from view when it reared up on the horizon. The dull leaden sky pressed down from overhead and the glistening expanse of the fast-moving River Thames resembled a current of churning razorblades.

Once the trucks, pushed by vampires to maintain covert silence, rolled through the gates and into the shadow cast by the towering walls, it was too late for protest.

It's low tide; that is good. The sound of rushing water which rumbled through the structure at high tide created a claustrophobic womblike experience, but that was a few hours away. *They will have some time to adjust.*

When Frank leapt down from where he sat on the roof of the lead truck, Greg and Sampson followed suit and took up a station beside him. The pair stuck together and Frank could feel their eyes boring into his head. He was a stranger, so it was to be expected.

Tired humans, strung out with anxiety which tainted their scent, were hard to resist. It was part of vampire hunting instinct to torture their prey – terrified blood, rich with adrenaline, tasted so much sweeter.

Before the truck tailgates were lowered, Frank walked the line of vampire guards, porters, wardens, and crop reapers, and paused to stare each one in the eye. With a deep intake of breath, he washed their scents over his palette and gauged their stress levels. With a jerk of his chin, he sent the ones he decided could lose the battle to control their hunger out through the gates to return to London.

With sixty percent of the transport team dismissed, the remaining vampires took the gel-like transparent masks Frank handed out and pressed them securely over their muzzles.

"If you can't control your hunger, get out. Understood?" Frank's barely contained snarl drove the message home. There would be no trial; they would not get a second chance.

Greg and Sampson walked along the convoy of trucks, flipping the catches and opening the rear doors.

The smell of human sweat plumed in the air and one vampire abruptly waved a hand and set off across the enclosure in a blur of movement. The tall metal fence jangled as he scaled it, dropped down on the other side and disappeared into the distance before the humans had registered the scene.

Greg pulled open the final truck, hopped inside and dropped down to sit in a space beside Seth. "This is it, guys."

Seth punched his old friend on the shoulder and grumbled, "Wish I could join the front line."

Greg knew hiding was not the Marine way and nodded slowly. "You, Adam and Oscar have your work cut out, believe me." His voice dropped to a whisper. "Leizle, Sandy and the rest need you."

"'Oorah," said Seth and got to his feet.

The wagons rocked as the eco-shelter and tree-dweller communities filed out. Leizle stopped to offer Uncle Harry a hand, helping the old man to clamber down.

Sergeant Frank lifted a hand in welcome and Leizle faltered self-consciously. "Don't be surprised, my dear. Julian will have my head on a stake if anything happens to you."

"I can look after myself." Her green eyes glowed in the dim light of dusk.

"I'm sure you can, but you need to stay safe." Waving an arm in a chivalrous gesture, Frank waited for Leizle to walk by and then fell into step beside her. "You can talk to me, anytime. Protecting Connor and Julian's human family is important to me."

"Is Rebekah safe?"

Frank smiled. "She's a new vampire and has friends around her. I'm sure she'll be safe. Let's make sure I'm able to say the same thing if she asks about you, hmm?"

Leizle's steps slowed as the chill in the shadow of the storage facility made her shiver.

Frank dared to place a hand on her shoulder. "It's okay. Principal Julian chose this place." *Not entirely true, but Julian thinks it was his idea.* When Leizle looked up, Frank raised his eyebrows in faked innocence. "C'mon, everyone is waiting."

Up ahead, at the corner of the building, with the gray water of the Thames rushing along behind him, Greg frowned in their direction, his arms folded over his chest.

Frank knew the Marine could hear everything they were saying. "Greg and Sampson are your guards inside the facility. The other vampires will remain outside as lookouts. You have nothing to worry about."

Before night fell, everyone was inside and settled into a series of chambers. The furniture did little to soften the stark lines of the tomb-like interior, but rugs, couches, and mattresses taken from the long-abandoned department stores in London provided physical comfort, at least.

With Sampson and Peter easing the transition for the human farm stock, and Greg and Seth reassuring Leizle, Harry and the rest, Frank retreated and took up a position out in the dark musty corridor, alone.

Three hours passed before the sighing sounds of sleeping humans whispered through the air inside the storage facility. The murmuring voices of the few who fought exhaustion and tried to remain awake gradually faded.

That went well. Frank pushed away from the wall, made his way to where the warden guarded the front entrance – the only door in or out of the facility – and gave the man a salute. "I'm reporting back to Principal Julian. If anything happens, sound the alarm."

"Yes, sir."

When Frank stepped outside, the gusting wind blew the spray of the swollen river into his face and soaked his hair. He lifted his chin and embraced the ferocity of the elements. Pausing briefly to give the lookouts final orders, he ramped up to top vampire speed and headed along the river towards the London Docklands.

The super tanker nomad vessel would be under guard, but Frank would cross that bridge when he got to it. *My life will be easier if Captain Gerrard is not there.* He whipped through the built-up areas on the outskirts of the city, the cloudy night reducing the surroundings to a scattering of coal-black outcrops of masonry.

When he arrived at the dockyard, the hulking shape of the nomads' ship resembled a menacing oil slick smothering the rippled texture of the water. The harsh winds coming in off the river plastered the long-coats worn by the London Hive guardsmen to their silent immovable bodies.

Circling round to the rear of the compound, Frank slowed to a walk and climbed the bank which overlooked the guarded vessel, deliberately making enough noise to attract attention.

"Halt. Identify yourself." The voice cut through the wailing gusts.

"Sergeant Frank. Ident LV259472." He held up his hands and waited.

"Approach, sir." The sentry visibly relaxed and Frank could almost taste the officer's relief.

"Is it all quiet?" Frank asked, finishing the climb and arriving beside the vampire guard. "Who's in charge?"

"Captain Hugh."

"Very good." *Very good, indeed.* Frank set off down the opposite slope, dislodging a clattering cascade of gravel.

Locating Captain Hugh on the quayside was easy. His tall figure occupied center stage, flanked by two platoons, in an overt display of power. Hugh darted a sideways glance at Frank and said, "Good evening, Sergeant."

Frank clasped his hands behind his back and joined the captain in inspecting the glowering black ship, listening to the low mournful creaks as water lapped around it.

"All quiet, Captain?"

"Indeed."

"I'm looking for Principal Julian."

"He is at his Richmond home, I believe."

"Ah. Thank you, Captain." Frank remained still, apparently sharing a moment of silent contemplation. *Has Blake seen me?* He hoped so.

Turning away, at last, Frank chose the path along the quayside, idly looking over the edge into the pitch-black water until he passed behind where Julian's ship was berthed and he was lost to the sight of the platoon of guards.

Removing his boots and slinging them around his neck by tied shoelaces, he dropped silently over the edge of the causeway into the water. Leaving the stone wall of the quayside behind, Frank carefully picked his way over the slippery algae-covered stones. Overhead, slanting rays of moonlight pooled in hazy silver patches. Water conducted noise, so slow and steady was the name of the game.

The dense shadow of the tanker loomed above and, as Frank hoped, a nomad crewman waited on the rocks up ahead, his hair writhing in the lazy current like a nest of black snakes.

His eyes glisten like jet beads in his pallid complexion and as he watched Frank approach, despite the grit and algae floating past his face, he didn't blink once.

The nomad turned, grabbed the vertical fall of a rope weighted with a lump of metal and climbed it. Frank followed and both vampires skimmed into an open porthole on the far side of the vessel, just above water level.

Inside the cabin they fell into, Captain Blake and Tyrone waited.

"Good to see you, Sergeant."

Frank got to his feet and roughly dried his hair with the towel Tyrone held out. "Where is Jacob Pearce?"

Blake's throat gurgled and Tyrone said, "You mean Councilor Serge?"

"Good, he has told you."

"Why didn't *you* tell me?"

Frank laughed. "I needed him in London. As a hunted man, there was no other way to get him here."

"He says he is important to the plan?"

"He is, but not in the way he thinks. Where is he? I have his next set of instructions, but I'm glad you know. I need you to make sure he follows them to the letter."

"Come," said Tyrone, and led the way to Serge's cabin. Blake stayed behind, but Frank knew he was with them in spirit and would use the nomads' telepathic connection to speak through Tyrone, and could listen in just as easily.

Chapter 24

Frank sank back into the shadows beneath the ancient oak trees lining the street. The roots of each one had forced their way up through the paving slabs, turning the sidewalk into rolling hills of cracked concrete.

A damp patch gathered at his feet where his dripping clothes had soaked the ground, but he had been waiting so long, that he was bone dry and his hair fluttered in the breeze.

The clouds cleared and, in the moonlight, the windows of Julian's Richmond home gleamed like silvery pools of mercury.

The principal was at home, but he was not alone.

Frank settled into a semi-conscious state and let his attention roam. Set far back from the street, the lawn in the front garden of the Edwardian house was flat and featureless, cut into two parts by a hundred-yard long wide gravel driveway. Overgrown shrubs and hedges which ran riot in neighboring plots were starkly absent. Modifications made by the principal, Frank felt certain, as it made sneaking up on the house impossible. The gravel stones, in every shade from white to darkest brown, glittered with dew. At the left corner of the property, a deformed angular creature squatted beneath a damp tarpaulin. Frank passed the time playing a guessing game until a gust lifted the cover for a second and, with a fierce squint, he noticed the barest inch of an oil black tire. *A motorbike? Interesting.* Shifting position, Frank tugged the front of his double-breasted guards' coat straight, adjusted his leather gloves, and inhaled deeply. Curiosity piqued, he decided to take a look.

But, before he could make the first step towards the house, he heard movement inside. Scanning beyond the glistening glass, he paused at each bricked up window. The hair on his nape rose. *Was that a human movement?* Frank bared his teeth in a grin and venom gathered in his throat. The tendons in his body pulled tight when a fire started in his gut. He frowned, running his gaze slowly across the masonry as if he possessed X-ray vision, but it was on his sense of smell he focused, that and tuning his hearing into the sounds drifting on the breeze. *Thud*. This time there was no mistaking the noise – the wet sound of a heart muscle clenching. A fierce snarl cramped his features. But the next beat didn't come. *Not a human then, but what?*

Pulling swiftly back, Frank froze when the door of the house whipped open and two figures appeared on the front step. Julian shook hands with Captain Gerrard, who then turned and skittered across the gravel stones making them rattle underfoot. As he rushed towards the sidewalk and straight at Frank, the sergeant had a nanosecond to dip his chin, cloak his face in shadow and hope. *If he recognizes me…*

Gerrard took a sharp right, his attention already fixed on whatever task Julian had given him.

Frank, keeping his chin tucked into his coat collar, shifted his gaze to view Julian through a fall of hair.

The principal exuded agitation. Even from the hundred-yard plus distance, Frank noticed Julian's hand trembling when he raked back his blond hair. The principal's eyes glittered like green glass as he scanned the front garden and cocked his head to listen.

Frank stopped breathing until Julian closed the front door. *How long shall I wait?* After three minutes, a lifetime for a vampire, he strode up the driveway. The gravel crunched and before he reached the bottom step of the porch, Julian opened the door and glared down at him.

"Sergeant Frank? Why are you at my home?"

"Forgive me, Principal. I promised an update and asked Captain Hugh where I could find you."

"Come in." Julian blurted the words, but his grip remained tightly fixed on the edge of the front door.

He's dehydrated. Frank bobbed his head in deference. "If you're sure."

Finally, as if his boots were made of concrete, Julian took four steps back.

"Are you feeling alright?" Frank followed the principal into his study. The vials of blood lying on the Victorian desk winking in the light confirmed Frank's suspicion.

"Make it quick," said Julian.

Jolting to attention, the sergeant said, "The humans are safely contained in SF8. Only three vampires are allowed inside – Greg, Sampson, and myself. An eighteen strong squad are outside on lookout duty."

"Only eighteen? What happened to the rest?"

"Dismissed by me. They weren't strong enough."

Julian lifted a brow and grinned stiffly. "Better safe than sorry, thank you, Sergeant. Return to SF8. Things are moving fast here, so stay put."

"Yes, sir." Frank turned to leave, but glanced back before disappearing. "I've got your back."

When Frank hit the sidewalk and ramped up speed, a grin pulled his face tight. *Things will move faster than you know, when the time comes.*

◇◇◇

Julian stared at the closed door. *That was close.*

Reducing Gerrard to an errand boy, asking him to bring a blood feed to the house did not feel good, but he couldn't be seen in the council chambers struggling for control. Connor would have torn a hole in him for being stupid, but from the moment he arrived home, an obsession with human blood had settled in his gut like rats gnawing a hole inside. Julian clenched his fist, staring at the lamp on his desk and controlling the urge to throw it across the room.

I need rap-sleep. Scooping up the vials of blood, Julian, muttered, "Shit."

He knew Frank had seen them lying on the desk. *The sergeant isn't a fool.* But Julian dismissed the worm of discomfort. 'I've got your back' was an informal and personal remark of a man who could keep a secret. *Or was it a veiled threat?* "Jesus, Julian, get a grip."

With a grunt of exasperation, he strode down the hall and into his sitting room. When he dropped down onto the chaise longue the wooden frame made a sharp crack of protest. After unbuttoning his shirt collar and cuffs, he downed the vials of blood, picked up his lucky pebble from the side table, and laid out flat. The padded chaise had a Julian-sized crater worn into it, and the upholstery closed around him in a comforting embrace.

Tapping into his concerns for Leizle, Julian closed his eyes. *Will she do what she's told and stay safe?* As the human blood dose pooled in his gut, he braced his muscles and, breathing deeply, used his diaphragm as bellows to accelerate the process which forced the blood into his arterial network and up into his brainstem. His body jerked as the human blood cells penetrated the barrier at the base of his skull and red clouds billowed in his occipital lobe. He swallowed noisily then locked down his throat. The cerise clouds in his vision clumped and shifted, finally reforming into a sculpture of Leizle carved in pink. Opening the brain center for rap-sleep, Julian's jaw clenched until his teeth creaked and the mask of his face pulsed with a network of pink veins. The exhilaration of the blood rushing to his head filled his mouth with saliva and he snarled. The vision of Leizle solidified further, and his fingertips twitched as if he felt her naked flesh beneath them. His groin tightened in a physical reaction, and the vein in his temple began to pulse like a heartbeat, but it stuttered, keeping pace with an erratic rhythm which didn't make sense.

The apparition features of Leizle melted away, becoming a smooth egg-shaped face with no details other than a gaping mouth and two burning holes for eyes. The thump, thump, thump of a heartbeat thundered through his skull and Julian's eyes shot open.

What the Hell? Even though he knew it was not possible. *I would have smelled her if she was inside the house.* He leapt to his feet, set the stone down onto the side table and walked deliberately along the hallway to the back of the house.

At the door to his soundproof room, he pressed both palms to the warm wood and rested his forehead against it. He inhaled deeply and listened. *She's not here.* Julian chuckled. "I'm going crazy."

But then, a heavy thump stopped him moving. It resonated through the air like the beat of a drum, but just the one. Impatient to solve the puzzle, he opened the door and scanned the room. A square of linen on the table smelled of cheese, bread and fruit. An empty vial had dregs of blood, and a wave of annoyance knotted Julian's shoulders tight.

"Come out, I'm not in the mood for games."

A shadow crept across the floor beyond the plump couch and then a slight girl rose gracefully to her feet. "Forgive me, I-"

"Hera." Julian absorbed the silken mass of dark hair gleaming with chocolate-colored strands and the almond shaped eyes in an elfin face. "What are you doing here?"

"Doctor Con-"

"Of course, he did," muttered Julian, sweeping into the room and whipping around so fast the drapes hanging at the bricked-up windows flapped wildly.

Hera took a step back into her corner and he hissed. "Sorry. Sorry, I'm not irritated by you, just him."

Hera drifted forward, sank down on the couch and assumed her usual cross-legged pose. "He is a thorn in your side, hmm?" She smiled.

Turning to face her, Julian said, "He has his reasons, I'm sure. You are safe here, and when I find Doctor Connor, then I'll find out what the plan is." The casual smile that accompanied his words did not match the ramrod straight posture. He crossed to the door and paused with his hand on the handle. "Good to meet you properly, Hera. It has been a long time."

~*You remember me, then.*~ Reverting to her favored form of communication, her pearl white teeth gleamed in the dim light as her smile widened.

"Of course, once seen never forgotten." With a firm nod, Julian left.

Back in his own quarters, he unconsciously rubbed his forearm where, in the hospital corridor, almost a year ago, Hera had touched him when she accompanied the nomads on a trip to the blood dispensary. The psychic jolt she had delivered was certainly never to be forgotten. *Her powers were strong, even then.*

Julian shook his head. "Connor better have a damn good reason for bringing Blake's wrath down on our heads, or I'll kill him myself."

Grabbing his coat, he checked everything was in its place and locked the front door. Turning up his collar against the drizzling rain, he headed into the city to find Connor.

Chapter 25

Breezing through the main door of the hospital, Julian ironed the irritation he felt from his face, but still the vampire guard detail who manned the doors since Connor's return looked concerned.

"Evening, Principal Julian, is everything in order?" asked the squad leader, the urgency in his tone mirrored by the probing look he pinned on Julian.

"Yes, thank you. Is Doctor Connor here?"

The squad leader barely had time to nod before Julian whipped away across the polished marble tiles and shoved through the door opposite. The steel handle bounced from the wall and crushed plaster rained down onto the floor, but, Julian was already too far away to hear it, or the muttered curiosity of the ten guards in the reception area.

The arrival of Portia and Silas made the hospital a security hotspot, so Julian was not surprised to find another guard detail at the entrance to the surgical wing.

The guards took one look at their principal in full flight and sidestepped out of the way.

When he paused at the top of the stairs which led down to Connor's domain, and caught sight of his reflection in the glazed door – blond hair standing in hedgehog spikes and a manic glitter in his green eyes – he understood. Inhaling deeply, Julian ran his hands through his hair, returning it to the groomed golden cap he usually wore, but the rest, the embers of irritation burning in his gaze, only giving Connor a piece of his mind would diminish that.

At the bottom of the stairwell, he banged a fist on the security coded door. "Connor, I want to speak with you, now."

A beep disengaged the lock, and Julian was one barrier closer to getting answers. But he knew better than to breach the decontamination procedure, so he waited, pacing back and forth in the confined space like a caged lion.

Connor appeared, wearing green scrubs and a frown on his tight features. "Is something wrong? Rebekah? Malachi?"

Julian shook his head fiercely. "No, but something is wrong with *you*. I've been at *my* house."

"Ah, Hera." Connor's crooked grin begged for forgiveness.

"Yes, Hera. *Blake's* Hera. The 'Hera' that Marius told you to leave alone. Do you remember that meeting?"

Connor nodded seriously. "I do, but things are not that simple. She might be useful in the attack."

Julian snorted. "She has magic powers, perhaps?" His green eyes clouded and the tirade stuttered. "She can control Blake? Or knows how to kill ferals? I doubt it."

"We know she does have powers, and even if it turns out they can't help us, she *can* help us control Blake. She is leverage we can use." Locking eyes with Julian, Connor jutted his chin out.

"What else are you not telling me?"

Connor chuckled. "You got me. Hera can see through Silas' eyes. She just didn't know what it was at the time."

"How does that help us?"

Connor looked sheepish. Lifting the medical bag he held up into view, he said, "I'm headed, to collect blood samples from Silas. When added to the perfluorocarbons blood substitute compound, it might 'cure' ferals. But first, we need to catch one and try it out. That's where Hera and Silas come in."

"And where will you get a 'feral guinea pig'?" Julian folded his arms.

Brynmor emerged through the laboratory door holding a tray of filled test tubes, stopped at the sight of Julian and froze.

"It's okay, Brynmor, Doctor Connor is filling me in on the hare-brained 'let's catch a feral' plan." When Anthony loomed behind Brynmor, Julian added, "You too, Anthony?"

Driving Brynmor out into the corridor, Anthony closed the door behind him and turned around. "It's a plan, at least." In a sudden apologetic jerky gesture, Anthony brushed his brown hair away from his eyes and dipped his chin, knowing he had overstepped a line.

"Point taken." Julian focused on Connor. "Ferals are coming, so what are our options?"

Connor took the greatcoat Anthony had draped over his arm, and shrugged into it as he spoke. "Anthony and the zookeepers will round up the monkey and ape stocks we have in London Zoo. I need them in their holding pens for the back-up plan."

"We have a back-up plan?" Julian laid a hand on Connor's shoulder. "I'm sorry old friend, I've dropped the ball here." He shook his head. "Things are moving faster than I thought."

Connor frowned. "You have protected the humans, not just in London, but in the other hives, too. I think your ball skills are pretty damned good."

"Once the primates are in place, what's next?"

"As I said, I'm looking for a cure, but if that fails, we have one more shot. It's too complicated to explain, right now, so one step at a time."

Connor was already skimming up the steps and heading out into the corridor where Rebekah was waiting.

"I imagine you know about Hera?" said Julian.

But Connor's wry grin and Rebekah's wide-eyed surprise told him differently.

"At least, I'm not the only one," muttered Julian.

"Hera is here? I didn't know, but I'm sure Connor has good reason." She touched Connor on the forearm as she spoke, drawing his attention.

Julian could almost feel the static of silent communication in the still look the two shared and the sense of isolation made him scowl. *I wonder what it's like.* Recalling his advice to Marius that he should turn a human to give him a voice, it was a short hop to yearning for that close connection with Leizle. *One day.*

Julian watched Connor, Brynmor and Rebekah whip away along the corridor to start phase one of 'the plan'.

Leaving the hospital, Julian kept Anthony company on his way to London Zoo, the two traveling in companionable silence until Anthony said, as if answering an unspoken question, "If anyone can save Britain from the ferals, it's Doctor Connor."

"I know, Anthony." Julian laughed and some of the tension pressing down on him lifted. "I have faith."

They parted company with a waved salute, and Julian headed back to his own domain of the council buildings. He pushed in through the heavy oak doors to be greeted by Marius and Daniel, and the familiarity of it all focused his mind. As the jurors fell into step behind him, Julian said, "Marius, tell Gerrard to deploy a platoon of the Elite Guard to London Zoo. Daniel, issue weapons to the council guard and stand by." Julian glanced at his companions and was glad to see Daniel had his crossbow slung over his shoulder, and the bulge on his hip interrupting the sleek line of his jacket showed that Marius, too, was armed.

Alone again, Julian headed to his chamber, opened the drawer in the bottom section of the wardrobe and unwrapped a utility belt loaded with hand grenades. He extracted one egg shaped device, running his thumb over the ridges on its surface – weak points designed to fracture under force and widen the blast. His mind drifted back to his first vampire years, when he had witnessed the development of weapons in the early 18th century. It was only then that 'percussive' muskets – popular with sportsmen – were tested against the traditional flintlock design. *Far more deadly than blades and hand-to-hand combat. The appetite of mankind to find devastating forms of destruction saw no bounds.*

For what it was worth, Julian missed the heroism of wielding a sword and riding a charger into battle, but ferals would not fall beneath such a weak onslaught. The grenade belt fit snugly and, for the first time, Julian felt in step with those around him.

Connor caught hold of Rebekah's hand as they raced along the hospital corridor. The guard posted outside a distant room watched their approach and cleared out of the way before he was bowled over.

Stopping at the door with his grip on the handle, Connor let Malachi know they were coming in. *I have my lab assistant and Rebekah here, too. Are you ready?* It felt odd tiptoeing around Malachi, but the chimps were a game changer.

Yes, but move slowly.

Entering first, Connor scanned the scene. Behind a curtain drawn around a bed, a fuzzy shadow confirmed the location of Portia and Silas, clinging together in an embrace. Malachi stood in the center of the room, exuding the alertness of a fully fed vampire. *Don't worry, Charles provided my food. Silas is well rested.*

Not making eye contact with Malachi, Brynmor moved smoothly over to the trolley set against the far wall and began preparing the needles and empty blood vials Connor would need. The two had rarely met, and Malachi remained a disconcerting sight. His flesh clung to angular bones and his skin was the color of ochre-stained parchment, but it was the fish scale iridescence in his eyes that created the aura of being a monster.

Rebekah grinned widely at the elderly figure. His fierce expression did not fool her; they had been through too much together.

My dear, you go from strength to strength, I see.

Rebekah nodded. *I had good teachers.* Her glance took in Connor, too.

Bringing Brynmor into the conversation, Connor said aloud, "We all need to be strong. What is coming could end us all."

Malachi's throat crackled with laughter. "The end is nothing to fear, not if it is written."

"What do you mean?" asked Rebekah.

"Everything happens for a reason." Malachi blinked slowly. "I have faced many dangers in two thousand years, and the end I feared never happened." Locking eyes with Connor and reaching into his mind, for a fleeting moment, the room around them filled with water and a weak and shackled Malachi, pinned by nails through his feet and clamped around the neck to the man-made wooden wall which sheered up the bank of The River Thames reminded them both of how close to dying his mentor had come. "You saved me when I was certain all was lost. Fate is a power to be feared, nothing else."

Connor was the first to admit that he long ago gave up on controlling his path. "You're right, Malachi. All that matters, is that we go down fighting." Glancing at the drawn curtain, he said, "Will Portia let me take samples."

Malachi shook his head. "But she will let *me*."

You know how? Connor's jaw muscle twitched and Malachi laughed.

You will have to trust me. You cannot always be in control. Resting a hand on Connor's shoulder, he said, "You can watch, and instruct me if needed..." *But remember to be calm, Silas might hear your thoughts. He is your brother, in many ways.*

When Malachi collected the tray bearing the needles and vials with cork stoppers, Connor drew back the curtain and followed the elder vampire into the cubicle. Both chimps looked up. Silas' warm brown gaze remained steady, inspecting Connor's face. Portia held her son closer and made a soft 'oohing' noise that tore at Connor's heart. Without thinking, he extended a hand, and Silas reached for it. ~*I can see you.*~ The voice that said the words sounded familiar and Connor frowned. "Hera?" he whispered.

Silas' gaze twinkled with merriment.

You can control Silas? The notion seemed ludicrous.

~*No, but I can soothe him, and encourage him to do things.*~ The young chimp reached for Connor's hand again, turned it over and drew an 'H' on his palm with his index finger. Connor pushed his hair back and laughed aloud, regretting it instantly when Portia jerked back at the sudden movement. The bed frame clattered as Silas was pulled away into a tight hug and Portia turned her back, shielding her son from the interlopers.

Connor, focus. This time it was Malachi's sharp tone.

Smoothing Portia's ruffled fur, Malachi coaxed the mother to relax once more. With quick deft strokes, he found a pulsing vein in the arm Silas offered up calmly.

Connor felt sure Hera was in there making the process easier.

Silas merely blinked when the needle was pushed into a vein.

Blood flooded in to fill the first vial, then Malachi slotted another into place. It filled more slowly. Connor tuned into the chimp's steady heart and respiration and watched Malachi repeat the process until half a pint of blood was distributed between twenty vials.

Silas began to look drowsy, his blinks becoming slower and more frequent. Another five vials were filled and Connor called a halt. "That will do, let them rest now."

Malachi withdrew the needle and pressed an ice-cold fingertip to the puncture wound. As if both chimps understood it was over, in a tangle of arms and legs, they tumbled off the far edge of the gurney. When Connor peered over, he saw a mattress on the floor, strewn with torn rags as bedding.

The sheet on the gurney hung down in a flap, providing a cover to hide behind.

"Thank you, Malachi. I'll get these back to the lab. If we can get the hybrid blood into a feral brainstem without using blood substitute to open the gateway, it could be the breakthrough we need."

Brynmor packed the samples into a foam lined carry case and waited outside the door.

"Stay here, for now. The guard outside will tell you when we have to move you. Trust only him, Julian, or Gerrard."

Shutting the door behind them, Connor muttered, "We have enough samples from Silas to try out different ratios, but let's play safe. Get a stock pile of blood substitute sent over to the medical center at London Zoo for the back-up option. Hopefully we won't need them but... well, cure or kill, we'll take what we can get." Connor shrugged.

Brynmor accelerated away, and Connor took a moment to inhale Rebekah's scent and capture a sense of calm. The guard took up his post again as the pair disappeared around the corner.

"Have you fed today?" asked Connor.

Rebekah dipped a hand into her pocket and produced a vial of blood. "Share?"

Her teeth ran over her bottom lip and Connor pulled her up sharply against his chest. His hand slid down over her backside and when her head fell back, he grazed his teeth over her neck. His tongue tasted the cool hard texture of her silky skin, and her vampire scent was no less alluring than the honey sweet nectar that had tortured him when she was human.

In a blur of movement, he towed her along to where examination rooms lined the corridor in the surgical wing.

She smiled when they stopped outside Examination Room 2.

Connor traced a long finger over the metal number. "The day that changed our lives."

Feeling like naughty children, inside the room with the door closed, they shared the vial of blood. Connor let Rebekah push him down onto the examination couch and straddle his hips. His fingers shook as he pushed her shirt off her shoulders. He sat up and took her nipple into his mouth as she freed him from his pants, and he sighed as she took him inside her.

They froze, their muscles tight and their flawless skin glowing with translucence even in the gloom. Connor snarled as rap-sleep unleashed lust in a wave which burned through his gut. Gripping her hips and driving harder, he chased the moment when the world would explode, and the starburst would scatter tingling fire through his senses. Burying his hands in her hair and locking his gaze to hers, the hunger in Rebekah's eyes drove him on. Making love to the human Rebekah had been filled with guilt and left bruises on her flesh, but now he took her with him, kissing her and tasting her gasping breath when the tightness locking her muscles was no longer hydration but the searing peak of pleasure at his touch.

When her head fell forward to rest on his shoulder, he cradled her into his chest and slowly laid back. Tracing patterns over her skin, they lay in the silent world only vampires understood. The clouds of red inside Connor's head dissipated, the cell door to the hydrated brain center softly closed, and crystal-clear thought returned, bringing a soft smile to his relaxed features.

They had stolen mere minutes for themselves, but now, Connor felt ready to take on the world.

Chapter 26

Serge gazed out of the porthole; his only view of the outside world had commanded his attention for twenty of the last twenty-four hours. Like studying ants, he gave each black speck of a guardsman a number, and became absorbed in the concert of their movements.

A clunk on the gangway outside made his head jerk, but nothing more. *Why did I get myself stuck in this Hellhole?*

Frank's fleeting visit a few hours ago had left him in the dark, but a knot of dread had ignited inside Serge when the sergeant's intent looks had crawled over his skin. He wondered what the reaction would be if he walked up on deck and surrendered to Julian's men. *Can it be any worse than this?* He peered out over the escarpment and scanned the lookout tower, hoping the principal would appear. *Is it better to deal with the Devil I know?*

A sudden noise outside penetrated like a nail dragging down over a blackboard and Serge turned around in time to see Blake, the talking sidekick – as he now thought of the smug vampire glued to the captain – and Sergeant Frank walk in.

Frank and Blake stood close, and Serge realized the pair knew each other well.

"It's time to take your revenge, Councilor." Frank raised a brow and smiled. "The captain will create a distraction, and we'll leave the ship on the port side and go into the river."

Even though Serge had been waiting for this moment, his brain was having trouble grasping the process. "There's a boat?"

"You will see. Come." Frank left the cabin and Blake stepped further inside, away from the doorway, and waited. If it was meant to scare Serge out of the room, it worked. He could not get to grips with this silent organism of crewmen, and relief to be leaving was reason enough to trust Frank.

Scuttling along the corridors below deck, Serge caught up with the sergeant. Skimming down metal ladders, the pair arrived at the compartment which housed the anchor mechanism. The thick chain disappearing out over the bottom edge of the hatch creaked under the pressure of each rolling swell. Glancing over his shoulder to check his companion was paying attention, Frank gripped the frame on either side of the aperture and swung out into the gusting squall that raced over the undulating water. Climbing smoothly down the anchor chain without pause, he continued on until the iron gray waters closed over his head.

Resigned to following, or having Blake arrive at any moment, Serge copied Frank's example as best he could. Having only one hand, his progress downward was jerky and desperate. Using the large chain-links as footholds made his climb safe, even if it was cripplingly slow.

His coat filled with air and billowed around his body as the icy tide rose up his legs. Even his vampire flesh registered the bitter cold – the water pressing against his skin felt like a suffocating embrace.

The drifting currents dragged gray lank hair across his face as he reached the bottom and scanned the riverbed for Frank. The pluming trail of silt gave Serge the clue he needed and, knowing Frank would not wait, he darted forward in pursuit, crushing rocks beneath his boots in agitation.

Reaching an algae-covered concrete wall, where the quayside blocked his path, he stopped for a nanosecond, but then, a white hand plunged down from overhead, he instinctively grabbed hold of it and was hauled forcefully up out of the water.

Frank jerked his head and both vampires leapt across the five yards of exposed quayside to dive beneath a tarpaulin cover thrown over an upended boat.

Inside the cave like space, Frank pushed a parcel of clothes into Serge's chest, quickly shrugging out of his own wet garments and pulling on a clean dry guardsman tunic.

Serge found he had the same outfit but once the elderly vampire was bare-chested, Frank put a hand on his armless shoulder. Serge jerked back, as if burned, then saw the reason why. With dexterity Serge could only envy, the sergeant buckled a linen strap around Serge's chest and another around his neck to support the weight of a mannequin arm. Although, when he was dressed, the uniform still hung on the councilor's scrawny frame.

The two figures ducked out from beneath the cover on the far side of the boat and headed with certainty across the dockyard and out into the suburbs of London. Serge focused on swinging the mannequin arm in time with his real one and matching his pace to the sergeant's.

Both vampires remained on high alert, listening for other travelers. On a street corner outside the Wellington Barracks on Birdcage Walk, Frank sank back into the shadow beneath the trees in the park opposite and pulled Serge into the space at his side.

Before the councilor could ask questions, three guardsmen slipped out of the barracks and drifted across the parade ground. The iron gates wailed like a banshee when opened, but the trio slipped through and, in a burst of speed that made their movements a gray blur in the darkness, they appeared beside the sergeant.

"Good evening, Harold."

The small vampire nodded. "Sergeant Frank, great to see you."

The other two vampires shook hands with Frank and slapped his shoulder in a show of brotherhood.

Feeling like an outsider, Serge looked from one to the other and frowned.

"You know what to do?' asked Frank.

Harold and his companions inspected the councilor and, clearly in tune with each other, Harold said, "We know what to do."

Sergeant Frank tugged his gloves straight and turned to Serge. "I will be missed if I stay. Harold is here to help you, and when the hammer drops, I promise, Connor *and* Julian will know it was you that brought them down."

Harold wore a reverent half smile as he said, "Councilor, it is our honor to be part of this. I was there in the Albert Hall when your protégé, Sebastian, almost killed Doctor Connor. He will get his just desserts, at last."

Serge puffed out his chest as the trio surrounded him, as if he were a precious cargo.

Frank checked his watch. "Everything will be in place within the hour." Their gloved hands made a chorus of soft thuds as each of the brothers-in-arms shook hands, again.

Serge responded to the nudge on his back, and soon lost sight of Frank as he was guided through the park. When the streets became more familiar, the councilor gained in speed and confidence. Like a homing pigeon, he dodged cracked paving slabs and deep puddles with ease, and when he turned the final corner and saw the embellished facade of the Edwardian houses on Eaton Place, he grinned. Rushing forward, he thudded into an arm thrown across his chest and shot an annoyed glance at the hefty vampire blocking his path.

"Careful, we must check it is all clear." Harold smiled in apology.

It was a long time since Councilor Serge had been held prisoner there, but Julian's guardsmen could still have the place under surveillance.

The taller vampire shielded Serge from view, as Harold and his companion strode purposefully along the sidewalk. Seconds later, the vampire tugged Serge's sleeve and, side by side, they crossed the street to join the others on the front step.

Serge frowned. The door was closed, but a gouge in the glossy black paint beside the lock showed it had been forced.

Harold pushed it open. "Sorry, Councilor, we had to install the… equipment."

It made sense. Guardsmen could move anywhere around the city and barely raise an eyebrow. *Especially a band of brothers like these, who move like a well-oiled machine.*

Harold extended an arm of invitation towards the darkened entrance. "After you, Councilor." A gust of wind whipped open the flap of his coat and a gold emblem flashed into view.

"What platoon is that?" asked Serge, lightly.

"Old habits die hard. Disbanded now, so more of a souvenir." Pulling his coat shut, Harold exuded calm confidence, but something in his probing gaze prickled unease through Serge.

Rubbing his hand over his nape, the councilor tried to shake off the feeling of doom as he shuffled over the threshold, peered along the dark hallway and inhaled a strange aroma.

Static made the hairs inside his nose tingle and a dough-like odor clogged his throat. It came from behind the closed door to the front reception room and Serge automatically tried the handle.

Harold grasped the old vampire's elbow. "You can't go in there."

The door had not budged anyway and, on closer inspection, Serge noticed a hard, waxy deposit blocked the keyhole.

"For your protection." Harold grinned. "If you don't know what you're playing with you could trigger it. We wouldn't want you in the same room when that happened."

His companions nodded, all seemingly unfazed by being this close to the door.

"I see," said Serge, "and where do I wait for the sergeant's signal?"

Harold grinned. "We will wait with you."

The tight grip on Serge's elbow propelled him towards the study – the only room he had used inside this house in over a decade.

Serge embraced the feeling of home and security as, released by Harold on the threshold, he tracked the well-worn path across the dust-covered carpet, went behind his desk and sat in his old chair. He ran his fingertips over the familiar tooled-leather surface of the desktop and scanned the open hardback volumes laid out in front of him, which he had habitually pored over, looking for ways to outsmart vampires who possessed strength and power; attributes Serge longed for but had been cheated of by his 'creator'. The rejuvenation myths were a cruel lie and immortality was unbearable. *But, I get my own back, now.*

Harold remained in the doorway, surveying the room and the remnants of Serge's human treasures.

"Where will we hide?" Serge asked, lying a photo frame down flat on the desk and using the sleeve of his jacket to wipe the dust from the glass and peer at the sepia images.

"Hide?" Harold frowned.

"To be safe from… you know."

"Aah. We won't need to hide. Just 'stand well back', as they say in the movies. That will be enough."

Serge carried on rearranging books, pictures and keepsakes; a laborious process of using one hand to touch well-loved items, as if reconnecting with his past made this situation 'normal'. "So, my possessions will be safe here?"

"Yes, Councilor, we have taken great care."

The other guards had disappeared and when a shadow flitted across his window, Serge stood up and peered out through the dirty glass. Both vampires were positioned outside, resembling garden statues.

"What are they doing?" Serge sank back into his seat.

"Waiting for the signal."

The back door opened and the taller vampire appeared. "It's time."

"Good," replied Harold, pulling a black handset from his pocket as he crossed the room. "The operating procedure is simple." Standing beside Serge, Harold held out the detonator.

The old vampire blinked twice and then took it. It was heavier than he expected. It had a trigger button and a small unlit LED. "It doesn't look like much."

Harold smiled. "Radio controlled. You don't even need to get up from your desk. You press the trigger button to activate, and then, let go."

Turning it over in his palm, Serge struggled to get a firm grip on the unit. He couldn't line up his thumb with the trigger using only one hand.

"Here, let me help." Harold shifted the position of the detonator. "Now, press."

Serge noticed the other two guards had disappeared, again. "Now?"

"Yes."

Serge depressed the button and the LED lit up.

"The device will go off when you lift your thumb."

Harold checked his watch. "Detonate it in three minutes. I'll head out and tell the sergeant we are good to go. The blast will certainly get Principal Julian's attention."

"Blast?" Serge swallowed loudly. He felt the draft as Harold whipped out of the room. He stared at the closed door and then down at his hand, and the red LED burned a hole in his retina. *Dead man's switch.* Standing up, he grinned. *They must think I'm an idiot.* He wasn't wearing a suicide vest, and the bomb was in the house, so all he had to do was get outside the blast radius before he let go. My hand will not tire, and if the distance means the bomb does not explode, then so be it.

At the first obstacle of the closed study door, Serge delivered a swift kick and it sprang open. Outside the reception room where the explosive device was planted, he pressed his ear to the door. Silence.

The carpet dust he kicked up filled his nostrils and danced in front of his eyes, but Serge had the front door in sight. He kicked again, heard the wood creak, but the sturdy lock held. *Frank has used me as a patsy.* The location of the explosives made perfect sense, and so did the sergeant's help to keep him hidden. *But, why does he hate Doctor Connor?* Serge kicked harder and heard the doorframe crack. When the door burst open with a third kick, the jolt almost sent him reeling. *Steady.* Inhaling, ignoring the thick dust which filled his lungs, he stepped out onto the top step.

He heard the high-pitched twang of a tightly strung wire a nanosecond before a crossbow bolt whizzed past his ear. A second later, another nicked his shoulder, spun him around and the detonator flew from his grasp. With his back to the street, Serge howled. The white light uncoiled slowly, driving wood, plaster and brick fragments ahead of it as his vampire sight watched the world explode.

Sitting in a tree, five hundred feet away, Harold grinned as the blast singed the leaves and flattened his wet clothes to his chest. *Sergeant Frank would have put a bolt in the councilor's eye with the first shot.* Rain ran down over his tight features as he said, "Mission accomplished."

◇◇◇

The blast lit up the night sky above London, the rays of light shooting into the heavens like a starburst. The explosion pulsed through the air in a succession of bone-shaking tremors.

The warning siren at the council building emitted an ear-piercing scream and every guardsman in London left their barracks and whipped along the streets to their muster points. Across the city, platoons waited for the orders they knew would come. Their commanding officers stood at the barracks' gates, like hounds on point, they stared out into the night exuding fierce concentration and impatience.

In his chambers, Julian felt the shockwave as tremors racing beneath his feet and allowed himself one second of paralyzing fear. His footsteps echoed from the walls as he darted along the oak-lined corridor to the rear of the building. In the courtyard, where a corrugated metal awning provided shelter in sunlight, he found the Elite Guard lined up and waiting for orders.

Focusing on the officer in charge, Julian barked, "Update?"

Before the vampire could draw breath, a pair of scouts returned, skidding in through the open gate from the street beyond.

"Explosion. Eaton Place." The tall scout's report came in a barrage of bullet points. "A single blast-site. No one spotted leaving the scene. A squad from Wellington Barracks arrived as we did."

"Wellington Barracks? Eaton Place?" Aware he was repeating the information, Julian switched gear. "Search the area and set up a cordon." Turning to the squad leader of the nearest row of guards, he said, "Escort the bomb disposal specialists to sift through the wreckage. Tell them…" Julian snapped his jaw shut then waved a hand which sent a platoon rushing out of the gate. He knew the experienced bomb disposal crew would be alert to the electrical signature of another radio-controlled detonator. *If they are unsure, they will stay out.*

It was hard not to micromanage, especially when, in his gut, Julian knew something was off. *Eaton Place is Serge's district. Wellington Barracks is very close, but something does not sit right.* Sharing a sharp glance with the Elite Guard Commander, he said, "Take charge at Horse Guards' Parade. There are four sites to protect – London Zoo, SF8, Doctor Connor's laboratory, and the blood substitute manufacturing plant."

The officer saluted, whipped around to leave and almost collided with another pair of scouts hurtling in through the gate. They stank of sea-salt and their clothes and hair were stiff with the airborne deposits the fast run had crystallized on their skin.

The leading guard blurted, "Ferals are coming out of the sea. On the south coast between Weymouth and Southampton. Hundreds of them. It looks like the sea is boiling."

"Mobilize the troops." Julian swung towards the ordinance compound, relieved that truck engines were already growling into life. The well-oiled machine of the Elite Guard whipped around the yard. The wide barred gates scraped open, metal clanked as crates of artillery and bazooka shells were brought out and loaded onto the trucks. Within minutes, the train of armor-plated vehicles swept out in a squeal of tires and a rumble of fast moving boots, as outriders ran alongside like the footmen of horse drawn carriages had done a hundred years before.

"It's started. We're out of time," said Marius, from where he and Daniel stood, framed in the open doorway at the rear of the council building.

"Marius, you take charge here, I need to find Connor and Rebekah."

Racing out into the night, Julian powered along the streets, vaulting walls into long ago overgrown back gardens and courtyards to cut corners and miles from his journey. He unleashed the harnessed tension when he hit Hyde Park and ramped up to top speed, whipping beneath Marble Arch and creating a vortex that tossed banks of leaves into a storm of dancing movement.

London Zoo, under vampire ownership, now covered most of Regent's Park. A twenty-foot-high perimeter wall followed the 'outer circular road' and a row of floodlights made it impossible to escape the notice of the guards posted in the lookout towers.

Julian remembered when the zoo first opened to the public in 1847 – for twenty years the collection housed there was for scientific study only. When visitors were allowed, the zoo was home to over six hundred species and covered thirty-six acres; one of the largest collections in the United Kingdom.

Vampire ownership redrew the outer boundary. The almost two square miles of 'Gorilla Kingdom' became the largest habitat, closely followed by the lion and tiger enclosure.

The big cat species endangered by vampires were nurtured here to restock the safari parks in Dartmoor and Exmoor, so having rogue vampires eating the zoo livestock was out of the question. The guards posted on the walls were veterinarians with Special Forces skills.

At the huge stone archway where a grid of thick bars prevented access, Julian whistled loudly. A white face peered down from high above, disappeared fast, and the iron barred gate swung open.

Beneath his feet, Julian could still feel the aftershocks of the explosion. "Where is Doctor Connor?"

Following his guide, Julian hurtled through the zoo, skimming along concrete pathways which ran between enclosures and 'themed areas' where the old zoo met the new.

The 'Gorilla Kingdom' zone had become the gateway to a variety of outdoor and indoor habitats, where the apes were cared for, treated, and provided blood samples whenever Connor required them for his blood substitute experiment.

Stepping inside a dimly-lit barn-sized structure, Julian found Connor, Brynmor and Rebekah. Connor was frowning as he read the numbers displayed on a handheld unit. All three stood up when Julian appeared.

"What on earth was that?" The frustration radiating from Connor created a force-field of tension.

"They are coming." Julian waved to indicate the row of sedated primates hooked up to I.V. drips and fingertip clamps which took oxygen saturation readings. "This will have to wait. You can't cure ferals by the thousand, so we must deal with what's coming."

"Where are they coming from?"

"France, Cherbourg, Channel Islands. I don't know for sure, but from over there." Julian's eyebrows climbed to the height of 'what the Hell does it matter'.

Pulling off scrubs, Connor collected his shirt and coat from a nearby porter and pulled on clothes as he moved. "I have an idea that could buy us time."

Julian watched the trio sweep past and muttered, "It better be good."

Moments later, he had caught them up and gritted his teeth to hold back a tirade of questions as he concentrated on staying on Connor's heels.

The threat on the south coast was calling, and Julian's anxiety built as Connor headed west through London. When the greenhouse of Kew Gardens glittered like a floating glacier from across the lush green parkland, Julian stopped in his tracks. *What the Hell?*

Connor, Rebekah and Brynmor, in a dart head formation didn't falter. When Julian caught up, yet again, he grabbed the flapping fabric of Connor's coat. Without looking around, his friend threw back over his shoulder, "Trust me, Julian, we need Hera. Seren and Osiris are meeting us there."

"How-?" Julian stuttered then laughed. *Darned telepathy.*

Rebekah dropped back, and without realizing it, Julian slowed to match her pace. When they were jogging along a clear street, she said, "Yes, telepathy is a bitch." Her grin matched Julian's. "But trust *us* to deal with this. You have other things to do."

"The humans are safe," replied Julian.

"Yes, and Brynmor will head back to the hospital. *You* must get Malachi and the chimps to a safe place. Silas is one of a kind. Take them to SF8. Anthony will ride shotgun."

As if her words had called him back, Brynmor appeared, bearing down on them as he retraced his path.

"Trust us," said Rebekah, as she swung around and raced away.

Chapter 27

When Julian's Richmond home came into view, as Connor hoped, Osiris was waiting on the top step outside the front door. His composed features, bathed in moonlight, radiated calm. The gravel of the driveway spat into the air as Connor dug his heels in and skidded to a stop. Before the clattering noise had faded, Hera and Seren slid out from behind the partly opened door to join Osiris.

"Did you get the weapons I asked for?" said Connor.

"If you can call them that, yes." Osiris bent to flip aside the handles of a holdall lying at his feet. Squatting down and undoing the zipper, he pulled out three bolt guns and a dozen cans of pepper spray.

"Only three guns?" Connor's gray eyes glittered from deep shadows beneath his frown. "That will have to do."

Mounting the steps until he could reach, Connor picked up the hefty bolt gun and run through the retract and trigger action required to prime and fire it. He beckoned to Rebekah and put a gun in her hand. "No ammo to use up. They were used to stun cattle in an abattoir. Feral skulls are brittle. Believe me, in a tight spot, a bolt to the skull can put a one down instantly."

"You've done this before, then?" asked Seren, picking up a gun and trying it out. The sharp metallic crack rang out into the darkness.

Thinking back to the rushing tide of bodies he faced in Egypt, Connor nodded. "If one gets that close, save yourself at all cost." Handing out canisters of pepper spray and sliding two into the pockets of his own utility belt, Connor said, "Spray their faces and run, if that's all you've got."

Osiris frowned. "Their eyes will sting?"

"No, but the fluid will blur their vision."

~So, what is the battle plan?~

Hera buttoned up a combat jacket and yanked the belt tight around her middle before looking up.

For Rebekah's benefit, Connor said aloud, "You three head north to Salisbury and drive the deer and stag herd down towards Dartmoor. When you see ferals, cut one of the herd, and the ferals should track the blood."

"What are you and Mama going to do?" Seren copied Osiris, loading up her utility belt and scraping her own curtain of jet-black hair into a ponytail.

"We'll head to the south coast and drive the ferals down into the West Country. I just need to keep them contained in the safari park until daybreak. They will have to go into hiding at dawn and that will buy me time to run a final lab test. Then, we get to try it out."

The wind picked up and a distant wail jerked Connor's head around. "That explosion drew them across The Channel. Someone wants to make our lives Hell."

"Well, we've been *there* before, and they aren't going to win." Rebekah gave Seren a quick hug, hesitating for only a second before embracing Hera a little more carefully. Hearing the slight elfin girl's bones creak reminded them all that she was the weakest amongst them. Switching his speech to vampire speed, Connor said, "Keep Hera safe, we need her."

Connor wasn't sure of anything yet, but a plan was forming in his head, and Hera was the key.

With a final wave, both parties headed off in their different directions.

Connor and Rebekah raced across country in silence, taking turns to lead, and swooping in and out of the hedgerows in a flowing dance. Connor grinned, exhilarated by the joy of seeing Rebekah match him stride for stride. He missed her human fragility, but had become addicted to having a mate in whom he had met his match.

The silver-gray moonlit expanse of the English Channel glittered in the distance. As they picked a path through the seaside towns built on the slopes which led down to the shore, anguished wailing sounds drowned out the rushing noise of the wind. Rebekah faltered, her sudden deceleration almost derailing

Connor, who swung wide to avoid a collision, but when he saw what lay ahead, he too felt as though his boots were glued to the ground.

Down below, the golden sand was black with writhing waterlogged bodies. When a wave went out, more ferals rose from the boiling surf like decaying corpses being washed up on the shore. They staggered and walked over others who had fallen. The cleansing sting of salt in the air could not neutralize the stench of rotting flesh.

At the edge of the beach, the London Hive guard held the line. Whenever the front ranks knelt to reload their weapons, the rearguard took aim at the tide of rushing ferals. The bullets from the high-powered rifles shattered their brittle skulls, and if they were lucky, lodged in the flesh of the feral following on behind. But still, the guards were retreating one step at a time as the constant swell of attackers plowed up the wet yellow sand.

"We haven't got much time." Connor grabbed Rebekah's hand and the pair vaulted walls and barged through overgrown gardens, cracking trees as they went.

Sergeant Hugh was in the center of the rearguard, shouting the orders which kept the well-oiled machine turning over.

Connor stopped beside him and said, "Let them through, but force them northwest."

"There are so many. They keep coming."

Following the sergeant's gaze, on the shore line Connor saw the piles of bodies ranged along the beach, but more shriveled snarling faces appeared from beyond, climbing over the fallen as if they weren't there. The sickening crack of bones being crushed underfoot accompanied the wet sound of rotting flesh tearing.

"They won't stop." Hugh stood ramrod straight, his jaw dropping open as if he couldn't grasp what he saw.

"You're right, they won't. We have to funnel them away from London to where we can get the upper hand. Block off the side streets – knock the buildings down if you have to. They have no plan, they just march along the path of least resistance."

Hugh shouted to the back row of riflemen. "Fall back. Let them have the high street." To the vampire guard at his side, he said, "You heard Doctor Connor, block the side streets, anyway you can."

"Yes, sir." The guard disappeared into the sleepy seaside town.

Moments later, a series of grenades exploded. Choking brick dust filled the air and buildings collapsed, and a line of vampires shouldered back the tumbling stone to keep the main route clear. Masonry which fell into the high street was picked up and thrown back onto the piles of rubble.

"Good, keep the ferals moving and shoot the ones who leave the pack."

Hugh smile grimly. "Yes, sir." The rekindled light in the sergeant's copper-bright gaze radiated determination. He grabbed at the order as a mission upon which he could deliver. Swinging away, with a jerk of his head, Hugh led an eighty strong detail around behind the crumbling heaps of masonry.

Connor and Rebekah took a parallel course through the town to reach the front of the boiling tide of flesh eaters. "We need a blood trail." Connor darted into a nearby overgrown garden and returned with a rabbit which he gutted. Squeezing it like a sponge, he ran on ahead of the horde, dripping blood and then lumps of flesh when the carcass was dry.

From behind, they heard the sound of gunshot, or the hearty thump and crack of a hammer hitting flesh, and knew Hugh and the guardsmen were hard at work. *Will we get enough of them to follow?*

He tossed the rabbit away, and grinned when Rebekah swooped in ahead of him dragging a fox by its scruff. The guttural wailing of the feral tide rose to a nail screeching peak, and the shuffling and scraping noise of the press of bodies grew louder. They scented blood and surged forward, clambering faster and faster. The slower ones were trampled underfoot as the rolling heaving mass gathered speed. Connor climbed a tree and could not see an end to the churning column of rotting flesh. The coastline spread out in the distance was speckled black where pockets of ferals came ashore on different beaches, but the ant-like figures, like veins leading to the heart, seemed to be drawn towards the main body of the horde.

It's working. Outrunning the voracious bloodthirsty mass was the only focus Connor and Rebekah had. Twice, a clump of ferals broke away, following movement shuffling in the undergrowth and detecting the panicked heartbeat of a petrified mammal. Connor tore a hefty branch from a nearby tree and shattered the skulls of the first group of four. He thought about using a bolt gun, but decided stealth was better. It wouldn't do to attract the attention of the main clump.

Heading across the open countryside, the bait trail became hit and miss. Herding guinea pigs came to mind as the oozing flow of ferals resembled an octopus growing tentacles whenever they began to wander off course. *Shit, we need more.*

The ground beneath Connor's feet began to shake. It was a minute drumbeat, but he felt it in his chest, and so did the ferals. They dissipated. Scattering with their chins raised and saliva rattling in their throats as they scented prey, like hunting dogs, but the quarry covered so much ground, they roamed left and right.

Squinting towards the horizon, Connor held his breath.

"It's the deer herd," said Rebekah. She touched his elbow and grinned. "Look, there."

To the right, traveling at an angle which drew close but would rush across in front of the horde, were five hundred or more deer. The antlers of the majestic stags were easy to pick out as the bucks bounded along on the outer edges of the galloping pack, protecting the does from the terrifying threat of the dark-haired vampire warrior snapping at their heels.

"They did it," said Connor.

Hera was running along on the far side of the stampede, which made Connor feel easier.

The ferals, too, found focus, and accelerated forward, clawed hands outstretched at the hope of bringing down a meal before it whipped by.

The glint of steel caught the light as Seren drew a blade. She swooped in towards a large doe at the back of the herd and sliced across the velvet flesh of the ear. The doe stumbled, her knees hitting the ground as the shock sparked through her brain, but then survival instinct kicked in and she reared back up and kept running. Pearls of blood sprayed into the air as her pumping heart made her pulse rate gush. A black spear of bodies lunged forward from the undulating mass of flesh, clawed nails anchored onto the doe's rump and the animal screamed. The distressed deer hit the ground with a dull thud and was buried beneath the grease-stained shapes of ferals ramming their heads into their prey. The tearing of flesh attracted another twenty or so, and the snarls of hunters guarding their spoils stuttered through the early gray light of dawn.

If we sacrifice the back row of the herd, it could slow the ferals down enough for dawn to help us. Across the pluming dust which hung over the stampeding animals, Connor darted his attention to Hera, Seren, and then back. Their sudden change in direction as they slowed to let the main body of the herd pass by affirmed they had read his thoughts.

Within seconds, a spray of blood spurted into the air above five animals at the rear. The mist of droplets created hideous beauty to a vampire's gaze, and the sweet smell of adrenaline-soaked blood made even Connor's mouth water. Like a macabre game of leap frog, as the pile of bodies feeding on the fallen deer carcasses grew, others clambered over the top and chased after the healthy animals running on ahead.

Each row of deer Seren and Hera culled slowed the rushing feral tide by a few minutes, and a red line crept across the horizon on either side of the brilliant center point of the rising sun. Instinctively, Connor pulled his leather gloves up his wrists and checked his leather face mask was where it should be, pushed into the waistband of his pants.

At the head of the herd, Osiris guided the animals trying to escape back into the main pack – although guiding was more about growling and knowing his scent terrified them into running away from him. The Egyptian warrior grabbed the flapping edge of the long leather cape he wore, and flung the fabric over one shoulder, shrouding his bare chest and arms in protection. Hybrids, too, had to respect the dehydrating power of the rising sun.

In the distance, reaching from one coast to the other of the West Country peninsula, a dark smudge ranging across the landscape marked the fence-line of the Dartmoor Safari Park.

Connor and Rebekah constantly weaved back and forth to control their own side of the densely-packed fast-moving column of ferals, grateful when the dark band of the park boundary came into focus as it hurtled closer.

Shots echoing across the surrounding rolling green pastures relayed the hopeful message that stragglers were being hunted by Hugh and the guardsmen.

Connor squinted as the twelve-foot fence-line drew ever nearer. The organized 'checking in for hunting' procedures hive vampires adhered to were about to collapse beneath the coming onslaught. Heat haze hung like mist over the deer herd at the head of the stampeding mass as sheer panic drove them on; keening cries erupting each time a feral brought an animal down.

Behind the fence, a row of set white faces peered out from the courtyard in front of the 'checking in' outhouse. The wide entry gates whipped open as the ground shuddered and loose earth danced like dried beans on a drum skin. *That won't be wide enough, shit.* But as the thought raced through Connor's head, dozens of thick wire-mesh panels fell forward, leaving just the upright spines of steel fence posts in the way. *Someone has brains.*

The sun was warm on his shoulders and Connor tucked his chin into the collar of his greatcoat to shield his face. He slowed to let the deer herd thunder by, their bodies bouncing off each other and their eyes flashing white in the darker sweat-stained fur. Tuning in to the cacophony of heartbeats, Connor hoped that some of these animals would survive the day. Gazing back at the undulating feral mass, snarling features in their crazed blood-stained faces, Connor detected wisps of blood and bone fragments. Breaks appeared in the sea of bodies, figures clumping together like rocks being swallowed in an earthquake. *They are attacking each other.* The stench stung his nasal lining and Connor inhaled it with pleasure. Rebekah stopped at his side as the ferals headed into the safari park, crunching the fallen fence panels underfoot. The loud crack of splintering wood and shattering glass marked their path through the buildings the vampire safari wardens called home.

The noise persisted for the half an hour it took the roiling horde of hundreds to thunder through the opening, more fence panels crashing to the ground beneath the onslaught. From deep inside the safari park enclosure the distant howl of a tiger – puma or lion – Connor couldn't be sure which, became a blood curdling keening cry of pain and death.

"We did it," said Rebekah.

Connor watched Osiris, Hera and Seren meandering across the mile-wide tract of churned up earth as they checked each smoldering heap which marked the site of a trampled feral, to make sure they really were dead. The explosive crack of a bolt gun put an end to anything still moving.

What happens now? Seren sent her thoughts like a dart which hit Connor between the eyes.

"Now, we pray that before they eat every living thing inside the three hundred and fifty square miles of the safari park, we find a cure or a kill."

The smell of melting metal and a wave of heat drew Connor's attention. In bursts of purposeful action, small teams of vampires unbent, welded and replaced the buckled metalwork of both perimeter fences, but this time, the twenty-yard expanse of no-man's land between the two was crowded with vampire's bearing arms. Heavy artillery – guns humans would have mounted on wheels – were hefted around by broad-chested guards as if they were made of balsa wood. There was no doubt the odds were against the vampire force, but they would take down as many ferals as they could when the time came.

293

"Maybe they'll all die in the sun?" said Seren, when she finally joined her parents.

Hera and Osiris were only a second behind her.

Osiris dropped an arm around Seren's shoulders, tucked a strand of black silk hair back into the hood framing her face, and said, "Not all. There are woods, granite tors and manmade caves in there, but they won't all find shelter, either."

Another feline roar twisted into a keening cry.

Connor swore. "Such a damned waste. Let's head back into the city. This isn't all of them and they won't stop. Another wave could already be headed our way, but we've bought some time." Focusing on Hera, he forced a smile. "You three worked well together. Is there a strong connection?" *I expect Seren and Osiris to be close; Malachi's blood plays a part in both their DNA.*

Hera tilted her head. "I'm not sure if our connection is stronger than the one I have with Blake, but it is… easy." She frowned. "He wants me to return. I feel it."

"I'm sure he does." Connor laid a hand on the small girl's shoulder. "But that will wait. We have more pressing business, and so does Blake."

Setting off back towards the city, the damage left in the ferals' wake became clear. Villages Connor had skimmed through without noticing had become craggy mounds of stone and fractured brick. Felled feral corpses trampled underfoot by their own lay in mangled clumps of torn flesh and crushed bone.

On the outskirts of London, Sergeant Hugh's stout figure came into view. He waited for them to approach, turned his back to the rising sun and pulled his leather face guard away. "Keep your weapons close, Doctor, ferals came ashore further up the coast, but we should be safe now until dusk, at least."

"Thank you, Sergeant."

"Principal Julian is at the council building. He asked me to tell you all to stay together under guard at London Zoo – safety in numbers."

"Very well." Connor could use the help cataloguing the blood samples and checking on the sedated apes in their holding pens. "Are Malachi and the chimps safe?"

A sour expression crimped Hugh's face. "He's still at the hospital-" Holding up a 'don't shoot the messenger' hand when Connor scowled, he rushed on. "Malachi said you might need Silas. The storage facility is not an option. He refused to go."

~*Malachi is right.*~ Hera shrugged and dropped her gaze to the floor when Connor looked at her. ~*I can see through Silas' eyes. Feel him. We should keep them close.*~

Connor nodded. That eureka feeling of an idea igniting drifted like a spark on the outer edges of his mind. *I agree.* To Hugh, Connor said, "Escort Malachi, Portia and Silas to the zoo. If Julian needs us, we'll be there running tests."

Chapter 28

Human breathing disturbed the still atmosphere inside the storage facility. Instinctively, the communities had gathered on the first subterranean level. Already being used to living below ground made it easier on the eco-shelter inhabitants and, like adventurers circling a camp fire, hurricane lanterns became the focal points to gather around, where friendly faces were never too far away, and when exhaustion crowded in and their heads nodded, a supporting shoulder was always there.

Leizle woke up from just such a doze – she remembered leaning against Oscar, his arm around her making her feel secure, and then nothing. Her hearing surfaced first, as always when waking up. She lay there, feeling the weight of the sleeping bag cradling her body, letting the reassuring hum of conversation wash over her. Keeping her eyes closed and her breathing relaxation deep, she picked out the familiar voices first. Oscar and Evie, Adam, Sandy, Uncle Harry. It was harder from then as the distance meant deep tones drowned out lighter ones.

Finally opening her eyes and staring into the darkness, she realized the halo of light around the lamp didn't reach the ceiling. *What's up there? Bats?* A giggle gathered in her chest; the stuttering squeak drew attention and Oscar said, "Ah, welcome back, lass." The pat on her cocooned shoulder made her body rock. Reluctantly, she sat up, unzipped the sleeping bag and pedaled her legs until they were free.

She froze in the act of pushing long strands of tangled hair back from her face when she smelled coffee. The tin cup Oscar held out was a blissful sight. She smiled her thanks, shuffled forward to take her place, like a bead in the necklace of hunched bodies surrounding the lamp, and warmed her hands on the mug.

Blowing gently into the cup and feeling the steam damp on her face, she murmured, "What time is it?"

Oscar glanced back over his shoulder, then said, "Four in the morning."

Leizle twisted to check out who was keeping count and grinned at Greg. Even below ground, vampires knew where the sun was in the sky by some strange mumbo jumbo, it seemed. In reality, the elevated iron content in congealed vampire blood enabled them to pinpoint the location of the North Pole, like homing pigeons, and to detect where on the earth's rotation they were in relation to the sun. After all, it was life or death for vampires.

Sampson stood beside Greg, both vampires shielding the entrance to the dormitory. Sentinels guarding those who had become precious. The human farm community exuded nervous energy. For them, the claustrophobic element of living underground was an alien experience. Being condemned to darkness was stressful.

Leizle listened to their stuttering conversations and felt sorry for them.

A sudden thud of falling bodies echoed around the chamber when a muffled struggle broke out, and Greg jerked to attention.

Peter, the human leader of the farm group, leapt to his feet and hissed, "Knock it off, guys. We're all in the same boat, just stay calm. Take a deep breath for Christ sake and get a grip."

The grunts of annoyance stopped as suddenly as they had begun, and a few muted back slaps signaled that the hatchet was buried. Drama over.

As companionable silence descended again, Leizle rolled up to her feet and picked her way through the field of backpacks and bedrolls until she reached the wall beside Greg. "This is a tough gig, eh?"

Greg sighed and rubbed a hand over his jaw. "Windows would be good."

"Oh, I'm not so sure." Leizle grinned. "Landing a punch in the dark is tricky. That might be a good thing. It's a pity we don't have some soothing music. Don't suppose you can sing?"

"Afraid not, not in tune, anyhow. For now, this is all we have."

"Do we know how long we must stay here for?"

From where he stood at Greg's other shoulder, Sampson said, "Sergeant Frank and his men are guarding the main entrance. He'll update us when he knows anything."

Leizle nudged Greg with her elbow and winced when it felt like jarring her bone against a brick wall. Gritting her teeth, she said, "But, we'll be okay?"

Stroking her hair as a father would, Greg replied, "You're safe here. Go and try out your singing theory, I dare you."

"Yes, sir." With a mischievous grin, Leizle picked her way back to where the beacon of light cast her friends faces with ghoulish shadows. Leaning on Oscar, she dropped back down beside him.

Greg smiled as he watched her progress, until his head whipped around and he locked eyes with Sampson. Outside the range of human detection, a low rumble rattled through the structure and fine dust rained down from above.

Seth noticed both vampires' sudden jerk to attention and, with the shorthand of brothers in arms, Greg signaled to Seth to stand guard as he silently left with Sampson to investigate.

The two vampires whipped along the ascending corridor, frowning as the tremors grew stronger.

Making the final ascent to the main entrance chamber, they found Sergeant Frank and three of his men gathered by the closed door.

"What's happening, sir?" asked Greg.

"We'll know in a moment. One of my men has gone outside." Sergeant Frank exuded calm. His crossbow was propped against a nearby wall, but the loaded ammunition belt strung across his chest showed he kept other fire power close to hand.

At the whisper of footsteps outside, a tall guardsman pulled open the door.

Greg glanced round, wondering where the storage facility's usual doorkeeper was hiding.

The pale small figure resembled a statue standing in a corner, the subdued gleam in his eye radiating dull confusion. *I guess we are all struggling to adjust.* With all the vampire inmates cleared out, the warden and his staff felt redundant.

A gust of wind blew inside along with the returning soldier who was soaked by the spray of the churning river. He plastered his dripping hair back into place and, with a tight frown, said, "There's been an explosion in London."

"Where-?" Greg jolted forward to make a grab for the door and a solid figure blocked his path.

"Are the primary sites safe?" asked Frank.

Greg glared at the vampire obstacle, but waited.

"Yes. Council, hospital, zoo, barracks. All category 'A' sites are safe."

Greg relaxed. That meant Julian, Connor, Rebekah and Gerrard were also safe.

"What now?" asked Sampson.

"We do our job, soldier. Protect our charges and wait."

Greg wanted to protest, but commonsense prevailed and with a firm nod, he agreed to the plan.

Following Frank's orders, Sampson and Greg headed back to the human dormitory and their guarding duty. Outside the door, Greg said, "I'll just do a quick check down below. Make sure we are in good shape."

At the lowest level, where the metal-lined walls made it too cold for humans to stay, Greg found the warden resting back against the wall in a dark side-room.

Peering around the door, Greg surveyed the scene. The empty coffin shell sitting on a plinth looked to be a more permanent fixture than those in other storage rooms.

"Warden?"

The warden's dark eyes gleamed. "Marine."

Greg smiled. The man remembered him and that eased the tension gripping his neck. Going inside and shutting the door, he said, "Strange times, eh?"

"Indeed. The Butcher is gone – over a hundred years he's been here. Very strange times."

Greg inspected the coffin with renewed interest. "So, this is where he was kept?"

The warden nodded. "Except for the annual ceremonial viewings designed to drive home what interment in the storage facility means, yes."

Both vampires stood in silence digesting the magnitude of the changes facing them all.

Finally, Greg cleared his throat. "Do you think the storage facility is a safe hiding place?"

Pushing away from the wall and straightening his coat, the warden smiled. "The humans are secure here. There is only one entry point. Vampires have tried to break in *and* out, without success. What caused the earth tremor?"

"You felt it?" Greg lifted a brow. Tuning into the constant low rumble of the river rushing along behind the walls on this lower level, he was surprised. "An explosion in London."

The warden nodded. "London? Yes, I felt it, but I knew it was miles away. The storage facility is built to withstand heavy artillery, the humans are safe."

His companion's certainty made Greg feel better. "Thank you, warden. I'll let you get back to..." He wasn't sure what it was.

"Meditation." The warden grinned.

"Meditation," Greg agreed and, with a wave, he left the room and powered back up to where Sampson and his friends waited.

Sergeant Frank watched Sampson and Greg leave and his lip curled. *I think the Marine would be useful in a fight, pity.* Jerking his chin towards one of his crew, when the guard jabbed a thumbs up sign, Greg became a marked man.

The group stopped breathing, did not blink, and resembled a row of mannequins. Frank cocked his head, held a finger aloft, and then relaxed again. He glanced at his watch. *They should arrive soon.* Just as a flash of lightning heralded the crash of thunder, Frank knew the shockwave of Serge's explosion would be followed by the arrival of ferals in Britain. As more minutes ticked by, a worm of doubt crept through his brain. *Blake spotted them gathering on the French coast at Cherbourg. They must have felt it.* The sense of security shared by the British hives came from being off the radar of the mindless foe, thus far, but, the English Channel would not stop vampires. *Although, the terrain is hazardous.* When crossing the seabed on foot, walking down into the deep chasm of the shipping channel and up the other side was the biggest danger. The churning current and vibration caused by passing ships had eroded the bedrock, and the cliff-like rocky slopes were stacked like Jenga bricks. A careless step could cause an avalanche.

The ferals wouldn't take care on the crossing, but the numbers that might end up buried in the bottom of the trench would not be missed in a horde so vast. *They'll get here.*

The guard beside Frank nudged his shoulder.

When the sergeant refocused and tuned into the surroundings, he heard it, too. A cantering sound. Faint but rhythmic. Like the distant patter of scurrying rats.

"Do it." With a sharp nod, Frank's companion unsheathed a blade and slipped back out of the entrance door.

Facing the gusting squall which spat sea-spray into his face, the tall guard strode from the shelter of the storage facility to the edge of the stone platform and looked out over the River Thames. His wiry iron-gray hair darkened to ash as a wave crashing into the concrete plinth reared up and a white ghost of frothy water pummeled his still form. The pounding wall of spray sloshed around his feet as gravity dragged the watery beast back beneath the waves.

The low snarling rumble of inhuman hunger – a growl that rattled through the air – was still a long way off.

The vampire darted away, to where the trucks parked up in rows around the back of the facility were protected from the worst of the biting wind whipping across the wide river. Dropping the tailgate on a wagon, he jumped up and disappeared inside. Along the back wall, behind a pile of sacks sat three cages. Clamping the blade between his teeth, the gray-haired vampire opened the door on the nearest metal crate and reached inside. The vixen in the crate backed up, bared her teeth and a bark stuttered in her throat. With nowhere left to go, her jaws snapped as she lunged at the gloved black hand closing in. The crunch of shattered vertebrae drowned out the anguished shriek of pain when the vampire grabbed her by the throat. Her pulse throbbed beneath his palm and, before it died, he dragged the vixen out of the truck, slit her throat and tossed the carcass over the high fence thirty feet away. It landed with a thud in the rough pasture beyond, and the guard repeated the process twice more. The third fox took a lucky guess and managed to clamp its teeth onto the black glove of his tormentor, but suffered a cracked skull for his trouble.

The distant rumble resonating through the night air grew louder and, after watching the third bleeding carcass smack down onto the asphalt access road which led to the gate, the gray-haired vampire wiped the blade clean on his thigh and whipped back around to the thick door of the storage facility.

At the smart bang of his fist the door opened and he slipped inside.

"Trap is set," he said, his black gaze glittering with excitement.

"Stand by, men." Frank eyed the group of four. "Let about ten inside, then shut the door, any way you can."

Frank cradled his loaded crossbow in his hands, waited for each man in the squad to nod, and then walked away. The row of smoke canisters and hand-grenades strung across his belt clunked as he moved.

As the tremors through the ground grew stronger, grit skittered down the walls of the reception chamber and fragments of granite covered the head and shoulders of the vampires primed and frozen in place, waiting for the first wave to hit.

The perimeter gates shrieked as fence-metal twisted, and the gray-haired vampire nodded sharply. The remaining three braced their shoulders to the metal panel as their leader used both hands to pull back the hefty bolts securing the steel door. Carefully, they inched it open. The metal panel jolted inwards, bodies crammed into the space and crazed howls couldn't drown out the sound of bones splintering in the crush. The first row of snarling open-mouthed ferals, rammed in through the space too small for a human form by the ones behind, died. The manic light in their eyes flickered and their broken slack forms slid downward.

"The bodies will block the door," barked one guard, shoving his shoulder in harder as the leader swung his boot like a mallet at the carcass lying on the ground. Another feral reared up behind, swinging his legs in first as he tried to squeeze into the tight space. Rotting flesh smeared over the steel frame and a cheekbone crumbled as he forced his way through.

"Hold the gap," said the gray-haired vampire, gripping the greasy fabric of the feral's coat, then taking a half step back to pull him inside. The intruder's flailing clawed grip dug into the squad leader's forearm and the gray-haired officer landed a punch, shattering the feral's other cheekbone and spinning him around. The creature froze, lifted his chin, and a keening wail echoed around the chamber before he darted forward into the darkened mouth of the access tunnel.

"He's got the scent of the humans."

The hungry shriek triggered another surge of ferals, their blood-stained bony fingers curling around the edge of the thick door like spider legs, and the door panel shunted open another few inches.

"Hold the line, for Christ sake," shouted the gray-haired leader.

Three ferals shoved in through the tight space and surged to their feet.

Picking up a hammer in each hand, the squad leader swung at their skulls and dropped them where they stood. Other ferals clambered over the bodies and, flattening his back to the side wall, he counted them in. When the eighth figure staggered past him, he shouted, "Push."

Even with the lightning fast reflexes of the group, who threw everything they had at the creaking metal door, another two ferals were already wedged in the closing gap. The shoulder-blade of the last one snapped with an ear-piercing crack as he fell inside over the growing pile of the trampled dead. His limp arm swung erratically as the feral lurched up from where he had crashed down onto his knees.

Switching hammers for an ax, the squad leader hacked at the clamoring limbs of those outside still trying to claw their way in.

As the door inched shut, four more snarling ferals pushed into the gap, teeth grinding and saliva spraying into the squad leader's face. Pulling a pin on a grenade, he shoved it into the open mouth of the nearest feral, planted a boot on his chest, and grunted as he kicked hard and the feral fell back. "Now, shut the fucking door." He returned to hacking at the bodies on the threshold, flesh and bone crackling as the three guards shoved harder and the door groaned shut.

From outside, the splattering impact of exploding flesh ricocheted through the panel, making the metal hum in its frame.

The gray-haired vampire watched the last of the ferals stagger towards the access corridor to the lower levels as his crew slid the bolts back into place. "Jesus, I hope the sarge knows what he's doing."

Swinging around, the group armed themselves with hand guns and checked they were fully loaded.

Shoving his own weapon into his belt, the squad leader said, "Let's go, and remember, don't shoot unless sarge gives the order."

The square cut granite-lined corridor was pitch-black, but now it was familiar territory the guards didn't bother to collect a flashlight from the alcove cut into the wall. Flashlights would only give away their location.

"Stay together." Like hunters stalking prey, the squad leader led his men silently down the polished stone pathway. It evened out on level one and, hearing a gargling noise coming from inside the first dormitory, the squad leader raised a clenched fist and everyone froze.

Homing in on the wet sound of tearing flesh, one guard palmed his handgun, pushed the door open, and peered inside.

When he aimed the weapon, the gray-haired leader gripped his arm and slid forward to look for himself. A black figure crouching over the bleeding corpse on the floor continued to shove his face into a gaping chest cavity. The suckling sound – like an infant feeding – made the squadron leader's lip curl.

Easing back out, he mouthed, "Stand guard and wait."

The remaining group of three sidestepped along the corridor to the next human dormitory. The gray-haired vampire jerked back when Greg stepped out of a side-room.

"What the Hell is going on?" The Marine scanned the three blank faces with narrowed eyes. Craning his neck, he checked out the guard standing outside the door further back. He swallowed down saliva, because talking had let plumes of fresh human blood invade his senses and his gaze clouded with distraction for a nanosecond.

The group of three exchanged pointed looks and their leader raised two fingers.

Greg pulled his favorite weapon, a blacksmith's mallet, from his belt and said, "This is bullshit. You're fucking traitors."

"Not us." The lead vampire sidled closer. "You're looking in the wrong place."

"I'm looking in the right place. You let the ferals in." Taking a swinging blow, Greg caught the nearest guard on the elbow, felt the joint shatter, and visceral pleasure skittered through him. Stepping in closer, Greg slammed the mallet head into the vampire's face, opening up a crater where his nose should be.

"For God's sake, he's a new vampire, let's get the job done."

Abandoning the mallet wedged in his victim's skull, Greg swung around as the remaining two guards pulled their handguns. Shots rang out and, like a wrestler in the ring, Greg bounced from one side of the corridor to the other, hissing at the heat as a bullet grazed his ear. Pushing away from the wall, leaving a shoulder shaped crater of crushed granite, he barreled into his foe and grabbed a vampire by the hair.

When they both hit the opposite wall, Greg rammed the guard's head back into the stone. A cheekbone cracked in his opponent's face and the guard's gun hit the ground.

A thick arm closed around his throat and Greg felt the muzzle of a gun pressing into his torn ear – a bullet in the eye socket or ear canal into a vampire brain were certified kill shots. With a grunt, he went slack, dropped to his knees and the shot grazed through his scalp and bounced from the wall beside him.

A sudden rushing breeze flattened Greg's combat jacket to his body and Sergeant Frank burst into view, powering up the slope.

Faint sounds coming from down below of a human screaming focused Greg's mind. *Shit, how many are dead?*

The sergeant's fierce frown exuded rage. "Whatever the fuck this is, shelve it, fall in and fight the real enemy. Now."

Driven by only one thing, Greg sprang up, put his foot on the chest of the fallen vampire to yank the blacksmith's mallet out of the smashed skull and brushed past the sergeant. His human friends were dying.

Nudging the prone figure with his boot, Frank said, "We're a man down, you better get your asses into gear."

A tussle in the room behind ended abruptly, and the third vampire guard rejoined them, wiping feral blood from a bayonet spike onto his sleeve. He looked at the crushed face of his companion and his fist tightened around the spiked blade. "The Marine will pay."

With a sharp nod, Frank disappeared from view, heading back down towards level two.

The injured vampire's cheekbone shifted when he grimaced, and the squad burst into action to follow their commander.

The group locked their throats down and stopped breathing as they descended to where the heavy sweet smell of human blood hung in the air. One wall resembled modern art, covered in smears the shade of ruby, punctuated by splattered droplets in claret.

The vampires clenched their teeth, fighting the urge to lick the blood from the wall.

Up ahead, Greg delivered a two-handed mallet blow to the back of the skull of a feeding feral. The creature fell facedown onto his victim and the glassy stare of the dead human told Greg it was too late. "I'm sorry," he muttered as, grabbing the man by one boot, he dragged him from beneath his attacker and towed him down along the corridor. Greg moved fast, and the trail of glistening blood formed pools whenever he slowed to check for ferals.

Like beetles scuttling out from beneath rocks, four ferals emerged, fell to their hands and knees, and scraped their teeth over the granite as they pressed their faces into the congealing blood.

The guards dispatched the distracted feeders with ruthless efficiency, one with a bayonet spike to the base of the neck which pierced the brain, the others with a pointblank shot into the ear where the bullet bounced around inside the skull like a wooden spoon stirring a bowl of custard; the fate Greg had narrowly escaped.

Frank appeared again, his tunic stained with blood and a glitter of exhilaration in his eyes. A grin pulled his face tight and bared his teeth. The corridor behind him was all quiet. "We saved most of them."

Greg stood and his shoulders slumped. "How many did we lose?"

"Thirty."

"Shit. Where are the rest?"

"They are inside the death chamber. The ferals can't get past the reinforced door."

Greg nodded. He gently lowered the leg of the body he had dragged along the floor and picked the dead man up. Dodging passed Frank, he headed off to assess the carnage and face the worst.

In a side-room on a lower level, a row of steel coffin shells gleamed dully in the gloom. Although now empty, the recent vampire occupants had left gritty deposits in the base. Hoisting the slack body over the side, Greg laid down his human burden and straightened the limbs. His steps were heavy as he traveled the corridors and homed in on the thick scent cloud which hung over each slaughter site. At each corpse he gathered up, he steeled himself to look. After laying twenty humans into coffin shells, making some attempt to rearrange torn flesh and reunite severed limbs with their owners, a worm of hope crawled through his brain. All the human dead so far were farm dwellers he did not recognize, but, if Frank's body count was right, it was not yet over.

Where is Sampson? He shook his head. *We were foolish to not have more trustworthy vampire escorts. Anthony, Marius, Daniel. We should have protected the humans.* Heading down another level, the stainless-steel walled network of the death chamber wing loomed. Bloodied fingerprints dried onto the door handle were a bad sign. When Greg pushed at the door, it was locked so he called out, "Hello."

The metal rods of the locking mechanism retracted with a click, Greg entered and was greeted by the warden. He had deep gouges cut into the side of his face and his left sleeve hung in tatters.

"How many ferals got in?"

"Only one, thank God."

"The blood on the door?"

"I'm sorry." The warden stepped aside and revealed a fresco of bodies lying in awkward angular poses, like a modern sculpture. The feral was still moving but had no arms, and so it squirmed from side to side like a lunatic in an asylum rocking.

Two of the human bodies lay in an entangled mess, and Greg swallowed hard. He didn't need to go any closer to recognize the large solid frame of Oscar, and the woman he still clasped to his chest had blood streaked gray hair. *It must be Evie.* A surge of tight anger jerked Greg's body ramrod straight. Swinging around, he strode back out through the door and along the ascending tunnel until he found Frank.

Pointing at the guardsmen standing five yards behind their sergeant, Greg said, "They let them in. They are traitors."

Frank planted a hand on Greg's chest as he tried to lunge past.

When Greg glared, the sergeant raised an eyebrow. "Who is a traitor would depend on whose side you are on."

Greg frowned. "What-?"

"I'm sorry."

The vampire behind Frank, on the left, lifted a crossbow. Greg went to dive right, but grunted when the sergeant stepped in and rammed a bayonet spike up under his jaw, twisting to grind it through the tough vampire skin. Greg grabbed Frank's forearm, dug his nails in hard and grated out, "Why?"

The two guards approached, grinning. One broke Greg's fingers as he levered each one from the sergeant's torn sleeve. Impaled but conscious, Greg jerked his knee up into Frank's stomach.

"It's a shame," the sergeant said, as he twisted his hip to ward off the blow. "You would have been a great soldier." Pulling Greg in closer, he glared. "You want to know 'why?'. The answer is, Doctor Connor."

Confusion made Greg gargle in the nanosecond before his own blacksmith's mallet crunched down onto the crown of his head. The blow rammed the spike up through the roof of his mouth, and it took another two strikes before Greg's skull cracked open.

"Clear him out of the corridor, but then crush his skull. He deserves to be at peace." Frank bent to pull out the bayonet spike and slid it into his belt. "I'll reassure the humans they are safe and start coordinating the escape."

"The ferals outside won't leave, so how are we going to get them out? There is only one door." The gray-haired vampire lifted an eyebrow as if to say, 'it is why we chose this place, remember?'

Frank grinned and laid a hand on the shoulder of his second in command. "The humans are inside the death chamber. We just have to wait for low tide."

Racing down the corridor, Frank banged on the sealed door to the death chamber wing. The warden opened it and his mouth formed the perfect 'O' of surprise. "Sergeant." He fell back as Frank surged forward.

"The ferals are all dead." Frank slumped his shoulders convincingly as he said, "The Marine, Greg, was the traitor. He let them in."

"No." The word burst from the warden before he clamped his jaws shut.

"I don't think he wanted people to die. He just wanted to be a hero, but things got away from him. Don't tell his friends." The sergeant cast a searching look at the warden.

"Very well." The pallid gray skin on the warden's face visibly sagged.

He thought highly of the Marine. Frank shook his head, as if shedding a cloak of regret, and said, "We owe it to him to save his friends. Let's go."

The metal walls of the final approach to the death chamber were dripping with more condensation than usual. It was because humans needed oxygen – breathing created moisture; a stark reminder that the death chamber could only be a temporary solution. Blood speckled the walls like pink tear-stained rivulets and Frank eased the stiffness from his nape to cover a surge of excitement that clenched his gut tight. *We could have lost every human.* But all that meant was he would have lied to Julian and found another way to execute his plan.

The polished metal door slid aside with a whisper, and Frank scanned the sea of grubby startled faces. The one he sought was right there at his left shoulder.

"Where are they?" Leizle's voice shook, the pitch rising as she gripped Frank's sleeve and scoured his face.

"I'm sorry. No one outside this room survived."

Tears welled in her eyes and she swiped at them. Turning away, she hugged a thin boy, who started to cry into her shoulder. "He can't be dead. He can't be…"

A tall wiry man with shaggy graying hair and salt and pepper stubble stepped forward and squared up to Frank. "Greg wouldn't have let anything happen to Oscar. He and Evie will be hiding somewhere."

Let's hope the warden backs me up. Smothering his irritation, Frank lowered his voice and said, "Greg and my guards fought hard. We killed the ferals, but we lost men."

Seth's jaw muscle ticked as he jutted out his chin. "I'll take a look."

Frank put a hand on his chest and whispered, "You won't. You owe it to Greg and Oscar to help settle the group and get them to safety."

Seth held Frank's piercing gaze for ten seconds, then visibly sagged. "What's the plan?"

"The sluice gate." The sergeant nodded to indicate the rubber trimmed panel which covered most of the back wall. "It purges this chamber of its... contents at high tide, but at low tide in..." He checked his watch. "Three hours, the water level will mean I can get you all out of here without the ferals up there seeing you." Frank shrugged. "Keeping quiet is down to you." Assessing the rows of tired, drained faces, he could smell the after effects of plummeting adrenaline. *They'll be fatigued and easy to convince.*

Turning his attention to Leizle, the sergeant reached for her hand. "I'm sorry if you lost someone close to you." Her red-rimmed tear glazed eyes and blotchy face would have told him that, even if he could not tap into the hormones racing through her arterial system. "I promised Principal Julian I would keep you all safe and I failed." Stepping closer and pinning her in an earnest gaze, he said, "I will not let any harm come to you or your community from this day onward. I swear it."

Leizle swallowed noisily, her grip on his hand tightening until her knuckles glowed white in the gloom. "Thank you."

Casting a glance across the chamber at the huddled humans, so tightly packed into the space that the weary could only sink down into hunched cross-legged bundles, Frank said, "Rest while you can, and stay quiet."

Peter and Sampson were waiting for him when he turned to leave.

Darting a look over his shoulder, in preternaturally low tones, Sampson said, "Did we lose twenty-eight farm dwellers out there?" Peter, unable to hear anything more than a humming whisper, pulled on Sampson's sleeve. The young vampire held up a finger, telling his companion to wait. "As you can see, they need to know. The dead had family and friends."

"What do you want from me?"

"Nothing, just let Peter and I identify the dead, so we can tell them."

Frank frowned, assessing the pale face of the young man who peered back with gritty determination. Slowing his speech so Peter could hear him, Frank said, "It's not a pretty sight."

The pair nodded in unison, and the sergeant led them from the death chamber, telling the warden, "They will be back shortly."

Chapter 29

Connor left the medical block inside London Zoo and inhaled a deep lungful of fresh air. If he closed his eyes, he could recite every species living inside the boundary wall, down to how many beasts were in each herd, troop, pride, etcetera. The heyday of the conservation project, when there were over six hundred different species which Londoners flocked in through the gates to see, were in the distant past.

The strongest odor riding on the late afternoon air was straw, ether, and simians. He checked his watch and frowned. Four hours locked inside the lab had passed in the blink of an eye.

Inside every dull gray square-shaped building in the yard, were metal barred cages, or holding pens. The moment they arrived in the medical compound, Connor and Brynmor had selected and sedated potential simian subjects, until all the holding pens were filled.

Brynmor took blood samples from the primate subjects and catalogued the donors by sub-species, and in order of robust health indicators. Working side by side with Connor, his laboratory assistant had concentrated on filling I.V. bags with a synthetic blood substitute/perfluorocarbons combination – a proven compound which could pass through the gateway of the vampire brainstem and hydrate the brain. *Is it too late for the ferals?* Only time would tell.

Connor worked on the endgame option; combining simian blood/perfluorocarbons with various toxins. The downside was, the best delivery system he could think of meant the wholesale sacrifice of the zoo's primate population.

The first problem was to acquire a feral subject to try out the 'cure'.

Heading across the concrete courtyard, Connor ducked inside the dim interior of a nearby outbuilding. The group of figures gathered at the far end of the long line of animal pens rippled with movement as Rebekah looked up and nudged Seren.

313

A gnarled elderly hand appeared as it gripped a bar from inside the last holding pen in the row. *It will be sunset soon.* Malachi's thoughts cut to the crux of the matter.

I have something to try, but I need a guinea-pig. Connor strode the length of the large shed until he could look inside and see Malachi. Silas and Portia were sitting calmly in a bed of straw.

"What's happening?" asked Rebekah.

"Papa needs a test subject," replied Seren.

"A test subject? You need a feral?" Rebekah mused aloud. "How can we do that?"

"They are out there, hiding from the sun, right now." Connor's jaw muscle clenched. "We just need to lure one here."

"I can be the bait." Osiris stepped forward, eased the gold armlet down from his bicep and disturbed the sealed plug of wax in the catheter tube enough to release a plume of fresh blood fumes. Connor absently registered his mouth filling with saliva, but shook his head. "No, you are not indestructible Osiris. I won't risk a human or hybrid life."

Silas rolled over in a flurry of straw husks and padded across to the bars. In a human-like gesture, he waved to attract attention. His fingers skimmed quickly through a sequence of sign. 'I will go.'

Connor frowned. "What?" Scanning the others in a 'what on earth' glance, he found a row of expressions as dumbfounded as his own, until he got to where Hera lay slumped against the wall with her eyes closed.

Connor looked back at Silas, who rested on his haunches and then nodded sagely.

"Is that you?" Connor asked Hera.

~Yes. I can tap into Silas' consciousness at will. I only realized that when we spent time here. The visions I had of Malachi in Egypt through Silas' eyes were just the beginning.~

Feeling the irritation coming off Rebekah in a tangible force, Connor chuckled and repeated everything Hera had 'sent to him'.

Seren crossed quickly to Hera and laid a hand on the girl's shoulder. As if struggling her way back from a coma, Hera's lips moved in a silent litany and then her eyes slowly opened. Sweat beaded on her forehead and her gaze was dull. "It takes a lot of effort, but I can control Silas."

The chimp 'oohed' softly, loped back to his mother, and fell into Portia's embrace.

Deep in thought, Connor drifted to Rebekah's side, took her hand and idly played with her fingers.

"How does Hera being able to control Silas help?" Rebekah asked.

"I'm not sure," he murmured, but his gray gaze remained glued to the young chimp.

"Yes, you do. Tell me," said Rebekah.

"I need to ask Malachi, first." Seeking out his mentor, the two communicated in their familiar shorthand. The Dartmoor plains filtered into Connor's head, as he and Malachi agreed on the best location to 'lure a feral'.

"Marius should come. His battle experience will be invaluable, and he can read 'sign' faster than any of us. He'll know what Hera is saying through Silas," Connor said aloud.

Malachi's pearl glazed eyes sharpened and his paper-thin skin crackled as he frowned.

Connor glanced again at Hera – her color had returned and she appeared alert once more.

You are taking a gamble. What if Silas is… caught?

Malachi's question appeared as script carved across Connor's mind. Aloud, he said, "Have you got a better idea? We need to move fast."

Osiris stepped up. "I can lure one here." He puffed up his broad chest.

"We need one feral, not a thousand. This is a handpicking exercise." Connor nodded at Hera and Malachi. "Just us three."

"And Marius?"

"We'll collect him on our way through London. He's manning the blood substitute manufacturing plant with Daniel. Connor was happy to avoid Julian. Relating the plan out loud would sound like madness. *Heck, it already does.*

Rebekah caught hold of Connor's hand and squeezed. "You better get going. Seren and I can look after things here."

"We'll be quick," he replied, dropping a kiss on her upturned lips before heading for the door.

Outside, Connor eyed the cloud-cluttered sky, but still flipped up his coat collar. Malachi wound a wide swathe of fabric around his body into a sling which held Silas. The chimp wrapped his arms tightly around his surrogate father's ribcage. Seeking reassurance, Silas plucked at Malachi's skin with his lips and a soft 'oohing' sound became muffled by the cloak the elder vampire drew closely around his shoulders.

Connor could hear Malachi's bones creaking beneath Silas' hugging grip, and knew that a human escort would have sustained broken ribs – chimps were stronger than most humans could imagine.

Osiris appeared beside his mentor, dressed for the journey. His curtain of black hair cast a shadow over his high cheekbones, but the stubborn gleam in his coal black gaze was unmistakable. "I'm coming."

Connor chuckled. "Very well, but *no* blood trails and keep out of the way. Understood?"

"Understood."

The group of four skimmed along the gloomy streets and Connor darted an anxious look skyward. "Keep your eyes and ears open for ferals." He felt better saying it, even if it was obvious. "We just need *one*."

When the group arrived at the manufacturing plant building, the dark juror appeared on the top step outside the entrance, and Connor grinned. "Marius."

The dark intense vampire pinned Connor and his companions in a sharp glare, his surprise at seeing Hera clear. He signed, 'Where are you going?'

Connor was glad they would not lose time tracking the elder juror down. "We're headed to the Dartmoor safari park. We need your help to capture a feral specimen. I'll fill in the details on the way."

Marius swung back inside the building and emerged a minute later with Daniel, who was armed with his longbow and quiver of toughened steel arrows.

"I'll update Julian," said Daniel as Marius leapt from the top step of the concrete stairway, ready to burst into action.

Connor wasn't sure Julian would approve of the plan, but he didn't have time to argue, so he jerked his chin and said, "Let's get going."

Marius effortlessly matched Connor's hurtling speed, settling at his shoulder so they could communicate while they rushed onwards west out of London.

In tight formation, the group were soon racing into the buffeting headwind which blew across the open countryside.

Getting closer to Dartmoor, they wove a path through the piles of feral corpses.

Marius whistled to attract Connor's attention. 'How many are in there?' he signed, jerking his chin towards the distant smudge marking the boundary of the safari park.

"A thousand or more came across after the explosion, and more on other beaches." Connor frowned. "Sunset could bring another wave from across The Channel, so we need to be back in London where the guardsmen are patrolling before then."

Marius nodded.

Hera drew alongside the dark vampire. "You understand sign?"

With a flurry of hand signals, Marius gave his answer, and a grin softened his stern expression. He locked gazes with the slight girl and signed, 'How will this work?'

Hera's white teeth gleamed in the glow of a setting sun. "I'll see through Silas' eyes. When Doctor Connor selects a feral, we'll lure it close enough for him to sedate it with a blow-dart."

Veering towards a clump of trees, Connor led the group to where they could stop and survey the landscape ahead.

Malachi loosened the fabric sling and Silas wriggled free, dropped to the ground and stood oddly erect. Hera sank down into the soft earth at the base of a tree trunk, her body becoming slack. Her mind could only control one receptacle at a time.

Marius frowned. 'I've seen this before,' he signed slowly for Connor's benefit. 'She has left her body.'

Silas nodded, and the chimpanzee waved a hand toward the open ground.

'I'll protect Hera... Silas, until we find a feral.' Marius laid a hand on the chimp's shoulder and pointed west. 'Be ready with that dart.'

The pair set off.

As Connor prepared to follow, he muttered, "Well, here goes. The range on this thing is about a hundred yards." In the confines of London Zoo, hitting the target was simple, if anything, Connor had to be careful not to use too much vampire force and bury the dart too deeply into the primate's muscle mass. Thinking aloud, he said, "I've got to get this dart into an eye, ear, or mouth for it to work."

It was your idea. Malachi's harsh laughter rattled around Connor's head, but when he glanced back, both Malachi and Osiris were hunkered down beside the unconscious Hera. Osiris had placed his folded cape beneath her head, and Malachi's bony hand stroked the young girl's hair. Her olive-toned Spanish complexion had become so pale it looked yellow.

"And it's too quiet out there." Connor loaded the dart gun and jogged out into the open. He easily caught up with Marius and Silas at the newly repaired fence-line of the safari park and joined them in peering through the mesh, frustrated that the mounded debris of the reception buildings obscured the view.

"I can't hear anything." Connor nudged Marius. "We should hear something."

Marius indicated the pink haze of dusk on the horizon, and signed, 'You're right, the ferals hiding in the forests should be moving around by now, unless they are all dead.'

The idea was ridiculous, and would ruin their plan. Connor snorted. "They can't be so far gone they would all walk out into the sun and die?"

Climbing the fence, Connor dropped down on the other side. Jogging across the divide, he tapped the metal frame of the inner gate to attract a guard. *Nothing.* Graveyards were quiet, but this was beyond that. Tuning into the metallic smell of blood, Connor realized there was only profound silence. Every living creature – pumas, tigers, lions, bobcats, and even the rodents, rabbits and foxes which shared the parklands – every living thing was dead. The air hung heavy as if the wind could not move it. Gripping the bars, Connor peered through the window of the nearby changing station and saw a jerking movement. The door eased open and a park warden sidled out and glanced left and right. In a blur of strangely creeping movement, which barely stirred the dried silt on the ground, the warden appeared in front of Connor. They have killed everything in a two-hundred-mile radius. They disappeared when the sun came up, but-" He shot a glance at the dull pearl colored sky. "At sunset, they'll start moving again."

"Where are your men?"

Copying Connor and gripping the bars of the gate, the warden said, "Half of them were trampled underfoot, the rest are tracking the feral herd at a distance. The artillery made hardly a dent, and we haven't got the fire power to do much more but they'll warn us if the ferals swing around and head back up the Cornish peninsular."

Connor noticed the bullet scarred tree trunks and swathes of trampled undergrowth in the distance, for the first time.

"Cattle prods are our only defense in hand-to-hand combat. Sheer numbers of the horde make that a suicide mission."

"Have you got tranquilizer guns in the veterinary compound?"

"Yes."

"I plan to capture a feral specimen, and you can help. I have a team ready with a lure."

Connor turned and gave the signal, and Silas and Marius made an odd pairing as they too scaled the outer perimeter fence and ran forward to join him.

With a sharp nod, the warden squared his shoulders and determination glittered in his eyes. Pulling a key from his belt, he let the visitors in through the gate. With renewed purpose, the group dashed across to take cover beneath the overhang of the roof of the changing block. 'Wait here' signed Connor and, at a crouched run, followed the warden around to the back, hugging the walls. Holes had been punched into the brickwork in places and they had to step over piles of rubble.

Darting across a small yard, the warden unlocked the door, entered and relocked it once Connor had whipped past him.

In a storeroom, the pair sorted through the equipment store and found hunting rifles and tranquilizer and muscle relaxant cartridges. Their prey was undead, so he loaded up with the relaxant version, but the warden tapped him on the shoulder.

At Connor's arched look, the warden whispered, "Tranquilizers work faster… we don't know why."

"Interesting." Feral physiology really was a matter of guesswork. With an 'in for a penny' nod, Connor loaded another hefty gun with hollow point rounds as a precaution. His own blowdart he shoved into his waist band.

"How do we get one away from the pack?" The warden frowned. "They are like an organism."

"There must be stragglers. Every herd has them. We'll track one and use Silas as a lure. We literally just need something with a firing brain cell." Connor grinned.

Coming back out into the open, he beckoned to Marius and Silas, and both skimmed swiftly across the space between the buildings.

'Follow closely and keep an eye out for any movement. We are looking for a feral we can separate from the herd,' signed Connor.

The group of four emerged from the shelter of the veterinary block and fanned out into a straight line, like a row of police officers conducting a search for a dead body. The ground was scattered with mounds of soft earth which made Connor frown, feeling uneasy. He had hunted here often enough to know that was unusual. Scanning ahead, there was no movement as far as his vampire sight could see – so fifty miles of nothing, apart from the flapping of bird wings as they skittered around in the tops of the trees that were still standing.

The group skirted around the spiny grid work of branches made by fallen trees, using them as cover as they silently moved forward. Maintaining a line of sight between him and the others, Connor set a steady pace. The darkness of nightfall thickened and Silas made a gentle 'ooh' sound. Hera brought the small chimp closer to Connor and, in a smooth move, Silas leapt up onto Connor's back and wrapped his strong wiry arms diagonally around Connor's chest from shoulder to waist, anchoring the chimp tightly in place.

Silas' heart beat like a drum against his back, and Connor understood why Hera wanted the chimp close to him. *This is what the ferals will hear and I have to protect him.*

In the center of a line, now, Connor continued on. All three stopped abruptly when in the near pitch-black, they heard the shuffling sound of pouring earth. Raising his tranquilizer gun, Connor rotated on one heel. The dark shape rising from beneath the ground beside him smelled of damp soil and flesh. Gargled dirt fell from its open mouth and in the second before the feral lunged, Connor lined up the tranquilizer gun. Before he could pull the trigger, like a knight falling on his sword, the feral flung himself forward, and the metal point on the cartridge shunted into his gaping mouth.

His clawed grip latching onto Connor, the feral kept pushing until the gun barrel began to grind a hole through the back of his head.

From nearby, the warden leapt in and smashed a rock down on the feral's skull, cracking it in two. The creature's arms fell and he hung slack, brain matter oozing in a slug trail down over his features. *Shit, we needed the brain.*

Letting the weight of the body pull the gun barrel down, Connor watched the feral slide away. It flopped back onto the earth with the cartridge protruding from its mouth, as if impaled to the ground.

Marius drew closer and signed, 'I'll take Silas. You won't get a shot off if you're too close.'

The chimp instantly switched vampires, and Connor paced slowly forward. When the next mound of earth erupted, he was ready. He swung around and heard the wet sound of the dart piercing the feral's eyeball. This time, the chemical smell confirmed the cartridge had discharged in a direct hit. The moment the feral hit the ground, the warden darted in and secured a wire noose around the creature's ankles and dragged him along behind as Connor continued forward.

Another feral broke up through the soil close behind Marius, and Silas unleashed a piercing shriek. The smell of blood plumed into the air and dozens of piles of earth began to shudder as if the ground was boiling. The shuffling sound of running feet swelled into a chorus of guttural groans as more ferals burst from their makeshift burial places and others joined the approaching tide, crawling out from beneath rocks and fallen trees.

"We have to go." The sound of bullets whistling through the air gave Connor a moment of relief.

The warden's men were picking off ferals from the high platforms of the granite tors in the park. With each one felled by a successful shot, the progress of the feral herd stuttered as they sniffed the carcasses. Some bit into the dry undead flesh, driven to satisfy voracious hunger, before staggering back into motion. Clusters of bodies fell like angry drunkards, instinct driving them to fight over food that didn't exist.

It bought Connor time.

Silas hung onto Marius' back by one arm, his other hand covering the bleeding wound trapped between their bodies as he clung on. Another feral lunged in and the tall vampire swung round to face it, shielding his face with a forearm. The feral buried his teeth into Marius' hand, the vibration of gnawing jaws grinding through stone hard flesh made the vampire shudder.

The chimp slid to the ground and staggered back, with both arms clamped around his body to cover the grazed flesh of his side. Blood oozed down the chimps' thigh when Silas used sign in ragged stutters of movement. 'Save Silas or I'll die.'

Connor read the message at the same moment that Malachi's words exploded like a grenade inside his skull. *Hera is dying.*

"Marius, take Silas to safety. If he dies, Hera dies... she's inside him."

The dark juror glared at Connor, pulled a hefty blade from his belt and buried it in the feral's throat. The jaws remained locked shut, the teeth wedged in between the bones in Marius' hand. The anchored feral pinned Marius to the spot, dragging his arm down. A sea of shadows drew closer, like a rolling bank of black fog. With a whistling yell, Marius hacked at his wrist joint until it tore and the hand fell away.

Turning and scooping up Silas into one arm, Marius disappeared in a blur of movement.

"Take the specimen," Connor yelled at the warden as he turned to follow the trail the dragging body made on the ground, firing darts at random into the nearest ferals. *They're gaining.*

The horde became thicker and when the moon broke from behind a cloud, seeing the surging tide of pale snarling features almost made Connor stumble. Facing forward, he focused on speed. The perimeter fence loomed up ahead. Marius and Silas were through the gate and the warden was close on their heels. But the fence wouldn't stop this stampede, and Connor knew it. *Shit.* They would follow Silas' blood scent. He felt a clawed grip of a feral snatching at his coattail and accelerated.

"Here." The word rang out far to the left.

The trampling herd of ferals fractured into fingerlike strands.

Squinting, Connor glanced along the fence-line. He could smell it, too. Fresh blood. Lots of it. *Dammit, Osiris.*

The splattering sound bounced inside Connor's head and, stopping, he turned and watched the ferals swerve and head towards the stream of ruby red flowing blood.

Shit. His helpless anger clouded his brain as a feral collided with him, almost knocking him to the ground.

"Come on, Doctor, this way." The warden waved from the gate. Marius had disappeared and so had their captured specimen.

The flow of ferals around Connor thinned as the distant fence-line began to rattle. Dreading the moment when Osiris would scream out, Connor lifted the gun, aimed at a nearby herd straggler and shot the dart into his ear. His prey fell to the ground and Connor grabbed him by the back of his greasy blood-encrusted coat, dragged him along behind, and burst into a pumping run.

Slipping through the gate, Connor heard it clang shut and set a course for the tree where he had last seen Hera. *Damn you, Osiris.* Guilt tore him in two. *If Hera dies...* Connor could not bear the thought.

He fixed his attention on the potholed ground, feeling the jerking pull of the unconscious feral bumping along behind him. With gritted teeth, he made a last dash as the tree-line drew closer. When the leafy canopy overhead cut out the moonlight, he looked up and saw Julian.

"What-?"

"Another hare-brained scheme." But Julian was grinning. Without taking his eyes from his friend's stunned face, he shouted, "Fall back, men."

Connor felt the weight of the feral being taken from him and, suddenly, he and Julian were alone beneath the tree.

"Come on, the others are safe. We need to get behind the front line."

Noticing the retreating platoon of guardsmen for the first time, Connor made a sudden about turn and fell into step with Julian. Catching sight of movement away to his right, he located the racing figure of Osiris keeping pace with them, some fifty yards away. He too was racing towards the line of guardsmen. Smears of blood mottled his skin with dark patches, but his movement was smooth and powerful as always. *Thank God.*

The safari park fence-line behind them began to rattle and the metal fractured in an ear-piercing screech. Shrapnel, like pelted confetti, bombarded Connor's head and shoulders.

A line of crouched guardsmen ranged across in front of him and he frowned in confusion. *What the Hell?* He wanted to ask

Julian, but had no time. As the pair burst through a gap in the ranks, closely followed by Osiris, an explosion tore the air apart.

A glance back revealed the orange and red glow of napalm. The mass of ferals dropped to the ground as if their legs had vanished, before the fire ate their clothes and desiccated their flesh to the point of granite.

Connor grinned with relief. *Claymore mines and hand held napalm guns.* It was not a war winning solution, but it provided breathing space, right now.

A mile further inland, Connor finally took stock.

Malachi was standing in clear view beside a distant tree trunk, but his crossed arms and the blackout curtain of thick silence exuding into Connor's head did not bode well.

Finally, Malachi blasted, *You almost killed them both.*

"I'm sorry," he whispered.

Rushing forward into the cover of the clump of trees, some of which were torn from the ground by their roots, he found the group huddled together. Hera looked as if she couldn't keep her eyes open. ~*I'm okay.*~ Her lips twitched in a small smile. ~*I didn't know I couldn't get out if Silas was so far away.*~

Dropping to his haunches, Connor took her slender hand in his. "No. I'm sorry. I should have thought of that."

Hera shook her head. ~*It is new to all of us.*~

"Where are our feral specimens?" asked Connor.

"On their way back to the zoo," said Osiris, and added with a frown, "Marius is in pretty bad shape."

Julian coughed. "Focus, Connor. Get back to the zoo. Rebekah said you have a possible cure, so get to it. I'll deal with this, but more ferals will be coming over The Channel, so hurry."

Shaking his friend's hand, Connor thumped Julian on the shoulder. "We've been through tougher things than this. Hang in there."

Connor didn't look back as he powered his way through a drizzle of rain which soaked his hair. His speed laid a mask of frost over his stern features. When he reached London Zoo and entered the medical center, he was relieved to see a drowsy Silas laid out on one gurney and Marius sitting on another with his stump being attended to by Anthony. *Julian has been busy.*

Looking up, Anthony grinned. "I thought it was quicker to do a house call than have Marius come to the surgical wing." With deft movements, he used glue to seal the end of the humorous bone and then each exposed blood vessel, stopping the further loss of fine pink grains of crystallized blood which had been trickling out.

"How *are* things at the hospital?" asked Connor.

Anthony frowned, concentrating on preparing a buffing tool and polishing the rough end of the patient's stump until it looked like glossy stone. "Running as smoothly as they need too. Charles has set up a triage system and sends away patients who can wait until after the feral threat has been neutralized."

Connor grinned at his assistant's certainty. Anthony's faith in Julian and Connor remained steadfast.

Marius whistled gently through his throat and threw his legs over the side of the examination couch, forcing Anthony to take a step back.

"I haven't finished, Marius."

The patient nodded, and Connor said quietly, "Yes, you have, Anthony."

The oil black pool of resignation was back in Marius' dark stare. Connor had tried to ignore the pact he made with the elder juror after the battle at St Michael's Mount, but now his friend had lost another form of communication. *First his voice, and now he can't sign.*

Connor shook his head. "Triage, Marius. We'll talk when this is all over."

Marius' clenched jaw required no interpretation, but Connor ignored it. "How's Silas doing?" It was only then that he noticed how pale the chimp looked. His soft brown eyes were half closed and for a moment, Connor felt a heavy weight in his chest as he feared the worst. Tuning into Silas' vital signs, he detected a slow heart rate and depressed breathing. "How much blood did he lose?"

"Enough," said Anthony, "but I've stitched the wound and given him a mild sedative. He'll be okay."

"Thank God," Connor murmured, "and where are the ferals?"

"In the operating theater, heavily sedated." replied Anthony.

Passing through the scrub room without pausing, Connor shoved the swing doors aside and stopped. Both ferals were still 'asleep'. Metal bands clamped around the chest, hips and knees of each patient gleamed in the strip lighting overhead. Connor recognized the restraints from the supplies at the vampire hospital, and metal-caged muzzles were a nice touch – they were from the veterinary supplies.

"Nicely done, Brynmor." He nodded at the younger vampire who watched over the subjects.

"What, now?"

"We try out the blood samples we blended to see if we can hydrate the brain centers and put the genie back in the bottle, so to speak."

"Will they be 'normal' again," asked Anthony.

"Not completely, but calm, docile, or at the very least, manageable. But we'll see. Pushing out through the theater doors and back again before they could swing shut, Connor brought with him a tray of loaded syringe barrels, a drill, and drill bits.

Brynmor took up a position on the opposite side of the first guinea pig.

"The problem is, we need to bring them round after each compound, so we'll try out three on each patient." Connor lined up three syringes on both trays and peered at Brynmor. "Everyone ready?"

Putting his thumb on the eyeball of the first feral, he pushed back the eyelid and measured the pupil size. Framing the subject's skull with his hands, he calculated the level of electrical activity inside the brain and Anthony noted them down as baseline readings.

"Okay." Picking up the drill which Anthony had already plugged in, Connor selected a drill bit, and a high-pitched whine filled the air as he adjusted the speed.

Brynmor turned the patient's head and used both hands as a clamp.

Lining up the drill with the base of the skull, Connor applied constant force, stopping when pink fluid staining the drill bit indicated he had entered the vampire's cerebellum.

Switching sides with Brynmor, Connor moved round to access the point between the feral's eyebrows and applied force which pierced the skin, but within seconds the motor seized. Retracting the drill plumed bone dust into the air. He deftly changed the bit for a new one and resumed his excavation, finally piercing the skull and cerebral membrane, and penetrating the frontal lobe.

Connor muttered, "Anthony, inject the first primate/perfluorocarbon compound into both sites in the brain, then take new readings. I'll prep the other feral."

Anthony selected a syringe from the metal tray and injected half the dose into the hole in the brainstem and discharged the remainder into the site between the feral's eyes and waited.

Connor had drilled both entry holes in the skull of the second patient by then and repeated the experiment with the second syringe.

Raising both hands in an unconscious gesture of a surgeon remaining sterile, Connor stood still for a full five minutes. Approaching his subject, he lifted the eyelid again, and took measurements. *No change.*

Loading a syringe with naltrexone/xylazine – a reversal drug for the opioid based combination sedatives Anthony had used on the vampires – he injected the feral in the relatively soft tissue beneath his jaw, near the carotid. The crunch of crystallized blood being shunted aside crackled loudly. Within sixty seconds, the feral's eyes shot open. His body clenched in spasm and rattled fiercely against the restraints. Like a dog caught in a trap, the feral shook his head until the metal muzzle started to buckle.

Stepping in fast, Connor aimed his air-propulsion dart gun at the feral's straining neck and pulled the trigger. The feral writhed for what felt like an age, to vampires, before his body became slack again.

The reaction in both patients was the same.

"Try the next syringe," said Connor, quickly taking up the drill and using it to make new holes in the feral skull.

The process was performed again. This time with a different ratio of the primate blood/ perfluorocarbon components. The patients' reaction when revived was equally violent.

Anthony took more readings of brain activity when the ferals were sedated again and shook his head.

"Shit," muttered Connor. "That was Silas' hybrid blood. Let's try it again with blood substitute doses." The drill shrieked through the air and the forehead of the feral Connor worked on collapsed under the pressure. Not what he wanted, but the experiment could still go ahead.

The pupil measurements and cerebral electric activity were different this time.

Priming the cartridge of the penetrating captive bolt gun he found so effective in the super tanker battle, Connor nodded to Anthony. "You revive him, and if there is no change, I'll put him down."

The feral opened his eyes and laid still this time. Connor frowned, holding the weapon a half inch from the feral's temple. A minute ticked by and Anthony drifted over to the side of the other patient, but focused all his attention on Connor's face.

"Okay, revive the other one." Connor jerked his chin in a decisive nod.

All three clinicians in the room had stopped breathing and remained stone still. *What if...?* Darting a glance at Anthony, he realized it was too late to stop him. Connor clicked his fingers in an explosive crack of sound and the feral leapt into movement. The seizure like contractions made the gurney rattle and the metal legs began to buckle as the convulsions lifted it off the slick shiny floor and then slammed it down again, hard. *Damn it.*

The crack of the bolt gun against the feral's head brought a mere instant of silence to the room before the other feral snarled, venom gargling in his throat. As if the louder noise triggered a more violent reaction, the trolley toppled sideways and the straps around the feral's knees stretched until the brittle restraints fractured. Rolling to his feet, the bed became a protective shell as the feral bent double and darted forward. Anthony dived to one side and grabbed the upright leg on the gurney, buckling the tubular steel in his effort to hold on. He dug his heels into the rubber skimmed floor, but was still dragged across the room at an alarming rate.

Sliding into a rugby tackle, Connor took out the feral's legs from beneath him and the table crashed down. Wriggling around, he got his gun hand within range of the feral head just as a clawed grip tore into the fabric of his pants.

The bolt made contact, and the feral's eyes widened. The tendons in his neck bulged like cords and then he slumped.

Pinned at the waist beneath the motionless patient and the gurney, Connor flopped back on the floor and stared at the pair of shocked faces looking down. "Sound. Why the Hell didn't I think of it earlier?"

Anthony flipped the table and the feral over in one move, and Brynmor pulled Connor to his feet.

Brushing down his clothes, Connor was glad there were no other witnesses to the fiasco. "They are too far gone. We can't save them, so we have to kill them."

"How? Not like that, one at a time, I hope," Anthony blurted.

Connor laughed harshly. "Certainly not. But we haven't got a victim to try my 'weapon' out on, and we haven't time to catch another feral."

"But you have a weapon? Thank God for that."

"I think we need a lot more help than God has offered so far. Come on, let's give everyone the bad news."

Both vampires tore off latex gloves and burst through the theater doors to confront Malachi, Osiris, Seren, Hera and Rebekah. The hope on the row of expectant faces melted at Connor and Anthony's grim expressions.

Rebekah crossed to Connor's side, pointed at the torn pants and the sticking up mess of his dark hair, and said, "Didn't go so well, hmm?"

Connor caught her hand in his, dropped a kiss onto the back of it and murmured, "You know what they say, it ain't over 'til it's over. The good news is, Silas is off the hook."

Rebekah beamed, sharing Connor's relief. "His hybrid blood didn't work?"

"No, so now, onto plan B," he said.

Chapter 30

As Frank knew it would, the feral attack on the storage facility made the humans see him as a steady rock to cling to.

He stood against the wall inside the death chamber, like a sentinel carved in stone, exuding certainty, as he waited for the tide to go out. Distant bumps and crunches far above kept the humans on edge.

Sampson was quick to reassure them. "They can't get in. Not now."

He shot a sharp glance at Frank, and the sergeant knew he was questioning *how* the ferals broke into the facility in the first place. *It will be a shame if he doesn't buy the 'Greg's foolish mistake' scenario.*

The rushing sound of the river faded until it was a mere whisper and, even though the chamber would still flood by a couple of feet, Frank decided it was time to move.

"The metal tables are bolted to the ground. Find something to hold onto. I'm opening the sluice gate."

A wave of disbelief and horror ramped up human heart rates, causing a flush of blood to redden their cheeks, and Frank paused to inhale in appreciation. There were so many humans crammed into the space that a few could go missing without being noticed by anyone other than their 'friends'. *The men could do with a reward if this goes smoothly.*

Frank thumped a fist several times on the internal metal door to the chamber, in the agreed signal to the warden. Like the captain of a ship, the warden would stay behind and face the music when the London Hive demanded answers. *If there are any of them left.* Frank felt the vibration as the warden hit the red button on the wall outside the chamber and the sluice gate whipped up.

The gray water rushed in over the floor, patches of froth gathering on its boiling skin, and Frank and Sampson stood as if welded to the ground.

The humans linked arms and held on tight, shrieking and whimpering in panic as the undertow of the icy tide tried to drag their feet from beneath them. The steadier ones fought to pull up friends who slipped and disappeared under the water. Sampson and Frank acted fast to save the few who lost the battle to hang on from being swept out through the sluice door and into the churning current of the river, the force of which would have thrown them back against the facility's concrete wall and broken their ribs.

Frank yanked a tall man up by the scruff of his neck and used his own body as a water break until the human could stand again.

"Thank you," he gasped, clutching onto the vampire's arm.

Once the water level settled, the humans standing in thigh high cloudy colored water were breathing heavily and gray-faced with fear and exhaustion, but alive, at least.

Frank grinned. *If only they knew. That was merely the first hurdle.*

A flotilla of lifeboats rowed by vampire guardsmen approached fast. Larger fiberglass crafts hung back, but inflatables which could take fifty humans at a time skimmed in over the submerged floor without difficulty. The pilots helped the nearest humans to clamber in as the inflatables bobbed on the shallow water inside the death chamber. In a seamless flow, when each one was full, the vampire crew ferried them out to the larger boats, repeating the process until they had everyone onboard. The last wave rowed back out to join the flotilla of crafts heading up river.

Once the death chamber was empty, the sergeant again pounded the door in a signal and the sluice gate slid down. In a dart of movement, Frank and Sampson rolled out beneath it and scaled up the embankment wall and on to dry land. Setting off along the riverbank, the sergeant enjoyed the exhilaration of his plan coming together. No one, but he and his men knew where the humans were being taken, and his squad was faithful to him. At intervals, he leapt up onto the derelict roads which looked down over the riverside properties and the wide promenade. From that vantage point, he checked on the progress of the cluster of lifeboats powering along as near to the riverbank as the wharfs and jetties allowed.

The choppy dull gray water glittered as if razor-like teeth tried to devour the boat-shaped morsels cutting a swathe across the surface, and in some ways, devour them it could. If a human fell overboard, their survival chances in the icy currents were slim to none.

The mudflats hidden beneath the ebbing tide were another hazard which the lifeboat pilots expertly avoided; the same color as the water, but a different texture. The vampire rowers wove in and out, navigating a path through the channels with ease.

The bridges arcing across the River Thames gave London its iconic atmosphere, but the bridge Frank looked for would be better described as an eyesore – Battersea Railway Bridge.

Passing by Chelsea Harbour, where the rotting shells of privately owned cabin cruisers, speedboats, yachts, and water taxis wallowed like dull-colored icebergs, Frank veered down onto the Thames Pathway which ran along the bank, passed beneath the railway bridge and took the spur out onto the water at the Imperial Wharf Marina. The platforms and jetties were deserted. The abandoned boats at this exposed location had long ago been swept away.

Like a magician's transportation illusion, Frank and Sampson materialized on the wooden walkway in time to greet the arrival of the first craft, and the huddled humans exuded relief when they saw familiar faces.

Leaping from the lifeboats, the rowers secured the mooring ropes to any protruding metal cleats or wooden posts which were still usable. Like officials charged with crowd control, the vampires offered their arms to enable passengers to haul themselves out of the swaying boats and directed the stream of wet, anxious humans down the jetty to the asphalt path beyond. Guiding the meandering snake of trudging figures along the road, Frank caught up with Leizle beneath the concrete railway overpass. She walked arm in arm with Uncle Harry, and her wide glassy stare made it clear she was struggling to hold it together.

Falling into step beside her, Frank shrugged out of his grimy coat and laid it around her shoulders. "I'm sorry you lost friends, but Julian will be happy you are safe."

Swiping away a tear and pulling the collar of the coat closer around her, Leizle's face twitched as she tried to smile. "I know, and we have you to thank for that."

The glass wall of the Imperial Wharf railway station building loomed ahead, and Frank said, "You'll all be safe and sound, very soon."

At the top of the stairway leading up onto the platform, Leizle gazed around with a spark of interest. "So, this is a railway station."

The tracks were intact and four train carriages sat at the platform. Although the paint had cracked and the metal rusted, the doors slid smoothly when their guides forced them open. The vampires wiped the freshly applied grease from their hands onto their coats as they stepped back.

A cold wind blowing through the station whistled through the cracked and missing panes in the glass wall barrier, and wearing damp clothes made Leizle's teeth chatter.

"Get inside and huddle together," said Frank gently, arranging his face in a reassuring smile. "There are dry clothes and clean beds waiting for you when we arrive at our destination." Glancing down at Leizle beside him, he added, "Of course, I forget. It's hard to imagine that you've never been on a train before." Frank watched his crew beckon the steady flow of humans forward as they emerged up onto the platform. "It won't be quite as it was, but you get to ride in a carriage, tonight."

The shivering figures filed in through the open train doors, too tired to ask questions. It reminded Frank of a stream of lemmings rushing towards the abyss – they had no idea what lay before them.

Handing Leizle up into a carriage, Frank saw her and Uncle Harry safely onto their threadbare moth-eaten seats, then leapt back down onto the platform and pulled the door shut.

With a quick exchange of orders, Frank took charge of the first packed carriages, assigning three guards to the rear of each one. The locomotive engine had been removed a decade before, but they didn't need it – vampire power was reliable, and faster.

Sampson appeared at Frank's shoulder. "Where are we going?"

The sergeant grinned. "The most secure place we have left. Wormwood Scrubs."

"The maximum security prison?" Sampson's eyebrows climbed in stunned surprise. Running a hand over his jaw, he said, "It could work."

"It's perfect, so let's get going. I'll need your help. We have to change trains to pick up another railway line. The next set of carriages are waiting under the Westway. There's food and dry clothes at the Scrubs."

"I can see you thought this through."

Frank shrugged, his gesture taking in the vampire guards working in unison. "Being prepared is in the blood, so to speak."

With a sharp nod, Sampson said, "I'll bring up the rear. You set the pace."

As Samson walked away to the last carriage in the row, Frank hopped down onto the tracks behind the leading one and joined a team of two vampires. All three braced their hands on the metal panel and pushed the carriage along in a smoothly gathering pace. The miles were eaten away at a steady speed, until the dim light of early dawn descended to pitch-black when they passed beneath the six-lane wide flyover complex called Westway.

Frank dug his clawed fingers into the metal, crimping the steel panel into handgrips. Applying the brakes by using the heels of his boots, he ground a channel in the wooden sleepers and gravel traps between the rails, and the shudder of wheels stuttering along rusted tracks rattled through his skull as the coach screeched to a halt.

Stepping out from behind the carriage and onto the wide path of sharp stones beside the rails, Frank raised a 'wait here' hand. He dived into the belt of trees and shrubbery planted alongside the tracks by railway companies as a sound absorbing barrier. Out on the other side, the wind whistled across the huge expanse of a disused depot where a few dilapidated storage sheds still stood on one side of the yard. As Frank crossed the exposed area, rustling sounds grabbed his attention. He pressed his back to one wall of a storage shed, edged his way along to the back corner and peered out.

Behind the sliding metal concertina gate in the perimeter wall, half a dozen ferals stood, rocking from one foot to the other, as if in hibernation.

He doubled back and frowned. *Slow and silent is the name of the game. But will they smell the humans?*

Frank ran through options. He had grenades on his belt, but an explosion would draw hundreds more ferals, not to mention other attention he didn't want. *A sacrifice could work.* Heading back to the train, Frank stopped and peered left and right, scanning the thick bank of trees and shrubs which ran for miles along the tracks in both directions.

Stepping out into view, he drew Sampson's attention with a wave. "Stand guard, watch the humans."

Signaling for a team of four to follow, Frank scoured the belt of undergrowth for decoys, feeling irritated when they came up woefully short, catching only a fox and two rabbits.

"We could kill a human?" suggested a vampire, holding up a skinny rabbit carcass by its ears to inspect it and grimacing.

"Not an option," Frank hissed shortly, with a shrug. "This will have to do."

Gathering the men alongside the train carriages again, Frank said, "We're moving them out. Tell the humans to keep to the boundary wall on the right side of the depot, and to be as quiet as possible."

Before he could dismiss the men to follow the order, Leizle appeared at the window of her carriage door, peering out through the glass. She waved her hand and raised a bottle of pills into view.

Frank eased open the sliding door a crack, wide enough to see half Leizle's face and one green eye. "What are those?"

"Uncle Harry. He brought modified beta-blockers with him." Jerking her head towards the human crowd at her back, she said, "We've all taken one, but there's enough for the people in the other coaches."

Frank frowned. "How long do they take to work?"

"You tell me, have they worked?"

Leizle jerked back when Frank shoved his nose and mouth into the space, inhaled deeply, and saliva gurgled in his mouth. Pulling back and tilting his head, Frank tuned into the slower, thicker heartbeats, and found it needed more concentration. Holding out a black-gloved hand, he took the plastic bottle Leizle fed out through the gap. "Thank you. I'll pass them along."

Sharing a wide grin with his men, Frank strode to the next carriage to where he saw Peter pressed back into the metal doorframe by his closely packed companions.

Catching his attention with a wave, the sergeant eased the door open and gave him the container of pills. "Make sure everyone takes one, then Sampson can pass them on to the next carriage. Leizle sent them."

The doubt evaporated from Peter's face at the mention of Leizle. *Maybe, he has a crush. I wonder what the principal would think about that.* A low laugh rumbled through Frank as he turned away to rejoin his squad of men.

Once all the humans had taken a beta-blocker, Frank gave the signal to open the carriage doors and put his fingers to his lips in a warning to be silent. The first few humans sat to swing their legs out first and then drop carefully down onto the gravel stones before turning to help others. They moved in a steady stream across to the thick grass of the wooded verge.

Moving like a colony of ants, the string of humans stayed close to those in front and focused on making no noise.

Frank detached himself from the seemingly endless procession, took the dangling fox carcass from one of his men, and returned to the spot where he could see the gathering of ferals, who appeared to have lost touch with their horde.

The scuffing sound of human footfalls crossing the depot yard stuttered through the air, but the ferals didn't seem to notice. As each new cluster set off across the yard, the sound became a whispering constant, settling into background noise, and Frank relaxed.

Slinging the fox over his shoulder, he turned to walk back.

A thump, like a sandbag hitting the ground, followed by a human grunt, pulled Frank up short. *Damn it.*

In a scurry of movement, a tall man scooped the girl who had fallen up into his arms and darted a look across the yard. Frank could almost see the deep calming breath the man took as he forced himself not to hurry and resumed a slow careful walk.

The metal gate behind Frank rattled. He looked around to see a feral face pressed in between the crisscross of bars, the open mouth gurgling as it inhaled and searched for the scent of prey. Slipping the fox back down to his side, Frank tore a hole in the pelt and tossed it a hundred yards to land behind the group. The tumbling missile galvanized them into a snarling clambering mass. The beads of blood which dropped like rain whetted their appetite, and the ferals darted after the lure. *But, for how long?*

The first of the humans were clambering into the carriages on the other train track. Seeing the back of the line eased the tension for Frank, but the growling snarls behind him grew louder. Rushing over to the last few in the human procession, Frank hissed, "Run."

The metal gate at the far side of the depot shrieked as it rattled. The first feral leapt to the top and another forced his head through a diamond space in the concertina of bars, tearing the flesh and his ears from either side of his skull.

"Run," shouted Frank.

The grinding sound of rusted wheels started up; the first carriages were full and being pushed away. As Frank hefted the last two humans up under his arms, a couple of his men rushed past, pulling weapons from their belts. "Don't use a gun," Frank barked, "we don't want more of them to find us."

He swung the human baggage up into the waiting outstretched arms of their agitated companions. As he pressed on the glass and slid the train door shut, the stuttering cries became quiet sighs of relief and the mass of human flesh sunk to the floor as if their legs had melted.

He heard the crack of bone and feral snarls being viciously cut short.

As Frank began to shove the last renaming loaded carriage along the rails, pumping quickly up to a fast run, two pairs of blood-stained hands lined up beside his. He shot a glance either side and grinned. One guard had lost an ear, but both grinned back at him.

Hurtling around the curve in the track at speed caused the human cargo to shunt sideways, but a few bruises were a small price to pay for safety.

Pulling the carriage to a halt behind the ones already parked up at their destination, Frank stood back and slapped his companions on the nearest shoulder. "Phase two," he said. *This is the easy part.*

The humans poured out of the opened doors and followed the vampires like ducklings imprinted on their mother. Losing sight of their protectors was unthinkable. The short walk took them through trees, across deserted car parks, and finally through open gates in tall black railings embellished in gold.

Towering turrets framed the imposing entrance doors at the far end of a courtyard. As the last sight of the outside world, the impressive structure of interlocking red brick and cream stone would crush the spirit of prisoners entering Wormwood Scrubs, a high security prison where the blackest of hearts served the longest of sentences. As a gateway to Hell, it mocked the detainees with its striking, forceful beauty.

A huge wooden door swung open and the stream of figures were ushered through and into the cavernous enclosed space where prison vans would have stopped to unload the newest arrivals. The roof leaked in places and dripping water echoed.

As protection, Wormwood Scrubs was perfect, and Frank had control of everyone inside. The humans milled around until a vampire guard led them through a door and began handing out parcels.

"Clean clothes. We don't know how long we'll be here," Frank said to Leizle when she wove her way through the ambling crowd and stopped at his side.

"I'm that easy to read." She laughed.

"Questions are natural, given the situation." Frank shot a glance down into her enquiring face. "We have prepared the prison wings for habitation. It's grim, but where else are there hundreds of beds, an industrial kitchen and a dining hall?"

"You have thought of everything."

"And it is safe. My men will man the guard towers and no one can come near without us knowing about it."

The last of the humans trickled through the door leading to a prison wing, until only Uncle Harry, Thomas and Evie remained huddled in a group waiting for Leizle. Standing nearby, Seth, Adam, Peter and Sampson exuded reassuring determination.

"What now?"

"I go and inform Principal Julian of the feral attack on SF8, and tell him you are safe."

"Not all of us," whispered Leizle.

Meeting her gaze, Frank said, "There are always casualties in a war. I'm sorry you lost friends, but Principal Julian will be relieved that *you* are safe."

He smiled stiffly, and Leizle nodded. "True. Thank you."

Frank watched her walk away to join the others, noticing the squared shoulders and ramrod straight posture, despite the exhaustion she must be feeling. *She's got spirit.* It made him smile. *Julian will fight for her.*

Finally, Frank gave up on lurking in the shadows outside Julian's Richmond home. His hope of having a low risk meeting by catching the principal alone was clearly a non-starter. *It was worth*

a shot. Setting the most direct course east, he breezed past Wormwood Scrubs once more, taking a moment to check all appeared quiet before heading back into the city.

Ten minutes later, after crossing paths with Juror Daniel in the corridor of the council building, and learning that Julian was meeting with Gerrard, Frank melted into hiding again. *Gerrard can't see me, not yet.* Peering out from behind the statue he blended into, Frank was relieved when, fifteen minutes later, the captain passed by. The man was frowning. *Things must be gathering pace.*

Stepping out into the corridor, Frank composed himself. His clothes were wet and salt stained, the dirt kicked up from the railway tracks had turned his gray hair to grimy ash, and his beleaguered appearance suited his plan. He knocked on Julian's door.

"Come."

Before he could obey, the door whipped open. "Sergeant Frank, what the Hell-?"

The principal's shocked expression was satisfying. Striding boldly forward, he shut the door and turned to face Julian. "We were attacked, sir. Ferals."

"What? At the storage facility? How, in God's name?"

"We can't be sure. But they got inside somehow." Frank knew that knowing too much would sound suspicious. *The time for answers will come.*

"The humans?"

"Most of them are safe." He tacked on quickly, "Leizle is safe."

"Thank you, for that." Julian dragged his hand down over his face, clearly feeling bad that his relief showed. "Where are they?"

"Wormwood Scrubs." Frank smiled at Julian's sharp look. "My men are standing guard."

The principal digested the distances involved in the evacuation and nodded, inspecting the grimy tattered appearance of the figure in front of him. "It must have been a huge task, thank you."

"We did what had to be done. How are the drug trials progressing?"

At Julian's waved invitation, the sergeant crossed to a chair and sat down.

"Slow. And at sundown, more ferals will come."

"The Scrubs is secure and nowhere near full. If I may speak freely, sir?"

"Go ahead."

"You are our principal. I believe you and your key staff should move central operations to Wormwood Scrubs, sir."

"I need to stay in touch with Doctor Connor, but thank you."

"I see." Frank ran a hand through his hair and dirt scattered over the floor. "Pardon me, but is Doctor Connor's maker here? The Egyptian, Malachi?"

Julian blinked slowly; his green gaze sharpened.

"They can communicate telepathically?"

"Yes."

Frank sat stone still and let three minutes tick by. "I would be neglecting my duty if I didn't stress the potential danger we face. High value targets, such as Malachi, Rebekah, and Seren should all be protected." Standing up, Frank said, "Time is running out. We may only have until sundown to prepare a fallback position in the event that the City perimeter is breached."

"I understand, Sergeant. Return to Wormwood Scrubs and hold the fort."

"Yes, sir."

When the door closed behind Frank, Julian pulled a coat from the wardrobe. Captain Gerrard had brought worrying news reports from the coastal lookouts. Along the shoreline, ferals could be seen waiting beneath the waves. That in itself was disturbing enough, but Gerrard himself had seen some ferals stumble out of the water in full sunlight and die, as if shoved from behind. *How many are out there, beneath the sea?*

Wheeling around, Julian headed to the guardroom and walked in without knocking.

The guards packed into the space jerked to attention and saluted.

"Carry on, Captain Gerrard," said Julian, settling back against the wall to listen. As the updated reports came in, the tension in his gut became a tight knot.

The captain turned to Julian. "If the feral numbers are as high as indicated, then let the suburbs go. We must hold the line around The City of London."

"What is the strategy for that?" Julian asked.

Gerrard replied quickly, "We have target buildings wired for demolition, to create a wall."

"Good, good, but wait for my order," muttered Julian.

He and Gerrard had already agreed on the prime sites to protect. The vampire hospital where Isaac and Charles were fully occupied feeding the troops. The Blood Substitute Manufacturing Plant which was under the protection of Juror Daniel and the Elite Guard. London Zoo, for obvious reasons.

The squad leaders filed out to instruct their men and, left alone with Gerrard, Julian asked, "Where is Anthony?"

"Back at the hospital. The experiments to cure the ferals failed. He's arranging a transport of blood to the zoo. He's looking for samples with signs of thrombosis rejected by the dispensary. Doctor Connor has another plan."

"Thank, God." Relating the news brought by the sergeant, Julian shook his head. "The survival of our human stock is imperative. I want to check all is well. Malachi and Anthony must accompany me to Wormwood Scrubs before nightfall."

"Why Malachi? He will not leave his chimps." Gerrard frowned.

"I might need to think on my feet. I need a direct line to Connor, and he is it. If you can persuade Rebekah to join us, then do it." The muscle twitched in Julian's jaw. "It is an order, Captain."

"Yes, Principal."

Leaving the room, Julian whipped along the oak-lined corridors at top vampire speed. The tension pressing down on him eased as he leapt the flight of steps outside the council building. As he hoped, Anthony was still at the hospital dispensary when he swung in through the jelly-like plastic flaps of the doors and surveyed the room.

Anthony and Charles were poring over a loaded trolley, deep in discussion.

They looked up when Julian approached, the surprise on their faces obvious.

"Anthony, I need to talk to you."

Within the hour, Julian and his small traveling party approached the main entrance to Wormwood Scrubs.

Sergeant Frank waited in the courtyard. "Good to see you, Principal."

Thick gray clouds gathered overhead and Frank glanced up. "You made it in time, sir."

Julian grinned wryly. It had been hard to convince Malachi to come, and Gerrard failed with Rebekah, but he should have known that.

"Please, enter."

Once Julian, Anthony and Malachi were inside, the doors swung shut and were bolted by two vampire sentries.

"The humans are in the wings to the left, but first..." Frank turned right and through a door which led outside, once again. The group headed across the access road and into one of the buildings where prisoners were once kept. From an aerial view, the accommodation wings resembled tines of a fork. The recessed gaps were filled by auxiliary buildings, an exercise yard, and lawned gardens.

Inside the third accommodation wing, Frank led the way along a short corridor. Passing through an unlocked door, they entered the high security part of the prison. A wall of thick bars blocked the hallway. The gate Frank unlocked creaked when he pushed it open. The musty air in the high-ceilinged wing beyond coated Julian's nose, so he stopped breathing. Looking up, beyond the welded iron walkway which protruded overhead, he could make out cell doors lining a succession of upper landings. From the false ceiling of wire mesh, cobwebs hung like angel's hair. When the creak of the gate closing behind them faded, the silence was eerie.

"There is space here to house the Elite Guard. The humans are in similar accommodation."

Walking to the first cell in the row, Julian peered in through the barred wall. The thin mattress on the bunk was furry with dust and the stagnant toilet bowl was stained black.

"The human wing is clean, of course."

The group returned to the main building and waited for Frank to lock up and rejoin them.

"How do we get up onto the perimeter wall?" asked Malachi, his opaque stare reflecting impatience with the 'visitor's tour'.

"This way." After ascending the stone stairway of the tallest tower, Frank rested his hands on the thick wall.

Straight ahead the purple gray ribbon of the river Thames glittered in the dying light. Down below, a thick wall crowned with wide coping stones ran from one tower to the next, creating a fortress-like perimeter.

Malachi leapt from the tower and landed on top of the wall with the agility of a cat. Julian followed, but discovered Malachi was much swifter of foot than he anticipated, as the Egyptian rushed away to the rear of the prison compound. From the high vantage point, the pair looked out over the vast expanse of Wormwood Scrubs Park. Covering over a quarter of a square mile, the area had become an overgrown wilderness. The sports pitches were gone, the children's' playground was strangled by weeds and the foot paths were barely detectable. The eighteen hectares of tree cover rose up in places, like iceberg tips floating on a green sea.

"There's a lot of cover for ferals to hide in," Julian muttered. "How is Connor getting along?"

Malachi laughed harshly. "Give him time."

Julian watched the darkness descending. "Time? We might not have much of that left."

As night fell over the vast field of green, the moving shadows of the taller 'iceberg trees' oozed across the overgrown acres like an oil slick.

Even before Julian noticed the flash of paler orbs in the field of green – faces lifting to scent the air – the low rumbling chorus of snarling ferals was unmistakable. "They are searching. The beta-blockers are working for now, but pretty soon, this place will become one huge heartbeat. It is as I feared, we can't keep them here long."

"Where can they go?" asked Malachi, scanning the landscape as if counting ants.

"There is only one place, but it's the last place on earth I'd choose."

Malachi looked at Julian's tight features. "I see."

"Feed this information to Connor. I'll update Frank and Sampson to prepare for evacuation."

"I'm sure the humans would be pleased to see you." Malachi shrugged. "A friendly face."

As Julian retraced his steps along the wall, he chuckled. *Wily old buzzard.* After an endless half hour of relaying the updated plan to Sergeant Frank and Sampson, and a much slower human exchange with Peter and Seth, as the leaders of the groups, Julian walked along the newly cleaned wing where the humans were trying to rest.

In many of the cells he walked past, human huddles were packed onto each bunk, some talking quietly, others just resting against each other and enjoying the comfort of being close. Some cells were empty, containing only rucksacks, lying where their owners had dropped them. Julian recognized Seth's boy Adam lounging in an open cell gateway up ahead. A chorus of muffled laughter echoing from above made the youth glance up. On the upper landing, beyond the wire mesh ceiling, more cells were occupied. Tension pulled his jacket tight and Adam pushed away from the doorway. "I better tell them to-"

Swinging around, he came face to face with the principal and grinned widely.

"Adam." Julian nodded.

"Hey, Leizle, look what the cat dragged in." As he passed by, Adam said, "I'll leave you alone, I've got high spirits to pour cold water on."

A rustle of scrabbling movement made Julian grin. He barely reached the wall of bars before Leizle swung out onto the walkway and threw herself at him.

He lifted her carefully off her feet and returned to the privacy of the cell, but, those across the landing could look in.

Even as he registered the intrusion, Leizle squirmed out of his arms and tied a sheet across the bars by the corners, creating a screen.

"Why, young lady, I hope you aren't going to ravish me." Julian waggled his eyebrows as he sat down carefully on the steel bed frame and she slipped onto his lap. Wrapping her arms around him and pressing her face into his chest, she murmured. "Nothing kinky, I've just missed you."

Resting his chin on her head and stroking a hand down her back, he said, "Ah well, a guy can hope."

The ripple of laughter which made her body shake lifted his heart. For the first time in many days, he felt happy. Leizle's breathing became deep and steady, and Julian wondered if she was falling asleep. He could smell the salt and dirt in her hair, and knew the journey here must have been exhausting.

With a wriggle, she shifted and looked up to meet his tender gaze. Her eyes welled with tears. "Did you hear about Greg? And Oscar? We lost too many loved ones, Julian."

He stroked her cheek with a long finger. "Yes, they told me. I'm sorry, my love." His features tightened as he clamped his jaws shut.

Leizle searched his face. "I know. It's not over yet."

Hugging her in close to his chest, Julian chuckled when she squeaked, "Ow."

"You'll need your fighting spirit a while longer. We could get the signal from Connor to move out at any moment."

"What-?" The prospect alarmed her, and Julian guiltily enjoyed feeling her sluggish heart jolt in her chest and the sudden flush of blood warming her skin. It filled his mouth with saliva.

Rolling slowly down onto the thin mattress and entwining his leg with hers, all Julian said was, "Sleep, now, while you can."

He knew he should get back to the council buildings, but he did not want to leave just yet. *I'll tell her to stay with Seth and Sergeant Frank during the evacuation, but for now...* He closed his own eyes and lost himself in the rhythm of her breathing and the scent of her warm skin.

Chapter 31

Inside the London Zoo lab, which felt like his second home, Connor ran a finger along the line of test tubes, selecting the next sample for testing. Pressing a droplet of blood between two glass slides and inspecting the smeared blot, he muttered, "This one might work." He slotted the vial into a tray of samples inside the glass-fronted refrigerator unit and stood back. "Is that enough?"

"We have enough to run the next round of trials." Brynmor pushed his glasses up his nose. "We know blood clots cause seizures in vampires, so it is reasonable to assume that the altered clotting factor will have an effect on ferals."

"But will it work the same way?" Connor ground his teeth in frustration. "I need another sample from primate subject A to prove the theory."

Brynmor crossed to the door of the laboratory and stopped as he touched the handle. "You know Malachi will be alright with Principal Julian, and Hera is looking after Silas."

Looking up from an examination of the next slide, Connor inhaled deeply. "I know Malachi is tough, but he's not indestructible. I should know."

"Really?" Interest glittered in Brynmor's eyes. "How do you know?"

"In 1910, I saved him from dying at the hand of his brother, Numu." Connor froze. "No, I didn't. I *thought* I did. I was a new vampire and he was beneath the water of the Thames with six inch nails through his feet pinning him to the embankment wall, and a wire noose around his neck, but I remember now…"

When Connor stopped talking and remained statue still, Brynmor coughed.

"That's it. Malachi *looks* frail but is strong. I *thought* his brother tried to kill him but Numu was just holding him prisoner until he had finished me off. I had everything backwards." Connor spun around, peered at the test tubes, and blurted, "Get me new samples from subjects A *and* B. I took something for granted that I shouldn't have. Let's try again."

"Well, as an epiphany goes, that was a lightning strike. I'll get the samples." Brynmor opened the door, letting a gusting breeze scurry inside. Through the window, Connor watched his companion head across the straw strewn yard to the operating theater block.

Connor opened the storage cupboard and began sorting through the contents, looking for the drug he needed. *I hope this works.* Every few minutes, Malachi's updates filtered through his mind, like the swelling of background music, Connor registered the messages, but didn't allow them to interrupt his train of thought.

"Yes." Connor grinned at the 'eureka' moment. Reaching in and gathering up half a dozen vials, he felt pleased he didn't have to waste time heading back to the hospital for supplies.

A breeze kicked up and fluttered his lab coat. "You got them? Good."

Brynmor arrived beside him, but when Connor looked up, a searing pain shot through his head. Malachi's pictures rifled into his mind like a scattering pack of playing cards and the vial Connor held dropped from his hand.

Brynmor darted forward and caught it. "Doctor Connor?"

The white walls of the lab grew darker and the moon appeared overhead. The floor disappeared, and he was looking down over a wall. Twenty feet below, the black shapes of trees and bushes shifted as if they boiled, and then each shadow became an open-mouthed baying face. Fragments of stone spat into the air as ferals trampled their brethren underfoot, using the bodies to climb higher and reach up to dig bony clawed fingers into the mortar between the bricks. Connor heard bones crack as the person he was 'seeing through', threw a boulder that smashed down onto the scrabbling outstretched arms and knocked the climbing bodies back down into the thick carpet of shrubs.

Wisps of mist inside his skull solidified into Malachi's face. *We need to leave here, now. Send help.*

"Okay, I will."

"Connor? What do you see?"

The scene melted from the laboratory walls as the vision evaporated like rolling fog, and Connor felt in control of his own body again.

"Get the samples prepared, I've got to find Rebekah." Connor vanished, leaving the door bang shut behind him. Across the yard, he went through the iron gate into the primate enclosure, skimmed along the concrete paths, and entered the indoor habitat. The air was thick with odors of straw, pee, and faeces, but that was 'zoo smell' for you. His vampire senses also detected the scent of tranquilizer fumes and warm simian blood.

"Honey?" He glanced into each straw covered cage as he went, but still she appeared as if from nowhere."

"Hello, Doctor-" The teasing smile dancing around her lips faded, and she said, "What's wrong?"

"The humans are in trouble. They are under attack."

"Oh, God." She shrugged out of her overalls and handed the bucket she carried to Seren, who had arrived at her side. "Hera, Seren and Osiris can keep the apes comfortable. What do you need me to do?"

Connor frowned.

"C'mon, you can't be everywhere and you are needed here."

"Okay, but take Gerrard with you."

"Where?" She fixed her eyes on his and her certainty calmed him.

"To Captain Blake. Tell him to sail up The Thames and take the humans onboard. It is the only safe place Julian and Malachi can think of, and I have to agree."

"Into the lion's den?" Rebekah shook her head, but by her expression, he saw she understood. "Okay, I'll go now." As she turned to power past him, she grabbed his hand. "I've got this, now get back to the lab and save the world."

Within minutes, Rebekah was passing along the eerily quiet city streets. She slowed to a human walk. Tuning into the buildings around her, she recognized the unusually wide sidewalks, so much wider than the roads, here in Piccadilly Circus. She had been foraging in the nearby pharmacy on the day her and Connor's paths collided in a life changing encounter. *It's still here.* On impulse, she pushed on the door and stepped inside, remembering the mix of determination and fear that had knotted her stomach. The floor was still coated in dust and cobwebs hung from every surface. *I was a different girl back then. A human girl.* She smiled gently and made her way back out onto the street.

Tuning into the sound of the shuffling leaves, the ruffling noise of birds brooding high in the trees, and the creatures scuttling in the undergrowth of the nearby park land, she realized that even vampires had left the inner boroughs. *They'll be guarding the perimeter.* They would hold the City of London against the coming invasion. It was a sobering thought. Like the survival mechanism in the human body, all the crop reapers, human farm wardens, and safari park rangers would retreat to protect the London Hive – the main organ of vampire survival.

She cut through the side streets, passed along pitch-black alleyway entrances, and arrived at the council building. Leaping the steps and thumping through the main door, she called out at the top of her vampire lungs, "Captain Gerrard."

When he appeared round the far corner, accompanied by ten purple clad Elite Guards, Rebekah froze. "Where are you going?"

"More ferals are coming ashore on the east coast. We're sealing off the city."

"You have to come with me. I need your help. Our humans are in danger."

At his sharp nod, the guards swept past and out through the door behind her to complete their mission without him. "Fill me in on the way."

As the pair approached the guarded perimeter fence of the London Docklands, Gerrard barked a command that cleared the gates from their path.

In the darkness, the rusted loading bay machinery and mounds of coiled chain took on eerie shapes which Rebekah automatically checked for movement; the enemy could crawl out from under any stone.

From the quayside, Rebekah scanned the length of the massive hull rising up into the night sky.

The nomads' vessel wallowed gently like a jagged berg of coal in water that rippled like torn silk in the moonlight. A row of white faces emerged on the deck of the container ship. Looking down from high above, they appeared to float like balloon-shaped lanterns.

"What now?" asked Rebekah, "How do we talk to the Captain?"

Before her words died away, the hatchway in the hull snapped open and Tyrone appeared on the threshold. Without extending the metal walkway, he spoke into the still night. "You need to talk?"

"We need your help, Captain Blake's help, to save our humans."

Tyrone's smile cut a black gash across his moonlit face. "Come aboard, Captain Blake will be happy to help."

The mechanism of the gangplank creaked as it inched towards the quay. Losing patience, Rebekah leapt across the divide and landed beside Tyrone. "We don't have time to waste, weigh anchor and untie the mooring ropes, or whatever you seafarers call it, we need to set sail now."

Tyron chuckled until Rebekah glared at him.

As the pair turned away from the edge, Captain Gerrard also made the jump aboard.

Rebekah darted him an 'are you sure' look, her brows raised.

"My men have everything in hand. We'll both be needed to coordinate a human evacuation." The probing gleam in the captain's eye said everything he couldn't voice out loud.

Glad not to be alone in the lion's den, Rebekah nodded in thanks.

After following a silent Tyrone up through the vessel, they emerged on deck.

Rebekah barely registered the wind snatching at her clothes and turning her hair into a nest of writhing snakes as she mounted the exposed stairway which led to Blake's domain up on the bridge. Barging in through the door ahead of Tyrone and Gerrard, she blurted. "Battersea Railway Bridge. How close can we get?"

Blake turned to face his visitor, tilting his head to one side, as if his shiny, distorted features still functioned.

Tyrone followed Gerrard in over the threshold and pulled the door shut, his words stuttering with grim laughter. "The Captain is searching for Hera. He assumes that if you are demanding help, you are returning her in exchange."

Stepping closer to the nomad captain, Rebekah lifted her chin and ground out from between clenched teeth, "Your deal is with Connor, so let's cut the crap, save the humans and argue about it later."

Saliva rattled in Blake's throat in what Rebekah took to be laughter. The captain gripped her arm and leaned in so close his rancid breath fanned her face. She quelled the urge to jerk away before she gagged. She stopped breathing instead, blocking out the smell.

"You could take Hera's place." Tyrone delivered the message, deadpan.

Rebekah tore her arm away, her eyebrows raised in irritation. "Take us to Battersea Railway Bridge."

The hull began to creak as the vessel shifted into the flowing current of the river. "Thank you." Rebekah released an exasperated 'at last' breath, spun on her heel, returned to the deck and gripped the hand rail. Until she saw the humans, she would not rest.

Scanning the wide expanse of choppy water, Rebekah felt as if a stone sat in her stomach. The river whipped by and clumped islands of debris riding the current made her think of corpses. *I hope we are in time.* When the railway bridge came into view, she focused on searching the riverbank, until suddenly, a change in the pattern of ripples on the water drew her attention. She saw the first boat. Her spine became rigid. She had not expected them to be out on the water. "They are using boats," she called out.

Gerrard appeared at her side, and then Tyrone.

Tyrone said briskly, "That is good." His facial muscles twitched as if he searched for a thought, but the deck behind erupted into movement and Rebekah realized he was communicating with the crew.

The metallic clank of chains skittering down over the hull was weirdly musical. The black clad nomads launched themselves over the handrail like bats taking flight. When Rebekah peered over the side, she saw the vampires stop with their coats skimming the surface of the water, their boots braced against the steel hull.

A lifeboat rowed by a vampire easily defied the dragging current and quickly approached the ship. The waiting nomad reached for the rope the vampire pilot threw, and the tethered boat fell into step with the ship, in strange synchronicity. Rebekah was so absorbed watching the flotilla of inflatables and fiberglass boats create an intricate daisy-chain like huddle, that the ship came to a graceful stop without her realizing. More nomads climbed down the chains until the tied-on lifeboats resembled a floating island. There was a breathless moment of relief, when the rows of tense human faces peered up the towering wall of the ship's side.

"What happens next?" asked Rebekah, sensing the arrival of Captain Blake. As Connor had before her, he exuded such power, she forgot he could not talk.

"It will take a little time, but they will come aboard via the landing ramp hatchway." A dull vibration shook the deck as the hatch swung open, and Rebekah watched the balletic dance of each boat being reeled in and the passengers disappearing.

Finally, the group she searched for arrived at the front of the queue. Uncle Harry, Thomas, Leizle, Seth, Adam, shared their boat with others who were once *her* human community. *Where is Oscar?* A lump blocked Rebekah's throat as she guessed, without being told. *He's dead.* Vampires could not cry, but her face suddenly felt so stiff it hurt and her grip on the handrail buckled the metal. Gerrard put his hand over hers and said, gently, "There will be time to mourn when all this is over, now is the time to be strong for those who survived."

Rebekah glanced at the distinguished older vampire. "You are right. Thank you. I'll go and find Leizle."

As Rebekah made her way along the deck, her steps slowed at the tearing sound of human sobs. Rounding the corner of the metal walls enclosing the bridge and storage areas, she inspected the endless rows of container units. Following the noise, she swung along the gangway between the steel boxes until the clamor of human hearts and the aroma of adrenaline-soaked blood made her hurry.

She collided with the solid chest of a nomad when she turned the final corner. "What is going on?"

The tall nomad stared down at her, tilted his head as if listening, then turned back to his task.

A crowd of exhausted figures shuffled along, penned in by nomad guards. The metal doors of a container stood open and though their footsteps faltered on the threshold, the humans behind forced the ones ahead to move inside.

Tyrone appeared at her shoulder. "It is the safest place for your humans. If ferals get aboard, they will be protected. Keeping them alive is the goal, is it not?"

Surveying the scene, and realizing the nomads had formed an intimidating wall of flesh, but were not laying a hand on their charges, Rebekah felt better.

"You're right," she said, reluctantly. Staying behind the nomad wall, she followed the trail until she reached the door through which the lifeboat evacuees were emerging. Pushing her way in until she formed part of the lineup, she looked for Leizle. The smaller girl appeared with Uncle Harry beside her, leaning heavily on her arm, and Rebekah reached into the throng and caught her free hand.

Too tired to talk, Leizle raised a puffy face with red-rimmed eyes to Rebekah and gave her a watery smile.

Rebekah said, "I know. I'm sorry, but you're safe now."

In a hoarse whisper, Leizle said, "I wasn't sure if we were jumping out of the frying pan and into the fire, but you're here, so..." her voice cracked and the tears brimming over trickled down her grubby cheeks.

"This is infinitely safer, trust me."

Seth deliberately shoulder bumped into Rebekah. "Well, look who's here." The deep sadness in his eyes robbed the remark of its playful lilt.

"Hello, Seth."

"Good to see a friendly face. How is Connor getting on with saving the world?" A grim smile took the sting out of the words.

"He's working on it, so take care of everyone until it's done, okay?"

"'Oorah," muttered Seth, and slipped back into the stream of plodding figures to catch up with Harry, Adam and Thomas.

"I'd better go too." Leizle squeezed Rebekah's hand and then looked over her shoulder and blurted, "Sergeant, I thought you had gone."

Rebekah spun on her heel and came face to face with a tall, gray-haired, distinguished looking vampire. Even in a grimy uniform, he exuded quiet assurance.

"You must be Rebekah. It is good to meet you at last."

Sensing how Leizle had relaxed and her heartbeat slowed when the sergeant arrived, Rebekah knew she trusted him. "This is the sergeant Julian sent to look out for us."

Frank smiled and jerked his head towards the dark cavernous interior of the container. "I don't think Principal Julian would want you to be inside one of those. Come. Captain Blake has provided a cabin." Turning his gaze on Rebekah, he said, "You can both catch up in comfort. I'll guard the door." He half turned and lifted an enquiring brow.

"Where are Malachi and Julian?" asked Rebekah.

"Malachi wanted to get back to London Zoo, and Principal Julian went with him. Doctor Connor might need them."

Frank took a step back, and Rebekah found herself being towed forward by Leizle. *He got them this far, and that took some doing.*

She reined in her vampire speed and matched her pace to Leizle's as they followed him below deck, passing through a metal door and along a corridor lined with cabins. She found it amusing that this sergeant did the same, essentially walking along at a snail's pace.

The sergeant pushed open the door of the fifth cabin and waved them through it. "When we reach the Docklands, Principal Julian asked me to look after you, to take you off the tanker to a secure location. He'll come for you after this is over."

"No, I'll stay with the others," said Leizle, slowly.

"Please, he doesn't trust Captain Blake, and I have my orders." He frowned and ran a hand over his jaw, and the tension in his face belied the cajoling look in his eyes. *He's worried Julian will be annoyed.* With the shoe on the other foot, Rebekah could see how caring for a fragile human who was strong willed was a nightmare. *Connor has others helping him, and Gerrard can keep an eye on things onboard with Sampson's help.*

"I'll go with you, Leizle. Julian will be happier if you are somewhere safe."

The sergeant darted a look at Rebekah and, at vampire speed, beyond Leizle's range of hearing, he said, "Thank you. The principal was very clear. I will be grateful if you can smooth the path."

Rebekah nodded as he withdrew and closed the door.

Sitting on a bunk and drawing Leizle down beside her, Rebekah said gently, "You are tired, rest."

Leaning into Rebekah's side, Leizle mumbled, "No, I'm okay." But within minutes her body sagged and her breathing became deep and relaxed. Bracing an arm around the girl's shoulders, Rebekah hung onto the moment and savored a feeling of peace.

Chapter 32

Blocking out everything but the blood he was combining into test samples, Connor moved around the laboratory in seamless determination. Brynmor stayed out of the way in the corner, but watched every step so he could replicate the process if the trial worked.

When Connor finally stopped, the exhilaration in his gaze was unmistakable. "If this works, then we can win."

Blinking slowly, Brynmor pushed his glasses up his nose. "What is the next step?"

"We need a guinea pig." Resting his hip on the counter where he had a line of loaded syringes lined up, Connor sneered. "Catching another feral is impossible, but we need to test it on a vampire." An inhabitant of the storage facility would have made a good subject, but they were all gone. *Shit.*

"What effect are we looking for, exactly?"

Connor chuckled. "Of course, sorry. I've been in a world of my own, haven't I? We know blood-clots in human blood trigger seizures in vampires, which provided an obvious path to explore. But, then, I realized, the opposite effect would be more effective. An anticoagulant compound to make the ferals bleed out. Ingesting the blood substitute should open the vampire brainstem, but the chemical reaction of the altered composition will break down vampire blood cells and make them collapse."

Brynmor looked thoughtful. "So, the dehydrated vampire receptors will recognize the blood as food but can't lock onto the altered cell structure. All the brain centers will be opened at the same time. Clever."

"If it works." Connor grunted.

"How are we going to inject it into ferals?"

"We aren't." Connor took a deep breath. "We inject the primates and use them as bait. They'll bleed out if bitten. It will draw in other ferals. The blood of one ape will infect hundreds, if it works as I think it does."

"That's a big sacrifice," said Brynmor, his sad expression reflecting how Connor felt.

"Before I sacrifice our primate population, I need to test it on a vampire."

Brynmor rolled up his sleeve. "Use me."

Connor, time is running out. His mentor's thought triggered irritation and he blurted, like a sufferer of Tourette's, "I know time is running out. I'm ready."

Brynmor's brows shot up and Connor laughed. "Sorry, I was talking to Malachi. He is back."

Swinging out through the laboratory door, Connor registered the gloom of late afternoon and felt tension, like a noose starting to choke him. *Nightfall will bring another wave, and this attack could overwhelm us.*

Malachi, Anthony and Marius clanged in through the distant arched gateway to London Zoo, and a breeze kicked up as the three vampires rushed towards the primate compound and stopped in front of Connor.

"You better be ready," Malachi said with a dry grin.

"I hope you are ready," was Anthony's more respectful outburst at the exact same moment.

"We are all set," said Connor with gritty determination.

From the laboratory doorway, Brynmor shot a penetrating glance at the gathering, and Marius whistled through his throat and flapped his remaining hand.

Anthony, frowning, said it for him. "Have you injected Brynmor with something?" The rolled up sleeve was a universal sign.

"Not yet, and I'm not going to, but I do need a guinea pig to test out the serum." Looking at Anthony, Connor asked, "Are there any patients on the surgical wing past saving? Or has Julian sentenced anyone after trial? Connor's gaze gleamed with hope. *The muscle relaxant will make the reaction less violent, but it will still give us a clue.* When prepped for surgery, muscle relaxant immobilized the vampire body, but their brain function remained sharp. They did not feel pain, so it simply served as the solution that stopped the patient lashing out in panic and breaking their surgeon's bones.

"No, everything has been suspended until after…"

"Damn it."

Marius stepped forward and jabbed his chest with a thumb.

"No, there is no coming back." Connor glared at the tall dark juror who had become a friend. "The test subject will not survive."

Shoving Connor to command his full attention, Marius again thumped his hand on his chest twice. His throat whistled as he grinned and nodded.

"You're too valuable."

With a shrug, he cast a glance around at the gathered vampires, then gesticulated towards the primate house where Osiris, Seren, and Hera were working. Finally, Marius stared Connor down. 'Who then?' was the clear message.

Reluctantly, Anthony said, "We are out of options."

"Connor, he's ready." Malachi laid a hand on the dark vampire's tense shoulder.

Marius wanted to die.

Looking his friend in the eye felt like falling into the abyss; the darkness seeped into Connor's mind like coal dust. He had talked the juror round many times, but this time, he nodded. "You win."

Whipping around, Connor led the way to the veterinary surgery. *The patient won't survive, so no need to scrub in.* Jerking his head to Brynmor, he said, "Prepare a bovine syringe with muscle relaxant, we might need it."

Marius' stride did not falter as he entered the theater and laid out on the operating table where the restraints were at the correct settings for the previous simian patient.

Because apes had longer arms, Connor quickly made adjustments, clicked the solid metal shackles around Marius' knees and forearms, and tightened leather straps across his hips and chest – the thing apes and vampires had in common was strength beyond the human range.

Connor measured out a dose into a plastic cup. "I plan to administer it by mouth – just as a feral would ingest it – and time the response in Marius."

"How do you expect it to work?" asked Anthony.

"The sample, drawn from a simian subject, has been combined with a blood substitute/anticoagulant compound to create the serum. If bitten, the host ape will bleed out. This will attract more ferals. When the ferals feed, if it works, the blood substitute element will unlock the vampire brainstem, let in the anticoagulant to destroy the brain."

"I see." Anthony shuffled his feet.

Knowing Marius had heard, Connor crossed to the restrained subject and asked, "Are you sure you want to do this?"

Marius nodded, his throat whistling in answer.

"Okay, here goes. "He could not look his friend in the eye as he poured the measured dose into the juror's mouth.

Marius swallowed noisily.

Brynmor stood by as Connor took a step back and everyone waited.

The clock ticked round for seemingly endless minutes, and even Marius raised his eyebrows.

"How long…?"

"I don't know," snapped Connor, cutting Anthony short. He stared at the patient, torn by desire for success and the relief of failure.

"Maybe, we need to adjust the compound?" Brynmor spoke quietly.

"You could be ri…" Connor snapped his jaw shut when, abruptly, the metal frame of the operating table rattled as Marius' body began to vibrate.

Blood-stained saliva ran from the corner of Marius' mouth as his lip curled back and a snarl grated in his throat. When violent jolting seizures kicked in and the metal cuffs began to buckle, Brynmor darted forward with a syringe of muscle relaxant, and Marius jerked his head round, his jaws snapping as he tried to bite the laboratory assistant. Brynmor dodged back out of range, but before he could go in and try again, the juror's body tightened in a cramped spasm, then sagged and Marius lay stone still.

Connor approached and pushed back the hooded lids of Marius' eyes to inspect the blown pupils. Framing the dark vampire's head in his hands and pressing thumbs to his temples, Connor nodded. "No brain activity. The anticoagulant dose worked."

Sadness thickened the silence in the room.

Only Connor moved as he closed his friend's eyes and cleaned away the thick vampire blood that oozed from his nose, mouth and ears.

"What is the next step?" asked Malachi, quietly.

Brynmor had already left the theater to collect the syringes of serum from the veterinary laboratory.

"We inject all the sedated primates in the habitat, wake them up and release them where there are most ferals." As he spoke, Connor led the way across the courtyard to the shed of straw-filled pens, where the apes were waiting. Osiris greeted Malachi with an outstretched hand, leading the elder vampire to where Silas and Portia shared a pen with the barred door propped open.

Seren and Hera were already taking syringes from the tray held by Brynmor.

"Inject each animal before we wake them up," said Connor.

"How are we going to make sure the ferals find the apes?" asked Osiris. "Will their heartbeats be enough?"

"There is no way to know, and they'll bleed out too soon if we cut them," said Anthony.

"We'll have to get them close, very close." Osiris frowned.

The sound of a vehicle rolling into the yard outside galvanized every vampire into action.

Going outside, Anthony dropped the tailgate of the flat bed lorry fitted with a wire cage that created an overhead box. He hopped aboard, broke open the straw-bales stacked at one end, and used it to pad the metal floor pan where the apes would be lying while they came too from their sedated state.

Inside the shed, Connor used a stethoscope to check each animal before Osiris, Seren and Hera carried them out and loaded them into the lorry.

When they were alone for a moment Connor beckoned Anthony closer. "Can I have a moment?"

Leading his assistant back to the laboratory, he said quietly. "That tooth you repaired, I need you to do some more work on it."

"This is a great time to be worried about your devastating smile. Open up, let's see what we've got." His eyebrows lifting in an innocent expression, Anthony said, "I could always pull it out."

He laughed as Connor glowered.

"Have you seen Malachi's grin? I don't care if it makes me vain, and anyway, vampires need their teeth." Dropping the cover of humor, Connor opened his hand to reveal a gel capsule sitting in the palm. "I'd do it myself but I can't see. Just do a quick glue job and put this inside the tooth."

Anthony looked suspicious. "One heroic suicide is enough, what the Hell is that?"

"It's an insurance policy." Connor lifted his chin and dropped his mouth open.

"Even so, you better damn well know what you're doing." Gripping the tooth with surgical pliers, Anthony winced when the troublesome molar cracked in two. "Serves you right," he grumbled as he completed the task and ran a line of glue along the seam. "That will have to do."

Manipulating his jaw and clenching his teeth, satisfied, Connor said, "Thank you, and this is our secret, okay?"

A few seconds later, the pair returned and jumped up into the back of the lorry to watch over their charges as they woke up.

Malachi, stay here with Portia and Silas.

Osiris, Seren, and Hera ran alongside the truck as it rolled out of the yard.

The grumble of the engine echoed through the deserted streets and attracted a squad of curious guardsmen as they drew near to the newly fortified perimeter of the city.

Captain Hugh appeared on a street corner and beckoned them forward. "You'll need an escort, there are only a few unblocked roads left."

Even before they passed through the final chasm between the mounds of concrete and metal that used to be buildings, they sensed the desolation beyond.

The squad escorting them scanned the area intently. The bulky backpack each guardsman wore reassured Connor. Flame throwers or Napalm, he didn't know or care which, it would get them out of a tight spot.

The truck trundled through the suburbs, rocking gently when it passed over potholes and debris. The streets were mostly residential, two floored dwellings, with boarded up doors, windows and shop fronts.

A guardsman on the left discharged a burst of Napalm which lit up the night sky and took out an entire row of shops. Wisps of glowing ash danced in the air and the stinging scent of charred wood and brick filled Connor's sinuses.

The startled waking apes reacted to the dragon-like roar and the rush of heat that puffed straw up into the air. Simian hearts pumped faster and they struggled to regain their feet with a harsh screech. One animal grabbed Anthony, but the solid boxer-honed vampire withstood the force and gently calmed the ape with a whispering mantra.

A few miles outside the suburbs, the scenery became a sea of rolling fields, Captain Hugh fell back and rejoined the escort party.

Attracting Hugh's attention through the wire cage, Connor asked, "Where are we headed?"

"There is a dense concentration of ferals about twenty miles outside the Greater London area, centered around one of the old towns. A good place to release your primates, before other ferals come across from the east coast."

Connor noticed the guardsmen falling back and giving the truck a wider berth as they left a country lane and traveled along a high street through what was once a bustling English town. The

366

truck rolled to a stop when the landscape changed to farmland. Connor leapt out, leaving Anthony to keep their primate cargo calm.

Osiris approached, his face set with fierce concentration. "We'll go ahead, perhaps we can draw them in this direction." Seren and Hera arriving at his side made his intention clear. In explanation he added, "We have heartbeats."

"Be very careful." Connor laid a hand on his son-in-law's solid shoulder.

"There's something-" Osiris shook his head. "Never mind, my imagination is playing tricks, we know where all the humans are."

Confused, Connor watched the trio run quickly away across the fields and into the distance. *Humans? What did Osiris mean?* Closing his eyes, Connor ranged his senses over his surroundings. There were hotspots everywhere, but they were temperature changes caused by a natural process; stone and metal absorbed heat during daylight hours – a fraction of a degree in most places. He switched his focus to hearing alone and froze. A sound like cantering hooves, muffled and indistinguishable, grabbed his attention. Like beads of moisture floating on the breeze, it tempted him and filled his mouth with venom. The confusion grew. Like Pavlov's dog, his vampire conditioned response said 'human food'. *But that's impossible.* Just when the frustration consuming him made it hard to stand still, a rumbling snarling wave of sound snatched his focus back. *Ferals.* Judging by the ground shaking beneath his feet, there were a lot of them.

"Anthony, release the primates."

With Anthony's urging, the ambling creatures rose one by one, and then in enthusiastic groups. Sensing freedom, at last, they swung out of the truck, landed on the ground and scanned their surroundings. But their bead black eyes shone with intelligence and, when fear seeped into their body postures – making some apes sink to the ground and others puffed up, as if to intimidate an oncoming predator – Connor felt the weight of regret.

When the truck was empty, swinging round, Connor called out

to Hugh. "Use the truck as a platform. Train the fire throwers on the incoming horde."

The suspension of the vehicle moaned beneath the weight of the guardsmen climbing aboard. The wheel arches pressed down onto the tires and made driving the truck impossible. As if it was made of fiberglass, the guards punched holes in the walls and roof of the wire cage, and aimed their weapons out through the gaps like cannons on a ship.

The troop of primates began shrieking in a discordant tribal chant, loping forward, and then galloping away to where instinct told them safety might be waiting.

Osiris appeared. His black hair streaming back and his chest heaving as his arms pumped in time with his driving stride.

"Damn him." It didn't take a second look to see his gold armlet was dislodged from his bicep. The stink of sea spray and rotting meat could not conceal the odor of the fresh blood trickling down to Osiris' fingers to spray in a wind-tossed shower behind him.

When the scent of blood hit, the truck lurched as even the vampire guards primal reaction was to leap after the alluring scent trail.

Swinging around to take the same direction as the apes, Osiris turned the forty feet wide column of chasing ferals.

Connor leapt on to the roof of the truck cabin as one feral who could not stop slammed into the metal door panel where a second before he had been standing.

Seeing Seren running towards the truck, with feral stragglers rushing along behind her, Connor reached down and swung her up beside him.

"Fire," yelled Hugh.

The ground on that side of the truck lit up as the guards discharged their flame throwers at a height through the buckled metal cage, angling down from ten feet or so above the ground.

With Seren anchored to his side, Connor scanned the battlefield from his own high vantage point on top of the cabin. *Where the Hell is Osiris? And Hera?*

When the flaring blast stopped, hungry flames continued to devour the ferals' clothes, although many writhed and crawled out of blackened pools of melted leather and fabric. The vitreous fluid of their eyeballs leaked down their faces and, much like Captain Blake, their senses were destroyed.

Connor's gut churned as the mindless swarm became a black sea of undulating flesh. More were coming in from the coast and the truck became a metal iceberg in the flowing mass of feral bodies. The shuddering chassis began to crack and the truck cabin rocked beneath his feet as the floor pan of the vehicle splintered.

The guardsmen dropped down from their perches, their flame throwers spent. Shrugging the empty tanks from their backs, they drew close combat weapons – pistols for the most part – and launched themselves from the crumpled wire structure.

Connor hugged Seren close.

I'm so sorry, squirt. I never wanted it to end like this. Another thought cut deep. *Please God, let the serum work.*

The dust kicked up by the hundreds of ferals rushing by clogged Connor's nostrils. He framed Seren's face with his hands and stared into her slate gray eyes. She was not scared. Her hybrid heartbeat was slow and steady and he felt a rush of pride that he had fathered an amazing young woman.

Seren suddenly smiled and held a finger aloft. *Papa, Osiris said the warriors are coming.*

Connor frowned. *Who?*

The stream of ferals flowing around the vehicle thinned. Connor heard them before he saw them – their steady heartbeats were in sync with Seren's. The dull thump of flesh hitting stone confused Connor, at first, until the frontline of Earth Walkers drew closer and he saw the daggers they wielded were similar to the one he had used in combat with Sebastian – seemingly a million years ago. The dagger's blade protruded as an extension of a clenched fist.

An Earth Walker picked off a straggling feral with a driving punch to the back. The vertebrae shattered and the spinal cord made an audible twang to vampire ears.

The countryside was strewn with fallen ferals, many alive and crawling, but sunrise would remedy that. Other corpses were dotted around, too, and ferals clawed their way on their bellies to feed on the fallen bronze-skinned warriors lying in the mud trampled grass. Another Earth Walker strode along with a trickle of blood oozing from a stab wound in his arm. Connor quickly realized some warriors had offered themselves up as bait, although, by the vampire remains splattered over their bare chests, they were not precisely sheep to the slaughter.

Imhotep and the Earth Walkers? Osiris' father? Connor's jaw hung open in disbelief.

"Yes. He has been hunting ferals across Europe." Seren frowned. "Osiris says he is here to see *you*."

"Wait here, I'll be back." Drawing his bolt gun and leaping from the roof of the truck, Connor set off across the field at a fast run, passing through a gap in a trampled hedgerow to follow the tracks of the feral pack. *I need to know if the serum worked.*

Coming up fast behind a back marker, Connor put his bolt gun to the back of the skull and with a click of the trigger, punched a hole in the feral's head. It fell to the ground like a puppet with severed strings.

As the crowd of bodies grew thicker, and he still had not seen a primate casualty, Connor climbed a tree. From fifty feet up, he scoured the landscape until he located a clustered mound of ferals, all lying motionless, the ground around them stained with a dark ruby-colored paste. *The apes bled out.* Even as he watched, other ferals staggered like drunkards weaving a jagged path, stumbling over stones or other bodies until they fell and didn't get up again.

The anticoagulant is working. Hearing Osiris inside his head, Connor darted a look around until he saw the Egyptian waving from a similar perch, high in a tree some twenty feet away. On a neighboring branch, Hera sat exuding relaxation, as if resting on a comfortable cushion and not abrasive bark.

Connor grinned widely, relieved to see his son-in-law had replaced the wax cap on the catheter buried in his brachial artery.

The blood smeared across his bare chest had dried. *You know Seren would have killed me if you died.*

Osiris shrugged. He spoke aloud, knowing vampire hearing exceeded his own capability many times over. "I had to give my father a chance. Seren knows I will never leave her."

Looking back out over the scattering stampede of dying ferals, Connor sent a heartfelt thought back to Osiris. *Will you take Seren to the Docklands to wait for Rebekah and the super tanker to return? I thought I'd lost her today. If we have to do this again tomorrow night with the next invasion, I'd rather not have to worry about her.*

Osiris grinned, his teeth flashing white in a blade of moonlight. "I'll be happy to. I can make you the bad guy, but I want her away from the frontline, too."

Connor sat, swinging his boot and savoring the feeling of triumph. It was a good day. He had found the key to killing the ferals, and his headstrong daughter might actually do as he asked. *Win/win.*

As the battlefield below became still, Connor jerked his head and leapt down to land gracefully on the muddy grass. Like a general looking for his men, Connor stepped over twitching bodies until he found a feral without obvious injury, but lying on the ground racked with shudders.

Dropping to his haunches, he observed the specimen, who displayed an extreme reaction to the serum.

Osiris and Hera joined him and Connor murmured, "Their ligaments and soft tissue is more wire than elastic." He pressed a finger on the juddering jawbone. "Lock jaw. It snapped shut so fast it broke his teeth." As the group watched, the feral ground its jaws until the lower mandible crumbled.

Pulling a bovine syringe from his jacket, Connor stabbed it into the feral's brain via the eye socket.

Hera winced.

"Sorry," Connor said automatically. "A sample will enable us to fine tune the serum compound in the next group of primates. Make it more effective."

Replacing a plastic sheath on the needle and dropping it back into his pocket, Connor walked quickly back through the battlefield. His mind moving onto the next challenge; meeting Imhotep, at long last.

Chapter 33

Gathering the sample from the feral proved to be worthwhile. Connor swallowed his impatience to sit down with Imhotep and focused on adjusting the blood/anticoagulant combination to slow the rate at which infected ferals would die. Letting them live longer would maximize the spread by increasing the window in which they could pass on the infection when they bit their brethren. Connor had seen it at first hand; when in a feeding frenzy, attacking one of their kind was a common feral reaction.

Standing back and surveying the trays of vials, each filled with the new serum doses, Connor grunted his satisfaction. "Brynmor. Anthony. You can take things from here. Get Hera and Malachi to help inject the apes. We need to infect around eighty to use in the next wave of the attack."

The lab assistant stacked the trays into towers of three and waited as Anthony followed his lead.

"We've got this." Brynmor blinked from behind his spectacles and nodded firmly.

"I'll be back before nightfall." With a final salute, Connor set off at full vampire speed, heading back into the City.

Stopping off at the hospital, he put himself through the decontamination system at the laboratory twice, the scalding steam washing the feral remains and dirt from his skin and leaving his granite-like flesh warm to the touch. *I wonder what Rebekah would think of that?* For so long she had been the warm human and he the cold vampire, although not when they 'made' Seren. He grinned and shook his head to push away the thoughts of touching Rebekah's warm body. Once this war was won, then his mind could turn to family, love, and happiness once more.

Stepping out of the tiled chamber and into the dressing area, Connor pulled on fresh clothes and swept the damp wing of dark hair into place with his fingers. The knot of excitement in his gut made his eyes glitter.

The feral threat had brought with it a longed-for event; he was meeting Imhotep, at last. There was no fitting setting for the encounter. Osiris' father was akin to Egyptian royalty, but the gravitas of the jurors' 'hearing chamber' at the court building was the best they could do with London on shutdown.

When Connor arrived outside the door, he took a deep breath. Entering slowly, for a vampire, he could not help but smile when Julian, sitting in his customary throne-like chair at the dark lacquered wooden table, wore a similarly awed expression on his face.

Imhotep rose smoothly from a seat beside the principal.

Connor held out a hand. "It is an honor."

Julian stood and grinned. "This is Doctor Connor, but I believe you met, briefly, on the battlefield."

Imhotep wore a clean white linen tunic. The oiled skin of his forearms glistened as the muscles moved when shaking hands, and he may not be undead, but his strength registered with Connor. The regal Egyptian's sleek curtain of black hair moved when he nodded.

"I have waited a long time to meet the man my son admires more than any other."

Osiris, resembling an Egyptian statue positioned at his father's shoulder, smiled. "Doctor Connor is a great man."

Connor shook his head sheepishly. "You said, you need my help. Anything I can do, will be my pleasure."

Julian sank back into his seat and Imhotep followed suit. "Great One," said Julian, using the Earth Walker leader's formal title. "You saved many lives in Egypt, across Europe, and now here in England. Name your favor and you have it."

Imhotep's dark obsidian gaze fixed on Connor's face. "If you will permit me, it is simpler if I show you."

The humility Imhotep radiated hit Connor like a sledgehammer in the chest. Whatever the favor, he knew it would mean the world to this magnificent warrior and fear that he could not deliver laid heavy on him.

"Please, yes, show us."

Osiris crossed soundlessly to an internal adjoining door, opened it, and beckoned.

A bare-chested Earth Walker entered, carrying a slight figure tightly bound in animal hides, secured with thick rope. A leather mask covered the young man's lower face, but holes had been gnawed through it.

Connor easily detected the shuddering muscles fighting against the confinement and looked to Imhotep for an explanation.

"He was bitten, and he is my youngest son."

"Bitten by a feral?" Julian came around the desk, concern lowering his tone.

Connor laid a hand on the boy's shoulder and a jerking spasm of aggression tightened every muscle, causing the Earth Walker warrior carrying the burden to sway gently.

"What is the story?" Connor murmured, sitting down, again. "How old is he, really?"

With a wry grin, Imhotep inclined his head. "You are correct, he is not a boy in your human years." Casting a regretful look at Julian, the Egyptian said, "I'm sorry, principal, but can Doctor Connor and I talk in private, as family?"

Julian knew the Earth Walker tribe were steeped in secrecy and their longevity was beyond explanations found in nature, so he was not entirely surprised.

"Of course, Great One." To Connor, he said, "I'll be at the docks, keeping an eye on Blake. Come and join me, after…" Julian waved a hand when he couldn't find the right words, left and closed the door behind him.

"You are *connected* to my son, Osiris?"

Connor knew he meant by the telepathic link of both sharing Malachi's blood, so he nodded.

At the rate of an express train which pressed Connor back in his seat so hard that the wooden struts of his throne chair began to crack, a sand-colored scene flooded into his head.

He could see the spectrum of colors in each grain and realized he was buried beneath them. The angle of his face had created an air chamber and the sand shifted as the ground above him shook. When the noise died away, the figure he inhabited pushed steadily up and broke the surface of the gritty ground. Squinting, he watched the stumbling rolling gait of hundreds of ferals as they meandered away, weaving right and left as if searching for a scent trail.

This is Egypt? Connor watched strong bronze-toned arms push aside the weight of sand and, as he climbed from the hole and stayed low, he saw dozens of Earth Walker warriors doing the same. Fitting the 'punching knife' over his fist, the warrior gained speed, and in a crouched run, darted towards a straggling back marker of the feral horde. The feral died soundlessly. The next one he tackled, darted sideways, turned, and clamped its jaws onto the warrior's forearm.

Both bodies fell to the ground and Connor could feel the tendons in his own hand going into spasm as fire whipped along the veins. *Ferals have venom.*

The picture cleared away in gold-colored wisps of smoke and Connor stared into Imhotep's serious dark gaze.

"He *was* bitten by a feral?"

"Yes. We have 'bled' him. Used leeches. But with limited success." Imhotep shook his head. "Malachi has always held you in high esteem, so we came to England for help."

Connor smiled stiffly. "The timing of your arrival was lucky for us, and I will do what I can." His voice dropped to a whisper. "I need to take blood, but before I do, can you tell me about-" Connor waved gesture took in all the Earth Walkers in the room. "-your physiology." The thrum of slow steady heartbeats illustrated the point.

"I am the father of all Earth Walkers." Imhotep rumbled with low laughter when Connor looked confused. "My blood runs through them all in the 'gifting ceremony'. Their extended lifespan comes from my heritage. Call it magic, wizardry, paranormal. My father was a shaman, who learned that mind over matter, if honed to its ultimate conclusion, controls the cells in the body."

"How long can you live?"

Imhotep grinned. "The answer to that question is yet to unfold. We only die at another's hand."

The bundled casualty jerked into spasm in his captor's arms and Connor burst into movement. "Lay him on the table. I'll take blood."

To examine the patient, Connor directed the bearer to uncover the warrior's chest and hold him still. "Great One…" he muttered, while pressing his fingertips into the warm solid flesh and detecting the presence of crystalline grains of encroaching vampire cells.

"My gift name is Imhotep, please, we are family."

"I can do a blood transfusion, but I'd like to try a 'cure' Brynmor and I developed which did not work on the ferals because their brainstems were too far gone." Connor tempered the glow of hope with caution. "There is no guarantee, but it could work."

Connor grabbed hold of the chance to do something useful. Waiting for news that the ferals infected with the serum had died was hard, and until the guardsmen reported success, the humans would remain onboard Blake's ship. Connor was not foolish enough to believe the release of the London Hive herd would be accomplished without a fight. For now, he embraced being a doctor who could make a difference.

"We'll perform the procedure here. Osiris, tell Anthony to bring the samples used in the feral trials and I.V. bags from the hospital, quickly."

Osiris left the room, and Imhotep became still.

The wait seemed endless as they stared at the patient straining against the Earth Walker warriors holding him down, but in truth, it was mere minutes.

When the pair rushed in through the door, Anthony surveyed the scene and seamlessly began unpacking the crate he carried.

Once the youth was sedated, the blood substitute/simian compound was shunted into the carotid artery using a syringe. Framing the warrior's skull with his hands, Connor monitored the patient and waited for the sparks of electric activity in the brain to change to a frequency he recognized as 'normal'.

"I think we caught the cerebral atrophy early. The signs are good. The circulation around his body; that is more straightforward."

Connor laid out I.V. bags of human blood in a row and injected each one with clear liquid from a vial. Laying the syringe down, he turned to Imhotep. "The perfluorocarbon added to the I.V. can force blood through the crystallized tissue and restore the circulation, but infusing him with some of *your* blood might help."

When Imhotep nodded, Connor sat beside him holding a needle at the ready.

Locating a vein, he filled five vials with blood carrying DNA peculiar to the 'Great One'.

Connor shook a vial, inhaling the scent to wash it across his palate, feeling sure it should smell or look different. Magical.

Imhotep laughed gently. "I am a man, Doctor Connor, the rest is in the hands of the Gods."

With a sheepish nod, Connor stood, injected the samples taken from Imhotep into the I.V. bags, and deftly set one up to deliver the contents into the patient via a catheter inserted into his 'bitten' arm.

The warriors performing the role of restraints froze in place, and would do so until the process was complete and the patient came round.

"All there is to do now, is wait." Connor sat down again. *Please God, let all be well.*

"Let us talk of wars and how to win them," mused Imhotep. "You are worried? There is more darkness to conquer?"

"Our humans are in the hands of our enemy. It was the only safe place." Connor frowned. "I believe that getting them back will require a sacrifice. I'm unsure who will have to pay that price."

"Take control." Imhotep held Connor's attention without moving. "Inhabit your enemy's mind and tell him what choice to make. Decide, and make it so."

Imhotep's quiet strength calmed Connor and freed his mind. Each scenario he considered, suddenly had purpose... and solutions.

Chapter 34

The metal hull of the container ship glinted in the late afternoon sunlight. At the top of the dock-master's tower, Julian gripped the safety rail, his fingers crimping the tubular steel to fit his hands as he scoured the vessel.

"There's no movement," said Daniel.

"I know." Julian grunted from beneath a leather face mask, trying to ignore the sense of foreboding settling like a dark cloak over his shoulders.

"It is still daylight. The nomads will be taking cover, and the humans…" No one but Blake knew for sure which of the many dozens of containers they were being held inside, if indeed they had not already been moved into the bowels of the ship to join his own captive herd.

"I've searched the vessel before," Julian said, "If he's moved them, I know where they keep their humans."

"We just have to wait."

"Even though Rebekah and Gerrard are onboard, that's not enough to guard our interests." Slamming a hand down and leaving a fresh dent in the steel rail, Julian spat, "Where the Hell is Connor?" He snapped his jaw shut. *It's been four hours. I hope that's not bad news for Imhotep.*

"Leizle will be okay on the ship, sir. Rebekah will keep her safe."

"Thank you, Daniel." Julian laughed harshly. "I can't deny, I'm worried about her. If that mutant lays one finger…"

Daniel switched his attention to the quayside below. As each platoon returned from the feral hunt with good news, the numbers lining up along the concrete platform grew. "We have a sizable force, if it comes to a fight."

"You are right. We just have to wait until dusk."

Seren climbed the metal stairway and stood beside Julian, settling the cowl hood of her coat into place. "I wish we could contact them."

He draped an arm around the girl's shoulders. "Your Papa has saved the vampire race, so this is a mere hiccup. Don't fret, my dear."

"Do you think Hera should be here?"

Julian glanced down into Seren's serious gray eyes. *She's a bright girl.* "Hera is our ace in the hole. We'll produce her when the time comes." Julian felt the dark cloud thicken around him. He liked Hera and did not want to see her back in Blake's clutches. *But if there's a choice to be made?*

As if she read his mind, Seren said, "I don't think Hera should go back to Blake."

Her chin lifted in a determined gesture Julian recognized well. "We'll think of something. It's not for you to worry about."

"We are negotiating from a position of force," said Daniel with a smile.

Seren darted Julian a wide-eyed look of obedience and he didn't buy it. *Shit, Connor, even Seren can see we're whistling in the wind. You better get here, bloody soon.*

"What will Papa do when he finds out Mama is still onboard?" asked Seren, unlocking the door to Julian's worse nightmare.

"I'm sure he'll stay calm and use his head. He knows your Mama can look out for herself."

"Not how it works, in my opinion." Seren shook her head slowly.

Julian was beginning to wish the girl had stayed at the zoo.

"Look." Daniel pointed across at the tanker. Ripples streamed away from the hull as the vessel began to move. "Where are they going?"

"Docking at the quay," Julian answered, more confidently than he felt.

He heard the whisper of steel as Daniel loaded his longbow and trained it at the ship's deck. They both knew there was no target to aim at, but the warning gesture made the young vampire feel better.

Captain Hugh moved quickly down from his vantage point on the escarpment to the concrete yard below. "What are your orders, sir?" His gaze remained pinned to the shifting hunk of steel as it rotated like a blown leaf.

"Hold your fire." Julian ran through the odds. Seren had called it; Blake running without Hera was unlikely.

The mammoth vessel wallowed like an iceberg, pirouetting slowly until the gap between it and the quayside began to close. *Thank God.*

The ship drew closer until it lined up with an empty berth, and then, as if on cue, Blake appeared on the bridge observation platform, adopting the pose of one looking down at the hive forces gathered in the compound. A sneer crumpled his slick shiny visage.

From his position on the deck, Tyrone shouted, "Where is Doctor Connor?"

Julian bristled, glaring at Blake as the origin of the demand. "You will deal with me, as principal. Dock and release the London Hive human herd."

"We wait for Doctor Connor, unless you have Captain Blake's property and are ready to make the exchange."

About to blurt that Hera was not 'property', Julian realized the futility. *All humans are property.* He tried another tack. "Hera asked for sanctuary."

"That is a pity. We cannot feed your entire human herd for long, but if we don't make the exchange, then our crew can use *them* as food."

"Doctor Connor will not negotiate while you are holding Rebekah hostage." Julian shrugged. "The humans we can live without, thanks to Connor's blood substitute. Let's hope your own food supply never runs out. You will find no welcome on our shores."

The smoke-gray light of dusk crept across the sky and like beetles crawling out from under stones, the pale gray faces of the nomad crew appeared and ranged across the length of the vessel like a string of dull pearl drops.

"They are closing ranks," said Daniel.

"Their own show of force," agreed Julian, grateful that he could take off his mask, at last.

Suddenly, a human man appeared on deck. The thunder of his heart peaked above the background noise of his companions, and he yelled, "Let me go."

He almost fell over the rail when he was shoved in the back, and Julian winced, even before the man grunted at the impact, then hissed with pain.

Captain Hugh took a step forward, his boots crunching on the concrete.

"Wait," murmured Julian, barely loud enough for Hugh to hear.

Tyrone arrived at the rail beside the figure, who exuded aggression, fighting against the vampire nomads holding his arms.

"Return Hera to Captain Blake."

As Julian took in a breath to speak, Seren blurted, "She is dead."

"Damn it." He gripped the girl by the arm until the bone started to creak. "What are you doing? You are a *child*. You will not speak again."

A sudden rustle of activity put paid to the hope that they had not heard her outburst.

The nomad crowd parted as Blake strode to the guardrail, gripped the human by the back of the neck, and pushed him down until his head was lower than his hips and his boots scrabbled for purchase on the deck.

"Help. No. No. No." The man's words became a stuttering cry.

"Stop." Julian jerked up a hand.

"You have nothing to bargain with," Tyrone said flatly.

"Take me. Let our humans come ashore. Take me," shouted Seren.

"What the...?" The space beside him was empty and looking down, Julian saw Seren at the edge of the quay, waving her arms, like a child attracting the attention of a giant.

Julian launched himself over the rail and crunched down onto the ground beside her, a shower of fractured concrete spitting into the air. "What the Hell are you doing?" Julian barked, glaring. "Hugh, take Seren away."

"Agreed," said Tyrone.

"No, there is no agreement," Julian snapped.

The man's whimpering cry became a high-pitched scream as Blake tossed him over the side onto the concrete. Blood splattered over Julian's face and the sound of crunching bone rang through the air.

Everyone froze.

"The doctor's child in return for half your herd. You have one minute."

Shit, shit, shit. Turning to Hugh, Julian said, "Where is Connor?"

"I'll send Daniel to bring him here."

"Now." Julian frowned.

A human woman with dirty clothes and salt-encrusted hair screeched when a nomad dragged her forward.

"Stop." Julian held up a hand and locked gazes with Seren. "Find Rebekah and stick to her like glue, do you understand?"

"Yes."

"Connor is going to kill us both," he muttered, refocusing on Blake's still form. "Release half the humans, and Seren comes aboard until Doctor Connor arrives."

"Very well." Tyrone turned away and the nomads began darting across the deck in purposeful movement.

Descending from the dock-master's tower, Daniel acknowledged Julian's order to find Connor with a stabbing thumbs up gesture and disappeared.

Julian gripped Seren's hand as the noise of grating metal began, each scrape vibrating through the hull in a high-pitched symphony which put his teeth on edge.

The hatchway swung open and the gangplank winched out across the divide. A stream of figures shuffled along it, each one gripping the handrail for balance. The glazed eyes in their grimy faces radiated exhausted relief.

At Hugh's signal, guardsmen guided the freed hostages across the yard to where they dropped to the floor, huddled in groups waiting for whatever should happen next.

Tyrone appeared and beckoned to Seren. "Come."

"That is not half," said Julian. "The girl comes aboard and then the next group will be sent over."

Pulling her hand away, Seren was gone before Julian could find a way to stop it. He raked his fingers through his hair, clenching his teeth tightly. The stream of hostages began again, and as each one appeared, he felt the tightness in his chest clamp tighter. *Where is she?* The grating of metal began again, the hatchway closed, and Julian shut his eyes, his shoulders slumping as he tried not to dwell on Leizle.

The huge vessel became a silent hunk of steel.

The loudest noises he heard were sniffles coming from the relieved humans huddled behind him and the shushing sound of their hearts pumping blood around their chilled stiff flesh.

Captain Hugh and the guardsmen handed round blankets until a fleet of trucks could take the hostages somewhere safe and warm.

Blake might have Rebekah and Seren, but at least Sergeant Frank and Sampson are on there, too.

Julian could do nothing other than stare at the tanker to make sure it didn't disappear. *I should go and hurry Connor along.* But he could not bring himself to leave.

He became aware of Hugh standing beside him, and said, "We need to prepare for the worst. Make sure the guards up on the escarpment have the nomad crew in their sights. Target Tyrone and Blake as a priority."

The captain grunted his assent, but neither of them believed Blake would show himself if the tanker were to set sail.

A statue carved in granite, Julian stood guard until his coat flapped wildly in the rush of fast-moving air that signaled a new arrival. He whipped around and darted back to intercept Connor before his friend broke cover from behind the loading bay station and let Blake see him. "About bloody time, Connor, where the Hell have you been?"

"We saved Imhotep's son, but I couldn't leave until I was sure."

"Bloody Hell." Julian scowled.

Tapping into the tension emanating from Hugh, Connor moved to where he could furtively scan the dockyard, and seeing the huddled humans raised an eyebrow. "You opened negotiations without me?"

"No." Julian stabbed a finger at the hulking ship. "Blake did that."

Connor inhaled to confirm the black pool staining the quayside was human blood. "Shit, Julian, who?" He held his breath, his face a stiff mask.

"A farm human." Julian shook his head in regret. "I didn't even know his name."

"I'm sorry. Where are we?"

"Seren went aboard as a trade for the human lives." Julian glared and raised his hand as Connor reared. "I told her to find Rebekah and stick together."

"And that's supposed to make things better, that my *entire* family are hostages?"

"Now you are here, we can negotiate, again."

Connor had taken one stride towards the quayside when Julian muttered, "Oh, and Seren told Blake Hera is dead."

"For God's sake. Any other missiles to dodge?"

"Well, if all else fails, you can dazzle Blake with your devastating smile," said Julian.

"If only you knew," muttered Connor.

Striding out into open space, he spread his arms wide and shouted, "Blake, what will it take to release the rest of the hostages *and* my family?"

A clanging sound deep in the belly of the ship was the only indication that they had been heard.

Connor smothered his surprise when the hatch door in the hull opened and Captain Blake himself stood on the threshold. Like an out of sync movie soundtrack, Blake's jerking hand gestures accompanied the disembodied voice of Tyrone.

"You will come aboard alone, now."

"I can't do that." Connor peered into the darkness behind Blake, hoping to reconnect with Tyrone. It seemed a lifetime ago, but he felt like the captain's right-hand man and he understood each other. "You know I can't do that, *Captain.* You have to give me something. Release the rest of our humans."

There was an oddly frozen moment when, by the expressions undulating over Blake's ruined face, Connor guessed he and Tyrone were having a discussion. He decided to throw a spanner in the works. "Seren is young and impulsive. You shouldn't believe everything she says."

"The humans will go ashore, your child will stay until we have talked, in private."

"Very well." Connor retreated to where Julian waited.

"What just happened?"

"He wants blood. My blood," replied Connor. "As I suspected."

"What's the plan? Tell me there is a plan." Julian stared at the ship, watching the scene as more humans staggered out into the moonlight.

"There is a plan, of sorts."

"Comforting," grunted Julian, but the probing glance he fixed on Connor was dim with worry."

"You won't get rid of me that easily, old friend." Landing a hard slap on Julian's shoulder, Connor returned to his spot out on the quayside and waited until the stream of humans had shuffled past.

When Tyrone beckoned, Connor started up the gangway. *Stay with your Mama, Squirt. We'll be out of here soon.* His projected thought held more confidence than his true feelings.

Footsteps echoed around him as he stepped onto the ship, and two figures he recognized emerged from the gloom, escorted by grim-faced nomads.

As Gerrard and Sampson were forced to march past Connor towards the gangplank, Gerrard dug his heels in and stopped. "I don't like this, sir. We've lost enough good men, don't end up being one of them."

Connor gripped Gerrard's hand. "I'll do my best, Captain."

A shove from a nomad broke the handshake, and Connor watched until the pair disappeared from view. As the door began to close behind him, Seren's thoughts arrived in a rush. *Mama's not here.*

What? Glaring at Tyrone, Connor asked, "Where is my family?"

The vampire's grin was weary. "The Captain is waiting."

The sensation of his chest filling with concrete accelerated when Connor heard Julian shout out from the quayside. "Leizle is missing."

What the heck is going on? Tyrone's bland expression confirmed Connor's fears. *He knows something.* Connor also knew that Tyrone would not talk. Bragging rights would lie firmly with Captain Blake.

The hull began to creak and shift. The vessel was leaving the dock.

"Where is the Captain? The agreement was an exchange, *me* for Seren *and* Rebekah."

Without answering, Tyrone picked up speed and accelerated up through the levels of the ship.

Connor hoped they were headed for an enclosed space, somewhere he could maneuver Blake into a corner, but the wide-open barn-like cavern of the storage compartments whipped by and they continued upward. Connor realized this would not be a private encounter. *I'm an example, then. A prize.*

Sure enough, when Tyrone shouldered open a door against the rushing wind to where the Captain waited on the deck. The quayside was already two hundred feet away, and getting further each second. Not a great concern, if his own escape was all Connor had to worry about.

Making a quick assessment, Connor calculated the odds. *The guardsmen have us in their sights. Daniel will be primed and ready.*

"Where is Rebekah and Seren?"

"You flatter me with more power than I have. Rebekah and the red-haired human girl left the ship many hours ago, while we were kicking our heels waiting for you to grace us with your presence."

"Left? With who?"

"One of your guards. An emissary of your Principal, it would seem."

"And why would you let them leave the ship?" Connor sneered, unable to hide his suspicion.

"The sergeant convinced me Principal Julian would be grateful if I let his girl go. I hoped one good turn would deserve another." Conveying Blake's derision, Tyrone waved both hands in a 'ta-da' gesture. "And, here you are."

"Here I am," agreed Connor. "When Seren is onshore, we can talk."

Blake took a sudden stride forward, and Connor stepped back and collided with a broad chest. The nomad crew had closed in and created a wall of pallid bodies.

At a sharp nod, two nomads grabbed Connor by the arms and another patted him down. The weapon search turned up a loaded syringe, but nothing else

The syringe was handed to the blind Captain, and Connor wished he had not put the plastic sheath on the needle. A jab in the finger with the anticoagulant serum would have taken longer, but like all poisons, a little would still get the job done, eventually. *It would have been worth the risk.*

Connor's eyes tracked the strokes of Blake's fingertips as he investigated the contraband. His throat gargled when his chest vibrated with wet laughter. "What have we here? Is it poison?"

Taking the syringe when Blake held it out, Tyrone ran it under his nose as if appreciating a Cuban cigar. "It smells of blood and chemicals," said Blake's sidekick. Wrinkling his nose, he added, "I do believe the Doctor came with evil intent."

Connor lunged forward, and the nomads tightened their hold, digging their fingers deep into his tense muscles.

When the prisoner hawked and spat in Blake's face, the captain merely grinned. "It's clear, now, why you wanted to be the *only* hostage on the ship. But let us negotiate, as I promised. The deal was, I help your hive survive the feral attack and you return Hera and supply me with a stock of your blood substitute, correct?"

"I saved The Reverend in return for help rescuing Malachi. That's the *only* deal."

Blake shook his head. "But then, you took Hera."

"Release my daughter." Straining forward until his face was a fraction of a centimeter from Blake's, Connor ground out through gritted teeth, "Let her go, and then we talk."

Like a narrator at a play, in a reasonable tone from the sideline, Tyrone said, "But you can't return Hera. Your *daughter* told us that. We have been here before, Doctor. I want an eye for an eye. I keep Seren as my new mate, and you-"

"Use the poison and rid yourself of this monster. Do it." Connor locked eyes with Tyrone. *Will he listen?* "Do it," Connor whispered harshly.

With barely a stutter in the delivery of Blake's speech, Tyrone continued, "...and *you* will inject yourself with the poison. Happy ending all round."

Connor bellowed, kicked back and heard the knee cap of the nomad on his right shatter. Shocked, the other lost concentration for a second, and Connor shunted his elbow back and cracked the nomad's sternum. Six crewmen took their places and forced Connor to the ground. A foot pressed down on the side of Connor's head, and all he could see were rows of salt-stained boots.

Just when he thought his skull would crush, they yanked Connor back up to his feet.

Tyrone carefully uncovered the needle and said, "I am not foolish enough to trust you. If you had infected one of us, it would have spread like wildfire."

"*I'll* infect you all, too." Connor bared his teeth.

At a nod from Tyrone, large hands clamped Connor's head into position and when the needle jabbed into his ear, Connor felt the eardrum pop.

Locking eyes with the prisoner, the sidekick said, "Not if we throw you overboard."

Suspended between the nomads, Connor's body jerked in spasm. His face contorted into a tight snarling mask and a sudden snap of tension pulled his head back, the tendons in his neck bulging.

The nomads darted looks at Tyrone. "They can't hold him much longer, Captain."

"Throw him overboard and set sail."

Hanging onto his last thread of conscious thought, Connor felt as though the plummet into the cold water lasted an eternity. As his body spiraled through the air, the rows of blank nomad faces looking down broke into identical gloating grins, as if responding to the flick of a switch.

The black steel wall of the hull and the choppy surface of the water blended into a hypnotic kaleidoscope and then he was encased in the freezing current. His body kicked up clouds of silt when it hit the bottom of the river.

Focused on moving one hand, it took more effort than he expected. Gritty water rushed in as he opened his mouth. Gripping the tooth Anthony had fixed, Connor cracked it open, taking in more water as he swallowed the capsule tucked inside the cap of enamel. His survival hinged on the properties of the desmopressin hemophiliac medication it contained. *Will it work? Did I take it in time?*

His world continued to plunge into darkness, a blanket of coal dust filling every space. He felt the stones on the riverbed dig into his hard flesh, but then, lying prone and gazing up at the navy velvet surface of the water, blue gray holes tore into it. His vision cleared and the frothy white blobs moving from right to left became Earth walker warriors swimming overhead.

It's working.

Clenching his fists, Connor fought the paralysis of seizures and found it easier with each movement. His hair wafted in the driving current when he was finally able to roll to his feet and start the run along the rock-strewn underwater landscape towards the black torpedo shape of the moving container ship. The number of swimmers powering through the waves above boosted his confidence. *He must be onboard.* As if in answer to his prayer, a nomad plunged into the water on his back, his weight taking him downward in a cascade of bubbles. The gray bloated flesh resembled a drowned corpse, but he leapt up and, seeing Connor, bolted forward in attack.

Connor ducked to pick up a boulder as the nomad lunged forward. Using both hands, he smashed it down on the nomad's skull. This time the body fell and stayed there, with puffy clouds of brain matter seeping out into the water.

Creating a tornado stream when he turned, Connor resumed his chase. Gaining on the tanker, he scanned left and right at the wide stern for a clue of which side to head for, and then he saw it. A thick weighted rope flaring out behind the vessel crossed his vision at an angle.

Grabbing hold of the trailing tether yanked Connor off his feet and he immediately started to climb. As his head broke the surface of the river, he looked up into the deep brown gaze of an Earth Walker. The warrior wound in the rope, accelerating the climb until Connor could vault over the rail.

Dashing across the deck to one of the metal storage boxes he remembered from the time when he and Greg took their lives in their hands and bluffed their way onto Blake's ship, Connor crushed the padlock to dust in his palm and lifted the lid. He frowned, disappointed that there were no flare guns. *Maybe having a ruined face has made the Captain more cautious.* There was however, a fire ax.

Shoving the ax into the belt of his pants, he crouched low and ran towards the sound of battle. The Earth Walkers' had improvised a defense using chains, ropes, and metal lids of storage boxes. They could not match the nomad vampires in strength, but the joint consciousness of the crew appeared overloaded, sent reeling by the human hearts they heard beating in intermittent erratic pulses which they could not process.

Connor realized the warriors were weakening and falling back. He easily picked out the tall regal figure of Imhotep in the thick of the action. The Great One pointed to an elevated platform above where Connor stood, so he darted up to the observation deck, ducked down behind a metal storage chest and waited.

When the warriors were driven back to the metal wall at the stern, one sliced open his forearm and let blood splatter onto the deck. In a frenzy, the nomads lost concentration and a few more were culled by the warriors who swung thick chains before dodging away into the grid-work of channels between each of the massive cargo containers.

Up on the bridge, Blake appeared with Tyrone at his side, and like dogs called to heel, the nomads lost interest in fighting for a share in the pumping blood, dropped the dead warrior onto the deck, and reformed into regimented lines.

When Imhotep strode forward, silence fell.

Darting around to the blindside, Connor used the rivets in the metal panels to scale the wall of the bridge. Once on the roof, flat on his stomach, he commando crawled across it, stopping short of peering over the edge. *If the nomads below see me, then Blake sees me, too.*

Blake and his companion gripped the handrail of the observation platform and, like snakes enthralled by their charmer, all the faces on the deck below tracked every movement. Blake raised a hand and, in a fluid action, the nomads turned as one and closed in on Imhotep.

Here goes the 'snake head' theory. From the experience of fighting the nomad, Viktor, Connor calculated it would give Imhotep sixty seconds of interrupted telekinetic feed.

He rose silently to his feet, pulled the fire ax from his belt, and leapt down behind Blake. He swung the ax in a driving arc. The grinding noise of stone shattering screamed through the night as the blade gouged a trough in Blake's neck. The Captain's shocked face twisted towards Connor, the sightless eyes glowing like milk-colored glass.

As Connor hoped, the nomads below stuttered to a halt, as if the power was cut.

Imhotep stood still and crossed his arms over his solid chest, curiosity ablaze in his stare.

Connor launched himself over the handrail, landed beside Imhotep and grabbed his arm. "Let's go." But, even shoving the warrior couldn't shift him.

The nomads' glazed eyes began to gleam. *Shit, they're waking up.*

Tyrone recovered first, glancing down at where Blake lay at his feet, and his face became a mask of confusion. *Maybe, he is the first link in the nomad chain.*

The others rocked from foot to foot until turning slowly, they disappeared below deck. 'The Two', his wingmen from the battle in Egypt were the last to move, and Connor could've sworn they nodded in greeting before they disappeared.

As Tyrone descended the metal stairs from the observation platform, Connor kept him in his sights.

The Earth Walker warriors emerged from the maze of containers and lined up in a wall of solid muscle behind Connor and Imhotep.

Nodding, Tyrone said, "You want your daughter, but leave us our herd."

"Very well."

"Do you trust him?" Imhotep watched the nomad disappear through a metal door.

"I do, but if he doesn't return in two minutes, then get off the ship and I'll find Seren myself." He knew where Hera's quarters were, and where the nomads kept their human herd, so there was little point in Tyrone breaking his promise.

The ship starting to move back in toward the quayside was the clincher that the vessel was under new management, and seconds later Seren burst through a door and flung herself into Connor's arm.

Chapter 35

As the sun descended, Frank pushed back his frost stiffened hood. The rising bubble of elation he enjoyed burst with a shudder. *He's still alive.* Where he sat overlooking the London Docklands, perched high on the sloping pyramid roof of One Canada Square – known as Canary Wharf – the wind speed had laid ice over the folds of his thick cape. The ice-shell fractured when he burst into movement, climbing up the steep slope to where a light beacon shone out through the opening at the peak of the skyscraper roof.

Swinging inside, he dropped to the floor and descended by the direct route he had used going up. Having already wedged open the doors to the elevator-shaft, he made short work of a free-running descent, whipping past the succession of derelict dirt-ingrained floors until he burst out onto the pavement.

He raced through the streets until he was within sight of the quayside at the docks. With a grim smile, he accepted that his fall back plan was extreme, but necessary. *If Doctor Connor would just die, then no one else needed to get hurt.* The grudge he bore infected his psyche. Deep respect for his slain commanding officer focused him on revenge and nothing less would do. It had taken three years to engineer this moment – which was nothing when compared to his vampire lifespan – and he could almost taste it.

Smoothing the sneer from his lip, he made his way to the top of the embankment and nodded to the Elite Guardsmen holding their position on the bluff. The uniform he wore and insignia identified him as one of them; an officer in the London Hive.

Silently, he scanned the yard below.

Spotting the blond hair and upright bearing of Principal Julian, Frank took a moment to also pinpoint Captain Gerrard. The quayside was the holding area for the hundreds of humans who had been released from the nomad ship. *The perfect smokescreen.*

Skidding down the slope of scree, clattering stones as he went, Frank joined his own corp of men.

Harold saluted his commanding officer and said heavily, "It failed. The doctor has nine lives."

The muscle ticked in his jaw as Frank said, "Captain Laurence taught us better than that. The puzzle pieces are in place, it is merely the picture that has changed."

All loose ends had been tied, Serge, the mad surgeon, and the fake identity ploy, had worked to bring them here, but now, they had another hurdle to jump.

"You know what to do, Corporal."

Harold nodded. "Sir, yes, sir."

Spinning on his heel, Frank wove an efficient path through the wandering clumps of humans and vampires towards the river's edge where Julian stood, gazing out intently at the tanker.

Before the vessel, which had begun to drift towards a mooring berth when the fight onboard ended, got too close, Frank touched the principal on the arm.

Switching his focus from the narrowing expanse of water, where Connor and Imhotep could clearly be seen on the tanker deck, Julian turned around.

"Principal," said Frank, his face a mask of tension.

"Sergeant, where the Hell is Leizle?" Julian physically jolted, as if resisting an urge to grab Frank by the throat. "Is she safe?"

"Neither Leizle or Rebekah are on board the tanker, but they *are* both safe."

"Where are-?"

An explosion rocked the ground beneath their feet, tore a hole in the perimeter fence, and the shrapnel raining down around them blew craters in the concrete.

Instinctively ducking low, Frank and Julian darted looks around, but saw only smoke and mangled loading dock machinery, and then the wailing began. The smell of blood told the tale. Broken human bodies lay in mangled heaps, charred by flames, and walking wounded wandered with dazed expressions on grimy faces.

Grabbing Julian by the arm, Frank tried to drag him away. "Sir, until we know what's going on, you must come with me. We've lost key members of the council, but *you* must survive. I'll take you to Leizle and Rebekah." Julian resisted until Frank said, earnestly, "Sir, I saved your humans, and your human woman, as you asked. Trust me."

Julian's steady regard sharpened, then wavered.

Frank hoped he had not overplayed his hand. Dropping a syringe down his sleeve, he tensed, looking for the second he could take Julian by surprise.

The water beyond the quay became a mass of splashing foam as Imhotep and his warriors swam towards the quayside.

When Julian turned to look, Frank jabbed the thick needle up into the space under his jaw.

"What the f-" Julian's knees buckled and Frank grabbed his victim around the waist, pulling a slack arm around his shoulder. He tried to make the helpless principal move forward smoothly. "Muscle relaxant, Principal."

Knowing his captive remained alert inside his skull, Frank grinned with pleasure. *His mind will be overloaded with questions he can't ask. Poor bastard.*

Frank scanned the scene. Juror Daniel and Captain Gerrard were rushing wounded humans into dockside containers for their own protection – to lock them away from the vampire guards who struggled for self-control. Steering away from where Captain Hugh and his men searched the rubble for answers to who set the explosion, Frank tagged onto the rear of a fast-marching stream of guardsmen and then peeled off behind a collapsed loading crane.

He had a small window of opportunity to get his captive to where Leizle was hidden. Hoisting Julian up over his shoulders, Frank powered forward, and straight into the path of a tall broad guardsman.

"Who goes there?" the guard planted his feet wide and trained a high-powered rifle at Frank's face.

Shit, I should've known the perimeter was shut down. Taking another step, Frank yelled, "Clear out of the way, Principal Julian is hit. I have to get him to surgery, now."

Recognizing the principal's flopping wing of gold blond hair, the guard caught a glimpse of Julian's still features and jolted out of the way. "I'll escort you, sir."

The guardsman began running alongside Frank, who ramped up to top speed. As the sergeant expected, once they entered the quieter streets, out of nowhere a crossbow bolt whistled through the air and the escort flung forward, landing heavily on his chest with the shaft of the bolt protruding from the base of his skull. Frank barely broke stride as the body fell.

When he entered his own familiar terrain, the buzz of excitement made him grin. He was grateful that Julian had been spared a similar fate. He respected the principal, even if his choice of friend was repulsive.

Harold is right, the plan was sound, and anyone else but Doctor Connor would be dead by now.

◇◇◇

When the shockwave of the explosion in the docks rattled through his skull, Connor leapt overboard and the slimy boulders on the riverbed cracked beneath his aggressive propulsion. Glancing up, he tracked the torpedo-like dives and powerful driving movement of Imhotep and his warriors as they made short work of swimming to shore.

Rearing up from the river, Connor stood bolt upright, water streaming from his black hair down over his tightly composed features as he looked for familiar faces. He grabbed the arm of the nearest vampire guard. "What happened? Who set off the grenade?"

Shouts went up at the perimeter fence-line and Connor peered through the billowing clouds of dust draped over the crumbling debris. A dirt encrusted guardsman emerged, being dragged along between Captain Hugh and Captain Gerrard.

The smell of blood distracted Connor until Imhotep laid a heavy hand on his shoulder and said, "My men will guard the wounded humans, your vampires are making their hearts beat faster."

Connor spared the Great One a grateful glance before addressing Gerrard.

"Tell me," he barked shortly.

The vampire prisoner appeared to be cooperating, but the smirk on his face was hard to ignore.

Grabbing the vampire by the front of his uniform, Connor grated his words out. "What the Hell did you do?" As he glared into the complacent brown gaze, Connor froze. "I know him."

Gerrard nodded. "I'm sure he remembers you, too. Guardsman Harold. You broke his shin bone in the fight outside the eco-shelter."

A fierce frown etched deep lines into Connor's snarling face. "So, what the Hell is this all about?"

Harold lifted his chin and said clearly, "Revenge for *our* captain. Captain Laurence. You might remember him. You killed him when you revealed your impregnated cow."

Connor punched the vampire in the face and shattered his nose. "Rebekah. Her name is Rebekah."

The smile never shifted. "It's time for you to pay," said Harold.

Every nerve ending in Connor's brain suddenly buzzed with apprehension. "Where is Julian? Tyrone said Rebekah and Leizle left the nomad ship with an emissary of Julian's. Where is The Principal?"

"We can't find him," said Hugh.

"Julian asked *me* for the name of a sergeant he trusted, the officer in command of Serge's detainment in London. But *that* detail was given to Sergeant Frank, and this man is not in his squad." Gerrard looked from one face to another as he tried to fit the pieces together.

Connor focused on Harold, again. "You set off the grenade as a distraction, so *you* know where Principal Julian is."

"He's with my sergeant."

Gerrard swore softly. "God damn it. *Your* sergeant has been using Frank's name?"

"Has anyone seen this sergeant with Julian? If he's not Frank, do we know who he is?"

"Sergeant Barker. He served in the S.A.S unit under Captain Laurence, as we all did." Harold puffed up his chest, planted his boots wide and pulled his arms from the grasp of Hugh and Gerrard. "We've waited three years. We nearly got you at the duel in the Albert Hall – but lost a couple more men instead." Harold shrugged. "Revenge is best served cold."

"Jesus," muttered Connor, "you're like rabid dogs chasing a bone. I've done nothing but protect my family."

"People around you die," replied Harold.

"So, what is the plan? You have an ultimatum, I assume." Connor tapped a finger on his temple. "The clock is ticking, so let's have it, where are they?"

Harold grinned.

Captain Hugh grabbed him from behind, his powerful forearm clamped across the shorter vampire's throat. "If you're not going to talk, we don't need you." The strangle hold tightened.

"Wait," said Captain Gerrard, "he knows more than we do, at this point."

Connor rammed his face in close to Harold's. "What *do* you know?"

Hugh eased his grip and Harold croaked, "What time is it?"

Frowning, Connor replied. "Two in the morning, why?"

"As I said, people around you die and if you kill me, Julian, his red-haired whore and your vampire bitch die."

Connor put one hand around Harold's neck and glared at the sneering smile; His thumb pressed the Adam's apple until he felt it starting to crumble.

"Don't, Connor, he's baiting you." Gerrard laid a restraining hand on his shoulder.

Connor stepped back, dragging his fingers away as if defying a magnetic force.

"You must go alone, or they all die," said Harold.

"Not a chance," barked Hugh.

"I'll go alone. Now, where?"

"Smithfield Market."

"That's a big place," replied Connor, already preparing to turn and run.

"You'll work it out." Harold shrugged.

"Keep him locked up," Connor shouted, as he headed to the rear perimeter fence and vaulted over the top.

He had never been to Smithfield Market. Reminiscing about animal slaughter did not ring his bell. The choice of venue felt macabre and dark. *How the Hell did this Sergeant Barker – Frank – whatever he calls himself, suck Julian in?* As Connor tried to relieve some of the tension cramping his muscles, he struggled with a stark reality. This showdown bore the hallmark of a patient and ruthless mind.

When he rounded the corner on Charterhouse Street, he made himself stop. *Rebekah?* He closed his eyes and opened his mind, looking for the tremble on the thread of their psychic connection. Like a spider could sense the lightest touch on a silk strand, he was used to feeling her before he tuned into actual words. *Nothing.* His jaw muscle ticked. He refused to believe she was dead, but the cold weight in his chest made walking forward again harder when he could not find another explanation to latch onto. Vitriol had exuded from Harold like poison gas. *She must be alive.* He switched the focus to Leizle. Scanning the ground before him as he walked along the Grand Avenue, he concentrated on finding clues. *Did Frank choose the East or West Market?* He froze when he heard faint knocking. A rhythmic noise. *A message?* It came from below ground so Connor headed quickly to a descending elevator shaft.

Taking the downward journey in one leap, he walked out into the dark cavernous space of a deserted underground carpark. He slowly inhaled the disturbed dust floating in the air. *Someone has passed through here.* As if sensing the faint warmth of a candle, Connor began to feel like he was getting somewhere.

The biggest piece in the puzzle was the human heartbeat he now felt vibrating around the space in an echoing drum beat, but scanning the flat black expanse of the surrounding walls revealed nothing useful. He checked the bolt gun tucked into his belt was primed and moved forward. After each step, he used every sense to scan for movement. *This sergeant won't allow me to live. He's drawing me in.*

Connor realized he had no choice. "Sergeant, I'm here alone. Let the hostages go and I'll come in."

Movement caught Connor's eye, and a tall dark figure appeared in an open doorway at the far end of the cavernous space.

"Doctor Connor, you will come inside or the hostages die." The vampire shrugged. "They mean nothing to me."

Shit. "How do I know they aren't already terminated? I only know Leizle is alive."

"Ah, it is good to know my cage works." The sergeant pushed the door to the industrial-sized cold store wider, turned, and retreated inside.

Looks like I have no choice. Striding forward, he darted in over the threshold and froze. It was almost pitch-black, except for a green LED light emitted by a sensor on the ceiling. The right wall of the cold store was filled with an arsenal of crated weapons, all locked inside metal cages, which would slow Connor down if he tried to grab one.

Just inside the entrance on the left, a sarcophagus sat in an enclosed, walk-in metal box. An open padlock swung on the hasp of the bolt fitted to the metal door, and Connor guessed Frank used it to lock himself inside. *So, this is his lair where he takes grave sleep.*

"Connor."

Rebekah strained forward, touching the meshed wall of her prison with her fingertips. The buzz of ionized air vibrated through Connor's head and it fell into place – the current passing through the metal fabric broke the telepathic link.

Connor approached in a swift crouched side step until he could touch Rebekah's fingertips, registering the live current as the tingle of pins and needles. "Thank God. Are you okay?"

"I'm so sorry." Dull anger sparked in her gaze. "We were so stupid."

"None of that matters. Where did the sergeant go? He only wants me. You just have to sit tight." Inhaling, he detected the odor of muscle relaxant and heard the clink of metal when Rebekah shuffled her feet.

"He's a sick son-of-a-bitch, but smart. Be careful," said Rebekah.

Tearing his attention away from her tense face, Connor scanned the cells beyond. On the floor of the next one, he saw the crumpled body of Julian. Beyond that, in the darkest corner of her cage, Leizle lay slumped on a bunk bed.

With a deep breath, Connor gritted his teeth and stepped back. "You've gone to a lot of trouble to get me here, Sergeant. Let's talk." He backed away to where a large steel storage box sat, opposite the row of three cells, hitched a hip against it and swung one boot in a relaxed pose. The metronomic clunk, clunk, clunk of his boot making contact was the only noise apart from Leizle's shallow breathing. "You really are a coward."

A crossbow bolt whistled past Connor's left ear and vibrated as it gouged a hole in the steel skin of the refrigeration room. Narrowing his gaze, Connor zeroed in on where his nemesis stood, blending into the surroundings. Three things gleamed in the dim light; the sergeant's jet-beaded eyes and the silver tip of the next bolt.

"Thank Christ, for that." Connor stood up and spread his arms wide. "Go for it. I thought I'd have to listen to you whining about my being a murderer. Your Captain Laurence lost because he was inferior. Your squad members died because they were stupid."

The string of the crossbow sang as the sergeant fired the next bolt. Connor dropped like a stone. Rolling over and punching a hole in the wall of the nearest cage packed with weapons, he forced his way through, bending back the wire mesh like the petals of a metal flower. Once inside, he ducked behind a crate and waited.

Scanning the stenciled labels, he read descriptions of types of grenades, claymores, but, he found nothing that wouldn't kill Leizle in an instant, even if vampires stood a chance of survival.

Peering around the crate, Connor caught a glimpse of Julian. His hands fluttered, paused, and then fluttered again. Connor frowned. *He's using sign.* Focusing on the movements this time, he read the communication. *The muscle relaxant has worn off.* Connor clenched his jaw, irritated that the messages could only go one way, because he had a plan.

"I'm coming out," he said evenly. Pushing his way back through the hole, he stood tall with his hands raised. Walking forward, he stopped three yards away from the barred wall of Julian's cage. This one was not a faraday type contraption. *Frank did his homework.* The sergeant knew which vampires shared Connor's DNA and a telekinetic connection.

"Let's talk."

The dark figure of Frank appeared, his arms bare where he had shed the restrictive fabric of the guard tunic and hooded cape.

"You want to fight me? Is that the plan? Will that satisfy your sense of honor and revenge, to kill me in combat?" While speaking, Connor shrugged out of his greatcoat and unbuttoned his shirt cuffs. "Will you release the hostages if you win?"

"Yes," Frank said with a wide grin.

Liar. Connor narrowed his gaze. "Hand-to-hand combat, then? I'll beat you fair and square, as I did Captain Laurence."

Frank laughed harshly. "I don't think so."

"Stop, no more fighting. Just save Julian, please." As if she had just noticed Connor, Leizle leapt up from where she huddled on the bunk and staggered across her cell, sweeping her hands blindly in front as her human sight detected only darkness. Her waving fingertips touched the wall of her prison and she threw herself forward, using the bars as support in a white-knuckled grip. She pressed a tear-stained face into the space between the metal rods, her red-rimmed eyes brimming over with more. Her pupils were blown wide, reminding Connor how terrifying it must be to only be able to *hear* the sounds of fighting echoing in the dark.

"It's okay, Leizle. Julian is in the cage beside you. He is safe."

In the split-second Connor darted a glance towards Leizle, an explosive shoulder charge rammed him back into the metal wall of the munition store. His ribcage creaked beneath Frank's barreling weight, and Connor grappled for a hand hold to push him away. Connor jerked his knee up, making contact with a solid thigh, and the sergeant's balance shifted.

Twisting sharply, he grabbed Frank's steel gray hair and pulled until the scalp separated from the skull. As the crackle of disintegrating vampire flesh filled the air, Frank bellowed, surrendering to the force lifting his head up. Connor landed a right hook and heard the sergeant's cheekbone crack.

When Frank staggered back into the bars of the cage behind, Julian flew up from his twisted collapsed pose, lunged forward, and grabbed the sergeant round the neck, anchoring him to the metal bars.

Frank's eyes opened wide and a croak of laughter grated in his throat.

Connor stared into the manic gleam of Frank's stare and swallowed loudly. Before he could stop him, the sergeant flung an arm out sideways to where Leizle still gripped the bars of her own cage, and closed his hand over hers.

The girl screamed.

The sound of cracking bones popped like corn kernels on a stove, and Julian froze.

"She'll lose the hand if you don't let me go." Frank smiled.

Instantly, Connor stepped back and held up both hands.

Julian hesitated a second, but when Frank tightened his grip and Leizle dropped to her knees with a sobbing shriek, he had no choice and released his hold.

Rebekah moved forward, dragging the hefty chain behind, although she could barely reach the sides of her cage. "Sergeant, what do you want?"

Leizle's howling cry grew louder."

"You said, you'd let her go." Connor sneered. "You're here for me. Let them all leave."

"I *said*, 'she'd lose a hand'." Frank shrugged.

"Please," sobbed Leizle.

With his grip still crushing her fingers, Frank swung around to face her as she struggled back up to her feet.

"Please."

Connor locked eyes with Julian, both vampires feeling helpless. Under cover of Leizle's grating sobs, Connor reached into the back of his belt and pulled out the bolt gun. *She'll lose the hand anyway, the crush injury is too severe.* Looking to Julian for agreement, Connor slipped closer, raising the weapon.

Frank released Leizle suddenly and her scream, when the blood rushed back into her broken fingers, was cut short as he reached through the bars and clamped his other hand around her throat.

"Put the gun down, Doctor," Frank said calmly. Turning his head to where the barrel was inches away. "Or the girl dies."

Heavily, Connor said, "We all know the girl dies whichever way this plays out." He closed the gap, pressed the barrel into the base of the sergeant's skull, and pulled the trigger. The resounding crack of bone shattering drowned out Leizle's guttural cry as her spine crumbled in his clenched fist and both their bodies slid to the ground.

"Noooooo." Julian gripped two bars on the wall separating them and pulled hard, his face contorted with rage and pain. They bent enough for him to ram his shoulder and one thigh through into her cage, but no more. He sagged suddenly, animation draining away as he stared down at Leizle's face. Her copper hair covered one eye and the other stared up at him.

"I'm sorry, Julian."

"How could you? How *could* you?" It was Rebekah's tight voice which sliced through the darkness. "I'll never forgive you."

"Honey." Connor dropped the bolt gun with a resounding clatter. "I had no choice. You could smell the internal bleeding. The bone-marrow seeping into her bloodstream. He would have killed her anyway."

"You don't *know* that," yelled Rebekah, her chains rattling as she tried to get closer.

"I think you should go, Connor." Julian supported his own weight once more, pulled back into his cell and turned to grip the front wall of bars.

Like a slowly unwinding spring, he increased the pressure until the gap he made was wide enough for escape.

Connor stared at Rebekah's set features. *That damn cage.* He couldn't read her thoughts, feelings, or send his to her. "I'm sorry."

"Go," said Julian, finally stepping out into the storeroom. As if Connor was not there, he dropped to his haunches, patted Frank down until he found the keys, opened the cell door, and walked inside.

Falling to his knees, he gently pulled Leizle's slack body onto his lap and rocked her. "It's okay, Red. I've got you. I've got you."

Connor turned and went to the doorway. Looking back, he felt invisible. Julian stroked Leizle's chalk white face, and Rebekah sat on the other side of the dividing mesh barrier and rocked in time with their grief.

His footsteps echoed as he set off across the cavernous underground chamber. He heard a whisper and knew what it was, but didn't care. *Of course, Frank would not be here alone.* Spreading his arms wide, he welcomed it, and when the impact of the crossbow bolt spun his body around, he prayed he would be dead before he hit the ground.

While he lay staring at the rows of burned-out fluorescent tube lights, resembling soot-black poker straight snakes crossing the ceiling, that last thought seared a path through his brain. *Frank was not alone.* His fatalistic acceptance vanished and fear for Rebekah and Julian gripped the fibers in his prone body.

Air wafted around him as the shooter passed close by, pausing to inspect Connor, aiming a bolt at his head, but then firing it into his bicep, instead. It tore through the muscle and the tip lodged into the ground beneath. *Where was I hit?*

Waiting until the vampire had gone, Connor used his good arm and found the first bolt had shattered his collarbone and was buried in his neck. Pulling it out was not an option. *Shit.*

Straining every sense and using the muffled sounds which marked the progress of the creeping vampire to track him, Connor began a rhythmic scraping of his diamond hard nails over the rough concrete. *Please God, let Julian hear me.*

◇◇◇

Julian buried his face in the silken strands of auburn hair and whispered his pet name for Leizle. "I'm so sorry, Red, so sorry."

Rebekah stared in silence, not wanting to intrude on the grief pouring from him as he sat, clutching the body to his chest.

Jerking his chin up, Julian stopped rocking. "What's that?"

Rebekah focused on the faint noise. "A rat?"

Julian clenched his jaw but shook his head. "It's too measured. Rebekah, play dead." As he said the words, Julian toppled over, pulling Leizle with him, and the pair became a fresco of death akin to a scene from Romeo and Juliette.

Feeling her soft body mold to his, Julian trapped a coarse sob inside his throat. *I'm so sorry, baby.* This time, he was begging forgiveness for what might come. *Someone is out there. Frank had backup.* Keeping his eyes wide open, peering across her profile and trying to ignore the long lashes of Leizle's open glazed eyes, he waited.

A tall vampire moved quickly across the storage area. *He knows the territory, so one of the team.* When he drew alongside Rebekah's cage, he paused, but moved smoothly on with a faint grunt.

Julian examined the black boots when the guardsman stopped beside the fallen sergeant. "We got him, Sergeant. Mission accomplished."

The guard dropped to his haunches and laid down the crossbow he had swung with each stride onto the ground. Pulling on the prone body, he straightened out the sergeant's limbs, and for a moment, Julian dared to hope. *Will he leave?*

Turning away, the guard entered a munitions cage and broke open a crate.

At the sharp crack of splintering wood, Julian burst into action. He dived towards the open doorway and made a grab for the crossbow. The weapon scraped away across the concrete and the guard jerked back up, holding a grenade in each hand.

"Jesus," he shouted, darting forward. One grenade hit the ground as he lunged to take back the crossbow. Twisting from his belly and onto one hip, Julian swung his leg and kicked the weapon out of the guard's reach, and rolled up onto his feet.

The guard watched the crossbow skitter across the floor, pulled the pin from the grenade he still held and shrugged. "I thought you were dead. The place will go up like a Roman candle when I set this off. I hoped to survive, but this was always billed as a suicide mission."

Rebekah abandoned the pretense of being dead and said quietly, "What was the mission, exactly? The last I saw, Connor was alive and well, so 'mission fail' fits the bill."

As if on cue, the noise of a scuffing boot echoed through the parking level outside.

The vampire looked around, and Julian launched himself forward, wrapped his arms around the guard, and trapped the grenade between their bodies. He clamped his fingers over the guard's, fighting to stop him from releasing the trigger.

"Rebekah, go."

"The door is locked." Rebekah rattled the mesh of her cage in frustration. She could see the keys, but the Faraday construction didn't have bars with spaces.

"Damn." Julian frowned fiercely. The few seconds the grenade would take to explode was an eternity for vampires. Julian had no plan to save himself, but could he get Rebekah out in time?

Everyone froze when Connor appeared in the doorway, his arm swinging uselessly at his side, the shredded flesh of his bicep hanging.

Like Frankenstein's monster, the crossbow bolt protruding from his neck, with a labored stride, Connor picked up his abandoned bolt gun and came up behind the guard. He rammed the barrel into the vampire's shoulder socket and shot the bolt, tearing the tendons and crippling the nerves controlling the hand. Dropping the gun and pushing his hand in-between the pair of bodies, to where only the pressure of Julian's fingers still held the guard's fist clenched, Connor took over. Using his weight as a battering ram, he wedged the guard face forward into the caged wall of the munition store.

"Get Rebekah out and shut the door."

Julian stepped away, scooped up Frank's keys and rifled through the bunch, trying to tune out the staggering dance of Connor struggling with the guard.

The vampire fought to free the fist clamped around the grenade, but Connor forced the guard face first into the steel cage and used the weight of his solid body to pin the guard still.

"You're all going to die," the guard said, and even with the linked metal squares digging into his features, he managed to grin.

"Connor," said Rebekah, her words a low whisper of distress.

"It's okay, honey, I love you. Julian, you have to get her out of here," said Connor, through clenched teeth.

Julian gripped Rebekah by the arm. "I'll come back, but let's go."

The guard rattled against the metal, his body jerking and twisting, and the grenade fell to the floor.

Connor yelled, "Get out."

Julian shoved Rebekah out through the doorway and dived out after her. He slammed the refrigeration unit shut, twisting the handle to seal the room just as the ground beneath their feet shook and they felt the 'oomph' of the shockwave of an explosion.

Rebekah froze, staring at where Julian still had his shoulder pressed against the door.

"You can let him out, now," Rebekah croaked. "Let him out."

Julian turned to face her, his hands dropping to his sides.

She tried to dodge past, but he grabbed her and held her tightly to his chest.

"Let him out," she whispered.

"I'm sorry. He's gone. He's gone."

Rebekah went slack in his arms and Julian rested his chin on top of her head.

As if he was all that stopped her falling to the floor, she held on and buried her face in his chest. He stroked her feathered hair and tried not to think about the wreckage lying behind the closed steel door.

Chapter 36

The purple-clad Elite Guardsmen marched Harold into the courtroom and Julian examined the defendant through tired jaded eyes. *What is the point?*

Glancing left and right at Daniel and Anthony, both dressed in their jurors' robes, the tight expression on their drawn faces hit home. Everyone here felt crushed by the loss of colleagues and friends. *Justice doesn't bring them back, but it makes the knife of grief more bearable.* Julian swallowed hard. This was where his own stupidity would be laid bare. The sick feeling in the pit of his stomach was caused by the writhing fear that he had let the serpent into the garden.

The gallery remained empty for this closed session, so at least only a select few would hear the worst.

A cough from over his shoulder cut through his musings, reminding him that Captain Gerrard stood to attention behind the throne chairs on the dais.

Shuffling in his seat and sitting straighter, Julian said heavily, "Corporal Harold, you are charged with treason." He met the stare of the accused head on. Images of Leizle's death played out in his mind, superimposing themselves over the backdrop of the court, and Julian closed his eyes. A heavy hand on his shoulder jerked him back.

"Principal, do this for all of us." Anthony's steady brown gaze was dulled with his own pain. Connor was his mentor, his hero, and he struggled with the fact he was dead.

In a stronger voice, Julian said, "Before sentencing, the court will hear your testimony."

The glee in the prisoner's eyes confirmed what the jury hoped for, they had found a canary who wanted to sing. Harold puffed up his chest, taking a deep breath to charge his vocal chords, ready to take pleasure in his story.

"Doctor Connor thought he was God. When the *jurors*-" He sneered the word. "Witnessed him kill our Captain, he went unpunished. He maimed a councilor, tore off Serge's arm, and no

412

one did anything. He was a cancer and we decided to cut him out."

"You decided back then? Three years ago? Why wait so long?" asked Julian.

"We were under Captain Laurence in the S.A.S., he turned us and gave us eternal life. We had all the time in the world to wait for an in."

"What was the in?" asked Julian. His heart felt like a stone. *Here it comes.*

Harold grinned. "*You* were. Sergeant Barker replaced Frank on the house arrest detail of Councilor Serge, and suckered you. All we had to do was avoid Captain Gerrard."

Gerrard leaned forward. "Where is the real Sergeant Frank? What do you mean by replaced?"

Stroking his chin, Harold said, "Intercepted is a better word, I'd say. We crushed his skull, of course, and the two men in his squad went the same way. Getting Councilor Serge onside after we 'saved him', was easy."

Julian slumped in his chair. "I've heard enough. Take him down and execute him."

Captain Gerrard leapt over the handrail around the dais and landed two feet in front of Harold. "I'll perform the execution myself, with pleasure."

Gerrard shoved Harold towards the door, grabbing him by the scruff of his dirt-engrained tunic and the Elite Guard followed them out.

As if lining ducks up and shooting them down, Julian said aloud, "The feral invasion was a lucky break. They tried to take Connor out in the Albert Hall duel and lost two men, so they bided their time. Serge was an easy pawn, and Captain Blake. Frank – sorry, Barker – was a master manipulator. The ferals provided the chaos they needed, but I let him in."

Julian slammed a hand down on the desk. "I handed Leizle over to his care like a sacrificial lamb. Connor was right, she was always going to die."

The room remained eerily silent. The truth was, Barker was a ghost. None of them but Julian had seen him or spoken with him. The blame was his to bear.

His chair grated as the principal jerked to his feet. "Court dismissed," he muttered, and swept from the chamber. Striding along until the corridor became a blur, Julian was inside his private room in seconds. He tore his robe from his shoulders and flung it into the corner. Staring into the mirror, he saw the face of a broken man. The abyss in the stare he looked into sucked him downward. *I don't want to live.*

Dropping to his knees, he covered his face with his hands. The human Julian had wanted to die when he lost Eva, his human wife. Now, he had killed his love, and let in the monster who destroyed so many lives. *So many.*

Getting up, he opened a drawer in a side table beside the hearth and pulled out Connor's bolt gun. He had scooped it up when he dashed from the refrigeration unit. He didn't even know why. *Yes, I do.*

He put the barrel to his temple, but when he closed his eyes he heard a heartbeat. A voice whispered. *Leizle?* But he knew it couldn't be.

A gentle knock on the door gave him something else to concentrate on, interrupting his spiraling descent into self-loathing. A wry grin twisted his lips.

"Hello?" a female voice called. Hearing it felt like inhaling a fragrant flower and chased the tension from his body.

"Come," said Julian, returning the bolt gun to the drawer and facing the doorway with a look of wide-eyed innocence.

Hera entered, glued her searching gaze on Julian's face, and said, "We are all hurting."

It was not a wild leap, so Julian nodded. "We all lost friends."

Hera glided closer, her bare feet brushing over the carpet. ~*You have a heavy burden. I feel it. But you are the beacon they need to see in the darkness.*~

Bitterness tightened Julian's features as her thoughts felt like a chisel carving the script into his skull. "If you can read my mind, you'll know I can't lead anyone. I have nothing left." Lowering himself into a chair, he said, quietly, "I'm tired, Hera. Two hundred years and I'm back to emptiness. My dearest friend died thinking I hated him. My love died and I was helpless. I can't lead."

Dropping to her knees at his feet, Hera rested a hand on his thigh. ~*Stop lying to yourself.*~ Aloud, she cajoled, "Connor knew you loved him. Leizle knew death would come."

Julian jerked back in his seat at the sound of their names, but Hera pushed on.

"But what of Rebekah? What did she lose? And Seren? None of them are here demanding your head on a stake. No one blames you, but they *are* waiting for you to show them a way through this."

Looking down into her earnest gaze, he asked, "And what of you? What do you want?"

Hera smiled. "To stay in England. Tyrone will allow it if the London Hive has not disintegrated into lawless chaos." The look she sliced up through lashes was laden with sarcasm.

"So, this is your message? Stop bleating and get my arse into gear."

Hera nodded emphatically and gracefully regained her feet. "Precisely. You have work to do, and people who love you are waiting for you to guide them."

◇◇◇

Rebekah entered the dining cavern, looked across to the table she had often shared with Leizle, and then froze as the truth slapped her in the face. Leizle was gone.

Seren touched her elbow. "It's okay, Mama."

"Of course it is." Smoothing away her fierce frown, Rebekah scanned the room full of exhausted weary humans who were staring at her. The wall of dull acceptance broke her heart. The missing faces of the eco-shelter community shrieked through her mind, and she knew the dead surely haunted the minds of each human, too.

Delicious odors of food wafted, blending with her favorite aroma of human blood, and the silence was broken by Thomas carrying a huge steel dish of fried chicken through from the kitchen and depositing it on a central table. "Dig in," he said, "Oscar always said this is soul food."

Thomas spotted Rebekah, hesitated, and then grinned. "So good to see you home again."

The boyish frame was gone and the man he had become when Rebekah wasn't looking gave her a steady encouraging stare. Whipping across the room as slow as a vampire could manage, she hugged him carefully. The three children who grew up here, were just two, now, but her sadness eased a little the moment she held him.

"I miss her, too. Oscar, Greg, Evie, all of them. And God, Connor, I'm so sorry, but he did it. He killed the ferals and saved us all."

Releasing the young man and holding him at arm's length, Rebekah said, "He did. He saved us all, and left us with the tools to stay safe."

Seth's boots grated as he stood up. "Sit awhile. I know you don't eat, but that's why you're here, eh? To be with loved ones."

Adam thumped the bench seat next to him and jerked his chin. "I saved this one for you."

Uncle Harry was sitting opposite and he grabbed her fingers as she sat down. It was a big thing for the old man. He shied away from vampires, determined to keep the strange beings at arm's length.

"So good to see you, Uncle Harry. All of you."

Seren slipped in beside her and the hubbub of conversation started slowly and became the hum of hope. Rebekah absorbed the heat of the human bodies, the slow thrum of heartbeats pulsed through her skull, and the melody of their voices calmed her. *I'm home.*

The vampire world could wait awhile. Brynmor, Charles and Isaac were a medical team Connor could be proud of. His legacy of the human blood substitute would change everything, on the

British Isles, at least. Imhotep and Malachi would take the serum which killed the ferals across The Channel. *You saved the world, my love.* Rebekah swallowed hard and Seren squeezed her fingers tightly.

"He knows, Mama, he knows you love him."